SEAL TEAM BRAVO BLACK OPS IV

ERIC MEYER

First published in the United Kingdom in 2012 by Swordworks Books.

ISBN 978-1-909149-08-3

Typeset by Swordworks Books
Printed and bound in the UK & US
A catalogue record of this book is available from the British Library

Cover design by Swordworks Books
www.swordworks.co.uk

SEAL TEAM BRAVO
BLACK OPS IV

ERIC MEYER

CHAPTER ONE

The dust cloud swirled behind the small, slow moving convoy. Four trucks traveled along the rutted road, brightly painted, decorated in garish colors, and votive images. They were equipped with brass bells that hung from the windshield, like streamers from the tail of a child's kite. These vehicles were known as jingle trucks, except that now the bells and chains that made the cheerful tinkling sounds were silent, tied with strips of dirty rag. The drivers were watchful, for even though the Islamic Republic of Waziristan belonged to them, there was always a danger the Americans would mount a raid. Hasan Khan, driving the lead truck, searched the landscape ahead, the endless landscape of dirt, sand, and scrub. He looked up again, as he had every minute since they'd started their journey. The ever-present drones had been murderous of late. Too many of their fighters had been lost to the cowardly attacks from the air. He searched the surface of the road ahead, looking for any signs of an ambush, paying particular attention to the low hills and piles of scattered rocks that could conceal an enemy. Nothing. He relaxed slightly, hawking a gob of spittle out of the window, and then he took a second look around. Still nothing. He smiled to himself, this time they would get through to their comrades in Parachinar. The brave fighters who'd suffered so badly from repeated efforts by the Pakistani Army to dislodge them, as well as the drone strikes that had decimated their numbers. The heroes of Islam had held fast, and now the relief convoy was only two kilometers outside the town, ready to arrive in triumph with their four truckloads of supplies. He pictured himself for a second or two, carried on the shoulders of a grateful population, a true warrior of Islam. They had ammunition, weapons, and some food, of course, for the starving population, although there'd been little room for food. Most of the space in the trucks was taken up with assault rifles, RPGs, and hundreds of thousands of rounds of ammunition. There were mines and explosives too, with which they could manufacture more of the IEDs to continue killing the infidels who dared to attack their country with their deadly UAVs.

Truly, there will be celebrations in Parachinar when we arrive.

He turned to his companion and smiled, showing an array of crooked teeth.

"Nearly there, Tahir. We've made it this time. The infidels cannot stop us now."

Tahir Lashari, the battle-scarred deputy commander of the Waziri Taliban grunted. He was not a man given to much celebration, even when there was something to celebrate. Life was hard for a soldier of God. People should understand that simple fact and accept the sacrifices that were necessary, not make light of their achievements.

They'd done well to get this far, he knew that, but he was uneasy for some reason. He scanned the ground around them again and looked up at the sky, again. He relaxed slightly and turned to his companion.

"Tell me that when we drive into the main square, Hasan. There is still time for an attack. You should be vigilant searching for the enemy, not talking to me. Remember who gave the order for these supplies! It would not do to fail the Sheikh."

Hasan nodded half-heartedly and gazed ahead again. It would certainly not do to upset Commander Lashari. Tahir was a morose man, a vicious fighter, and a ruthless killer. He never smiled, never had a good word to say to anybody. He'd become even worse after he lost his wife and two sons to an American attack helicopter, an Apache gunship. It had been a bitter blow, for one of his sons had been preparing to be a martyr for Islam, to wear a suicide belt when he next crossed the border into Afghanistan. His life was a vicious, single-minded crusade, dedicated to ejecting the NATO forces from what he regarded as lands that rightfully belonged to the Taliban. Tahir was a Taliban fighter even before his family was killed, and in a war, people were killed. Did not the prophet himself say, 'If you do good, you do good to yourselves? If you do evil, you do evil to yourselves'. It was true that Tahir Lashari had spread plenty of evil. Plenty of innocents had died at his hands, victims of collateral damage during any number of actions against the enemy. Hasan wished his commander would lighten up and talk about something other than war, just for a change, like soccer. They were nearly there, so he should relax, especially, when a long, dangerous journey such as this one was clearly at an end, and there would be celebrations for the next few days. Time to bask in the warm praise and gratitude of the townspeople, to enjoy their adulation, and not least the feasts that would be laid out for them. They had little enough food, but they would spare everything for the brave fighters. It was healthier that way. Allah be praised, life could be good. All he needed would be a woman to make it perfect, but he grimaced inwardly. On that road lay the path to certain death. It would be safer to mount an attack on the Pakistani Army than to toy with a Taliban woman.

* * *

"Convoy at twelve hundred meters. I count four trucks, no sign of any escort."

"Copy that. "

Chief Petty Officer Nolan, US Navy Seals, did a three hundred and sixty degree sweep, but the area was clear. The Waziri Taliban would be disappointed this day, for their supplies were about to explode in spectacular fashion. He smiled to himself.

The Fourth of July will have nothing on this. If it all goes right, that is.

He cautioned himself to be careful, for overconfidence was a cardinal sin. He grimaced as he heard the officer complaining.

"The marker, Chief, I can't see it!"

Nolan sighed. As if he didn't have enough on his mind, his lieutenant was next to him, trying to put his personal stamp on the operation. They were both wearing ghillie suits, covered by a loose sprinkling of dust and foliage, and in a forward position where they could observe.

"It's a hundred meters ahead of us, Lt. Those two rocks, with the small bush in the center."

"Yeah, okay, I see it."

Lieutenant Boswell still couldn't get it right, even after three missions with Bravo. He'd done a law degree at Harvard and was considered to be a coming man, first in the Navy, and then he'd undoubtedly follow the well-trodden path through a corporate Wall Street law firm and into the murky world of politics. He sure looked the part, a neat, smooth-faced Ivy League professional. He wore his blonde hair neatly trimmed and sported a small, blonde mustache. Boswell was slight in build, like many Special Forces operators who were of less than average height. Their trade required subtlety and stealth, not muscle-bound apes. But what was most in evidence was his smooth and easy confidence, at least, when he wasn't in the field, the product of a moneyed upbringing. Not that he was totally inept as a Seal, the Lieutenant had scored highly in the aptitude tests, and even survived 'Hell Week', the fourth week of BUD/S training that saw most Seal recruits drop out, nursing sore limbs and bruised egos. But it wasn't the test scores alone that forged a man into a Navy Seal. It needed a certain something, a freebooting spirit, an attitude to life and to war that said, 'Fuck the odds, I'll get the job done, no matter what'. He still didn't grasp that simple philosophy, although Boswell was still learning, thanks to his high-ranking connections that had leaned on the Admiral back at Coronado, San Diego, to 'help him along'. Part of that help lay close by, camouflaged like Nolan and Boswell in a ghillie suit; a new guy, Petty Officer Second Class Lucas Grant, sent to 'stiffen' Seal Team Bravo, following concerns about Boswell's performance on a recent mission. There was no doubt Grant would get results. His previous assignment had as a member of Seal Team Six. Following the killing of Osama bin Mohammed bin Awad bin Laden, the world's most wanted terrorist, any man from that particular Team Six could do no wrong, except that Nolan, Bravo's number two, and one of the unit snipers, was still uncertain about the new guy; a superb soldier, without doubt. He'd been there and come back with the scalps still hanging from his saddle, but something about the guy made him feel uneasy, or perhaps it was just Boswell. The guy was a wind-up. It was time to call in.

"This is Bravo Two, listen up. The moment that lead truck hits the ambush, make sure you take out the rearmost vehicle. We don't want them to run, not with what they're carrying."

A brief reply came from the second unit sniper, Vince Merano "Copy that."

The jingle trucks came closer, garish in their peculiar splashes of psychedelic color. Nolan felt the familiar surge of adrenaline that preceded every firefight. He made an effort to relax. The adrenaline surge was the sniper's main enemy. It caused tiny tremors in the body, and holding a rifle rock steady was one of the main requirements for pinpoint accuracy. He sighted along his scope, the Leupold Vari-X Mil-dot riflescope that gave him a clear view of the enemy. The target. He saw the driver of the lead truck making conversation with his passenger, an older man, wearing a black turban over his scarred, bearded face. Maybe he was a local commander. It was logical to have him in the lead vehicle, and it would make the strike that much more worthwhile. Senior officers, commanders, they were the preferred targets of the professional sniper. He checked the clip in his SWS Mk 11, the precision semiautomatic Sniper Weapon System that could deliver a lethal 7.62mm round out to a range of almost a mile. Unconsciously, he made the minute adjustments to his stance in preparation for the shoot; going through the rituals he'd performed a thousand times before. His earpiece clicked on.

"This is Bravo One. Stand by. Target is thirty seconds from ambush point. Nobody move until that first truck is stopped."

Boswell again, handing out unnecessary orders. Never mind, he's making an effort, and it was a valid order; except that elite troops don't need a reminder, they're usually busy with real soldiering.

Nolan watched the man through his scope. Yes, he was definitely a commander. The man's expression had a dulled, long stare, the look familiar to veterans of battlefields the world over, the look of a man who had killed many, many times.

Maybe he lost family in the never-ending war. Yeah, that's probably it. Yet it's a war they created, he reminded himself. Life is tough, sure, but there's always a choice. If the guy had stayed at home, the folks he lost may have survived. Still, he'll be joining them soon, in the paradise these people are so fixated on.

He focused on the driver, a younger man, who seemed to be irritated at something the older man had said. His irritation wouldn't last much longer. Nolan checked distances, working out angles.

"This is Two, ten seconds. You all set, Bravo Four?"

"That's affirmative."

They'd set Claymore mines, two of them hidden in the center of the road. It was all they'd had time for. The thin detonator wires were covered with a fine layer of dust and tracked through to a small, dish-shaped hollow in the ground fifty meters away. It was a simple plan. When the first truck came abreast of the marker, Will Bryce, the tough, hard PO1 would fire the Claymores. All being well, they'd destroy the leading truck, along with the convoy commander. The Claymores would sure make a mess of the crazy paint job. Vince Merano, the other unit sniper, was positioned to take out the rearmost truck, along with Dan Moseley, who had the unit's machine gun deployed, the M249 Minimi. The SAW, Squad Automatic Weapon, was a lightweight and reliable gun that spat out a hail of 5.56mm bullets at a devastating rate, making it the perfect support weapon. Between Vince's heavy sniper rounds, which would take out the driver first, and Dan's machine gun fire that would rip through any other fighters who may be along for the ride, they were confident of stopping the rearmost truck. That would leave the remaining two trucks in a trap. There was an irrigation ditch either side of the road, preventing them from escaping cross-country. It should be like shooting fish in a barrel. But how many operations had gone south, in spite of that optimistic prediction, 'should be'?

He keyed his mic. "Five seconds, stand by."

He refocused on the lead truck and turned away as the shock wave hit them with stunning force. He looked up again, in time to see the cab disintegrate in a torrent of smashed metal, shattered glass, and melted rubber; decorated with the body parts of the driver and passenger. It slewed to the side of the road, partially blocking both lanes, smoke and flames pouring out. Nolan heard the sound of firing as his blocking force, Vince and Dan, opened fire. He glanced back and was satisfied that the rearmost truck had come to a stop in the center of the road.

Good, the middle two trucks are blocked.

He focused on the lead truck. The magnified image of his scope enabled him to make out the telltale bloody red smears painted over the wreckage of the cab. A half-dozen armed men were tumbling out the back. Boswell had seen the threat, and he was shouting more unnecessary orders on the commo.

"Fire, open fire, that lead truck, kill the bastards!"

Nolan swept his gaze over the two surviving trucks, already under fire from the rest of Bravo's men. They also carried men, at least a half-dozen in each, but these men were not shell-shocked from an exploding Claymore.

"Belay that! I say again, belay that. Hit those men in the center trucks. Dan, are you clear to take them on?"

"I'm good. Vince is finishing off a couple of stragglers. We can hit the rearmost target from here, Chief. Our line of sight to the second truck is not so good."

"Copy that. Will, you got it covered?"

He looked across at Will Bryce, the unit PO1. He was immensely strong and always dependable, the unit rock. He'd had a difficult start in life and had been forced to fight his way out of the Detroit ghettoes, slogging through the lower deck to achieve his reputation as one of the most respected in the Seals, if not the entire Navy. Will was one of the finest soldiers Nolan had served with. The African American had a strong, crag-like profile, with big bones and a jutting chin under a powerful, almost regal countenance. His huge body was clad with slabs of hard muscle, the result of constant physical training to keep him at the very peak of physical fitness and skill. Strangely for a black man, he had gray eyes, undoubtedly a throwback to some long forgotten mixed ancestry. Will stared out at the world from under thick, bushy eyebrows topped by wiry black hair. When people stared at him, they saw a man of massive strength and authority, a man who carried his inner confidence and power like an aura. Already, he was something of a legend in the service, and Nolan couldn't even consider how things would get done without him. Bryce looked across at him and replied.

"We're shooting up the truck, but the men in the back were out of sight. They bailed out and took cover on the other side of the road. We'll have to go in and finish 'em the hard way."

"Copy that. I'll ask Dan to deploy the SAW to cover you as soon as he's secured his target."

"That would be useful, Chief."

Nolan looked up startled as Lieutenant Boswell abruptly got to his feet, along with Lucas Grant. He heard the officer bellowing orders on the commo.

"Will, bring your men here and form up behind me and Lucas. The rest of you, stay off the commo and remain clear. We're going in to finish those bastards."

Nolan spoke urgently. "Lt, no! They're behind cover over there, it's not..."

"I said stay off the commo, Chief."

He watched as the rest of Bravo ran to Boswell's position and formed up. He cursed under his breath. Ever since Lucas Grant had been transferred to the Platoon, Boswell had seemed to acquire a reckless courage, spurred on no doubt by the heroic tales of the bin Laden raid. It wasn't Grant's fault, but whatever the reason, he was heading toward getting men killed. Nolan jumped to his feet, ducked as a stray round whistled past his head, and ran back to where Vince and Dan were deployed. They were still laying down suppressive fire, but there were no return shots. The men in the rearmost truck were dead or dying, maybe one or two were running like hares for the hills, or maybe hiding. The two Seals looked around as he slithered to the ground next them.

"The Lieutenant said to stay off the commo, so I had to come on over. Our guys won't make it in a head-on attack. We need to flank the enemy and hit them in enfilade if we're to give our men a chance. It looks like you're done here. Let's go!"

He didn't wait for a reply, just ran across the road, past the wrecked truck, and charged across the broken ground, fifty meters, until he was abreast of the Taliban survivors, one hundred meters away. Sporadic shots whistled around him, but they didn't seem to be aimed. The hostiles were hunkered down on the reverse slope of a crease in the ground, waiting for Boswell's charge which they knew was coming. They were wise enough to hold their fire, as the Seals were still out of sight behind the vehicles, and there was little chance of hitting anything. But they were waiting, and as soon as the Seals appeared, it would be a slaughter.

"Dan, get that Minimi set up and working. We need to shake their aim. Vince, we have to thin them out some. Let's get to work!"

Merano grinned, relishing the fight. "You got it, Chief."

They lay down on the dusty ground and put their sights on the hostiles. They opened fire, and within seconds, three of the enemy were down. But the others, seven fighters, had seen them and dived for cover, preparing to hit back. Nolan saw a familiar shape poke out from behind a pile of rocks.

"RPG, down!"

The shooter was shaken up, or he was a rookie, maybe both. The missile impacted the ground ten meters in front of them, but the blast was enough to lift them physically a couple of feet into the air. Nolan felt the breath 'whoosh' out of his lungs as he smashed into the ground with a bone-jarring crunch. He brushed dust and debris out of his eyes and swept his gaze around the immediate area. Vince and Dan had been tossed aside by the force of the explosion, and they were picking themselves back up and checking their weapons. He ducked as a volley of shots cracked overhead, and when he looked again at the enemy position, they were shouting to each other, readying to press home the advantage the missile had given them. The RPG shooter stared at Nolan's position and saw that he hadn't completely destroyed the target. He shouted to a nearby fighter who was clutching a spare missile. They began to load ready for a second shot, and two more hostiles began firing short bursts in the direction of the Minimi. The other three men were staring in a different direction at the wrecked vehicles, waiting for Boswell's charge to materialize. He felt a chill in his guts as he recognized what they were doing. They were setting up a Russian Degtyarev DP light machine gun, the model with the distinctive pancake magazine. An old weapon, developed for the Second World War, and exported all over the Third World ever since; a heavy weapon, slow and not always reliable. But the vintage machine gun was still devastating, and able to spew out a hail of 7.62mm rounds.

More than enough to destroy Boswell's lunatic charge, or was it Lucas Grant's idea? Either way, they should have heeded the lessons of the valiant but ill-advised General Pickett at Gettysburg. Some lesson about not charging into the teeth of enemy guns, something about firing from behind cover whenever possible.

He had to do something. He leapt up, snapping out orders to the two Seals.

"I'll vector in from the far side to try and divert them, so pour it on, and give 'em everything you have. Keep trying to get through to Boswell. Tell him the enemy is dug in and just waiting for them. They have to stay behind cover until we have them boxed in."

As he ran, dodging from side to side, and keeping low to put the enemy gunners off their aim, a vicious burst from an AK-47 kicked up the dirt close to his boots, and he almost burst his lungs getting to his new position before they corrected their aim. He heard Vince passing on his order to Boswell, and it wasn't well received.

"We've got them on the run, Merano!" the Lieutenant shouted back, his voice filled with the excitement of the chase. "We aren't stopping on Nolan's say so. Keep moving!"

All of them could hear the emotion in his voice as the Lieutenant raced forward, panting and gulping in deep breaths of air, ignoring the deadly danger that faced him. Lucas Grant's voice came on the commo.

"We're good to go. If we don't hit them hard and fast now, they'll get away. That's the way we did it in Seal Team Six."

"You heard that, men, keep going," Boswell shouted. "Let's finish off these fuckers."

There was a short silence in his earpiece. They were surprised to hear him swear, as it was known that he considered himself above that kind of language, but it was a measure of his excitement. Nolan threw himself down just before a renewed burst of firing from more than one AK-47 tore past him. Vince had begun to shoot back, keeping up a steady rate of fire. He couldn't see the hostiles, but the way he laid down the pattern of bullets left them in no doubt that if they poked their heads up, he'd blow them off. Dan had moved to a new position with a better field of fire, and he'd begun spitting out long bursts of fire to keep up the pressure on the enemy. Then his box mag ran out of ammo. Nolan stared across at him, willing him to hurry while Dan wrenched the empty mag out of the breech and rammed home a replacement. He took aim and pulled the trigger. The gun jammed. There was a stunned silence, and Boswell's voice sounded in their earpieces.

"Drop it, man, both of you get over here."

Dan's frustration boiled over, and he exploded in anger as he finally lost patience with Boswell. He kept low and ran over to where the platoon leader was waiting to launch his idiotic charge.

"The fuck you say, Lieutenant! Listen to me, get your stupid fucking head down. Chief Nolan is out there drawing fire to try and save your stupid ass, and if the hostiles don't blow your stupid head off, I will!"

His voice was loud, ringing around the battlefield. Nolan nearly choked. If he hadn't been trying to stay alive, he'd have had a good belly laugh. But it stopped Boswell who muttered, "Okay, we'll do it his way. Nolan had better be right."

They all knew he'd deal with Dan later, but at least there'd be more of them alive. Nolan crawled forward, following a shallow depression in the ground, and finally reached a position where he could see the hostiles. Seven black-turbaned men, one armed with the Degtyarev, another with an RPG, reloaded and ready to fire again, and the rest of the enemy with AK-47s. One of the men, he assumed it was their leader, was shouting orders and pointing at the Seals' positions, giving them some kind of a pep talk. As far as he knew, they didn't realize he'd got in so far behind them. He keyed his mic.

"This is Bravo Two. I'm in behind them, to the south of your position. They look like they're about to launch an attack, so if you stay there, they'll fall on your guns, but that RPG could be a problem. I suggest we leave Vince and Dan to take him out, and the rest of you deal with the AKs. Is that Minimi clear, Dan?"

"Sure, it was nothing, just a bad piece of shell casing. I'm ready."

"I hope you got it right this time," Boswell cut in. "We'll try it your way, Chief, but if you're wrong again, there'll be fucking hell to pay when we get back."

Jesus Christ, I'd like to kick the little snot's ass.

"Copy that, Lt. Vince, I want you and Dan in position right now. I figure they'll show themselves anytime. I'll target the RPG before it does any real damage. Make sure you thin them out some before they get to Boswell's position."

"We're on it," he heard Dan reply.

It was one of those times when men on both sides for

some reason stop shooting all at once. Usually, it was just before one or other side was about to launch an attack. Nolan could hear the sighing of the wind, sweeping across the open plain surrounding the town of Parachinar. He stared around him. It was a desolate place, just dust, dirt and scrub, with patches of rock scattered in a random pattern. In the distance, he could just make out the roofs of Parachinar, a piss-poor heap of rubble and misery.

There'll be fighters in there. We need to finish up here before the Taliban defenders come out to help their buddies.

His mind had been wandering, and the shouts tore his attention back. And then they came, five Taliban fighters. They charged in a wedge, directly at where they believed their greatest threat lay, Boswell's unit, sheltering under cover behind the wrecked truck. They were firing single shots from their assault rifles to conserve ammunition. Their sole intention was to keep the Seals' heads down until they reached them, and then get in close and kill. But Dan Moseley and Vince Merano were not in front as they supposed, and the two men opened fire immediately. Nolan waited for his target, but the missile shooter was in the center, making him the most difficult man to hit. Two of the fighters went straight down, but the survivors made it to the drainage ditch and disappeared into the gully. Nolan jumped to his feet and began to run, shouting, "Hold your fire. I'm going in after them."

He heard Boswell shouting, but the blood pounded in his ears, adrenaline coursed through his veins, and the only thought in his brain was to reach the fighters before they were ready to start shooting; before they realized there was a crazy American sprinting toward them from behind, bringing death a little nearer with every stride. He was almost at the ditch. He dragged out his Sig Sauer, held it in a firm grip, and then leapt down and kept running along the floor of the gully. The ditch was narrow, very narrow. He tossed his sniper rifle out onto the earth above; this was no place for a long gun. With his free hand, he unclipped a grenade from his webbing and primed it ready. Then he came face to face with a fighter, a grizzled, older man with a huge beard, black turban, and teeth that were every bit as black as his headgear. The man snarled as he saw Nolan hurtling toward him, and he tried to deploy his weapon, the Degtyarev DP machine gun. But the Russian gun was no more practical for this kind of fight than a sniper rifle; the two men's battle had become no more sophisticated than the most basic, brutal trench fighting. The barrel snagged in the dirt of the gully wall, and the man cursed. Nolan shot him twice. The two rounds punched the man back, and then he ran on, searching out the next target. A burst of gunfire from an AK-47 streaked past him and buried a half-dozen rounds in the dirt, barely missing his chest. A piece of stone was chipped from a rock, and he felt the sting as it buried itself in the back of his neck. He jerked out of the line of fire, tossed the grenade, threw himself down, and put his head in the dirt. The grenade detonated, and the force of the explosion slammed into him, a pressure wave that compressed his rib cage and drove the air from his body. He gasped and sucked in more oxygen, got to his feet, and wiped his eyes clear of dust and dirt. As he vaulted over the dead Degtyarev gunner, still clutching the weapon in his lifeless hands, he glimpsed another fighter only a few feet away. The guy was badly wounded, but he still held on grimly to his assault rifle.

The man turned painfully to look at the American, his enemy, and snarled a challenge. He tried to raise his rifle to shoot the hated foe, but Nolan got there first. He shot him with another double tap, and the two 9mm bullets buried themselves into the man's body, one in the chest and the other in the head. He ran on, only to find the gully had emptied. Then he heard more shooting.

Nolan darted a fast look over the edge to see the remaining two fighters had crawled out and were sheltering behind the wreckage at the front of their truck. He knew that at the other side of the vehicle, Boswell's squad was deployed behind cover, waiting for the enemy to arrive.

Jesus, what a situation! One grenade and they'll be finished. And the missile shooter is among them, loaded for bear.

He keyed his mic.

"This is Nolan. You guys have two hostiles right behind that truck. They're about to attack, and one of them is holding the RPG."

There was a stunned silence, and then Lucas Grant replied. "Can you get to them? If we throw a grenade this close, we'll all go up with it."

"That's a negative. I can't see them. They've got in behind cover," Nolan answered. One of the men looked up and raised his Sig, but he ducked back down inside the shelter of the wreckage. The shooter with the RPG showed himself for a second, too quick and too far away for an accurate pistol shot. But his intentions were obvious; he was preparing to fire, maneuvering himself into a good position. The other fighter was behind him, arming the missile. They were about to shoot into the guts of the wrecked truck so they'd send themselves to paradise and destroy everything, Boswell's squad included.

"Vince, can you see them? They're about to blow themselves up, and the rest of our guys will go with them."

"Negative, Chief. I can just about make out a patch of their clothing, maybe two yeah, but it's not a clear shot. I can maybe wing them, that's about all. It's a risk."

"Take the shot, and don't miss. Do it, Vince, now!"

The two shots rang out. Vince had removed the sound suppressor for maximum accuracy and velocity. There were two simultaneous yelps of pain and surprise, and Nolan was up and running, straight for the wrecked truck. He rounded the twisted, burning remains and there they were, both men bleeding profusely from Vince's bullets. One round had entered the left femoral artery of the missile shooter; the other fighter had taken a hit to his right elbow. They were painful wounds, and both men were screaming in pain and anger. He put them both out of their misery. It was no time for fancy shooting. They were jigging around, a mixture of pain and fear, and he hit them with three bullets each to the chest. They went down dead, and seconds later Boswell, Grant, and the rest of the men rounded the side of the truck. Boswell stared at the bodies on the ground and then looked at Nolan.

"You okay, Chief?"

"Yeah, no sweat."

Boswell nodded. "You called it right, thanks. But I'll have a word with Dan Moseley. He should know he can't talk to me like that."

Nolan nodded. "Yeah, it's a real bastard, being insulted by someone who's saving your life. My advice, Lt, is to let it go."

He saw Grant's lips twitch in a smile. Boswell nodded

thoughtfully and looked at his number two man in the Platoon. Nolan made him nervous, that was obvious, but whatever the reason, he couldn't fathom what it could be. Except perhaps that he towered over the smaller man. Chief Petty Officer Kyle Nolan was tall, six-one, and lean, with the kind of features some people called chiseled. At first, people saw him as almost bland, but not all. More than one girlfriend had told him he reminded them of a young Clint Eastwood; a compliment he'd always accepted with some grace, even if they were plain loco. His angular face was again considered almost average, at first sight. But his strong chin and piercing eyes, the color of a clear, deep blue sky, were a hint that the man they belonged to was anything but normal. Despite his blue eyes, he had thick, dark brown hair, which some people found strange, but women frequently found attractive. But more than anything, it was probably the way he carried himself, a confidence, a strength and grace, which hid an inner core of hard, spring steel. Boswell hoped to acquire the same qualities but probably never would, although the men generally did their best to help and support him until he reached his goal. Or died in the attempt, but that was a risk they all took. The Lieutenant nodded.

"Maybe you're right. I'll let it go this time, but…"

He stopped, as the voice of their surveillance controller broke into their communications net. The unarmed Lockheed P-3 Orion was a four-engine turboprop surveillance aircraft, widely used in American theaters of war for its ability to loiter over a battlefield for up to ten hours at a time. Right now, it was circling in support of their mission a few kilometers distant, safe inside Afghan airspace.

"Bravo One, we have a drone report just in. They've sighted suspected hostiles emerging from the town of Parachinar. We estimate their number at one hundred. I say again, one hundred."

They swiveled around to survey the landscape and to check out the nearby town. It was too far away, and the ground was too undulating to see anything clearly, but the dust cloud swirling toward them was enough confirmation. The Taliban were coming, and this time in greater numbers.

Boswell reacted fast, rapping out orders. He tended to raise his voice to overcome his obvious feelings of some kind of physical shortcoming.

It's a pile of crap, Nolan considered to himself.

He was not a significant looking guy, pale and of less than medium height; there was little of the macho cowboy in the Harvard educated Lieutenant, with his blonde hair and neat, clipped mustache. As a result, the image he presented to the world was of a rather preppy looking senior clerk, maybe a junior attorney. But he was a Navy Seal platoon leader, and for most men it would be enough, more than enough. He just hadn't realized it yet. Nolan turned his attention to the Lieutenant.

"We need to clear the area. There are too many of them if they catch us here out in the open. You have to prepare the Platoon to move out, and we'll find a better defensive position." Boswell stared at him, uncertain, but Nolan ignored him and replied to the Orion. "Control, we require exfil ASAP. Send in the helos right away."

Boswell nodded. It made sense to get out. They'd carried out their mission with no loss of life, so it was time to bail. Except that the Orion crew had other ideas.

"Negative, Bravo. The images show those hostiles equipped with RPGs. We can't send in helos until they're taken care of. They'd be sitting ducks on the ground."

Nolan tried again. "Do you have air support in the area? Anything we can use?"

They could all hear the controller's irritation. "Bravo, you're in Pakistan. We can't overfly the country without the permission of the Pakistan military, and we don't have time to ask them."

"What about a drone?"

"Well, it was a drone that spotted them, but it's unarmed. Look, we have enough trouble with the Pakis, without shooting up the country with Reapers. Sorry, Bravo, you're on your own."

Nolan saw Boswell's expression darken, and the Lieutenant took over.

"Feller, listen up. This is Lieutenant William Boswell, United States Navy. Now you get off your ass and mention that name to your commanding general back at Bagram. He's an uncle of mine, and he likes to look out for his nephew. For some reason, he gets mighty angry if he thinks people are fucking with him. Or do you want him to find out how you refused to offer assistance to your own people, and maybe got some of them killed? What's it going to be? Do we get some air support, or are you looking for a new job sweeping the tarmac in some Godforsaken airfield in the far north of Alaska?"

There was a long silence. The controller came back.

"Hang on there, pal, wait up. We have a pair of A-10 Thunderbolts looking for some trade. I can arrange for them to lose their way and detour over the border. I mean, it's unauthorized, but I'll support you any way I can."

"That's good, Mister, you'd better vector them our way. How long before they can get to us?"

"I estimate they'll be with you in ten minutes, give or take. Can you hold until then?"

"We'll be fine, but you'd better make sure they're no more than ten minutes," Boswell replied.

"Copy that, Bravo. Before you sign off, I want you to stay to the south of the hostiles. I repeat, stay to the south. I'll order the Thunderbolts to attack the large group of insurgents north of your position and closest to the town of Parachinar, so we don't get any foul-ups."

"Understood."

Boswell stared around at the squad. Vince and Dan had come up and joined them. Boswell gave Dan a sour look and then ignored him.

"We'll find a new position to cover those hostiles, somewhere that'll give us a good field of fire. Chief, we'll form a blocking force to prevent them getting too near. If we keep them boxed up, it'll make the job that much easier for the A-10s."

Nolan nodded his approval. "It's a plan, Lt."

"It will be if those A-10s turn up on time. Let's move out. We'll find suitable ground and take up new positions."

They grabbed their gear and started moving at a tangent, off on the flank of the enemy approaching from the town. The dust cloud had resolved itself much as they'd been advised; a large group of men, heavily armed with a collection of Soviet, Chinese, and even American made weaponry, and all of them thirsting for vengeance. Nolan could easily make out four RPGs, together with numerous AK-47s, AK-74s, and a few M-16s, probably stolen. Somewhere in that group they'd no doubt have at least a couple of light machine guns, as well as a sniper or two. The Taliban learned fast, and they'd employed long-range snipers to deadly effect, their weapon of choice being the venerable British .303 caliber Lee-Enfield. The solid old rifle was heavy, basic, and easy to maintain in the field. The sniper variant was also deadly accurate in use, as many ISAF troops had found to their cost. Nolan walked close to Boswell, constantly surveying the ground around and ahead of them. He caught the Lieutenant's attention.

"This should be near enough. Any closer and they'll see what we're up to. There're enough of them to come around on our flank and do some damage."

Boswell grunted in agreement. "You're right. We'll deploy half the men in the rocks the other side of the drainage ditch. Split the men and keep the other half this side and stagger their positions. I don't want anyone caught in our own crossfire."

Nolan managed to keep his cool. "Yeah, I got it."

Yeah, I'd never have worked that one out. But the guy is trying, and I have to cut him some slack. He noticed the amused twitch again from Grant. Is the Seal Team Six guy grinning at our rookie Lieutenant, or at me for having to swallow his shit? Maybe the guy is just trying to keep sane like the rest of us.

Nolan ordered the men to their positions, and half of them took cover among the uneven piles of rock littering the ground the other side of the ditch. All the while, Nolan could see the crowd of hostiles getting nearer. It was eerie. They were keeping up a fast pace, but they made no noise. There was no shouting, no curses, no threats, nothing. He felt uneasy, but he couldn't explain why.

Maybe I'm just tired.

He checked his watch, five minutes before the A-10s arrived. It was going to be a close run thing. He'd need to keep those hostiles well away from their position, and by definition, well away from the incoming fire from the ground attack aircraft. The Fairchild Republic A-10 Thunderbolt had achieved almost legendary status in the Iraq campaign. It was an American single-seat, twin-engine jet aircraft, developed by Fairchild-Republic in the early 1970s. Intended to stay in service for at least another fifteen years, it had proved itself devastating in use against ground troops and armor.

The A-10s armament was a single gun, but it was no ordinary gun. The General Electric GAU-8 Avenger was a 30mm hydraulically driven seven-barrel Gatling cannon that was mounted exclusively on the Thunderbolts. The GA Avenger was one of the largest, heaviest, and most powerful aircraft cannons in the United States military arsenal. Designed primarily for the anti-tank role, the Avenger delivered very heavy, powerful rounds at a high rate of fire. The result was awesome, total devastation wherever it was employed. Nolan fully intended to keep his people as far away from the target area as possible. The A-10 took no prisoners. He made a final check of their positions, glancing back up the road to the approaching enemy.

What the hell are they doing? If I were in command of that warband, I wouldn't bunch up like that. It's an invitation to get shot to pieces, and the Taliban are anything but stupid. What gives? This is wrong, all wrong!

He glanced over at PO1 Will Bryce, the mainstay of the Platoon through countless missions.

"Will, does this look right to you?"

Bryce shook his head. "It sure don't smell right. What are they up to? Committing suicide? They know we're here, and they must know we'll call in air support, Pakistan or no Pakistan. It's like they have a death wish."

"Yeah, it's weird. So what's going on?"

Will shrugged. "I'll be damned if I know. Maybe they're just having a bad day."

Nolan grinned. "Make that a very bad day. When those Warthogs come in, they'll tear 'em to pieces."

He looked at Boswell. "They're near enough, Lt. We should hit them now. When the shooting starts, they may come at us for protection from the air attack."

The Lieutenant nodded and looked across at Grant for confirmation. "Sounds right to me, what do you think, Lucas?"

Nolan struggled to hide his frustration. We're a SpecOps unit, for Christ's sake, not a high school debating society. But he let it go.

"Looks fine to me. Like the Chief said, it would be best if we stayed well clear of those A-10s. So yeah, we should stop them here. The sooner we kill 'em, the sooner we can call in our ride home."

Boswell nodded. "Give the order, Chief. They don't get any nearer."

"Lt, there's something wrong," Nolan objected. "I don't like it. They're up to something. I only wish I knew what it was."

Boswell looked unconcerned. "It looks fine to me. Give the order, Chief. Tell the men to open fire. Let's corral them ready for the airstrike."

Nolan nodded and keyed his mic. It was true; they couldn't let them come any nearer.

"Listen up, men. We have to halt that group and hold them until the Warthogs come in. Commence firing, try and hold them back."

He'd retrieved his SWS Mk11, and he dropped to a kneeling position where he could rest the bipod on a flat chunk of rock. It made a perfect sniper stand. He sighted through the Leupold riflescope, and the group of hostiles came up large in his field of vision. The Platoon opened fire. A hail of lead slashed out at the oncoming group, and the enemy fighters slowed. Some fell as the massive combined firepower rippling out from Bravo Platoon smashed into their ranks. Dan opened up with the Minimi, firing in short, even bursts that tore into the oncoming crowd, and the noise of the gunfire was interrupted by the quick, accurate bursts from the men's Heckler and Koch 416 assault rifles. Vince's rapid, single shot sniper fire punctuated the roaring bursts of the machine gun. He'd removed the suppressor, and the whip crack noise of his shooting provided a lethal accompaniment to the din of the gunfire. Nolan kept his finger off the trigger. He still couldn't work out the feeling of unease that tore at his guts.

"Aircraft coming in, our guys are here!" someone shouted over the commo. "Yeeh-hah!"

He felt even more uneasy. It was far too easy. He looked up in time to see a pair of A-10 Thunderbolts hurtling in fast and low from the northwest, their fuselages painted in mottled light-brown and green camouflage. The marines had arrived. As he watched, the two aircraft banked to port and dived in for their first attack run. He looked back at the hostiles, and his mind went numb. It was all laid out in front of them to see. A massacre was about to happen at high speed, a collision of jet-powered technology with an almost stone age primitive people. The surviving fighters had jumped into the irrigation ditches either side of the road. In their center was a large group of Afghan civilians, mainly women and children who'd been kept hidden from the Seals. The Taliban had outsmarted them.

Oh, Jesus, no!

He keyed his mic and shouted, "Abort, abort, there are civilians in the firing line!"

"Belay that! This is Bravo One, press home the attack!" Boswell was shouting into the commo patched through to the controller on the Orion. "Do not pass on that order. The attack is to proceed as scheduled."

"Copy that, Bravo One," the controller's voice came back to them. The platoon commander had spoken, and then the Warthogs opened fire. The effect was devastating. The aircraft seemed to slow in the air as the Gatling guns poured out their heavy caliber rounds into the target. People ran screaming, desperate to find cover, but there was to be no respite for them. Some made it to the irrigation ditches, only to be forced back by the Taliban sheltering there. Some were shot down by their own people rather than allow them to escape the massacre.

"Lt, for Christ's sake, you have to stop this," he shouted to Boswell.

There was no reply, and he looked into the officer's eyes. They were glazed with excitement, satisfied that America's mortal enemies were being mown down like wheat before the harvester, except these weren't the enemy. They were a Taliban sacrifice and an American public relations disaster. Finally, Boswell came to his senses, but it was too late. They watched the A-10s come to the end of their attack run and looped in the sky for the return, pumping out bunches of flares in case of ground to air missiles. Then they came again, and the nauseating hammering of the Gatling guns echoed across the dusty plain. Once again, Nolan could see the civilians running, screaming, bleeding and dying. He heard Boswell shouting at the controller, "This is Bravo One, abort, abort, abort. I say again, abort!"

But the Warthogs were already turning for home. The pilots hauled back on their sticks, and the squat, ugly killing machines zoomed up into the sky to separate in a 'V' formation, prior to forming up for the return journey to Bagram Air Base, outside Kabul. They would know that too much time spent in Pakistani airspace invited disaster, in the shape of a visit from a squadron of Pakistani F-16 Fighting Falcons, more than a match for the A-10s. The firing had stopped, and in the distance, Nolan could see the surviving Taliban fighters climb out of the ditch and start to jog back towards the town, leaving the casualties bleeding and dying in their wake. He turned to Boswell.

"Lt, there never was any intention to fight us. That was a public relations battle, and they sure as hell won it. Why the fuck didn't you stop those Warthogs?"

The Lieutenant shook his head. He ignored the Chief's hostility. "I thought, well, I thought they were using them as a human shield, not a sacrifice. And then," he faltered. "I just…it was all too late. Chief, I never would have let it happen if I could have stopped it. Jesus, how can they do that to their own people?"

"That's the nature of the beast," Lucas Grant offered. "These people are animals, Lt. Don't let it worry you; killing their own comes as second nature to them."

If only it was as simple as that. Can't they see? We were

led by the nose.

"We need to check for survivors," Nolan asserted. "Some of them will need medical help before we leave. We're running short on time. We have to take care of it and call in the helos for exfiltration. It's time we were outta here. When the Pakistanis get wind of this, we'll hit real problems."

Boswell nodded. "Yeah, I'll call them in now. They're about fifteen minutes out, so that's how long we have left."

Nolan nodded and turned to Will, who was hovering nearby. "I need four men to come with me and check out those poor folks, see if there's anything we can do for them."

Behind him, he heard Lucas Grant murmur; "A bullet in the head might do some of them a favor after those Warthogs have shot them up." He ignored him, and keyed his mic.

"Vince, you and Dan round up the rest of the men and form a defensive perimeter, in case any of those Taliban decide to double back and take pot shots at us."

"Copy that, I'll get right on it."

He started up the road with Will and three other men, among them Jack Whitman, a promising new recruit to the Platoon. He was slightly above average height like Nolan, and finely muscled with the body of a martial artist. Whitman had one ambition in his life, and he'd achieved it. To become a Seal, and he hardly ever stopped smiling. Except now, his expression had changed as they approached the grim pile of bodies to survey the butcher's bill, the grim toll of death, and the dying. At first, he thought Whitman was sickened, and then he looked again. His eyes were glazed.

With what, horror, or something else? What is it?

Whitman caught him watching him, and his expression changed.

"Someone will pay for this screw-up," he muttered.

"Maybe, Jack. But who?"

The Taliban, for sending their people out to be murdered? Who will hold them accountable? Maybe it was the fault of those A-10 jockeys, or Boswell for not calling a halt. But we're all to blame, all of us. These poor bastards just want to live in peace. Instead, they have to deal with a constant flow of soldiers from both sides. Hard men, with hard faces set like stone against the task they're ordered to do. Armored and heavily armed. The devastated infrastructure of Afghanistan, and Waziristan, which counts itself an ally, is a grim testament to the level of destruction we'd wreaked. Or did Jack Whitman mean something else entirely? Is he horrified or enthralled? No, that's not it. He's horrified, like the rest of us.

"Help me, please, help me!"

He ran over to where a man was trying to extricate himself from underneath a pile of broken and ruined bodies. Nolan struggled to free him, and Jack Whitman joined him to help. They finally freed him, looking in horror at the bloodied wreck of humanity they'd saved. The man opened his eyes. He shook his head and stared at them. His lips moved, and he spoke, in English.

"It is not as bad as it looks. The blood is mostly someone else's. By a miracle, I was spared the worst of the attack. I believe I was shot on the right side of my body. I went down, and other bodies fell on top of me and took the worst of the attack."

"Exactly where were you hit?"

He pointed to a place just under his shoulder blade. "That's where it hurts most, anyway."

Nolan bent down to look and discovered a shard of metal, a fragment from the casing of a cannon round from the A-10 strike, had fallen from the sky at high speed and embedded itself deep into the man's lower shoulder.

"I'll need to put a dressing on this, Sir. It won't take a minute."

"Thank you."

He closed his eyes. Clearly he was in a lot more pain that he'd admit to. It was going to hurt even more in the next minute. He was bleeding badly, yet the metal fragment stuck out in such a way that the only way to strap on a dressing was to remove it, and fast. Before the man's body literally emptied of blood.

"I can do it."

He looked at Whitman. "You sure?"

"Yep. I spent a couple of years as a Navy Corpsman. They said it'd help my application for the Seals."

"Right. Did it help?"

Whitman grinned briefly. "Not a bit."

Nolan grunted. "Okay."

Jack bent down, unwrapped a sterile dressing, and gave it to Nolan to hold. "I'd ask you to keep it clean, but I guess that's out of the question."

Nolan looked at his filthy hands and nodded. "It is."

Whitman felt around the wound, looking for vulnerable organs, anything that was at risk of further damage. The man's eyes flicked open with the pain.

"What are you doing?"

"I'm about to put the dressing on, Sir. Nearly there, but I have to remove the metal fragment."

"Will it hurt?"

"A little. Best if you close your eyes."

"Very well."

As his eyelids closed, Jack jerked out the shard. Immediately, a fresh spurt of blood jetted out of the open wound. He was ready for it and jammed the dressing against the hole, staunching the flow.

"If you'd put your hand on the dressing, Chief, I'll strap him up."

"Sure."

Jack stood up to take out another dressing from his pack. Something caught in the corner of Nolan's vision. It was more an unconscious feeling than something he actually saw, but years of battle experience fired off the alarm bells.

"Jack, get down! Sniper!"

The warning probably saved Whitman's life. The heavy .303 caliber round fired from a Taliban sniper rifle, a Lee Enfield, hit the Seal just as he automatically dodged sideways in response to the shout. The bullet was aimed at the area of his neck. Instead, it struck him on the side of the chest, square on the ballistic plate in the center of his armored vest. Whitman was flung back by the force of the heavy bullet. Nolan ignored him for the present and keyed his mic.

"Enemy sniper, estimated position three hundred meters due north. It looks like he's hiding in an old stone building, probably a ruined shepherd's hut, just before the town. Nail the bastard. He just shot Jack."

"Is he okay?" Boswell.

"I'm checking him out now. He took it on his ballistic plate. You have to take out that sniper, or he'll nail a few more of us, and next time we may not be so lucky."

"I'm on him, Chief." It was Vince. "I can see a gun barrel poking out from behind the stonework. We need to wait for him to make a move, then I'll take him."

"Make sure you all keep your heads down while he's still out there," Nolan warned.

He ducked low and crawled across to Jack. The man's eyes were open.

"How do you feel?"

"Like I went ten rounds with Mike Tyson, but the vest stopped the bullet. I'll be okay, but we still need to fix that guy's wound. He's leaking worse than a sieve."

Nolan looked at the casualty. The blood was flowing freely from where Jack had removed the steel fragment.

"What do I do, Jack?"

"Just like I was doing, strap a pad over it to stop the bleeding."

"It's a lot of blood, do you think it'll be enough?"

"If you don't do it right now, he dies."

Nolan nodded and rammed the pad back on the bleeding hole, using his knee to hold it in place. The man started to come to, then lapsed back into unconsciousness. He strapped the second dressing over the first one and tied it as best he could. The bleeding had slowed dramatically, but whether it was enough, he'd no idea. He looked up as Will Bryce crawled over to him.

"How's Jack doing?"

"He'll live," Nolan muttered, "but this Pakistani guy is touch and go."

"Yeah, fucking Muslims, murdering their own people."

"I am not a Muslim!"

They looked at the casualty. His eyes had flicked open,

and his brown face, pale and gray with pain and blood loss, looked outraged.

"You what?"

"I am a Christian." He managed a small smile. "My name is Danial Masih, and I can assure you I have never been inside a mosque in my life."

They were both surprised, at least for a few moments, and not altogether convinced. Will said casually, "Not many Christians in this place."

"You mean the town of Parachinar? No, I think you are right." He closed his eyes in pain for a few seconds and then reopened them. He spoke again, painfully and slowly. "I was visiting my elderly uncle who lives there. I come from east of here, the city of Abbottabad. At least, I used to, although my son still lives there. I was an engineer there, and I," he stopped again, working to martial his thoughts, "I…I worked for the city council."

The men exchanged glances. Abbottabad was a city whose name had gone into infamy, the place were Osama bin Laden had sheltered. Until Seal Team Six put an end to his notorious career. The man tried to speak again and failed. He lapsed into unconsciousness, but he was breathing, despite the massive blood loss. They could see his chest moving as his body fought desperately to stay alive.

"What'll we do with him?" Will asked.

"Do? We'll have to take him with us. If we leave him here, he'll die."

Will was about to say something but stopped, and they ducked down as a hail of 5.56mm bullets parted the air overhead. It was Dan, he'd fired a long, well-aimed burst at the estimated position of the sniper, and Nolan saw chips of stone fly off the ruined hut. It was enough, the man moved, unsettled by the stream of bullets that must have ricocheted every which way around his primitive shelter. The sniper moved to find better cover, giving Vince Merano exactly the chance he was waiting for. Three bullets cracked out in quick succession, three precision 7.62mm rounds, and each one struck its target. They heard the scream from three hundred meters away, and suddenly the man appeared, black turban, long, black beard, and filthy robes, threaded through with pieces of bracken to camouflage himself. Vince was not a man to miss such a gift, and clearly the target was only wounded. He sent three more rounds that each struck the sniper, but this time at least one hit a vital organ. The man was flung back and disappeared behind the ruin.

Scratch one Taliban sniper, Nolan thought.

"I can hear the helos. They're on their way in!" someone shouted.

"Stay down! Stay under cover until we can confirm they're ours and not the Pakis," Nolan shouted.

He craned his head to look up at the sky, to see a pair of Marine Black Hawks, Sikorsky UH-60s descending toward their position. They landed a short distance away, and the Seals began running toward them.

Nolan and Whitman carefully carried Danial Masih across to one of the Black Hawks, lifted him gently through the door, and a medic took over. He seemed surprised that Nolan and Whitman were watching him, as if they cared.

"What? What is it? Is this guy important to you?"

"It's be nice to see one survivor from the massacre back there, that's all," Nolan shrugged. "Will he live?"

"He should be okay. We'll have to re-open the wound

when we get back, and he'll need some transfusions to replace lost blood, but other than that, he should be over the worst of it pretty soon."

"Thanks, Doc," Nolan nodded, and then he recalled Masih saying he was from Abbottabad. "Make sure he's looked after. Our intel guys may want to talk to him."

The man nodded absently as he listened to a message from the cockpit. "If you're coming with us, the skipper says we're running low on time. I'd get aboard if I were you."

They climbed into the cramped fuselage and watched as the rest of Bravo boarded the two helos. The twin General electric T700 turbines were already spooling up, and the aircraft wobbled slightly as it rose slowly into the air. The racket inside the cabin of the roaring turboshaft engines woke Masih, and his eyes flicked open.

"Where am I?"

"It's okay. You're in a helo returning to Afghanistan, and we'll take you to a hospital to get you fixed up."

The man nodded weakly and closed his eyes again. Lucas Grant stood nearby, and he nodded across to Lieutenant Boswell.

"The last time I came out of Pakistan we were heading outta Abbottabad. Now that was one hell of a mission. That time it was the 160th Special Operations Aviation Regiment who brought us out. Those Black Hawks were quiet, too, not like these noise buckets. Real stealth jobs."

Masih's eyes flicked open again. He turned his head to look at Lucas.

"You were there? At Abbottabad?"

Grant grimaced at the wounded Pakistani, annoyed that he'd spoken out loud something that was supposed to be classified. "It ain't any of your business, Mister."

But the wounded man persisted. "Why did you not kill bin Laden?"

Lucas sighed in irritation. "Fella, Osama is history. Right now, he's feeding the fish in the Indian Ocean if you hadn't heard. Believe me, I know."

Masih gave a low grunt of pain as he shifted position to look at the Seal. "Yes, I know about Osama. We all heard about it, but my question was why did you not kill the other bin Laden? I meant Riyad bin Laden, of course."

"Who the fuck is he?" Boswell snapped. He'd been watching the wounded civilian carefully. "We've never heard of him."

Masih sighed. "That's a pity. The man you killed, Osama bin Laden, was sick. For the past two years he'd been preparing for his place to be taken by his half-brother, Riyad. He was already running many of the al Qaeda operations."

"That's a load of bullshit, Mister," Lucas snapped. "We got the right guy, no question."

Danial shrugged painfully. "As you wish. It makes little difference to me. After the raid, they singled me out as one of the few Christians in the city and accused me of sympathizing with the Americans. They said I was a spy and that I'd betrayed the Sheikh to the infidels. I had to leave the city, or they would have attacked and probably killed me. Fortunately, they did not threaten my son, so he is safe for the time being. He is still in Abbottabad. I think they did not realize who he was. But as a Christian, he is always fearful of attack if the Muslims decide they wish to harass him at any time. I had hoped to find work in Parachinar so he could travel north to join me, if I could persuade him to give up his job." He shrugged, and his face twisted in agony as the movement reminded him of his wound. "After today, I doubt it will happen."

The effort of speaking had been too much for him, and he lapsed into unconsciousness again. Boswell gave the man a derisive sneer.

"I guess he's aiming to cash in on more of that reward money Washington was offering."

He looked at Grant for consensus, but the former Seal Team Six member looked worried. He stepped closer to Nolan so he could speak above the noise of the engines.

"What do you think, Chief? I was on that operation, and we went through hell to terminate that bastard. I'd hate to think it was all for nothing."

"I don't know, Lucas. Osama was the pin up boy for terrorists all around the world, and no matter what state he was in when you took him out, it was a huge boost for all of us when he went down. The bastard deserved it, too, several thousand times over. I won't forget the Twin Towers in a hurry or the USS Cole, or any of the other murders he carried out. He was a disease that had to be eradicated. And besides, there's a new guy at the top, Ayman al-Zawahiri took over after bin Laden was chopped, didn't he?"

Grant nodded uncertainly. "Yeah, I guess so. But what if he didn't?"

"What do you mean, what if he didn't? Didn't what?"

"Take over. What if there was another bin Laden already running things, hiding in the shadows where we couldn't pick him up on our radar, but still able to use the bin Laden name to stir up the Islamist fanatics and loonies?"

Nolan digested that scenario for a few moments.

Another bin Laden! Jesus Christ, that's a nightmare scenario. The Islamists would be more motivated than ever to continue their trail of worldwide death and devastation. It could also mean the half-brother would likely be determined to avenge the death of his brother, the spiritual leader, and founder of the movement, racking up the action even more. Arabs are no slouches when it comes to the vendetta; they even put the Sicilians to shame. They sure enjoy killing, and they aren't too fussy about who they murder, as their own people often find out to their cost.

"Lucas, I'd sooner not think about it. It sounds like a shitload of misery to me. We'd best hand Danial over to our intel weenies in Bagram, and let them take care of it from here on in."

"I hate the idea of sitting back and waiting for the desk jockeys to get a grip on it," Lucas muttered, his expression anxious. "I mean, there could be a lot at stake here. Fuck it, I smashed down the door, and I saw the bastard's face. Did we miss the real target? Was it all for nothing?"

"No, my friend, Osama had to go. He deserved to go. As for this half-brother, let the guys with the computers go to work on it. Maybe CIA and NSA will get involved, but it sure is above our pay grade. Don't worry about it, they'll sort it out."

"Yeah, maybe you're right."

But Grant looked a very worried man as the helo flew fast and low over the Khyber Pass and into Afghanistan, and an uncertain future for all American troops in Afghanistan, if it was true.

That about sums up my future. What if it's true? And

that other thing. What the hell am I going to do about that?

Several days before, Carol had called from San Diego to tell him a couple of bulls were on their way out to Afghanistan to talk to him about a crime committed in the city. Carol Summers, his partner was a cop, a detective in the San Diego PD. He remembered feeling astonished; not only at what she'd said, but the way she said it. She sounded so cold and impersonal, and he couldn't work out why.

Doesn't she trust me? What about the future plans we made?

And then he'd understood. Nothing had really changed. She was just calling from the squad room, so she had to sound official. He tried to sound her out.

"What crime, what the hell do they want? What's it about?"

"A rape, Kyle."

"That's ridiculous. Why do they want to talk to me about something like that? I mean, me personally. You know that's crazy."

"We had a walk in. A girl claimed she was raped a few weeks before by someone she identified as a Seal. She was pretty certain about it. She said she was traumatized for several weeks, and it took her that long to pluck up the courage to come in and file a complaint. She managed to get away from her attacker, but it was pretty close. By the time she came in, it was too late for a rape kit, of course, but her statement was pretty compelling. That's why they need to talk to you."

"I still don't get it." Her voice still sounded strange and distant. "You don't think I did it, surely?"

She paused for a second. "She gave us a statement and a description, Kyle, and it fitted you, as well as two or three other Seals we know of." Her voice softened a little. "Look, I know it may be stupid, perhaps it's a crock of shit, but these guys have to go through the motions, and that means talking to anyone who fits the bill. Talk to them, and don't do anything stupid."

"Like what? Disappear, run away?"

She didn't sound amused. "Whatever. No, don't disappear. Give them your side of things."

Jesus Christ. Don't leave town, that's what she's saying. What is this? He forced himself to calm down. It's all a mistake, and she's upset, probably put on the spot by the other cops in her department. A thought occurred to him.

"I may not even have been in San Diego, Carol. That could clear me."

A hesitation. "I know you were here, Kyle. I checked. It was one of my work nights. I recall you stayed home on your own."

So he had no alibi, and he noticed her voice had cooled even more.

But shit, I haven't raped anybody. It's an act I find totally repulsive. Besides, women come on to me, so why the hell would I do something crazy like that?

He shut that thought off as soon as it surfaced. It sounded like what they'd all say. Even so, he had no motive, nothing. He realized she'd gone quiet on the other end of the line. There was something more, something she hadn't yet mentioned.

"Tell me, what is it?"

"No, it's nothing, I…"

"Tell me!"

He heard her sigh. "You went to see your physician the following morning. I remember you told me you'd talked about your problem with the blackouts and memory loss you'd had the night before. But it's nothing, I..."

"You think I could have raped a girl without knowing about it! Jesus Christ, what kind of guy do you think I am?"

She hadn't replied. He'd ended the call. He didn't want to talk anymore. It was crazy, lunacy to suggest he'd do anything like that.

But if I can't remember, Christ, how can I even deny it? And what if I did...? Shit, no, it's not possible! And Carol, she was so strange. What the hell was wrong with her, how could she even think it? Yet she did. She believes I may even have done it!

CHAPTER TWO

The two Black Hawks flew low over Bagram. They banked suddenly, plummeted downward for a landing but hovered over the helipad, waiting for clearance. Boswell went forward to the cockpit to talk to local command HQ. He came back into the cabin and called for them to listen.

"They say there's a security alert down there, and Bagram is locked down tighter than a girl's convent school. The air base has been reinforced with a company of American infantry, and outside the wire they've put in a couple of companies of Afghan regulars to guard the approaches. It's a pretty big deal. President Hamid Karzai is here to meet the Pakistani Foreign Minister. They chose Bagram because it's a secure area, and they want us out of the way." He grinned. "If the Paki Minister found out we'd been inside his territory, shooting up the locals, he'd be pissed. They assigned us a helipad on the far side of the field, well away from the terminal, so there's no danger of any contact. They'll send transport out to meet us."

They began their final descent, and Nolan looked out

of the cabin window at the huge expanse of buildings and tents. At men and women, who scurried from place to place, most carrying something, packages, and boxes, all of them carried a weapon. Small tugs pulled lines of trolleys laden with munitions and supplies, heading for the scores of revetments that dotted the thirty plus acre site. While he watched, a huge Boeing C-17 Globemaster four-engine transport aircraft began taxiing out onto one of the two runways prior to take off. On the other runway, a pair of FA/18 Super Hornets waited, their engines idling while they awaited final clearance. At regular intervals around the perimeter, they'd stationed a number of Humvees, fitted with the lethal M134 Gatling style machine guns, and manned by grim faced troops in armor. Outside, the Afghan Army, in their distinctive green uniforms were patrolling the perimeter wire on foot, marching up and down. With the high number of 'green on blue' incidents, Afghan soldiers firing on ISAF troops, it was no surprise they'd kept them outside.

He turned to look at Boswell.

"You mention the guy we brought back, Lt?"

He nodded. "Yeah, they're expecting us to bring in a casualty."

Nolan sighed. "Not that. I meant, what he said about Abbottabad."

"I did not." He looked indignant. "That was some kind of a fairy story to frighten the kids. Riyad fucking bin Laden, bullshit. They got the right guy. Lucas here was there. I'm not making waves by bringing in a report of a new bogeyman."

Nolan stared at him. "You have to report it, Lt. If you don't, I will. It's pretty important."

Boswell sighed. "Okay, I'll mention it at the debrief, but…"

Lucas Grant interrupted. "Lt, they need to know, right now, the second we step of this aircraft. When we were out chasing Osama, he switched locations like he was running from a process server. We can't waste any time."

Boswell nodded, finally convinced. "Yeah, okay, as soon as we're inside HQ, I'll talk to them."

"You need to patch a message through from the cockpit. As soon as we land, they'll need to put a guard on Danial Masih," Nolan added. "He could have intel that's worth its weight in gold." He caught Boswell's eye. "Providing it's handled real quick."

"Okay, okay. Anything else?"

Nolan stared at him. The Lieutenant ignored him and walked to the other side of the cabin, muttering, "Fucking ragheads."

The helo bumped down on to the pad, and the door slid open.

"Chief?"

Nolan looked around at Lucas.

"Yeah?"

"If this intel pans out, you know what it would mean."

"Another trip to Abbottabad to clear up unfinished business."

"Yep. And the second time around, it'll be much harder. They'll have early warning systems, more guards, and much better defenses."

"Probably."

"If they want to send Bravo in as we're on the spot, so to speak, there's also Boswell. He's not up to it, you know that, and I know that."

Nolan grimaced. "Maybe, but I thought you were helping him out."

"I'm doing my best. They said if his performance was improved, they'd jump me early to E-6, Petty Officer First Class, with a recommendation for early promotion to E-7."

"I'd assumed it was something like that."

"Yeah. It's important to me. I've got plans. I guess you know what it's like. You gotta wife and kids?"

Nolan closed his eyes for a brief moment and thought of Daniel and Mary, being cared for by their grandparents. Cared for, because their mother had been killed in a drive-by shooting, part of a drug war back in San Diego.

"Something like that."

"Right. So I gotta help push the guy along, but he's got a ways to go."

"He has that," Nolan agreed.

"Too far, in my opinion. He's not up to a strike mission into Abbottabad, Chief. You know it, I know it, and I guess he knows it."

"It hasn't happened yet, Lucas. You're jumping the gun."

"Maybe," the Seal said doubtfully. "But if they do send us in, it'll be a whole new ball game."

"No, it won't. It's the same game we signed up for when we joined the Seals. We go where they send us, period. We undertake the missions that are too difficult for regular units, and we go with the platoon commander assigned to us. End of story."

Lucas scowled at him. "That's the way to get us all killed, Chief. It's not the way we did it in my last outfit. We had good platoon commanders, the best, not gung ho college boys on the make."

Nolan sighed.

I'm not going to persuade the man, and he has a point. Boswell is something of a liability even though he's doing his limited best to sharpen up. He has sharpened up, too. He has the making of a good Seal officer. He's just slow getting there. But if they tell me to follow the Lieutenant on a mission, I have to go. Period.

"Let's see what intel finds out. We haven't been ordered anywhere yet. Bravo is due to rotate back to the States. Maybe they'll let us go on leave."

Lucas stared at him. "Yeah, right."

What the hell should I do? A kill mission back to Abbottabad would put us into maximum danger, especially if Boswell leads it. Christ, I didn't ask them to assign the Lieutenant to us. Yet if I agree with Lucas, it's insubordination, and his connections would sure come down hard. I could, no would, be kicked out of the Seals. If I fail to spell out my misgivings about Boswell, it could be a threat to the safety of the whole Platoon. What the hell do I do? Wait and see. What else?

He disembarked the helo with the rest of the men. Two corpsmen were carrying the gurney loaded with Danial Masih out to the tarmac, and Boswell had assigned two men, Zeke Murray and Dave Eisner, to accompany it and act as guards. There was an ambulance waiting to transfer him to the base hospital. At least Boswell was thinking about security, which was to be welcomed. Nolan slid out into the Afghan sunshine with the Platoon, and they started the long walk to the HQ building. There'd been a foul-up somewhere, and apart from the military ambulance, there was no transport for them.

Well, a walk never killed anybody, and at least it isn't raining!

Will fell into step beside him.

"I gather the new man was giving you a hard time?"

Nolan shrugged. "Not really, he's between a rock and a hard place. They've promised him promotion in return for helping Boswell along, but he feels the Lieutenant could be a liability to the Platoon, especially if we tackle something real hard. Like Abbottabad."

"Yeah, he's about right. I guess we'll manage, though, however things go."

That was what he liked about the big PO1. He always managed. Nolan could count on him to come through, no matter what.

"I guess we will at that."

They both looked up as a Humvee rocketed across the tarmac and screeched to a halt beside them. An officer climbed out of the passenger seat, a Marine Colonel. He looked to be in his mid-forties, tall, clean-shaven, pale-skinned, and as thin as a whip. He wore thick spectacles and looked for all the world like a college professor, than a military officer. His name on his tunic said, 'Weathers'.

"I'm Lieutenant Colonel Randall Weathers, Marine Intelligence Department. I'm looking for Chief Petty Officer Nolan."

"That's me, Sir."

The Colonel looked at him. "I'm told you spoke at length with the wounded Pakistani you brought in?"

"Yes, Sir, we chatted some."

"Something about Abbottabad?"

"That's right."

Weathers nodded. "I need you to come with me, Chief.

I'm going over to the sick bay to talk to him, and I suspect he may open up more if he sees a familiar face. I want you to accompany me. Climb in."

News sure travels fast, he thought. Boswell must have made the call from the cockpit. Dropped me in the shit, more like.

While the Lieutenant was taking a hot shower and eating his chow, Nolan would be sat in a hot hospital room giving Danial Masih the third degree with Lieutenant Colonel Weathers and his pals. He shrugged mentally.

It can't be helped.

"Sure, I'd be glad to, Sir. I can't wait."

The Colonel gave him a sharp look, but he kept his face straight.

They had to wait for twenty minutes until the physician allowed them into his room. Masih was lying in a cot with three drip bags suspended above him, and his chest heavily bandaged. He'd been pumped with drugs, and Nolan suspected one of them at least was some kind of a mild stimulant to make him alert and talkative. The old Pakistani grinned at the Seal when he saw him walking in behind the Colonel.

"You are the man who saved me. You have my thanks."

Nolan nodded. "No sweat."

"Would you tell me your name? I thought American soldiers wore their name on their uniform, like this man."

He pointed at the Colonel's nametag.

"Not all of us, no. It's Nolan."

"Nolan. Thank you."

The Colonel leaned forward and tried, unsuccessfully, to mask his impatience.

"Sir, tell me about this Riyad bin Laden. Have you

actually met him?"

"Oh, yes, of course. Sometimes, he would stroll around the town, always accompanied by his guards. On one occasion, his older brother fell ill, and I saw him with his Osama."

"And how do you know this Riyad took over command of al Qaeda?"

Danial looked puzzled. "It was talked about in the town. The fighters get drunk sometimes and boast about the Sheikh! They said Osama was sick, and we were to obey the new Sheikh, Riyad, and protect him if the infidels came."

"I thought Muslims didn't drink."

He laughed. "That's nonsense. Most of the fighters I've come across in the town drink heavily."

Weathers nodded. "I'd heard something like that. You're a Christian, Mr. Masih. Tell me, why did they trust you?"

Danial smiled. "I'd lived there for so long they'd forgotten. And I kept my religion secret, very private, for there is always fear of reprisals. But recently, things have changed, and they have started to take their security much more seriously."

"I bet they have. Okay, so you heard this Riyad was the new man at the top."

"Yes."

"What does he look like?"

"Riyad? He looks like Osama. It is difficult to tell them apart, except he is younger of course, by about ten years."

Weathers closed his eyes, and they heard him mutter a curse. "So that would make him about early forties, yes?"

"That sounds right."

"Tell me, where did you last see Riyad bin Laden?"

"In his house, close to the compound in Abbottabad."

"Can you tell us where that is? The address, or maybe describe it for us?"

"If you wish, but after the raid, I doubt he will be there."

"No? Do you know where he would be?"

Masih looked puzzled again. "Yes, of course. He will be in Osama's command bunker."

"And where is that?"

"It is beneath the house you raided when you killed him, underneath the compound. He was probably there when you attacked. He set up his command headquarters down there."

The Colonel looked to the ceiling for inspiration. He said one word. "Fuck!" Then he turned to Nolan. "Chief, would you come with me."

"Yes, Sir." Nolan looked at Danial and smiled. "So long, my friend. You're gonna be okay now. A few days and you'll be out of here."

"Yes. My thanks again for saving my life, Nolan."

"Yeah."

He picked up his rifle, followed the Colonel out of the sick bay, and they gratefully sucked in the open air, driving out the stinking taste of antiseptics from their nasal passages. The noise was deafening as a pair of Air Force jocks gunned their engines ready for takeoff. The jet engines crescendoed to a high-pitched scream, and they shot along the runway, trailing clouds of kerosene fumes in their wake. In the distance, the Black Hawks that recovered them from Pakistan were taking off for somewhere, and their turboshafts screamed as they clawed for altitude. They climbed into the Colonel's Humvee. The driver was still sitting inside, waiting for orders.

"Back to headquarters, Mathews. Make it fast."

"Yes, Sir."

The driver kicked down on the gas, and the heavy Humvee surged forward, jerking them backward in their seats. Lieutenant Colonel Weathers affected not to notice. He looked sideways at Nolan.

"You know what his means, Chief, if it's true."

"I think so, Sir. We've got a problem."

"You got that right. Can you imagine what the world will think if they find out we killed a sick old man? Killed him, and missed the main target who'd taken over his terror organization. And then he appears on the damned tube, or the Internet, and there's this bearded turd with the name 'bin Laden', telling the Islamists to go out and bomb the West. It would be like the second coming."

Nolan saw it all then. The Colonel was right. It would ignite a furor that would set the world alight. It would send the fanatics back into the fray with a new energy and determination. Just when the Pentagon estimated they had them beat, they'd come back, a Phoenix climbing out of the ashes of the fire. And ISAF would have it all to do again.

Another 911 maybe. Dear God, it's too much to contemplate.

He suddenly realized the Colonel was staring at him, and he knew what it meant. But this time, he had to say no.

Christ, there are other units, Seals, Delta, British SAS and SBS, so why Bravo?

"I understand what you're saying Sir. If he exists, this guy has to be stopped. But if you're thinking of Bravo, you need to think again. We've been out in the field chasing around Afghanistan and Pakistan for months, and the men are tired. We're due to rotate back Stateside. You need someone fresh, a platoon that's at their peak. And besides, there are other problems as well."

"You're referring to Lieutenant Boswell, I assume."

He looked the officer in the eye, trying to read his expression.

"I didn't say that, Sir."

"You didn't need to, Chief. We know all about Boswell, or at least, we know about the influence his people wield at the Pentagon. We can't do anything about it, I'm afraid. He has to stay with the Platoon, and that's the word from the top. What about the new guy, from Seal Team Six? How's he making out?"

The reason for his change of direction was obvious. He knew why Lucas Grant had been injected into the Platoon.

"He's damn good, no problems."

"That's fine. You know he was brought in to assist Boswell?"

"Yes, Sir."

"And is it working out? Is he helping him make out?"

You could give me lessons with Placido Domingo, but it wouldn't make me an opera singer.

"Grant is a good man, Sir," he replied carefully.

"Yeah, that he is. They didn't pick any second raters for Seal Team Six."

The Humvee screeched to a stop outside an anonymous concrete building. There were no windows, just a pair of heavy, steel doors and a marine sentry on guard outside. Weathers hustled through the doors, barely acknowledging the salute, and Nolan hurried after him. They pushed through into a well-lit room, cluttered with desks and computer terminals, and all manned by uniformed marines, men and women. He opened a door and turned to Nolan.

"This is where I work. Come on in, Chief."

Inside, another officer, an Asian woman, probably Japanese, sat at a desk at the side of the room. He stared at her, and then forced himself to look away. She was stunning, almost enough to take his breath away. Her hair was a shimmering dark brown, nearly black, and tied up in a bun at just above the nape of the neck. Her skin was without blemish, and instead of the typical Japanese coloring was more of a dark, cream color, like a pale California tan. Her eyes were wide-set, thick-lashed, and inky black. She wore no makeup. She was a woman who'd never feel the need to enhance what nature had provided her. She wore a uniform that had been carefully tailored to fit her curves to perfection. Clearly a girl who took pride in her appearance; a girl anyone would notice. She had a strange combination of simplicity and polish, almost a physical aura, yet he got the impression she'd have been shocked if someone had told her how pretty she was. Definitely a Marine pin-up, and the kind of girl who would make a success of anything she put her hand to.

The Marine Corps sure are lucky to have her.

Weathers dumped himself behind the big desk.

"This is Captain Noguchi, Chief. She's my number two."

Nolan saluted, and she returned the salute, but then she got up and held out her hand. "We're more informal in intelligence, Chief. It's Mariko. Why don't you put that rifle down and take it easy."

She indicated a spare chair, and he sat down, but he kept hold of his rifle.

"I'm Kyle Nolan, Ma'am."

His voice was hoarse, and he struggled to clear his throat. She nodded and looked at Weathers. "How did it go with that wounded Pakistani, Colonel? Is he going to live?"

So the informality is junior ranks and NCOs only. Fair enough.

"He is, but it's bad, Mariko. The big bad wolf lives again, if we're to believe this guy." He filled her in briefly on what he'd learned from Danial Masih. "Riyad bin Laden, how the hell did we miss that one? We knew Osama had plenty of brothers, but we thought we had accounted for them all."

"We only knew about the ones he wanted us to know about, I guess," she offered. "His brother Mahrous bin Laden seized the limelight when he was implicated in the Grand Mosque Seizure in Saudi. It was a direct attack on the Saudi ruling family at the Masjid al-Haram in Mecca. It shook the whole country to the core, and they killed hundreds of people at the holiest of the Islamic sites. It was alleged they used trucks owned by the bin Laden family to smuggle arms into the city, even though it was buttoned up tight at the time. It meant we mainly looked at Mahrous and Osama as the principal troublemakers. If this Riyad was born around that time to one of his father's many wives, it looks to me as if they kept him quiet. Kind of like a sleeper."

"And now the sleeper awakes," Lieutenant-Colonel Weathers mused.

"Yes, Sir. That he does. If he exists."

Weathers stared at Nolan. "I need to know the answer to that question, Chief. I have to find out the truth, if this bogeyman exists or not. I want Bravo to go into

Abbottabad and find out for me."

But, Sir, we already…"

"Hold on a second, hear me out." He held up his hand. "I'm not looking for a kill operation, nothing of the kind. All I want at this stage is information, a recon mission, something I can put to our superiors and ultimately before the President."

"Sir, I understand, but I take orders from Rear Admiral Jacks at Coronado Base, and he's specifically ordered us to rotate back to the US for R&R."

He wondered what Jacks would have to say about this attempt to go over his head. One thing was for sure; the tough, proud Seal commander wouldn't be all that impressed. He pictured his boss, currently in his forties, short and bow-legged, but with broad, muscled shoulders, and his trademark close-cropped spiky blonde hair. Jacks was a sailor's sailor. Where his men were concerned, he'd go to any lengths for them.

Weathers nodded slowly. "Yeah, I'm sure that's the situation, but I'm prepared to trump your ace, Son. I'm betting the President of the United States will pass an order to carry out this mission."

"I see, Sir, but that won't change any of the problems that we're facing in Bravo."

"You mean your unit being worn out after so long in the field? Or are you referring to Boswell?"

Nolan hedged. "It's complicated, Sir."

"I'm sure it is, but this is just a reconnaissance mission. What the hell could go wrong?"

How many times has a senior officer put a dangerous mission in those terms, 'what could go wrong?' They could be waiting for us to pull something just like this, and half the men could come back in body bags. Or wind up in a Pakistani dungeon.

"Well, uh…"

"It'll be a walk in the park, Chief. In and out, in a single night. Pick up one or two locals; bring 'em back for interrogation, and you can go home to sunny California. Besides, I'll get you some help, someone who knows the culture and language of that part of Pakistan."

"Sir?"

Weathers looked at the Asian-looking Captain. "Our very own Pakistan expert. Captain Mariko Noguchi."

Nolan almost laughed out loud. "Er, Sir, she's Japanese. She doesn't look remotely Pakistani."

Weathers smiled. "Not right now, no. Captain, show him."

"Yes, Colonel."

She got up and walked out the door. Weathers stared at Nolan.

"Well, Chief? You don't seem comfortable about this. Problems working in the field with a woman?"

"It's not that, Sir," he lied. "It's the whole operation. Lieutenant Boswell shouldn't be on it. He's still finding his feet." Nolan thought back to that moment outside Parachinar when Boswell could have halted the attack, and instead allowed the Taliban to sacrifice scores of civilians to the Warthog gunfire. "Besides, he's the platoon commander, so it depends on his say so, not mine. And another thing, while Captain Noguchi is out of the office, I should tell you I'm not comfortable about taking an unskilled woman on a Seal mission. You know how hard we train. It's no job for a rookie. Besides, she looks Japanese, so it doesn't matter how she plays it, she just won't fit in."

"Is that right?" Weathers looked at him calmly. "You're sure about that?"

"I am, Sir. If this deal goes ahead, I don't believe the Captain is an option. We'll be better off without her, but even then, there're too many problems for us to take on such a sensitive mission. At a guess, I'd say whoever goes in will need some kind of undercover support, someone with local knowledge who can blend in and give them an edge over the enemy. After all, no one knows yet what they'll face when they get over there."

The Colonel nodded but made no further comment. There was a knock at the door, Weathers shouted, "Enter!" The door opened. An Afghan woman walked in, clad in the traditional blue burqa, her face covered behind the mesh screen of the hood that enveloped her head. Her spine was bent, common for local women who lacked the Vitamin D that sunshine provided for healthy bones. Their menfolk were content to see them suffer the agonies of rickets and other related diseases, as long as they obeyed the centuries old customs. Her head was bent low too, in the abject way these women comported themselves in the presence of men, as if to underline the nature of their lowly position within the Islamic paradise of Afghanistan, and similarly in Waziristan. Nolan felt instinctively for his Sig. These women were not unknown to carry weapons, even suicide belts for the Taliban. He kept it holstered but ready for instant action. She looked at him briefly and said something in the harsh, guttural local dialect. Colonel Weathers replied.

"That's okay, Captain. I think the Chief has seen enough."

"Yes, Sir," Captain Mariko Noguchi replied.

She took off the burqa. Underneath, she was still wearing her khaki Marine working uniform. Nolan felt the astonishment that an American officer could change so quickly. It wasn't just the burqa. It was everything, the groveling posture, and the language. She could have made a fortune on the stage.

"What do you think?" the Colonel grinned. "Pretty impressive, eh?"

"She sure is. Yes, she'd fit in anywhere in Afghanistan or Waziristan; I've no doubt about that. But it doesn't resolve the other problem."

"I'll get Rear Admiral Jacks to speak to Lieutenant Boswell. There won't be a problem."

"That's not what I meant, Colonel."

Nolan felt both pairs of eyes on him. Weathers looked mildly amused. Captain Noguchi looked pretty hostile.

"What exactly do you mean by a problem, Chief Petty Officer Nolan?" she snapped out.

Nolan drew breath. It had to be said. "Ma'am, Navy Seals are trained to handle this kind of mission. I'm guessing you're not trained in CQB, and I don't want to take any rookies into harm's way. With all due respect, Ma'am," he finished.

She stared at him out of those huge, inky black eyes, and it felt as if she was using some kind of mental power on him. Or maybe it was just her overwhelming femininity, so startlingly unusual in this harsh and hostile masculine environment. Then she sighed.

"You don't know how much training I've had, do you?"

"No, Ma'am."

"I scored in the high nineties with both a rifle and a

pistol. I'm also a Black Belt Third Dan, and I graduated UCLA summa cum laude with Urdu, Pashto and Dari. All of which I'd guess could come in useful out in Waziristan. I'm no rookie."

"How many missions have you completed, Ma'am? How much Close Quarters Battle training and experience to you have?"

She was still staring at him hard. He felt like a fly pinned to a board, and she wasn't about to give in. He realized that. She was a woman who knew how to fight, but still, a woman.

"None. But even the much-vaunted Navy Seals have to start somewhere. You can't hold that against me."

"No. It's just that…"

He trailed off lamely. Her expression hardened even more, if that was possible.

"So it's because I'm a woman."

He shut up. They were both staring at him now, Weathers and the pretty Japanese American Captain, and he squirmed in embarrassment. Finally, Weathers broke the silence.

"Chief, you have to understand that…"

The explosion was unexpected, and the building rocked as a mortar bomb detonated close by. Another explosion hit the tarmac further away, at the opposite end of the runway. Alarm sirens began to wail, and in seconds, the orderly business of Bagram Airfield turned into total chaos.

"Incoming, take cover, everyone to battle stations!" Someone was running through the building, shouting. They sounded panicked. Nolan had picked up his SWS Mk 11 and was already hurtling through the door of the small room and out into the main office. In an attack, there'd be enemies to snipe at. The office was crammed with men and women running around, panicking, trying to grab documents and possessions, but Nolan ran past them and out the entrance doors, which were now unguarded.

Where the hell is that sentry now he's needed?

The sight that greeted him was astonishing. The airfield had gone mad. A pair of Humvees zipped past him, and the wheel of one clipped the leg of his pants; any closer and it would have done serious damage. The vehicles were headed for the perimeter wire behind the Marine Intelligence Department building, fifty meters away. Behind him, the airfield was erupting with panicking troops and sporadic bursts of gunfire. He ran around the side of the building and dived for cover in a shallow dip in the ground as he came face to face with the enemy. They were wearing the green uniforms of the Afghan Army and firing short bursts at anything that moved from their M16s, their American supplied rifles.

"What's happening?"

He swiveled around. Captain Noguchi had followed him out. She'd acquired an M16-A4, and it looked much too long for her. He recalled the photos he'd seen as a kid, Japanese soldiers with rifles that were longer than they were. He smiled inwardly.

Captain Noguchi's a woman, she's on our side, and she sure is beautiful.

"Green on blue, Captain, those Afghan motherfuckers are hitting our people again. Get down, before they blow your stupid head off!"

She joined him, and they lay prone on the ground. He pointed to where the two Humvees were heading, their top-mounted heavy machine guns firing long bursts at a break in the wire where an Afghan Army platoon had established a strongpoint with two trucks parked to give them cover. Another mortar shell whooshed up from behind the trucks and sailed overhead, exploding on the tarmac. The big 4x4s bored in, machine guns hammering at the trucks. And then two Afghans stepped out from behind cover, both men with RPGs leveled. They fired, and Nolan watched, helpless as the two missile trails flashed across. The warheads exploded to score direct hits on the Humvees. The American vehicles exploded, and they literally blew apart, leaving behind a heap of twisted scrap metal and broken bodies.

"Oh, my God, those poor men. There could be survivors. We have to go check them out."

Mariko Noguchi jumped up, only to be dragged back down into the dirt as Nolan reached up an arm and yanked hard.

"I said get down!" he snarled.

She stayed down this time, and habit made him check the load on his SWS. He had a full clip of 7.62mm ammunition, which was as it should be. It was time to go to work. He sighted through the Leupold Vari-X mildot riflescope, and the first enemy loomed large in the precision glass lenses. He squeezed off two shots, and a missile shooter went down. Two more rounds sped out of the barrel, and the missile reloader followed his master into paradise. The other missile shooter and the loader ducked behind cover as they realized the danger, but Nolan kept searching for targets, and he kept up a steady rate of accurate fire that kept the missile shooters heads down. Three uniformed Afghan riflemen went down, and then he ran out of targets. But now the enemy had got his range, and the machine gunner, firing a heavy .50 caliber M2, also American supplied, opened up on their position. The loader was carefully feeding the ammunition belt through the breech, and more .50 caliber rounds than Nolan cared to count hammered all around the shallow trough of ground he sheltered in with the Captain, throwing debris and chunks of concrete to rain on them like a heavy shower. To her credit, she didn't flinch, even though she had neither a Kevlar helmet nor an armored vest. Not that Nolan's armor would help him; the .50 caliber rounds were enough to pierce an APC. Personal armor was no contest for the Browning machine gun. He realized she was trying to say something above the racket of machine gun bullets smashing into the ground and nearby buildings; the roar of mortar shells as they exploded, and the crack of assault rifles as both sides exchanged fire.

"What was that?" he shouted back, not looking around at her.

"I said they're our Allies!"

"You don't say! With allies like these, we sure don't need to go looking for any enemies."

"But…"

"Shut the fuck up, and stay low. Don't move, and don't follow me."

He regretted the language as soon as he'd opened his mouth, but he was angry she was in position of maximum danger, and he wanted her to stay put.

"Where are you going?"

"That machine gun, it'll hurt our boys badly when they try to take it on. I'm going after it."

He didn't wait for a reply. Nolan put his rifle down in the

dirt, got to his feet, and ran crouched over. The machine gun was too well concealed for a sniper shot, but he had grenades clipped to his webbing. He still hadn't checked in from the last mission. It was time to put them to good use, and the only way to kill the enemy was close up and personal. The perimeter fence was already breached, obviously in preparation for a serious infiltration. He thought of the security lockdown. It couldn't be a coincidence. They were here to kill Hamid Karzai, or maybe Chutani Muhammad, the Pakistani Minister of Foreign Affairs, perhaps both of them. He saw a window of opportunity, as the Afghan gunner shifted his aim to easier targets, a group of MPs armed with M-16 A4s, running toward the action from the guardhouse next to the main gates. The MPs dived for cover as the hail of fire churned up the ground around them. Nolan couldn't see if any of them were hit, and besides, he had other concerns. He had to get inside the arc of fire before the gunner spotted him and turned the heavy weapon around. The breath seared in his lungs as he pounded on at a record breaking, heart bursting pace. The pain in his chest rose higher as he pressed forward, putting every ounce of his energy and strength into the sprint. Maybe it wouldn't have been enough to break any Olympic records, but he reflected it must have come close, especially for a guy wearing armor and a helmet. He was almost there, almost at the first truck that would give him cover from the machine gun. He snatched two grenades and pulled out the clips. And then the gunner saw him. The barrel started to traverse, as if in slow motion, nearer and nearer. He tried to estimate if he'd make it, or should he dive for the ground and hope he was beneath the next hail of bullets that came his way. It was close, too close.

But the ground offered no real cover; he'd still be easy meat. And then the barrel stopped, and he was staring into a round, black hole. As he ran, he waited for the heavy lead that was about to spit out and tear his body to pieces. There was no way he could make it. The thunder of gunfire made him flinch, and he froze, waiting for the impact of heavy caliber bullets tearing him apart. But he reached the truck unscathed, and when he looked around, he saw an astonishing sight. Captain Mariko Noguchi was in process of making a single-handed charge on the Afghan gun, her M-16 A4 firing short, three-round bursts at the machine gun. The gunner saw her, stopped firing, and ducked down to avoid bursts of fire that clanged off the metalwork of the truck he sheltered behind. Noguchi's bullets clanged off the engine block, and the Afghan realized he was safe from the new attack. He began to traverse the barrel back around to destroy this crazy American who seemed to have a death wish. Nolan saw it all happening and didn't pause for a fraction of a second to work out what was happening. Everything he did was instinctive after thousands of hours training, hundred of hours fighting the enemy in missions the world over. The M67 grenades had spherical steel bodies each containing 6.5 ounces of Composition B explosive. Weighing a total of 14 ounces, the lethal objects sailed through the air in an unerring arc, straight toward the intended target.

"Get the fuck down!" he shouted back to Noguchi. At the same time, he dragged out his Sig and leapt around the side of the truck, ducking down away from the spread of the fragments as the grenades went off. The twin explosions were huge, and he felt himself lifted off his feet by the blast. The gun had stopped firing. There was no way they could have survived that blast. He ducked as a snapshot whistled past his head. An Afghan soldier was peering around the side of the truck, looking for a target. He risked a quick glance back the way he'd come and saw to his relief that Captain Noguchi was still alive. He could see her huge black eyes watching him from where she'd dived to the ground.

For Christ's sake, keep your pretty little head down. You did well. They'd have killed me without that crazy charge of yours, but now they know you're there, and they'll want revenge.

He was out of grenades. All he had left was his Sig and his combat knife, which was not ideal against troops armed with M-16s. He heard Mariko Noguchi firing again, the characteristic three-shot bursts of 5.56mm rounds from her M-16 A4. The Afghans took the bait. There were three of them left, and they leaned around the side of the truck, setting up a furious rate of return fire, intended to kill the infidel who threatened to upset their plans. Once more, she'd given him an opening. He jumped up and zigzagged around the truck to come up behind the Afghans. He hit two of them with a half-dozen shots from the Sig. It was a precision handgun, there was no doubt, but a short-barreled automatic, firing 9mm pistol rounds, definitely had its limitations. He missed the third Afghan, who lifted up his M-16 to kill him. Nolan pulled the trigger, and the Sig jammed. It was the first time ever, probably a result of faulty ammunition, or maybe debris in the mechanism after the last mission. He hadn't had time to clean and oil his weapons. But a jam was a jam, and in the heat of a fight, a killer.

The Afghan saw him pull the trigger and that nothing

had happened. He smiled, a filthy leering smirk through the rotting stumps of his remaining teeth. He mouthed a few words, probably, 'this is for my friends', or maybe something religious. The Muslims always seemed to find it easy to summon up a religious justification for killing. And the man died, thrown back by two heavy caliber bullets. Nolan looked up and stared across the air base. Bravo Platoon had arrived, and Vince Merano lay prone on the ground, clutching his sniper rifle. He looked up and waved to Nolan, who returned the gesture.

I'm alive, Jesus Christ. Bravo looks after its own, that's for sure.

He checked around his immediate surroundings, but the only enemies in sight were all dead. Some had escaped. The attack had involved large numbers of insurgents, and the body count wasn't high enough to account for them all. It would be good to think they'd killed the Taliban commanders, but he knew those guys would have stayed at the back when the bullets were flying. The higher their rank, the louder they shouted, and the further back they stayed. He remembered Saddam Hussein, exhorting his troops to fight and die, in the 'Mother of all Battles', and Muammar Muhammad Abu Minyar al-Gaddafi, Colonel Gaddafi, the dictator of Libya. His long harangues were famous, sending his minions out to do battle. Until the bullets started flying, and then he ran like the yellow rat he was.

He started to walk back through the wrecked fence and toward Captain Mariko Noguchi. As he strolled along, he reflected that but for her intervention, he'd be dead. It felt strange. One moment he'd been preaching about the need for training and combat experience, the next, a rookie officer saved his life.

Weird!

* * *

He'd have given anything to avoid the ceremony. Politicians turned his stomach, especially these people.

"Chief Petty Officer Nolan, we are in your debt. My advisors tell me that without your heroic efforts, the insurgents could have come close to killing me."

Nolan looked at the man stood in front of him. Fifty-five years old, spare and lean, with a sparse gray beard, wearing the trademark Karakul hat and the long, traditional Afghan ceremonial cloak, the Chapan. Hamid Karzai, 12th President of Afghanistan, darling of the George W Bush administration, despised by the fundamentalist Muslims, and mortal enemy of the Taliban. Next to him was the Pakistani politician the Foreign Minister, Chutani Muhammad. He was plump, almost obese, a short man with a round face, supporting at least three chins, and a potbelly thinly disguised by his expensively cut coat. Both men had hugged him, which made Nolan cringe, and Karzai insisted on saying a few words of thanks. He looked the Seal in the eye.

"I assure you, Chief Petty Officer, we will remember your service to this country, and I will make it my business to ensure you receive the appropriate recognition for your bravery under fire. This is not the first time my life has been protected by the United States Navy Seals. I am indebted to all of you brave men."

There didn't seem to be any reply needed, so Nolan nodded at both men and eased back before they put him in another politician's half nelson. Colonel Weathers and Lieutenant Boswell came to his rescue and led him away. For some reason, the meeting had been held in a large office in the building beneath the control tower. Probably it was easier to defend from the attacks mounted on a regular basis by Karzai's Afghan electorate who didn't seem so happy with what their votes had brought them. Bravo Platoon was waiting outside, and they gave him an ironic cheer as he came out.

"They're proud of you," Colonel Weathers beamed.

"Not really. They know I'll owe them a few beers next time we wind up in a bar," Nolan corrected him.

"To celebrate your victory, killing those insurgents?"

"To celebrate staying alive. That's what it's all about."

He nodded to the Platoon. "I'll catch you guys in the bar later."

"Yeah, don't forget your billfold, Chief. We'll see if we can lighten it some for you."

The Colonel grunted in irritation. War was serious business, too serious to make jokes about. Maybe the guy should have been a cavalry officer about two hundred years ago, leading epic charges against the redskins, armed with bows and arrows; although the rules were no different back then. Dead soldiers didn't live to get back up to fight and defeat the enemy.

They walked back to the Marine Intelligence Department building. Crews were still clearing the damage, although the casualties had long been removed, dead and wounded, friendlies and hostiles. The acrid tang of smoke still assaulted the nostrils, a combination of spent nitrates, burning rubber and wood, and the sweet, disgusting stench of burnt flesh. Weathers' HQ had only sustained minor damage during the attack. Mariko Noguchi was back in the office where he'd seen her earlier. She'd taken the opportunity to wash up, put on a clean uniform, and tidy her hair. She looked ravishing, and the Chief was reminded of the filth that covered him, that he'd still not had time to wash off.

"Could I have a minute with Captain Noguchi, Colonel?"

Weathers nodded. "Sure thing."

He went across to Noguchi. "Captain, that was a brave thing you did back there. Without you, I might be dead. Thank you."

She nodded gravely. "Without me, you would definitely be dead, Chief Nolan, but you're welcome anyway." Her expression broke into a smile. "You can buy me a beer later if you like. We'll call it quits."

"Ma'am, that is a promise."

"Good. I'll take you up on that promise, Chief. I'm glad you're still with us. I'm going to enjoy working with you."

He looked at Boswell and Weathers. They stared back implacably. What was there to argue about? She'd handled herself under fire like a seasoned vet, and it was one hell of a test of her abilities. He was old-fashioned enough not to want such an attractive girl on a live mission, but he was also savvy enough to know that his objections about taking a female rookie into the field had been answered.

"Sure. What about Admiral Jacks, Lt, what does he say?

"He's gone along with the mission," Boswell replied. "The Pentagon put pressure on him, and there are no objections there. So we're green-lighted. We'll be going in tomorrow night, recon only. Colonel Weathers feels we need a good night's rest before we go back into the field."

"That's kind of him."

Captain Noguchi managed a small smile. Weathers didn't smile as he interrupted.

"I want you to go into Abbottabad, confirm the existence or otherwise of the target, and investigate any other terrorist infrastructure that exists in the city."

"Sir," Nolan interrupted him. "To be clear, I assume the principal target is intel about Riyad bin Laden?"

Weathers nodded. "That's pretty much it. I want you to confirm the existence of this man, and his location, of course. So far, all we have is the word of that Pakistani you brought back, and there are people here who are still pretty doubtful. I doubt you'll actually set eyes on him, if he's anything like as reclusive as his late brother. But someone in the area will know something, one way or the other, so try and bring back a prisoner who may have something for us. We need confirmation. Your job is to bring back any intel that confirms or denies this. Naturally, if by some miracle, you did happen to run into the guy, who may or may not be the new head of al Qaeda, we'd like you to deliver a heavy-caliber greetings card from the American government."

"Naturally, Colonel."

"But assuming you don't, we need to start building an intel packet on this character. If you're careful, you'll be in and out without anyone being the wiser."

"Things can always go wrong, Sir. If you recall Neptune Spear, one of the helos clipped the compound wall when they hit turbulence, and they had to destroy it."

Weathers nodded. "I know that, Chief. But let's hope for the best, and prepare for the worst. Captain Noguchi will go in with you, disguised as a Northern Pakistani in the burqa you saw earlier. She'll be able to circulate freely in the town, and maybe pick up useful info. It would help if one of your team could dress up as a local and accompany her. They're a bit sensitive about women going out on their own inside Waziristan."

"I'll take care of it," Boswell interrupted. "I'll ask for a volunteer, someone who can pass as an Arab without too many problems."

"They're not Arabs, Lieutenant."

He looked at Captain Noguchi. "They're not?"

"No. Arabs are a Semitic race of people who hail from the Mid East and speak Arabic. Pakistanis don't fit that bill. They're not Semitic, and they mostly speak Urdu. In Waziristan, they also speak a local dialect of Pashto."

"Okay, but they're all Muslims. I thought they all spoke Arabic. It's a kind of religious thing."

She looked amused. "Are you Catholic?"

"Yes, Ma'am, I am."

"And do you speak Latin?"

"No, Ma'am."

"I thought not. It's the same for Pakistanis. It would be best to bear it in mind. It's important to know both your allies and your enemies."

He looked irritated, uneasy to have been corrected by a woman. "They sure are our enemies."

"Allies."

"What?"

"They're our allies, Lieutenant, the Pakistanis. I know it's hard, but that's the official view."

"Is that right? An ally wouldn't harbor a wanted terrorist like bin Laden. I still see them as the enemy, until they prove otherwise."

Noguchi gave up.

Besides, maybe Boswell has a point. Not that the Pakistanis haven't tried to rid Waziristan of the Taliban, but they've had even less success than ISAF achieved in Afghanistan. The Islamist terrorists are tough nuts to crack, Nolan mused.

"I want you all to get some rest," Weathers continued. "I'll work with my staff to make the arrangements for infil and exfil, and I'll mark the mission down to jump off tomorrow night. Wheels up immediately after nightfall. We'll plan for two hours on the ground. Any more than that and you'll run the risk of exposure. We'll go over the details first thing tomorrow."

"How do you plan to get us in there?" Nolan asked, staring at the Colonel intently. "You know they'll be at heightened alert after Seal Team Six's attack."

"HAHO drop," Weathers said promptly. "We'll use a Chinook to drop you inside Pakistan, and you'll be able glide down to a landing site to be determined outside of the town. Remember, this isn't a kill mission. We only want intel about what these gomers are up to."

Boswell interrupted him. "I'm not happy about a Chinook, Colonel," he exclaimed. "The Paks were sore the last time we went in. They're likely to shoot first and ask question afterwards, and a helo makes for a mighty easy target. We need a C-130, Sir. Quieter, and we can jump from much higher. They won't even know we've come visiting."

Weathers looked faintly irritated. "I already put a call through about that Chinook. It's being serviced out on the field right now, and they've arranged for refueling facilities at Jalalabad on the way. It's pretty late to make a change to the infiltration platform, Lieutenant."

Nolan was surprised; the platoon commander was standing his ground. Boswell's face took on a stubborn expression. "That's too bad, Sir. We need a fixed wing. It's the only way. It's the quiet way."

"We have a V22 Osprey on the field. That'll fly fixed wing."

Both Seals laughed out loud. "What did I say?" Weathers asked, trying to hide his annoyance. Nolan put him right.

"The V22 Osprey is one of the noisiest aircraft I've traveled in so far," Nolan replied, trying to control his laughter. "You can forget any ideas about stealth. Dropping from an Osprey is a bitch, and the downdraft from the rotors is like being caught in a hurricane. If you're looking for a quick, quiet infil, it's the wrong aircraft. The Lieutenant is right, Sir. We need a C-130 or something similar."

"They tell me we don't have a Hercules available at Bagram, Chief. It's not that easy."

Noguchi caught his eye. "Sir, the Air Force has a couple of C-17s on the ground right now. One of those would be perfect for this mission."

Nolan nodded his agreement. They'd used them many times for high altitude infiltration. The C-17 Globemaster could carry up to a hundred and thirty four troops and even an M1 Abrams tank. Her four Pratt & Whitney turbofans gave the aircraft a cruising speed of 515 mph, a range of 2,785 miles and a service ceiling: 45,000 feet. For a SpecOps clandestine HAHO insertion, it was the ideal aircraft.

Colonel Weathers nodded. "Very well, I'll talk to the Air Force. The Marine Corps doesn't own any of those babies. It shouldn't be a problem."

"We'll be able to drop from 40,000 feet, using oxygen," Boswell continued, "They'll assume it's a Pakistani air force transport. It won't even raise any eyebrows."

"Good, consider it done. Anything else?" He stared at each of them. "No? Good, I expect you guys want to get cleaned up, you can report to me here at 0700 tomorrow, and we'll start your mission briefing and final checks. Chief Nolan, would you remain here. I want to speak to you about another matter."

Here it comes. Is this where my troubles start again? I thought I was rid of my problems with those damn blackouts, and now they're coming back to haunt me, like a kick in the butt from a spooked stallion. Carol Summers reckons I blacked out when that rape was committed, but there's no way I could have done it. No way! Except they'll want proof, and I can't provide it. Whose side will this Colonel be on?

"Yes, Sir."

"Although you're not in my chain of command, JSOC is concerned about a couple of detectives nosing around in Kabul, and they asked me to find out from you what's going on. These cops say they're here to ask you some questions. What's it all about?"

Nolan explained what Detective Summers had told him about the rape allegation.

"I can tell you here and now, Sir, that's it's all a pile of horseshit. I've never raped a woman in my life, never had the inclination, and never needed to. I despise all rapists for the scum they are. But I guess these cops have to ask their questions. It's just routine."

"You're sure this is going to go away?"

"I'm sure. I didn't do it. They're looking at the wrong guy."

I know that, but will they listen? And besides, how can I explain what I was doing on a night that I have no memory of?

"Very well, I'll pass it along. Dismissed."

He saluted and left the Colonel's office. To his surprise, Mariko Noguchi was waiting outside. She called after Nolan.

"Kyle, a word if I may."

"Sure."

"I just wanted to remind you about that beer you owe me," she smiled. "I'll call back later to collect, so don't forget."

She walked away, leaving him open-mouthed.

What's the deal with Captain Noguchi? I have a partner back home, and a pair of cops chasing down my ass for some wild rape allegation. I sure don't need any more female complications.

He went to his room in the Marine Facility at Bagram, stripped off his gear, and spent almost a half-hour under a powerful hot shower. Then he lay on his bunk naked and tried to grab a few hours shuteye. It wasn't easy. The base was still in turmoil after the raid, and there was constant noise from outside as clearing up operations continued. He managed a couple of hours, and then he went back into the shower and freshened up with a torrent of cool water and changed into a clean uniform. Normally, the prospect of having a drink with Mariko Noguchi would have been something to look forward to. Normally. Except for his girlfriend back in San Diego, Carol Summers, and an SDPD detective. And the two cops waiting to talk to him.

He thought of Carol back in San Diego. They'd shared a lot of their spare time together, not least with his kids who adored her. She'd also proved herself one tough cookie when they'd found themselves facing armed hostiles on a mission of revenge, determined to kill him and the people he loved. They'd won out that time, and she'd played a major part in it. He smiled.

There will be more than a few criminals serving time who'd underrated that petite and pretty detective.

His mind wandered back to the good times they'd spent together, and some of the not so good times. He pictured her tiny but perfect frame. Detective Summers was a fresh-faced brunette with a few freckles on her nose. She had dark eyes over a tiny scar on her face, just above the right eyebrow.

She's one great girl, and I'm a lucky guy to have a partner like her, but this allegation's hanging over my head. Something odd's going down, and I dread finding out how much her feelings for me have changed. Maybe gone away for good. Perhaps it's best I'm taking off on another mission, even if it's one the brass has no right assigning to the Platoon. Why Bravo? We desperately need some down time. Maybe it's something to do with Lucas Grant. The guy knows the ground, and he does have a proven track record. Also Boswell's contacts will be aware of the potential for good publicity if their boy pulls off a second successful incursion into Abbottabad. Boswell will make captain for sure. He's welcome to his carefully plotted career. It's enough for me to take care of my men. Bringing them back alive is more important than any promotion or medal.

He heard a knock on the door and answered it. Captain Mariko Noguchi stood there in front of him, a small smile on her lips.

"It's time for you to put your money where your mouth is, Kyle."

He nodded. "Hi, Captain, I'll be right there."

"Okay, but you can call the girl who saved your ass Mariko when we're off duty."

"Sure. Give me a minute. Mariko it is."

They walked the short distance to the building that served as a bar for all ranks inside the Bagram Air Base. In the distance, he could see the concertina wire that surrounded the base, and a team was still at work repairing the breach. At intervals, guard towers overlooked the entire area, all of them manned and on alert. And he saw the grim outline of the Parwan Detention Facility, also called the Bagram Theater Internment Facility. Formerly a collection of disused hangars, the place had been rebuilt after Red Cross complaints about prisoner abuse.

I wonder if any of those bleeding heart liberals have ever been on the wrong side of a gun barrel held by an angry Muslim. And the Muslims seem to be permanently angry. And they all seem to own a gun. Okay, no civilized person has any time for sadism, but why doesn't the enemy know that? I've seen enough unspeakable savagery, most of it committed by the enemy on their own people, often women, to have few illusions about the enemy we face. They want human rights for their own men when they're taken prisoner. That's no problem, but hey, what about a level playing field? Quit beating their women, or mutilating them, especially young girls, when they feel so inclined. Quit castrating and killing ISAF prisoners when they're unlucky enough to be captured.

After the raid, the base was getting back to normal, but there were still large numbers of soldiers patrolling both inside and outside. He noticed the Afghans had gone. They'd pulled them all out beyond the perimeter, and there were only American troops in sight. He recalled when Carol had visited Afghanistan. She'd come to Bagram and almost been killed. On that occasion, they'd beaten the odds, and more than a few of the enemy had bitten the dust. Now it was his turn, but this time it was a fight he didn't know how to handle.

What if these two cops don't believe me? How will Carol take that? Pretty bad, I guess. If it hasn't ended already, it sure will then.

"What are you thinking about?"

He turned to Mariko and realized he'd been lost in his own thoughts, worrying about problems back home.

"This and that, nothing special."

"That means you refuse to tell me." She smiled to take the sting out of her words. "It's okay, I won't press it. Look, this operation to Abbottabad. It shouldn't be too difficult. In and just nose around for an hour or so, and see if we can confirm the existence of this Riyad bin Laden. He may not even be there, in which case there won't be too much security in the town. We'll just breeze in and out."

He stopped her with a gesture. "Hold it! If that's what you think, you shouldn't be coming."

She stopped, and her face reddened. "What do you mean? I was only saying…"

He stopped her again. "What you were saying just shows your total ignorance of SpecOps. You never, ever assume there might be no opposition or lax security. You want me to spell it out for you, Mariko?"

Her expression was stony. "I guess you're going to anyway."

"Damn right I am. When we drop into that town, we'll be on a war footing. The only question is can we keep it quiet enough to stop this bin Laden guy, if he exists, from finding out we've been there? We'll sure do our damnedest, but there could be killing, a lot of killing, and that's something we have to prepare for. These people spend their lives fighting. They're born to it. Because they're always skirmishing between each other makes it likely they'll put any trouble down to a local disagreement. But there'll be units of the Pakistani Army, the local police, and as it's inside Waziristan, Taliban as well. Last time, they were pretty pissed after the event, but this time, they'll be mad as hell if guys in foreign uniforms go in there unannounced. We may not be able to help bumping into Pakistani security, and they'll be itching to put a bullet into any American who crosses their path. If that happens, we'll have to kill them. The alternative is they kill us. We'll need prisoners to interrogate about this bin Laden report, and that's a whole new ball game. They won't come willingly. And they won't want to tell us anything, which means interrogating them in the field. When we're pushed for time, often under fire, you know what that means?"

She nodded tiredly. "Torture."

"Yeah, damn right. When you're faced with the possibility of a few hundred innocent civilians being killed, along with some of your buddies, having to almost rip a man's balls off to persuade him to hand over the details, it's not a choice. Do you understand that? Because that's what we'll be facing when we go into Abbottabad. It'll be hard and probably very, very bloody. Got it?"

She stared at him. He could see her face was pale, but it was also calm.

"Ouch."

"You what?"

"The guy who's balls you threaten to rip off. It'd be painful. I said ouch."

"I…"

He could see her mouth twitching, and all of a sudden they were both convulsed with laughter. Nolan almost fell on the floor.

"Fucking ouch, yeah, you got that right."

He sobered as he recalled how she'd been ready to kill when the chips were down, almost did kill that guy out on the perimeter fence. She was prepared to get into harm's way when the job required it, and if that meant squeezing some poor bastard's nuts to get information that would save lives, he imagined she'd be more than ready to do the squeezing.

Ouch! Maybe I underestimated her.

They reached the building. It was air-conditioned, which was a relief to men washed out from working in the 100-degree heat. The food in the restaurant was of high quality, and there were even calorie figures posted on each dish. Signs pointed to the fully stocked fitness gyms and the halls where movies were screened. They passed the Post Exchange, the size of a small supermarket. It stocked everything from shaving cream to Weber grills, and soap to luxury items. IPods were one of the big sellers, as well as laptops to circumvent the Pentagon's ban on using military terminals to visit popular Web sites like Facebook and YouTube. There was a beauty salon, a Burger King, and even a local market where Afghan merchants hocked the standard Mideast bazaar items, including carpets, gems, perfumes, and jewelry. But they ignored the stuff on offer and headed straight for the comfortable saloon where Nolan paid for a couple of beers. They sat on stools at the well stocked bar. He held up his glass in a salute.

"A toast, Mariko, to one brave lady who saved my ass. I'm in your debt."

"You're welcome, Kyle. Anytime."

What the hell did that mean? It sounded like a come-on, but Carol's back at home, maybe. I'll have to watch out for this fiery little Captain, or I could find myself biting off more than I can chew. There's little to choose between Carol and Mariko; two strong, tough, and determined women who could make a guy's life descend into a world of pain if they were crossed. Give me the Taliban anytime, at least you know your enemy!"

The smile faded from her lips, and she leaned in closer to talk. "I've not been in the field before, that's true, not like this thing we have planned. Do you honestly believe it'll be as tough as you described?"

"Not with me along to take care of things," a voice said from right behind. He looked around and saw Brad Rose. A Seal PO3, he was the unit dandy, slightly below medium height, powerfully built, and no matter what clothes he wore, he always managed to look good; like a playboy or a California beach boy. His muddy blonde hair was thick and shaggy, and he kept it under control by always searching out the latest and greatest hair products that must stretch his pay to the limits. His hair was long even by Seal standards, and he held it in place with a thonged leather headband. Brad had fine, almost delicate boyish features that he'd once tried to camouflage by growing a mustache and beard before the Navy made him shave them off. When Bravo Platoon walked into a bar, it was Brad that most girls made a beeline for. Mariko looked at Nolan with a questioning expression, so he did the introductions.

"Mariko, this is Petty Officer Brad Rose. He's one of our demolitions specialists. And Brad, this is Captain Mariko Noguchi, so be on your best behavior."

They shook hands. Brad looked at her, concerned. "How come you know about tomorrow's mission, Captain? I thought it was classified."

"Captain Noguchi is coming with us, Brad."

His eyes widened. "You're not kidding? What's your specialty, Ma'am?"

"I look good in a burqa."

He looked puzzled for a few moments. Then he understood. "Got it. So you'll be undercover, so to speak."

She smiled. "Something like that. I also speak Urdu and Pashto, so I'll be able to listen to what the locals are talking about. And if Kyle here has to torture anyone, I can translate what they say while he's squeezing their balls off."

"You what?"

"I was describing the latest interrogation techniques," Nolan explained.

"Yeah, well that one usually works. How are we going in?"

"HAHO drop."

Brad nodded. "That makes sense. How many jumps you done, Ma'am?"

She looked flustered. "I, er, well…none."

There was total silence between them for a few moments. Nolan didn't even hear the sounds of talk and laughter from the other patrons. It was as if someone had just announced the death of a President or a favorite team losing the series. He stared at her.

"You're shitting me?"

"No, I haven't done a single parachute jump, Kyle. But I do plan to begin training."

"You're cutting it a bit fine."

Maybe she'll break an ankle. That would solve a heap of problems.

"Not at all. My training starts tomorrow night. It's called learning on the job."

"I'll say one thing," Brad said. "You've got guts, Captain. HAHO jumps are not the easiest way to make your first jump, neither is an infil into hostile territory."

"We'd better make it a tandem jump," Nolan said abruptly. "No way are you jumping on your own, not the first time."

"You want me to jump with you?"

"Yeah, we'll go out together. You just hold on tight and enjoy the ride."

"I don't want…"

"I don't give a shit what you want, Mariko. That's the way it's going to be. If you go out on your own and come down in the wrong place, maybe with a broken bone or two, you'll likely be picked up. They'll assume you're a spy, and you know what they do to spies? They behead them."

She looked at both men, clearly unhappy and wanting to take issue with him, but one look at their implacable expressions told her she was wasting her time.

"Okay, I accept your offer of a ride. But I'll get the next round in, so what're you having, Brad? Kyle?"

She called the barman over, a suspicious looking Afghan. Nolan wondered if he'd been thoroughly vetted. He could do without his beer being poisoned. He served up more drinks, and Brad held up his glass.

"We'll see the enemy in hell."

Mariko sighed, and Nolan realized she was less than impressed with the gung-ho attitudes of SpecOps operators. He smiled to himself.

Maybe she wants to talk about shopping?

But finally she raised her glass, and they touched them for the toast.

She smiled. "See 'em in hell."

But Nolan had a sudden vision, almost a premonition. It wasn't the enemy that was in hell. It was Mariko Noguchi, screaming in agony, her face contorted with terror as the captors tortured her.

It can't happen. I'll do everything in my power to protect her. Damn, she shouldn't be coming on the mission at all!

He fought to control the shiver that tore through him. They finished their beers, and he made an excuse and left. He knew that he'd have trouble sleeping, and the nightmares would return. Garish visions of women who were close to him calling out for help, and he couldn't respond; something always stopped him, got in his way. He also had a real life nightmare to get to grips with, the rape allegation. A statement to the cops made by someone he'd never met, about a time he couldn't remember because he'd suffered a mental blackout.

Life never gets any easier, that's for sure.

CHAPTER THREE

They walked across the tarmac in the gathering darkness and up the ramp into the waiting C-17. The hold of the giant transport aircraft was lit only with red lights that would not betray them to any watcher. There'd be no sense in advertising what they were about. A Seal Team embarking on a cargo aircraft heavily laden with weapons and 'chutes only meant one thing, a drop into enemy territory. Alarm bells would ring. They had plenty of room inside the fuselage. Either side of the huge space were jump seats, so they each found their preferred position and sat down. Mariko carried no parachute, just a small pack with her disguise inside, a blue burqa. Nolan sat one side of her and Brad the other. Although Nolan wore the same uniform as the rest of the Platoon, in his pack he carried a change of clothes, robes typical of the Waziristan region. He'd dyed his hair black during the day and used camouflage cream to darken his skin. It was all they could do and had to be enough. At night, he'd pass as a local. Just about. If the mission ran over into the dawn, they'd see through his disguise and shoot him on sight. He turned and watched as the ramp came up, and the four Pratt and Whitney turbofans began to scream as the pilot worked them up to full power. The huge aircraft began to roll, gathered speed, and took off into the night. They were heading almost due east to Pakistan, and their landing ground, Abbottabad. Nolan recalled the briefing earlier. Security had been as tight as a drum. If the Taliban got wind of where they were going, it would be a blood bath. And the blood would be American this time.

* * *

"I've arranged the C-17," Weathers had begun, standing on a raised platform in the briefing room. He looked tired. "I was on to the Pentagon for two hours. The Air Force weren't too happy about it at first. They had other plans for their precious aircraft. I gather the Chairman of the Joint Chiefs had to intervene to persuade them to reroute. He was in the Situation Room with the President at the time, so your insistence on the Globemaster caused quite a stir, Lieutenant."

Boswell didn't look in the least concerned. He nodded, "Yes, Colonel."

"We'll drop you from thirty-five thousand feet, so you'll be on oxygen. I gather Chief Nolan has arranged to tandem jump with Captain Noguchi. I'm sure he'll appreciate her assistance to get him on the ground," the Colonel deadpanned. The men laughed politely. They went over the rest of the briefing, covering the minute details of infil, exfil, and mission objectives, together with the all-important details of what to do when things went wrong. Toward the end, Nolan had one last question that had been troubling him, and he put it to the Colonel.

"Sir, in the event we eyeball this bin Laden guy, what are our orders?"

"Yeah, that's a good point. It's not likely you'll see him. We know that. Osama never came out into the open, and if this guy exists, I doubt he will either. Your orders are to capture him if you do run into him, and if he offers any kind of a threat, take him out. When I use the word 'threat', I mean it in its widest possible sense. Clear?"

They all nodded. If an unexpected encounter occurred, waste him.

"Chief Nolan, you'll dress in native clothes and accompany Captain Noguchi. Any problems with that?"

"I'm all set, Sir."

"Okay. Don't forget, you are to stay clear of that compound. This is an intelligence gathering exercise only. If you spook this guy, he'll start running, and it could take us another ten years to find him, in the event that he does exist. So stay away, clear?"

They chorused, "Copy that."

Weathers nodded. "One more piece of information, and this has nothing to do with the mission. Our guys found a body on the base this morning."

He stared at them, but they weren't surprised, there had been a furious firefight the day before.

"It would be a surprise if there wasn't a couple they missed when they cleared up," Boswell replied absently. "What's your point, Sir?"

"The point, Lieutenant, is that this guy wasn't killed in action. He was murdered. Someone slit his throat."

"One of our guys?" Nolan asked.

"No, an Afghan. He was one of the civilians who worked on the base. So it looks as if we have a killer on the loose. It could be an American. It's not impossible, so watch your backs, at least until they catch this guy. That's all," he finished up.

They saluted, and Weathers stepped down from the platform.

* * *

The C-17 droned through the Afghan night skies. They checked and rechecked their gear, and Nolan had an increased responsibility to concern himself with. Mariko Noguchi. He'd fastened a tandem harness to his body and tried to show her what she was required to do during the drop. To account for the extra weight, he'd also drawn a larger parachute from the stores, which added to his misgivings. He'd used the same 'chute since he first started in the Seals. So far, it had never let him down. He didn't like making changes when they were about to launch an operation. He looked across at Mariko.

"You okay?"

Her face was almost white, and it wasn't just the cold at high altitude. She managed a brief nod. "I'm fine. I'll be better when we're on the ground."

Except you don't know what we'll face down there. Not yet.

He nodded. "We'd better start strapping up. I want to make certain we get this right."

"But, we're still twenty minutes out."

"That's right, so the sooner we go through the drill again, the quicker we'll be ready when we get the green light. Stand up, let's go through it all."

She sighed and stood up. He showed her once more how to fasten and unfasten the harness, and what to do if the worst happened, and the 'chute failed to open.

"Is the reserve chute bigger to allow for both of us?" she asked.

"Nope, I'm already carrying too much gear. If I have to pull the reserve, we'll go down fast."

"What does that mean?"

"Don't ask."

She carried a pistol which she'd wear inside her burqa, a lightweight Glock Model 26 9mm Parabellum, the Baby Glock, to which the armorers had fitted a suppressor. It was a tiny pistol, one that would be easy to conceal. He made her slide out the clip, check the load, and make certain she knew how everything worked on the unfamiliar weapon. She stowed it back in her pack, but Nolan was worried, wearing a burqa would make a fast draw difficult. She had a solution.

"I'll just carry it in my hand. The arms and hands are hidden beneath a burqa. If anyone looks suspicious, my hand will appear with a gun in it. That should give 'em pause for thought."

He nodded and smiled. "Yeah, I guess it'd give any guy pause for thought."

The sound of the engines was a constant, whining roar through the cabin, but even more uncomfortable was the intense cold of high altitude. Nolan wondered how she was coping with it.

After all, it's all new to her, and she's a girl. Does that make a difference? Well, yeah, it usually did with most girls he'd known.

The jumpmaster came into the cabin.

"Skipper says ten minutes to drop point, switch to oxygen, and stand by for depressurization."

She pulled on her goggles, and Nolan helped her adjust the oxygen mask that was essential to stay alive at almost eight miles up in the sky. Then he fixed his own mask. He could hear her breathing, shallow, short pants.

"Are you okay? Any problems?"

"I'm fine." The reply was short and firm.

He smiled. Mariko's her feisty self. Good.

He felt the pressure changing in his ears as the cabin equalized with the sky outside. And then the red light winked on.

"Ramp is lowering, stand by."

The ramp wound down, and the chill night winds howled inside the fuselage. He grabbed Mariko, who was about to be tossed backward against the straps of the harness. She looked at him and nodded her thanks. Despite their heavy equipment and armor, her teeth were chattering. The temperature had plummeted as the interior of the aircraft met the icy exterior of the night sky. The jumpmaster held up five fingers.

"Five minutes to drop, move to the ramp."

It was difficult, shuffling along with Mariko strapped to the front of him in the tandem harness, but they made it and joined the crowd of Seals clustered close to the edge of the ramp. Below, they could make out lights on the ground. It was a cloudless night with little moon, and ideal drop conditions. He saw her shivering and briefly wondered.

Is it the intense cold, or is it fear?

"Two minutes, we're on course, thirty kilometers

from Abbottabad. Height is twelve thousand meters. External air temperature is minus one hundred degrees centigrade, winds north-easterly, speed one hundred and thirty kilometers per hour, wind speed on the ground is estimated at eight kilometers per hour. You're good to go, gentlemen."

They waited in that relaxed posture that Special Forces adopt before going on a mission. It was what they trained for, sacrificed for, and lived and died for. Except for Mariko. The jumpmaster held up one finger.

"One minute, stand by, watch the green light. Skipper reports aircraft on course."

He could feel the tension in her body. She was rigid, and inside the lenses of her goggles, he could see her eyes were dilated. She'd have to cope. The open ramp of a C-17 at twelve thousand meters above the ground, seconds before the drop, was the wrong place to harbor second thoughts. He held her body close to his, knowing that she'd want the reassurance of human contact. The green light winked on.

"Green light, go, go."

He shuffled forward with the men, feeling a slight resistance from her, but then they were in the opening, and he fell forward into space, pushing her before him.

She hung almost like a sack of grain at first, but the chute opened, and he made the adjustments for the long glide using his wrist GPS. He altered course slightly and used the lines to swing onto a heading that would take them directly to the target.

"This is fantastic!" she shouted suddenly. "It's truly amazing. I feel like I'm a bird floating free in the sky."

"It's a good feeling. You have a few minutes to reflect before we hit the ground."

"I could get used to his, you know. Having my very own parachutist to carry me down."

He was about to make a flippant reply, but he realized he had so many complications in his life to deal with, he didn't want to act like a guy on a first date, not dangling from a tandem rig, high in the night sky over Pakistan. He kept quiet and concentrated on steering a precise course. From time to time, he made adjustments, and soon he could see the faint lights of Abbottabad in the distance about eight kilometers ahead.

"Is that it?"

"Sure, we'll land just outside of the main area. It's a patch of grass they use as a cricket pitch. Makes for a soft landing."

"I'm pleased about that. So they play cricket in this hellhole, do they?"

"They have one of the best teams in the world, Pakistan. It's their national pride."

"Not baseball?"

He laughed. "Too American."

They glided in for a picture perfect landing, and he managed to keep her upright as they touched the ground. Two other Seals were already down. His night vision goggles were switched on, and as he unstrapped the parachute, he could see other Seals coming in to land around him.

"I need to change into my burqa. Is there somewhere private?"

He laughed out loud. "I'd guess here would be about right. You wander off somewhere, and you might trip over some sleeping goatherd, or something like that. At least here you have a Seal platoon to guard your modesty."

She gave him a look, then unstrapped her pack, and pulled out the long, flowing blue burqa. It took only a few moments to unbutton her uniform, slip out of it, insert her earpiece, and pull on the burqa. The effect was uncanny. One moment, she was an American officer, the next, a servile Muslim woman; as were common throughout Afghanistan and Waziristan. When she was ready, Nolan stripped off his vest and camouflage gear and slipped into his own costume, baggy trousers, ragged sneakers, and a long white shirt that came to his knees with a black waistcoat over it. He adjusted a traditional Pakul hat on his head and tucked his Sig-Sauer with spare mags, his combat knife, and radio into his robes. He inserted the earpiece and tucked the wire out of sight behind his hair.

"Radio check, this is Bravo Two."

"Bravo Blue, loud and clear," she replied.

He smiled in deference to her ethnic disguise. She had the call sign 'blue'. It seemed appropriate.

"Are you set to go?" Boswell asked him, looming up out of the darkness. Nolan had packed his night vision goggles away, and it seemed odd talking to the Lieutenant who was almost invisible.

"Sure. We'll lead off, Lt. If we see any problems, I'll call you. We have the directions, and I have my GPS stowed under my shirt, so I'll keep an eye on it. The plan is to head toward the vicinity of the bin Laden compound and look for a local. Someone Mariko can talk to."

Boswell nodded. "Good luck on that, Chief. They're not too comfy about talking to women in burqas. I guess they think the husband is likely to slit their throats, so I guess you'll have to persuade them otherwise."

"We'll manage. I think Captain Noguchi has a line on

strong persuasion. Twisting their balls off. Ouch!"

She'd kicked him, and in the dark he hadn't seen it coming. But Boswell saw it and gave him an odd look.

"That could work," he grinned. "We'll be all around you, so if there's any hostile interference, we'll deal with it. Good luck."

They walked into the darkness, threading their way through the lonely streets and alleyways. There were only faint lights showing from some of the houses they walked past, mainly security lights. The road was partly beaten earth, with short strips of tarmac where the owners of adjacent houses wanted something more than mud to enter and exit their driveways. The houses were as mixed as the road surface; some wealthy looking homes in their own manicured grounds, complete with pools reflecting in the moonlight, and opposite, a row of semi-derelict shanties. The one aspect of the landscape both rich and poor shared was the stench. Human excrement from blocked drains, or maybe there weren't any drains in parts of the town. Not this part, anyway. They walked on in silence, and then Nolan dragged her swiftly into a doorway.

"What is it?"

"Quiet. Footsteps, coming this way."

A middle-aged man walked toward them and passed by, his steps staggering slightly. Clearly, he paid little heed to the Muslim prohibition on alcohol.

"Can we…"

"Wait!"

They drew further into the dark doorway, and a cop came into view. It was tempting. A policeman would likely know about the compound and have an idea of who occupied it these days. Yet taking him would be a risk. If he failed to check in, the alarm bells could start to ring. Nolan decided to wait, and they let the cop pass by. There were no further footsteps, and they walked out onto the road, rounded the corner, and continued walking toward the town center; straight into the arms of the two more cops. Two Pakistani policemen were staring down at a body in the road. The body was that of yet another Pakistani cop. He lay in a pool of his own blood, which had apparently streamed from his neck. The Pakis whirled as they heard the footsteps, and one of them; a fat man with his uniform stretched over his paunch confronted them. His hand was held up for them to stop, and he shouted something at them. Mariko whispered in his earpiece.

"They want to know what we're doing here."

Nolan stopped next to her and waited. He understood Arabic, but his Pashto was limited to a few words, and he couldn't even make out whether they were speaking Pashto or Urdu, or whatever.

Who gives a shit? The next few moments are going to be tricky whatever was said.

The guy barked questions at Nolan. Mariko whispered a translation, the mic invisible to them inside her burqa. The man shouted at Nolan, standing only inches from his face while his comrade stared at them, scowling and suspicious. He lit a cigarette and stood back watching and waiting.

"That dead cop in the street, he's one of their pals. They're pretty angry."

"Uh huh." He was acting the mute and couldn't speak.

"He wants to know what we're doing out here at this time of night. I think he suspects we may have killed him."

"Uh huh."

He heard her reply to the fat cop.

"I told him you're a mute, so nod your head and smile."

Nolan obeyed, but it only made the cop sneer even more. He was an older man, maybe fifty or so, with a fat belly and a stack of chins that wobbled as he shouted.

"He's telling you that your mother was a poxed whore from the slums of Islamabad. He wants to see your ID card."

That's your mistake, buddy. You're not playing hardball cop with some dumb-ass goatherd who's just come down from the hills.

"Nolan, you have to give him something, or pretend you're looking for it. He's getting suspicious."

The other cop looked on with interest. Then he turned away, unzipped his fly, and pissed against the wall of a house. When he'd emptied his bladder, he leaned against the wall, still watching. Nolan made a note. He looked meaner than the fat guy. He'd be fast to react when trouble started. The first cop still hadn't stopped his tirade. He was building up to apoplexy, shouting, and spittle beginning to drool down his chin. A light came on in a nearby house, a window opened, and someone looked out. The cop who'd been pissing shouted at them, and the window was shut with a bang.

"He says you're under arrest. I'll try to persuade him to let us go."

She pleaded with him, begging, cajoling, as only a Muslim woman in a burqa can. The cop was unimpressed, and he called for his buddy to help him. Mariko continued to murmur a translation, and he gathered it wasn't working. They were about to arrest the two suspects. The thin cop walked toward him, and Nolan's hand slid inside his long shirt, reaching for his Sig. The fat cop shouting at Mariko hadn't noticed, but the thin cop saw the movement and leapt forward, shouting threats.

"He says you have a gun," she whispered urgently.

"Yeah, that's the first sensible word that's come out of either of their mouths tonight. I'm taking them both, so be ready with your peashooter. But remember, we need someone to question, so we have to keep one of them alive."

Before she could answer, he snatched out his long suppressed Sig. The cops looked at him, astonished to hear the ragged man with his burqa clad wife speaking in American English. Then reality hit them. The guy was a ringer, and the two cops clawed for their pistols. But Nolan was ahead of them, a mile ahead. He double tapped the thin cop, the one who looked more dangerous. The guy went down as if pole-axed, and the 'phut, phut' of the 9mm rounds sounded unnaturally loud in the dark, stinking street. Nolan pulled the fat cop close to his body while he whirled around, searching for further targets. The man he was holding murmured something in his weird dialect.

"He's pleading for his life," Mariko interpreted.

"Yeah, I guessed it was something like that. Tell him to shut up, or I will kill him. Don't worry; it's only a threat. We need him."

She spoke rapidly in Pashto while Nolan searched the man. He removed his service pistol; a Russian built Makarov automatic, and found a pair of cuffs that he used to fasten the guy's wrists behind his back. Then he called in.

"Bravo One, this is Two. We encountered some cops.

One was already down, and I had to kill another. We have one as a prisoner, and he's with us now. We need help to tidy up here."

He gave them his coordinates. Thirty seconds later, the Platoon materialized out of the darkness. Boswell eyed the two bodies and turned to stare at Nolan.

"This is not good, Chief. Orders were not to make any waves."

"The only alternative was to let them shoot me. Besides, I didn't kill the first cop. He was already dead. It's too late to second guess it, Lt. We must get these bodies away and take this guy away for questioning."

Boswell nodded and gave the orders. The men ran forward, picked up the two dead cops, and carried the bodies back to the insertion point. Two other Seals began to clear up the area, using their night vision goggles to search for any signs of bloodshed that would be hard to explain away. Nolan could see Boswell had placed snipers at either end of the street. They seemed pretty well covered. If any more cops turned up, there'd be more dead bodies on the streets of Abbottabad.

They began walking back to the insertion point, the cricket ground. Suddenly, he remembered the first cop they'd seen and turned to Boswell.

"There was another cop. We need to keep an eye out for him. He's probably still around here somewhere."

The Lieutenant nodded and gave the order, but they reached the assembly area without running into any more of the local law. The men gratefully put the bodies of the dead Pakistanis on the ground.

"How are we going to cover this up, Chief? Three cops missing. The locals won't wear that one. Christ, what a mess!"

"We'll handle it, Lt, take it easy. We'll fake up something to convince them." He looked around, but there was no sign of Lucas Grant. "Where's Grant?"

Boswell looked a bit shifty. "He, er, I sent him to check out the compound. Jack Whitman went with him to watch his back."

"To Bin Laden's compound? You're not serious! You know what the orders were."

"Yeah, I know, but Lucas has been there before, remember, with Seal Team Six. He wanted to take a look around, see if anything had changed. It could tell us a lot."

"Did Grant ask to go on this wild goose chase, Lt?"

"Er, yeah, he did. But it seemed like a good idea."

"The hell it is. Get him back here before he does any damage."

"Chief, you don't give me orders. I'm in command here. I'd remember that if I were you, feller."

"As I recall, the order to stay away from the compound came from Colonel Weathers. Last time I checked, a colonel trumped a lieutenant."

Boswell stared at him for a long moment. Then he clicked on his mic.

"Bravo One to Three."

After a long pause, Lucas Grant replied in a whisper. "This is Three, go ahead."

"Come back in, Lucas. Abort, I say again, abort."

"What the fuck!" he whispered back. "You're sure about this?"

"Yes. Report back, on the double. Where's Whitman?"

"I left him a few hundred meters back. He's watching my six, and he'll cover my withdrawal."

"Whitman, this is Bravo One, do you copy?"

"Whitman here, I copy."

"Get your ass right back here, right now. And you too, Lucas, get moving."

There was a long silence, and it was clear Grant was anything but happy about the recall.

"Copy that. I'll be back in five."

The two Seals came back in together, and Boswell looked down at two bodies.

"We'll have to take those bodies back with us. If they find them, it'll blow the operation wide open. Chief, give the order to move out. You can organize a rota to carry those corpses. Captain Noguchi, keep an eye on the prisoner, and see if he has anything useful to tell us. Jesus Christ, the shit will hit the fan when those cops don't report back."

She smiled. "Maybe, Lieutenant, but remember, Waziristan is like the Wild West. Do you want me to rip his balls off to get him to talk?"

"You what?"

Nolan and a couple of the men who were in on the joke chuckled, but Boswell didn't get it. He shook his head. "No, there's no need for that, Captain. We have specialists at Bagram to take care of rigorous interrogations."

"If you're sure," she smiled. "Look, Lieutenant, I wouldn't worry too much about the cops. They go AWOL all the time in this area. Don't forget, it's a Taliban controlled region, so they're always tangling with the local law and taking potshots at each other."

"I hope you're right. Just watch him and talk to him, that's all."

The exfil site was ten klicks outside of Abbottabad.

160th Special Operations Aviation Regiment (Airborne) was due to pick them up, using two of their advanced MH-60M Black Hawk helos, specially silenced to shield the noise from anyone on the ground. Nolan brought up the rear. He'd donned his night vision goggles, and he was able to constantly sweep behind them for any signs of pursuit. Grant fell in beside him, and Nolan had to ask him the question that had nagged at him since they'd left the town.

"Why did you disobey orders and go to check out the compound, Lucas? Didn't you hear Colonel Weathers give the order to stay away from it? If this bin Laden guy is there and thinks we're nosing around, he'll be off like a frightened deer."

Grant squinted sideways, staring back at him through the four lenses of his night vision gear. Nolan always thought they made the Seals look like some kind of space age monster, but the peripheral vision was superb.

"I heard the order, Chief. But Boswell's in command out here in the field, and he told me to go check it out. I agree, I thought it was a stupid idea." He shrugged. "But orders are orders."

Nolan nodded. So it was Boswell all along who'd suggested it and blamed Lucas for the idea. Their platoon leader was making progress, but he still had lessons to learn, especially about following orders and loyalty to his men.

"What did you see?"

"I guess there's someone living there, someone pretty important. The walls and gates have been repaired since our attack, and there's extra razor wire strung everywhere. I couldn't get much of a close look, but it seemed to me there were alarm sensors all around the perimeter, and there's a new guard position on the roof of the main house. I'd guess they have anti-aircraft missiles up there, certainly a heavy machine gun or two. It's well fortified, and surrounded by sandbags, so the roof is protected against incoming ground fire and grenades."

"So it looks like he may be there."

Grant shrugged. "Look, Chief, I went there once. We took down everything inside that house, and there was only one bin Laden. He's the guy that's feeding the fishes right now. So no, 'HE' isn't there. But there's someone there, that's all I'm saying."

Nolan saw movement and raised his rifle ready to shoot, but it was Jack Whitman come to join them.

"I'm curious about the compound, Lucas," Jack said cheerfully. "How do you rate the chances of a rerun of the Seal Team Six mission?"

Grant sighed. "Jack, there's no bin Laden left in that place. We got him first time around, and second, they'll be just waiting for someone to try again. It would be like shooting rats in a trap, and next time we'd be the rats. Christ, I remember that place when we went in the first time. I thought we were goners when that Black Hawk crashed. We managed to get to the house, sure, but it could have gone either way. Funny that, there was this inscription over the door. When we weren't sure which direction to go, we assumed it was his quarters, and it led us straight to him. Dumb, to put that over your front door."

Whitman nodded. "Yeah, 'God is Great', that's what it means. Maybe you're right. It's the last place he'd hole up."

Nolan thought about that.

That's a fair point. These al Qaeda folks are no

dummies. But they may be planning something else, like trying to lure us into a trap, which is a possibility. It's quite by chance Danial Masih survived the massacre. It's true that Abbottabad is the last place anyone would think to look for a new al Qaeda leader, and except for the chance survival of the one of the few Christians in Waziristan, we wouldn't have even suspected it. So maybe it isn't a trap. Is that what they're counting on? That it's the last place anyone would think to look? It's something to think about. And something else; the cop who had his throat cut? Lucas Grant. I could ask him, but that could invite a lie. I prefer not to let Lucas think I've any suspicions about him. And Jack Whitman? Where was he when the guy was killed? No, it's unlikely. Jack's a 'by the book' Seal. Navy Seals is his life. I'll keep an eye on Lucas. The guy could be a problem.

And then something else struck him, something Whitman had said.

"Jack, how did you know about that inscription over the door to bin Laden's quarters, someone tell you?"

Whitman shrugged. In the dark it was impossible to see his face. "I guess they must have. I think I heard somewhere it's what these people put over the doors of their homes. But he won't repeat that mistake, I shouldn't think."

It didn't seem likely, Nolan agreed. But he'd never heard that fact from anyone, and he'd been fighting and chasing down Islamic insurgents for years. He had a lot to think about.

The road narrowed, and the short stretch of tarmac became a rutted, rough track. Occasionally, they passed a stone farmhouse, and more than once set a dog barking like crazy, but they pressed on fast, and no one came out to challenge them. They were heading for a wide cluster of trees, almost a small forest. Vince Merano on point led them unerringly through the wood, using a combination of GPS and night vision to navigate. They came out into a wide clearing, a ragged square of about two hundred meters on each side. Boswell posted sentries and called in the Black Hawks. They were so quiet they were almost on them before the men heard the muted 'whup, whup' of the rotor blades, and the soft roar of the suppressed engine noise. Mariko took advantage of the wait and changed back into uniform. Nolan did the same, and by the time the helos were on the ground, they were once again in the familiar Multicam of the American Special Forces, with a Heckler and Koch HK416 in her hand and his trusty Mk 11 rifle in his. The burqa had disappeared into her backpack, and he'd thrust the musty old robes into his own pack.

Christ, how can these people wear these crazy clothes? Whatever they are designed for, comfort isn't the priority.

He felt better in his familiar kit, armor notwithstanding. The crew chief leaned out of the nearest Black Hawk.

"You guys coming home, or are you staying out here all night?" he grinned at them.

There was a rush for the door, and Nolan sat on the floor inside the cabin with Mariko beside him. Their helo took off and soared away into the night sky, and he felt a sense of relief that they were getting out of Pakistan. Maybe the Paks were allies, but somehow it didn't quite feel that way.

The throb of the engine note lulled him, and he started to doze. The craft lurched as it hit an air pocket, and his eyes flicked open. He saw Mariko staring at him.

"What?"

"What do you feel about the mission?" she asked him. "We're coming back with a prisoner they can interrogate. I'd say we aced this one, but I got the impression you're not that impressed."

Now that they were on the way out of hostile territory, she'd started to relax and enjoy the delicious post-mission feeling; when you realized you weren't going to be killed or wounded, and that you were going home with your ass intact. He was sorry to disillusion her on her first operation behind the lines.

"We're coming out with just one guy, a cop who may or may not know anything. Three cops got killed, and no matter what's going on back there between the various factions that are fighting each other, they're gonna wonder. And Lucas Grant went off to the compound, disobeying a direct order, so we don't know if they saw him or not. It's not a good result."

"But surely Boswell ordered him to go."

"He had no right to do that. You know Colonel Weathers ordered us to stay away from the immediate vicinity. If we get away with this one, it'll be pure luck, and that's about all we can say for it. We should have been in and out of there with no one any the wiser. We didn't do that. We fucked up, period!"

He saw her face fall, and she looked away from him.

If she wants some headquarters' bullshit, she'll have to look elsewhere.

The helo hammered through the night on the long haul back to Afghanistan. The 160th Aviation Regiment had organized a refueling stop on the way to the border, and they put down in a remote part of the Waziristan badlands while a third helo, a tanker that had already landed and was waiting for them, fueled up the two thirsty birds. Nolan scanned around the immediate vicinity while they pumped the fuel. The green landscape stared back at him, almost mocking him for worrying about a non-existent threat in a landscape that was as devoid of life as the moon. But he knew appearances could be deceptive, and he stayed watching. He noticed Mariko Noguchi staring at the distant mountain range, which he knew was the Hindu Kush, the high peaks that formed the border between Pakistan and Afghanistan. He was distracted by the stink of aviation kerosene, so pervasive against the background of the warm scents of the Waziristan countryside, and they moved further away from the aircraft. They stopped, and he looked at her.

"I'm sorry, I didn't mean to, you know…"

She turned to face him. "You mean to spell it out, the truth?"

He grimaced. "Something like that, yeah. You okay now?"

She nodded. "I think so. It was just disappointing, that's all."

"What about the cop, did you talk to him on the way back to the exfil site?"

"I did. What he told me was inconclusive. There is a bigshot staying at the compound. There's no doubt about that, but we knew that anyway. It's an expensive and prestigious property, and someone would have moved in there anyway after Osama went down. But whether he's al Qaeda, or indeed even a relation of Osama, that's another matter, and he had no idea. He's still shaken up. What with being captured, and one of his buddies shot, and the other with his throat cut."

Nolan digested that info. It seemed unlikely he'd told her everything.

The guy's a cop, so he'll know what's going down on his own turf. Rumors, threats, bribes, snitches, together they form an intelligence haul any cop puts together as part of his daily work. If he does know something useful, maybe the mission will be worth something after all. It's too many maybes. Not the way I'm used to working. But still…

He looked at Mariko. "I reckon there's a good chance he knows more, that cop. He just wants someone to pull the right levers."

She grinned. "Like…"

"Yeah, maybe. Threaten to rip his balls off, whatever. They'll get it out of him back at Bagram."

"You think they really will torture him?"

He smiled. "No, I don't. These guys speak a universal language. They'll just say the right words."

She looked puzzled. "I don't understand."

"The bribe. It all depends on the amount. Cops in this region are all on the take. That's it."

"At least it'll make the mission worthwhile."

"No, it won't. What'll make it worthwhile is when we take down a sonofabitch who thinks he can take over bin Laden's mantel and carry out terrorist raids against America. If the guy exists, we need to send him to follow his predecessor, and he can make himself useful feeding the fishes. When that happens, it'll be worthwhile."

They both looked up as the crew chief from their helo walked over to them.

"It's time to mount up. The rest of the guys are aboard and we're set to go."

They both nodded and went toward the waiting Black Hawk.

The Night Hawks delivered them safely back to Bagram where Colonel Weathers was waiting for them. He took Boswell to one side, and they talked at length. Nolan wondered what the hell Boswell could have to say about a mission that had failed in many respects. The Lieutenant rejoined them after a few minutes, looking happy enough, so he'd spun the entire operation as a success, which wasn't anything new. In the Afghan theater of war, getting a unit to return from a mission with zero casualties was often considered a victory, of sorts. Nolan recalled reading something like that about another war. That one was called Vietnam, where often the jungle swallowed whole companies of men. And the dire outcome of that war had gone down into history. Nolan looked around as the door opened, and a couple of soldiers carried in a portable table and three chairs. When they'd set them up at the back of the room, they left. A civilian, who looked like military, came in with a female Marine corporal. The corporal sat at the table and waited. The civilian remained standing and called for their attention.

"Good news, men. Lieutenant Boswell gave a good report of the operation. It was one hell of a job you did over there. The cop you brought back was taken straight into interrogation, and he agreed almost immediately to cooperate. He's spilling everything to a couple of CIA guys we had waiting to debrief any prisoners you brought back. It's too early to know for certain, but we're pretty sure there's a high-ranking al Qaeda operative living in bin

Laden's compound. I have an officer waiting at the back of the room. He'll have some questions for you, and then you can get some shut-eye. That's all. We'll reconvene here later today, and we can decide what to do with the intel we've uncovered. Before you leave, I want each of you to give me a brief report."

They stood and saluted. Will Bryce looked at Nolan, and raised his eyes to the heavens. They both knew Boswell had fed a pile of bilge to cover up an operation that owed any success to luck and coincidence more than any masterful planning and execution. Nolan pushed his way to the back of the room. He wanted to get the bullshit over with and get to his bunk. The Intelligence officer and his clerk were sitting behind a folding table, on which there was a laptop and a portable recorder. The guy looked up at him while the uniformed marine held her fingers over the keys of the laptop.

"Name?"

"Chief Petty Officer Nolan."

Is it my imagination, or did my name make them look at me sharply? What was that?

He gave a brief outline of his part in the mission. The clerk took it down, and he was conscious of the red light on the recorder. Best not to make any mistakes, there'd be a lot riding on this particular recon. He finished and waited for them to let him go off to bed.

"Did you see anything strange, Chief? Anything out of place, something that seemed off to you? Or did anything happen, anything you want to talk to us about?"

What the fuck is this? There's something strange, something they aren't saying. What do they want? Why are they looking at me so expectantly?

"No, I don't think so."

Should I mention Grant disobeying orders? Is that what they're looking for? No, that was internal, our own business, and the Seals will deal with it.

The civilian pressed on. "Those cops that were killed, tell us about them."

And then he remembered. The first cop, who'd been lying in the road. He pictured the scene, the guy lying in a pool of blood, probably from a cut throat. He recalled Colonel Weathers' briefing, warning them about the murder here on the base.

Christ, what a coincidence!

He told the Intelligence officer what he'd seen, and the guy's interest perked up. He was young, a thin blonde guy, with a lock of hair carelessly pushed of his forehead. A bit preppy, probably he'd been to an Ivy League college, then he'd go on to big New York law firm, after a short period of military service to put on his CV. But he had an underlying toughness, and he seemed more than just a backroom intel weenie. And Nolan suddenly understood he'd got it all wrong.

The guy is not intel, no way. He has to be a plain-clothes cop.

"What are you? Military Police?"

The preppy guy smiled and nodded, "United States Marine Corps Criminal Investigation Division. I'm Captain Lomax, and this is Corporal Donna Ekstrom. You know why I'm here?"

"I assumed it was just to take down the mission debriefs, but clearly that's not the case. There's something else. What's up?"

"What do you think is up?"

Nolan shrugged. "The body they found after the raid?"

"Correct, a civilian worker with close family connections to Karzai's tribe. They're pretty pissed in Kabul, and they want answers."

"But what's it got to do with the mission? It happened in a different country, for God's sake. This is crazy. There's no connection between them. I'm going to bed."

He got up and started to walk out.

"Sit down, Chief Nolan! That's an order."

"And if I don't?"

"Then I'll arrest you, and we can continue this from your cell."

Nolan sat down.

"Okay, I'm all ears. Shoot."

"You said there was no connection. The murdered guy here on the base had his throat cut. From what I gather, the first cop who died in Abbottabad was killed the same way."

Nolan remembered the bloody body.

"Yeah, it seemed that way."

The marine keyed in the details, and there was a short silence. He got up to leave.

"I assume that's it?"

"Not quite, sit down. Now, tell us about San Diego, this rape they're after you for."

He sat there for a few seconds, stunned. So they knew all about it. It must have been all around the San Diego PD, the NCIS, and the USMC CID. He wanted to tell them to go to hell, but there was something about the way this was going that made him decide to tread carefully.

After all, I have nothing to worry about, do I? The best way is to cooperate, to some degree, anyway.

He told them what he'd heard from Carol.

"So you know there are a couple of SDPD detectives looking for you?"

"I heard, yes."

"So why didn't you come forward and clear the air."

"I've been a little busy, Captain. You do know why we're here, in Afghanistan?"

Lomax ignored his sarcasm. "You'll have to talk to those cops and answer their questions. I've arranged for them to come here this afternoon. You can speak to them after you've had a chance for some sleep. Make sure you say nothing about the mission into Abbottabad."

"I was going to write it up and send it to the San Diego Tribune."

"Yeah, very funny. You have a lot of questions to answer, Chief. I'd take it a bit more seriously if I were you."

Nolan ignored him. The response 'fuck you' was on his mind. He was tired, and they were pushing him hard.

"One more question," the preppy investigator said abruptly. "Then you can go. Where were you when that Afghan was killed during the raid?"

"I don't know when he was killed, so if you give me a time, I'll think about it."

The Captain nodded. "Yeah, well, we're still working on that. Okay, you can go, Chief. Don't leave the base, not until those cops have talked to you."

Nolan got up and walked to the door. As he was pushing through, he saw Mariko Noguchi staring at him.

Does she think I'm involved in all this? No, she was with me almost the whole time in Abbottabad. But the rape in San Diego, will she be wondering? Probably. Fuck it!

He walked angrily to his quarters and lay down on his bunk. He tried to sleep, but it didn't come. All he could think about were the fingers of suspicion that were pointed at him. A half-hour of anguished worrying at the problem got him nowhere. He must have started to doze when a knock at the door woke him abruptly. He ignored it at first, but when the knock was repeated, he heard her voice, "Nolan? You there?" He stayed where he was. After a few minutes, he realized she must have gone away as everything went quiet, and he fell into an uneasy sleep.

* * *

The two cops wore skeptical expressions, as if they'd been in the job a long time. They both looked tough, one in his late forties, the other probably mid-thirties. Both men had the jaded expressions, etched with suspicion, of career detectives. They were also overweight, with blotchy skin, the result of too many missed meals, made up with coffee, hot dogs, doughnuts, and hastily eaten junk food. The veteran detective look was completed with creased suits, shirts with the collars unbuttoned, and no ties.

Maybe it's some kind of an overseas uniform, Nolan wondered.

One guy was short, below medium height, and the other about six feet. Other than that, they could almost have come out of a mold. The cynical, careworn, city detective mold. He entered the room, a borrowed office in the guardroom, and they invited him to sit at a single chair placed to face the window, and the afternoon sun.

Funny. Are they that naïve? Do they think it will make

a difference?

They shook hands, and he waited for them to start. The only decorations on the peeling walls were warning notices, what to do in case of fire, or an enemy attack, and the only furniture, apart from the table and chairs, a pair of locked steel filing cabinets. The MPs weren't offering their civilian counterparts any luxuries.

"Kyle Nolan?" the taller cop asked.

He nodded.

"I'm Detective Preston, this is Detective Ashe. You know why we're here?"

"I do now, yeah. The CID guy told me. The San Diego thing."

"That's right. On the night of February 12th, that was a Friday by the way, a young woman was raped in San Diego. She gave a description that matches you exactly. What do you have to say?"

"As I wasn't there, what can I say?"

The shorter cop, Ashe, looked at him with a nasty expression. "That's a fucking lie, Nolan. You were there, and we can prove it. Show us your left forearm!"

"What the hell for?"

Ashe looked angry, as if he was about to physically pull up the Seal's sleeve. Nolan was ready to stop him. The taller cop intervened.

"Chief Nolan, the victim identified a tattoo on the guy who raped her. Please, show us your arm."

Finally, he nodded and rolled up his sleeve, revealing the dolphin he'd had tattooed there right after he'd completed his BUD/S training. Ashe looked triumphant.

"This is a sketch of the tattoo the girl saw that night."

He showed Nolan a picture. It could have been his

tattoo, or not. Nolan laughed.

"You know how many Seals and former Seals have this dolphin tattoo? Hundreds, maybe thousands, as well as tens of thousands of wannabes across the US. It proves nothing, Detective. Except your ignorance of the way these things work."

They stared at each other. Ashe was red with anger, and Nolan got the impression he was about to launch himself across the table. Once again, the taller cop intervened.

Good cop, bad cop, not the most original technique in the police arsenal. But I'll have to be careful; they're trying to trip me up.

"Okay, take it easy. We can settle this now, Mr. Nolan. Just tell us where you were on the night in question."

And that's the sixty-four dollar question. Where had I been? In bed, of course, except that I blacked out and can't honestly say, not for one hundred percent sure, where I was. But still, they can't know that.

"I was in bed. All night."

"I see. Can anyone verify your story, like Detective Summers, for instance? Were you with her?"

"No."

"Is that right?" Ashe smiled, and both detectives looked like cats that had got the cream. They exchanged glances. "Why am I not surprised?" Ashe commented.

Preston intervened. "You understand, Mr. Nolan. We have to ask these questions."

"Damn right," Ashe interrupted, "and quite frankly, we're not satisfied with the answers we're getting. We…"

Nolan stood up, and they both flinched. "No, you cops don't understand. You come halfway across the world chasing the wrong man. I didn't do it, so you should be looking for the man who committed this crime, and go after him. And it's Chief Nolan, not Mister. If you want anything else, you can talk to my lawyer."

Ashe nodded, as if he was pleased with the sudden hostility. He stared at Nolan.

"Tell me, Chief Nolan. Why did you threaten to cut her throat if she refused to keep quiet? Is that the way you handle your women? You like it rough, do you? Or maybe you don't remember. What, did you lose your memory that night? That's convenient. Why is it that perps always seem to lose their memory when it comes to the crimes they committed?"

Nolan felt a band tightening around him, and it all came together.

No, it isn't possible.

He stared at them. "You don't really think I did this? Jesus Christ, ask my partner, Detective Summers, she'll…"

"We already did ask her, buddy. That's why we're here. Look, you're in a lot of trouble, so why not settle this and tell us what you did?"

What's going on? There's no way Carol could think I did this. Could she? What has she told them? He felt his anger rise again. They were shitting him, she couldn't have? Could she?

He tried again.

"The problem is, Detectives, I just did tell you what I did. I was in bed, asleep. And this is a complete waste of my time, your time, and the American taxpayers' dollars. Now go chase the real criminal."

Ashe nodded. "We're looking at him, Chief. I wouldn't go too far if I were you, my friend. This is isn't over. We'll be talking to you again, and the next time, we'll be reading you your rights. Savvy?"

Nolan stared him down. Their eyes locked, and neither man was prepared to look away. He'd have liked nothing better than to give the San Diego cop a lesson in the finer arts of unarmed combat. But he controlled his emotions and walked out the door. He had to talk to Carol, as soon as he could put a call through. He went outside and tried to use his cell, but there was no signal, as usual. He'd need to use one of the base phones as soon as he could.

What has she told them?

CHAPTER FOUR

He strode along the path that led to the operations room, from where Lieutenant Colonel Weathers was just emerging. It looked as if the guy had been waiting for him, which was no surprise.

"Chief, did you deal with those cops? Is it all over?"

"No, Sir, it is not. Could I have a word with you, in confidence."

"Sure, you'd better come on into my office before those guys get to you. Tell me what's on your mind."

Nolan looked around; Ashe and Preston were fifty meters away, watching him. He followed Weathers into the office and took the indicated chair.

"It's those two cops, Sir. It's more serious than I realized. I don't know how it will affect my work here."

"Yeah, I gather it's not just our Marine CID. Those civilian cops look as if they're after your ass. Tell me, Chief, what exactly it all about?"

Nolan hesitated. Was talking to him a wise move, especially after he'd told the SDPD detectives to talk to his lawyer? But he had to do something, needed someone on his side. Otherwise he'd go crazy. So he leveled with Colonel Weathers and told him everything, except for the blackouts. That was his business. Weathers didn't interrupt, just listened to it all. The murdered Afghan, the murdered Pakistani cop, and what they'd told him about the raped woman in San Diego. She may well have been another victim, had her rapist carried out his threat. When Nolan had finished, the Colonel sat back, deep in thought. Finally, he looked up.

"Chief, I'll be honest, none of this is new to me. When I heard about those civilian cops, I asked around. The Department of the Navy, who oversees both the Marine Corps and the US Navy, gave me the necessary authorizations to dig deep into the files. I wanted to know what those cops wanted, and why. Anything that may affect the efficient operation of this facility, and the missions we run from here, I have to make my business. The death of the Afghan who was murdered on the day of the raid is still under investigation, and I spoke to Captain Lomax about the progress of that. I was also in on some of the interrogations of that cop you brought back, and what he said filled in some of the blanks. We covered the little matter of him and his colleagues going missing, by the way. It was easy to arrange a large cash deposit into the bank account of a cop in Abbottabad, and the CIA is in process of spreading a rumor about an arrangement he made with a rival warlord. The story is he wanted those cops out of the way because of some family feud."

"Do you think they'll wear it?"

Weathers laughed. "It's the one thing they will wear. Happens all the time over there. These people slaughter and kidnap each other at the drop of a hat. Don't worry; we're covered, but back to your problem. There is a link to all of these crimes, and I'm surprised you haven't worked it out yet. The Navy Seals."

Nolan nodded thoughtfully as it all clicked into place. The dolphin tattoo, San Diego, and the Seals being present at both the murders in Bagram and Abbottabad.

"You mean Bravo Platoon, not just the Seals. So you think it is me? You think I'm a murderer?"

Weathers smiled. "No, I'm pretty sure you're not a murderer. It doesn't mean you're in the clear, but it's a start. As for that civilian matter, it'll have to take its course. You'll have to deal with it sooner or later, but if you're innocent, they've got nothing on you. What concerns me is our problem; one we've only just realized we have. It looks like we have a serial killer running around inside the US military, inside a Navy Seal unit, and Bravo Platoon is the common link."

"It's crazy. Bravo, I can't believe it."

"Maybe, but it's probably true. This guy kills for pleasure, that's what we understand, some kind of a perverted power trip. When I started to look into this, I found there have been two other women victims at least, and three more men murdered in the same way. Both of the women were raped as well. It looks like the same guy did it all. And he's not too choosy about his victims, men, women, any age, it makes no difference to him. He just enjoys killing."

"What about DNA? Surely that can help find him?"

Weathers nodded. "You're right, as a rule. But this guy is clever, very clever. He leaves no traces, nothing we can pin on him. By the way, have you any objection to a new

DNA swab?"

Nolan shook his head. "None at all. I just want this out of the way."

"Okay, I'll arrange for it to be done, not that it'll take us far. We already have your DNA on file, as you know. But we'd like a current sample to compare with the original." He stared at Nolan. "Chief, I want your help to catch this killer."

"I still don't believe it's one of our guys, Colonel. It doesn't seem possible. Every man in the squad devotes his life to the Seals. It doesn't make sense."

"I agree, but we have to face the facts. Someone is committing these crimes, and someone who's grown to enjoy killing people a little bit too much. The link is Bravo. We need to catch this guy, and fast. I need your help."

Nolan thought fast.

If it is someone inside Bravo, it could rip the squad apart, a squad that every man has dedicated his life to, and sacrificed everything to be the best. But how can I help when I've this civilian problem to get over?

He explained his dilemma.

"Colonel, I can't deal with both the Marine Corps CID and the SDPD, not when I'm under suspicion. Besides, the right guy to deal with Bravo is Lieutenant Boswell. You should go through him."

Colonel Weathers stared at him for a long, hard moment. "Lieutenant Boswell. Is he up to it, Chief? Leading the Platoon, I mean?"

Nolan couldn't meet his eye. He just mumbled, "I dunno, maybe, maybe not. But that's an internal matter, Colonel."

Weathers shook his head. "I'm not totally happy about

that officer. He's got a lot to prove yet, and so far the thing he's best at is leaning on his highly placed connections. No, it has to be you who deals with this, Chief."

"Then you'll have to call off the dogs, Colonel. Captain Lomax, the Marine Corps Cop. And I'll need to convince those detectives, somehow. Otherwise it'll be like working with a hand tied behind my back, trying to find a killer when I'm the number one suspect."

Weathers shook his head. "It ain't gonna happen like that. You're uniquely placed to help us, and you know that. If the real killer thinks you're the likely suspect, he won't realize we're looking for him, and hopefully, he'll become careless. If you're cleared, he'll be a lot more careful, and it'll be harder than ever to find him. Think about it. There are twenty guys in Bravo Platoon, and one of them is almost certainly our killer."

Nolan was thinking exactly that. The Colonel was asking was that he continued as the Platoon's number two while under suspicion for murder, and at the same time he had to find out who the real killer was.

"It's too much, Colonel. You don't know what life is like for an operator on Seal missions. We need to think fast and move fast. It's like nothing you've ever seen before. It'll be hard enough waiting to be cleared of this rape nonsense, but I guess I'll have to roll with it. This other thing, you really need to talk to Boswell."

He shook his head firmly. "I've already said that's a non-starter. Do you have any suspicions?"

Nolan's mind whirled with the possibilities.

Who the fuck can it be? I trust those men with my life. That's the way it works in the Seals. Only one name comes to mind, and it doesn't seem possible. Lucas Grant. He was out on his own, moving forward to recon the compound in Abbottabad when the cop got chopped. Yeah, he was here in Bagram during the raid, and he would've been in San Diego at the time of the rape. As for the other crimes, I've no idea, but even so. I'm not comfortable with the guy, true, but for entirely different reasons. He's a little too gung ho, if anything, but Christ, the guy had been there and carried out the impossible, he was entitled. He's an American hero, for Christ's sake! Seal Team Six set America and the world alight when they took out Osama bin Laden. The raid restored the reputation of America's military and intelligence services at a stroke. And the guys in Six are the absolute best of the Seals, itself an elite organization. They don't come any better than those guys. When the raid became public, every Seal was proud of what their service had achieved. At the same time, there was a twinge of envy we all felt, that we hadn't been on that mission.

Weathers seemed to read his thoughts.

"You think it could be Grant?"

He stared at the Colonel.

"I'm sorry, Sir, no, I don't believe it's Grant."

And there was something else that occurred to him.

This whole line of questioning from Lieutenant Colonel Weathers, a Marine Corps officer, it doesn't ring true. He has too much knowledge of our operations and personnel.

"If not him, then who?" Weathers persisted.

"I don't know, Sir, but there's one thing I do know."

"What's that?"

"If you're a Marine Corps Colonel, I'll resign and join the Parks Department."

They stared at each other. Finally, Weathers nodded and smiled.

"Very good, Chief. You're right, at least, partly right. I used to be a Marine Corps Colonel until I transferred."

"To where, Sir?" But he already had a pretty good idea.

"This is for your ears only. Clear?"

Nolan nodded.

"I transferred to DIA Counterintelligence, Defense Intelligence Agency, after I got my star. Technically, I'm a Brigadier General, but my work for DIA means I have to adopt whatever rank is convenient for my current mission."

"Just what is your current mission, Sir?"

"I was sent here to investigate certain US military activities in Afghanistan, specifically here in Bagram. The murders were something new, and then I got caught up with this Abbottabad business quite by chance, but DIA wants me to continue to run with it. That's why I want you to unravel it and find out where it all leads. Is there another bin Laden in Abbottabad? If so, is he the new al Qaeda leader, or just a local rug merchant? And is there a killer inside Bravo Platoon, or is that just another set of coincidences? That's your brief. It's a tall order, but I need it taken care of."

"And all the time I'm the number one murder suspect," Nolan said bitterly.

Weathers shrugged. "That's the way it goes, I'm afraid."

The phone rang, and he picked it up. "Weathers."

He listened for a few seconds. "Okay, he's with me now. You can speak to him when he comes out."

He put the phone down. "That was the San Diego cops. They want to talk to you again, and they're waiting outside my office."

"Shit. Sorry, Colonel, or is it General?"

"Here, it's Colonel. You'd best remember that."

"Okay, Colonel. I told those guys I would only talk to them with a lawyer present."

"Is that right? I suggest you tell them you've changed your mind. You need to lead them on, to keep pressure off the real killer."

What about the fucking pressure on me? Who gives a shit about that?

"I haven't decided to take all this on, Sir."

"No? You got any other options, Chief, you going any place?"

No, I've nowhere else to go, that much is true, and I'm boxed in. Except that if they want me on side, I have a bargaining chip.

"Maybe not. But if that intel on Abbottabad pans out, and there is another bin Laden who needs to be taken out, I want to be on the mission. I mean, Team Bravo."

"That's not an option, I'm afraid. The planners will decide who to send, and I doubt it'll be your outfit. I'm sorry, Chief, but that's the way it is."

"Then it's no go, Sir. I'll do my job, but no more. You'll have to get someone else to find your killer. You want him, you find him."

Weathers stared at him. "That sounds a lot like blackmail to me. Are you sure that's the way you want to play it with me?"

His voice was low and cold, but Nolan had been pushed around just once too often.

"I do, Sir."

The Colonel thought deeply. "Neptune Spear was put

together with guys from different squads. They were all chosen for their experience and service records. They literally were the best of the best. I could maybe get you on the team that goes in."

"Not good enough. Team Bravo may not be Six, but we've been places and done things that were every bit as challenging as Neptune Spear. It's Bravo or nothing. It's not negotiable. Sir," he added as an afterthought.

Weathers stared him in the eyes, but Nolan wasn't backing down, and he stared stubbornly back. The officer laughed.

"I guess what they say about you is true. You're one, stubborn, single-minded sonofabitch who always gets what he wants. Maybe that's what makes you a good Seal. Okay, you've got it. If the raid goes ahead, it's Bravo's mission."

"Thank you, Sir."

"But you'd better bring that killer in, Chief, or the DIA will be after my ass, not yours. And in the meantime, make sure they don't arrest you. Find that guy."

"How do I find him?"

"I haven't the faintest idea. Do what you're trained for, Chief. I'll let you know what pans out across the border in Pakistan. Dismissed."

He walked out the door and immediately ran into Preston and Ashe. They'd been sitting on two hard, uncomfortable looking chairs, and they jumped to their feet when he emerged. Their expressions were smug, so he knew that whatever they wanted, it wasn't going to be anything good.

"Chief Nolan," Preston began. "We need another word with you. If you want your lawyer present, that's okay."

Ashe was looking at him expectantly; as if he was about to fall into a trap they'd set.

Nolan shook his head. "That's okay, I'll talk to you. I don't need a lawyer."

Ashe looked puzzled. "You don't?"

"No, I didn't do anything, so I don't have anything to worry about."

Preston nodded. "Let's get somewhere we can talk. They gave us the go ahead to use that room in the guardroom. We can go over there and see how this pans out."

"Sure."

They were both suspicious at his sudden change of heart. Cooperation wasn't what they'd expected, and Nolan felt that Ashe was just looking for an excuse to play hardball. Preston led the way out the door and across to the guardroom, just inside the main gate. Ashe brought up the rear, as if Nolan may have been planning to run. He smiled to himself.

The guy is far too close to prevent me from turning fast and disabling him with a snap kick, pulling my Sig, and squeezing off a round at the other guy. Maybe I should show them how it's done, without the shooting part, of course. Ashe should know how to guard a suspect. I need to deal with these two cops and get them off my back, so I can carry on doing my job. After talking to Weathers, doing my job has just got a whole lot harder.

They showed him into the interrogation room, and once more he sat in the same chair, facing the sun.

Preston went first. "Have you decided to tell us anything more about the rape?"

He grimaced. "What would you like me to tell you? I wasn't there, so it's difficult for me to understand what you want from me. You're asking the wrong guy."

"We want you to own up and tell the truth, motherfucker!" Ashe shouted, leaning across so he was inches from his face. Nolan didn't flinch. He just stared at the man, keeping his expression neutral.

Is this guy for real?

He waited for the man to calm down.

"We want a statement from you, Nolan. We want to know everything you can remember about your movements on the night in question."

And that's the problem. I don't know, don't know anything. I blacked out and went to the doc the following morning to talk to him about it.

He shook his head.

"I already told you. I was home, on my own. All night. I can't tell you anything else. What more could you want?"

Preston nodded. "Okay, you were home. What did you do? Watch TV, a movie maybe? Tell us what you did until you went to bed, and after, when you woke up."

"I, er, I watched TV, but I can't remember what it was. I really can't remember."

That was true enough.

"Think about it, maybe you watched sport, a baseball game? Football maybe?"

Nolan shook his head. "I don't know."

Ashe pounced. "That's too bad, buddy. If you don't know what you were doing, you can't convince us you were at home, so we can only assume you're lying to cover something up. And if you're lying about that, you're probably lying about the rest of it. You're a lying shit, isn't that right? A fucking pervert rapist. You deserve to be locked up with the rest of the sickos."

The detective kept staring at him, waiting for a reaction. They wanted him to lose his cool and maybe say something incriminating. He had to disappoint them.

"I don't know any more than what I've told you," he repeated.

The two cops exchanged glances. "That doesn't cut it," Preston murmured. "See, we have to have something to take back Mr. Nolan. Sorry, Chief Nolan," he sneered. "We have to know what you were doing that night, at least, before you turned in for the night and went to sleep. The rape occurred late evening. It's important that you account for your movements. Tell us, what are you covering up?"

They know I'm covering, maybe it's instinct, or maybe Carol Summers told them. But they know something. I can't tell them; it'd be the end of my career in the Seals.

Ashe stared fixedly at Nolan. "What was it, Nolan, some kind of a blackout?"

Who the fuck could have told possibility told them? Someone has. So maybe it was Carol. My doctor is also a possibility. Or are they just fishing?

"Was that it, you have no recollection of that night? Which is it?" Ashe stood up and leaned over the table. "Did you have a blackout that night, Nolan? Is it the truth? Is that what happened?"

He shook his head. He didn't know, couldn't know.

"So you could have been watching TV or out raping that woman, correct, you've no idea what you were doing?" Ashe's snarl had risen to a shout. "If you don't know, how can you confirm or deny where you were, buddy? You were there, weren't you? You raped that woman!"

"No, I'm…" he whispered. He felt like a deer, caught in the headlights of a car.

"If that's the best you can do, we don't have a choice. You understand?" Ashe continued.

Yeah, he knew what the cop was saying. Give them a satisfactory answer, or they'd arrest him. He had to say something, had to. But he couldn't think of how to retrieve the situation.

I have to make this right, if I am to keep to the agreement with Colonel Weathers. How the hell can I do that? And if the Navy finds out about the blackouts, I'll be taken off active service.

He sat waiting for their next attack. He had to think of something, some way out of this mess, or he was finished. He saw Preston look at Ashe, who nodded.

"In that case, Kyle Nolan, we're placing you…"

The door crashed open. Will Bryce stormed in with Vince Merano right behind him. The two cops eyed them suspiciously.

"We're using the room," Ashe shouted at them. "This is a police interview. You have to get out."

They ignored him. "Chief, they just gave us a call. Wheels up in twenty. Let's go."

"You can't…"

But Will Bryce stood over Ashe, huge, hard, black, and intimidating. He stared down the detective. "Oh, but we can, my friend. This is what the President of the United States pays us to do."

"But this is…"

They were hustling Nolan toward the door. Will looked back at them. "You got any issues, take it up with out Commander in Chief. He's in Washington. You know the address."

Outside, a huge Galaxy C-5 transport was beginning

139

its take off roll, and the four huge General Electric CF39 Turbofans were deafening as they reached maximum power. The lumbering giant began to accelerate along the main runway. The air stank of burnt kerosene, and the noise was deafening. Enough to drown out the two detectives shouting after them to come back. Nolan had to wait until the aircraft had clawed its way into the air before he could talk to Bryce and Merano. They were hurrying him toward the main building that housed the shopping mall and restaurants. Nolan squinted sideways at Will.

"Okay, what gives? Why aren't we headed to the briefing room? You said we were wheels up in twenty."

"I did, yeah. It's true; we do have wheels up in twenty. Twenty hours, that is. I'd never lie to a cop," Will smiled. "Thing is, those MPs in the guardroom have that room miked up, so they can monitor conversations and confessions. I persuaded them to switch it on. We were worried about you. When it sounded as if they were about to make an arrest, we came busting in to get you out."

Nolan chuckled. "Thanks, guys, that was well timed. So what is this mission?"

"Let's get into the coffee bar first," Vince said. "We'll find a quiet corner and fill you in. You look as if you need a strong cup of Java."

"I do, yeah. Thanks. I thought I'd be in chains and on a plane back to San Diego, just before you busted in."

They found a table where they could talk without being overheard. Nolan sipped at his coffee and waited.

"It's about that raid on the base," Will explained. "They upset more than a few of the government people when they tried to knock off Karzai. Our intel people located the group who were behind it. The guy at the top, the warband leader, his name is Abasin Balkhi, and his village is about fifty klicks from Bagram. It's a place called Bandez, to the southeast, and in the direction of the Pakistan border. CIA confirmed it, using satellite imagery and cellphone intercepts, together with some of their local assets. It's definitely the guy, and he's holed up with about twenty or thirty fighters, all of them survivors of the Bagram raid."

"All these guys are Taliban?"

"No. Oddly enough, this Balkhi is on record as saying he hates the Taliban. But he's Dari, and Karzai is Pashto, as you know. It's some kind of a blood feud. He's vowed to kill Karzai, and when he found out the President was coming here, it was a perfect opportunity. Until he got his ass kicked, that is. They want us to go in at 0300 tomorrow and put paid to this murderous bastard."

"What're the plans for infil and exfil?"

"This is going to be a shock and awe job," Will grinned. "No pussyfooting around in the boonies. We'll fast-rope down from a CH-47 Chinook. The plan is to land right outside his front door. The village is almost on a straight line between Bagram and Jalalabad, so they are used to the noise of the heavies flying backward and forward during the night. We're using the entire Platoon, twenty of us, and we'll be dropping in two chalks, so that'll get us on the ground before he has time to pull on his undershorts. Our guys have arranged for overhead surveillance, and a Predator drone will be overhead for the entire operation. We'll be able to monitor the enemy before we go in and spy out anyone who looks like might cause us any problems."

"Sounds okay, what about exfil?"

Will nodded. "We go out on the same Chinooks. It's a short flight for them, so they'll have plenty of fuel. After we've gone in, they'll land five klicks out. As soon as we've cleared the hostiles from the village, they'll come back and pick us up. They don't want to hang around when the shooting starts. These Afghans tend to get too free and easy with the RPGs. Makes the crews nervous."

Nolan smiled. "I'll bet. It all sounds good, providing there are no surprises waiting for us when we reach that village. Where's Boswell?"

The two Seals swapped glances. It was Vince Merano who answered.

"He's gone into Kabul with Grant."

"Kabul? He should be here, prepping the mission. What does he want in Kabul?"

He looked at Bryce. "You tell him, Will."

The big, black PO1 sighed. "He tried his personal satphone, and it didn't work. Lucas said he knew a guy in Kabul who could fix it, so they took off."

"You're shittin' me!"

"That's the way it is, Chief. Boswell's the boss, so, you know..."

"Someone needs to kick his ass," Nolan said angrily.

Will shrugged. "The guys are working pretty hard to get everything ready, so we'll be okay. When we're done here, we're going over to intel and relieve them of a couple of their up-to-date maps. You never know when you might need them if things don't go to plan."

Vince agreed. "Fact is, I can't remember the last time things did go to plan."

Nolan nodded. "You got that right. We'll have to work through the rest of the morning, and after chow, we'll all need to get a few hours sleep. We need to be on top of this tonight, not a bunch of sleepwalking zombies. Did

Boswell say when he and Grant would be back?"

They shook their heads.

What the fuck is the Lieutenant doing, going to Kabul when we're in the field again tonight? It doesn't make sense. And Lucas Grant should have known better. He's one of the most experienced Seals in the Platoon, with the exception of myself. And who knows when they might try again to drag my ass back to San Diego?

"Okay, we'd better get started. Are we in the same hut inside the JSOC area?"

Will nodded. "Yep, our guys are in there right now. Just one problem, Chief. Those cops, they might get pretty pissed and come looking for you if they see you still on the base. You know they thought we were leaving on an urgent mission. I can't imagine why," he grinned.

"Yeah, that could be difficult. Okay, we'll make sure they don't see me. Can you rustle up a Humvee? I'll go out the back way, and we'll drive across to the JSOC compound."

"No problem, give me ten minutes. I'll meet you out back."

Will got up and strode away. "It ain't gonna solve anything," Merano pointed out. "Those cops will still be here when we get back, and they'll be madder than a wounded grizzly. We need to take care of this and put an end to it."

"You're right, Vince."

But he couldn't he put an end to it, if he didn't know and couldn't remember. He'd delayed the inevitable for a few hours, maybe a few days, but sooner or later they'd want to take him in for a crime he hadn't committed. A crime for which he couldn't provide an alibi, and because of that, it would be the end of his career.

It's a mess, a real crock of shit.

But for now, he had an operation to plan, which took precedence over any personal problems. He would put his worries behind him for a short time, knowing who his enemies were. It was so simple when they carried guns and took potshots at you. It was the other kind, the sneaky ones that were hardest to deal with.

"I'll iron it out with those cops, Vince. I'm okay, don't worry."

Vince looked back at him, and his expression was dubious, and no wonder. Unless Nolan got lucky, he was in deep shit. He'd have to worry about that after the mission was over.

The noise of the twin turboshaft engines, coupled to the twin rotors made the cabin sound like the inside of a steam hammer. The only way they could communicate was by using their personal commo systems. The two Lycoming engines that powered the big helo were at cruising speed, but still the noise was awesome inside the fuselage of the Chinook. They had space, which was one advantage of riding in the CH-47, and the Team was sprawled around the sides of the cabin, making last minute preparations. The Crew Chief signaled to Nolan and Boswell, and they went forward to speak to him.

"I'll lower the ramp in five minutes time. I know we've been over this, but let's do it once more. You'll be dropping in two chalks, One and Two. Chief, you're first out with Chalk One. Lieutenant, you'll lead Chalk Two. You're both going out at the same time, and there's plenty of space on the ramp, so it'll mean you'll get down on the ground that much faster." He stopped, listening to a message from the cockpit. Then he looked at Boswell. "Sir, message from

Bagram, the drone assigned to this mission. It had to be recalled, some kind of an electronics fault. It's unable to navigate properly. They say there's no alternative, so you'll have to manage without it."

Boswell nodded. "Tell them message understood. And if they can get it fixed, they're to send it along. We may still need it."

"Will do, Sir."

Nolan was surprised. Boswell had calmed down, and the bluster had almost vanished. It was as if he'd made up his mind, at last, to concern himself more with the Platoon and less with his career advancement. He heard the pilot announce their position as eight minutes out from the target. The crew chief acknowledged, and began to make is own final preparations for the drop.

"Okay, three minutes until I lower. Both chalks assemble on the ramp, and I'll give you the word when to go. As you know, we'll circle away to our pre-arranged LZ, and wait for the word to come and pick you up. Bear in mind, the skipper gets mighty nervous about those RPGs, so the second the last man is on the ground, we're outta here. Make sure you let go that rope, otherwise you'll be coming with us for a free ride."

He checked his wristwatch and held his finger on the button that lowered the ramp. And then he pushed it hard, and over the engine and rotor noise they all heard the whine of the ramp as it lowered. It was a sound that always sent Nolan's adrenaline racing. It was a sound like no other. It was the precursor to a jump into hostile territory, and a time to put into use all the skills and knowledge he'd acquired after long years of hard, often painful training. The red light winked on, and already the two chalks were clustered around the rope. The crew chief, fastened by a strong lanyard to the fuselage to prevent any accidents if the Chinook hit turbulence, held up four fingers.

"Four minutes. Target is in sight. No sign of hostile activity."

They did the things that all soldiers do before going into battle, a last check that the safety was on your weapon, and a quick prayer for a safe return. Any of a dozen different rituals that were calculated to bring each man back alive and uninjured, until the next time. Nolan held the rope firmly. He wore the gloves he'd worn on three previous fast roping missions. Maybe that was his own ritual; they were worn and battered, but each time he wore them, he came back alive. The crew chief held up one finger.

"One minute to target, still no activity on the ground. Pilot reports favorable wind conditions. You're good to go. Stand by, nine, eight, seven."

He counted down, and Nolan could feel the man behind him, Vince Merano, pushing against him, standing close so he could grab hold the rope and follow him down fast. He looked out of the wide ramp opening and saw the pitiful collection of stone buildings and mud huts that were the legacy of Taliban misrule. They showed a sickly green color through his NVG gear.

"Green light, go, go. Good luck, you guys."

The last thing in his mind as he slid down the rope was how close he'd come to not making it on this mission. He thought back to the scuffle with the cops at Bagram.

* * *

The two detectives had got wind of a Seal mission going

out, and they were waiting out near the helipad. They couldn't get back into the JSOC area, not without a pass, and Weathers had shuffled their request to the bottom of the pile. But they were waiting near the Chinook, and as he walked past the two cops stepped out of the darkness.

"Nolan!"

He was in full battle gear, his Multicam camo uniform covered with an armored vest and twin ballistic plates to protect his body. With a helmet, night vision goggles pushed up out of the way, and carrying a pack and his weapons, the Mk 11 Rifle and a Sig in his belt, he'd clean forgotten about Preston and Ashe. But they hadn't forgotten about him. The shorter man, Ashe, blocked him from moving forward.

"We have more questions for you, Nolan. I don't know what game you're playing, but you're not going anywhere."

It was almost farcical. He was about to leave on a mission from inside a heavily guarded strategic military base, and these two bulls were trying to block him. But someone had given them permission to be there, and someone had told them where they could find him outside of the JSOC area. Who? It was surreal. The Seal Platoon was about to go out and do battle with the enemy, and these two civilians were standing in the way. Someone should tell them they were in danger of being shot. The Platoon wasn't psyched up and prepared to go out to a dinner party. He smiled at the absurdity of the situation.

"Ashe, you can't do this now. I'll find you when we get back. You have to get out of here."

They had to shout above the rising noise of the Chinook's engines as they spooled up and the rotors spun around above their heads.

"We have authority from the …"

"What the fuck's going on here?" Boswell had hurried back from the waiting CH-47. "I don't know what you want, but you get out of here now. This is a classified mission."

"We have permission from the Department of the Navy to talk to this man," Ashe shouted back."

"I couldn't give a fuck about that. Get outta here now!"

"I told you, we…"

Boswell carried two weapons. He'd brought an MP7 fitted with a suppressor, extended magazine, and a reflex sight. It was slung to his chest, a fearsome looking, compact submachine gun, already popular with Special Forces throughout the NATO countries. The 4.6mm ammunition was unique among submachine guns in that the bullet was made almost entirely of a hardened steel penetrator instead of softer copper or lead. It was devastating in use, even against lightly armored targets. But Boswell did not need the MP7, he left it where it was and drew his Sig Sauer P226 and raised the barrel to point at Ashe's forehead. The cop froze. "I'll say this once, Mister. This is a warzone, and you shouldn't be here. You're out of order. Either you clear the area, or I'll shoot you down where you stand. I'm not bluffing, pal. This is the only warning you're going to get. Now get out of here! Scat!"

They stared at each other for a few seconds. Then Ashe abruptly turned away without a word and stalked off, followed by Preston. Nolan nodded to Boswell. The Lieutenant's actions had surprised him.

"Thanks, Lt. I appreciate it."

"Yeah, no worries. I heard about your problem, and frankly I think it's a total crock of shit. Those guys were way out of line there. I'm surprised they got so close to a live mission."

That's the question, how the hell did they do that? Someone gave them the how and the where. And the person who'd tipped them off could well be the real killer. That'd be worth looking into, except the cops are not likely to tell me their source.

"Would you have shot him?" Nolan was curious. This was a new, tougher, more warlike stance from his platoon leader.

"Hell, yes," Boswell replied firmly. "Anyone gets in the way of a mission, they go down. And I mean anyone."

Maybe Boswell isn't so bad after all, Nolan mused. He has a long way to go, but he's moving in the right direction.

* * *

Nolan descended into Bandez and hit the ground, the first man down. A second later, Boswell arrived adjacent to him. Both men released the rope and moved out fast to deploy and cover the rest of the Platoon as they dropped down the rope. The plan was for Nolan's squad to cover the outside of the village, while Boswell's squad split into pairs and went through the houses, one by one. There was already movement inside the village as the occupants woke up to the enormous racket of the twin engine helo hovering fifteen meters above them. They were late, much too late. Even before the last man had touched ground, Nolan saw a movement, a green shadow, sneaking around the side of a building. He whipped up the barrel of his rifle, sighted, and fired off a quick shot. The Mk 11 coughed once, and the man was flung back by the heavy

7.62mm round.

"Move out, move out," he heard Boswell in his earpiece. "I want both those M249s covering the approaches to the village! Make sure no one gets in or out. Anyone tries, shoot 'em."

"Copy that," the gunners replied.

Nolan could see them rushing to either end of the village with their distinctive weapons, the M249, the American version of the Minimi. Fed from a long belt inside the box magazine clipped underneath the breech, the weapon gave a huge boost to the firepower of regular infantry, marines and Special Forces when they went into battle against superior odds. Right now, it looked like they would need the raw firepower of the Minimis, once the hostiles woke up to the nightmare that had descended out of the night. He keyed his mic.

"This is Bravo Two. Vince, where are you?"

"I'm on the roof of the mosque, side of the village, about fifty meters from your position."

"Copy that. Anything moving?"

He heard the report of two suppressed shots.

"Not now, no. A gomer just came running out of a stone house, so I popped him."

"Copy that. They're slow to react, as if they weren't keeping much of a watch. I hope our guy is here."

"He…"

Nolan didn't have time to listen further. If they'd been slow to react, they were making up for it now. A group of fighters came hurtling around the corner, their AKs spitting bullets. He felt a round strike him in the chest, a direct hit on his ballistic plates.

Thank Christ for the armor. These guys are sure making

up for lost time.

The incoming fire started to churn up the ground around him. He flung himself to the ground and sighted on the first enemy. Then he shifted his aim. Behind him, he'd seen a missile shooter. He'd had the RPG ready and aimed at the Platoon that was still bunched up after dropping out of the helo. Nolan squeezed off a couple of rounds, and the man went down with the force of the double tap. His missile soared out of the tube and went high into the sky; at least one piece of Russian ordnance that wasn't going to kill Americans. Bullets were hissing and spitting over his head, the whiplike cracks of suppressed American 5.56 and 4.6 HK rounds, and the heavier unsuppressed explosions of the 7.62 Russian ammunition. He saw the guy who'd been his first target pop up again. He was heading toward a doorway in the side of a stone hut. Nolan popped a couple of rounds, taking him high in the chest, and the man went down. But more fighters were flooding into the center of the village; proof the mission had targeted the right place. This was no innocent agricultural settlement. Will crawled up beside him with more of the Seals coming up behind him.

"Those machine guns, the Minimis, we could do with them back here. Boswell sent them off in the wrong direction."

"Yeah. I'll call 'em back in."

"This is Bravo Two. We need the M249s back in the center of the village. A strong hostile force is putting up a lot of resistance. Make it snappy guys, and watch yourselves when you come in."

"Copy that."

He saw Boswell rush in to clear a house. Lucas Grant

followed him. There was a burst of firing, and they came out and moved to the next house. Throughout the village, the two-man teams were doing their work, rooting through the dwellings, searching out the hostiles and taking them down. So far, no one had called in a sighting of the big prize, Abasin Balkhi. He could hear Boswell on the commo, urging the men to keep moving and to watch out for Balkhi. Intel had said he'd almost certainly try to flee rather than fight. He couldn't be allowed to get away. He'd indicated his intent to kill Hamid Karzai, so he had to be stopped; the way you'd stop a rabid dog, by putting it down. It was the only way. A new burst of firing came from a position almost behind him. He looked around and saw four hostiles shooting at them from behind a battered old truck.

"Will, behind!"

"Yeah, I'm on it. Where are those fucking machine guns?"

"Right here, guys," Brad Rose sung out as he slid to a stop and hunkered down next to Nolan and Bryce. Dan Moseley dropped down behind him. "I see them, just a second," Brad murmured.

He sighted on the truck and looked sideways at Nolan. "Ready?"

"Go for it."

Brad depressed the trigger. A stream of bullets from the M249 smashed into the civilian truck, ripping through the unarmored body. There was a scream as one of the Afghans was hit. The other three ran for a new hiding place, and Nolan and his squad had their opportunity to see them clearly. He fired first, knocking down the first man to dart out from cover. The Seals opened fire, and their HK416 assault rifles stuttered out short bursts of fire that scythed through the remaining two hostiles, tearing them to bloody ruin on the dusty village street. The machine guns had done their work, and then Boswell's voice sounded in his earpiece.

"Bravo One to Bravo Two. We have located the primary target. He's holed up in a stone building. It looks like a schoolhouse on the northeast edge of town. Chief, I need four men to cover the rear. We're spread too thin here. Tell me when you're in position, and we'll go right in and try to finish him."

"Copy that, give us a couple of minutes. I'll call when we're in position."

He looked around for his men. Will stood to one side with Jack Whitman; the two men were covering his left flank. Brad lay on the ground behind the M249, watching for movement. Dan Moseley was behind him, and Zeke Murray stood in the doorway of a stone house nearby.

"Will, we're moving. You stay here with a couple of men and watch for any hostiles that try to get in behind us. The rest of you, come with me."

They'd heard Boswell's message, and they hurried after him. It was the endgame. If they could kill Abasin Balkhi, the mission objective would be complete. Besides, it was normal for insurgents to fall apart when their leader was killed, so it would mean they'd be able to make a clean exfil if the survivors were running for the hills. He led them along the street, turned into the beaten earth square in the center of the village, and ran through to the dirt as a vicious stream of machine gun bullets cut just above his head. He could hear the other three men leaping for cover, and he lifted his head to see what they faced. He could see the gun barrel poking out from behind a heap of sacks, probably rice, that had been thrown down as a makeshift emplacement. He ate the dirt as another burst of fire swept over his head, meaning the gunner had seen him. He couldn't move, couldn't lift his head to aim his rifle back at the gunner. The moon had come out from behind the clouds, lighting up the street, so the gunner would have no trouble finding his targets. And Boswell was holding the primary target, which could easily slip away if he didn't hurry.

"Dan, can you hit him with a grenade?"

"I can, but I'll be exposed for a second or two while I aim. I need covering fire."

"You got it. The rest of you men, I'll count to three, and we hose that bastard down while Dan fires the grenade. You set, Dan?"

"On your mark, Chief."

"Counting, three, two, one, mark!"

It was like the Fourth of July as the street lit up with the intense gunfire. The shooter wouldn't be human if he didn't put his head down, protecting himself from the storm of lead smashing around him. Dan stepped out, aimed, and fired. He stepped back as the grenade sailed overhead and dropped behind the emplacement.

"Fire in the…!"

He didn't have time to complete the warning. They were crouched down, knowing what to expect. The grenade exploded, and pieces of metal, mixed with dried rice from the destroyed sacks, flew up into the air. They rushed forward even as the debris was still falling, but the hostile was down, as well as his loader. The two ripped and bloody bodies lay near the ruined machine gun. There was no need to check for signs of life.

Nolan nodded with satisfaction at the devastation. "Let's move on. It's time to pay that Afghan mother a visit."

They skirted around the town and arrived behind the building Boswell had described. It wasn't hard to identify, as it was the only large building in the entire village of Bandez. Gunfire was coming from the front windows of the schoolhouse, but Boswell's squad was holding its fire so far. They deployed behind cover to cover the exits. There were four windows and a single door, and he called up Boswell.

"This is Two, we're in position."

"Copy that. We're going in the front. We'll give them a couple of bursts and then go in fast and hard. Either our target will try and fight, or he'll come out your way, in which case take him down."

"Copy that." Nolan turned to his men. "You all heard. Keep your heads down. Some of that lead could find its way toward us."

The firing started; shorts bursts from Boswell's squad tore chunks from the fabric of the building, ricocheting around the inside. Some shots whistled all the way through and overhead. The firing from inside slackened, and the Lieutenant's squad hit the door. There was a loud crash and a scream as they smashed through the entrance and ran in, shooting up everything in sight. Nolan's men waited, and then the rear window slid open. A head peered out cautiously.

"I see him," he murmured.

The guy was in his sights, but not a clear shot, not a killshot. He waited. The head disappeared and then came back, but something told him to hold his fire. A man slipped out of the window, but he was young, much too young to be Balkhi. The man turned to help another man out the window, and this time there was no doubt. The Afghan warlord was trying to slip out the back way, leaving his men to fight a rearguard action. And die.

"Okay, I'm on him. Hold your fire. We don't want him to be skittish."

"He'll be skittish with a chunk of your lead up his ass," someone said. It sounded like Zeke Murray, but it was no time for jokes.

"Quiet!"

He still waited, looking for a shot that would put an end to the murderous career of the Afghan warlord. The younger man kept getting in his way as they walked away from the schoolhouse. And then he stopped and pointed at something. Balkhi replied to him, and the youth knelt down. Nolan fired. The 7.62mm round smashed through Balkhi's forehead, straight through his brain and exited the other side in a shower of blood and tissue. But Nolan didn't see it. He was already changing his aim, and his second shot hit the target again, this time in the center of the chest. But Balkhi's heart had already stopped beating as the brain ceased to send signals through his nervous system. He fell, certainly dead before he hit the ground. The younger man with him whirled around, the direction of the suppressed shots was not immediately obvious, and for a split second wouldn't have registered in his brain as enemy action. He died in ignorance of what had hit his boss, as Brad opened up with the M249 and stitched a line of bullets all the way up his body to his chin. He collapsed without a sound.

Nolan stood up and went cautiously forward to check the body. He looked down carefully at the bearded face, but there was no doubt. He called Boswell.

"Bravo One, this is Two. Target is down. I say again, target is down."

"Copy that, Bravo Two. Well done, I'm coming over to join you."

Less than a minute later, he emerged and came up to Nolan.

"Have you heard from Will?"

"Not lately, no."

He keyed his mic. "Three, what's your status?"

Will Bryce answered at once. "We're holding on the southern edge of the village, Lt. No sign of any hostiles. I think we either killed 'em or scared 'em away."

"Understood. Can you..."

He was interrupted by a burst of gunfire to the south. Then the sky was lit up by a score of weapons firing at once, bright flashes like lightning. They were coming from Bryce's position where he was deployed with Whitman.

"What's going on?" Boswell shouted urgently. "Come in, Bravo Three, report!"

"It's all hell breaking loose here! There's a new group of hostiles just come out of a house, right outside the village. Looks like they were sleeping there, some kind of dormitory. I guess we woke 'em up. But we could do with some help. We're taking a lot of fire, and we're pinned down," he paused. "It sounds like Vince is whittling them down some. I've seen three go down so far, but there's a whole heap more where they came from."

"I can't see all of them," Vince interrupted. "They went to ground after I popped the first ones, and they're not putting their heads up. Will's in trouble."

"We're on the way. Two minutes."

He started to run, and Nolan sprinted after him.

"I'd suggest we flank them, Lt. If you'll keep them busy from the front, I can bring my squad around behind them. With any luck, we can hit them while they're still worrying about you hitting them from this side."

"Do it, Chief. We need to finish this fast and get out. We didn't come here to start a major battle."

"Copy that. I'll call you when we're in position."

Nolan peeled off and began to regroup his men. "Brad, Dan, Zeke, follow me. We're going to come up on them from the flank. As soon as they're busy worrying about Boswell's squad, we'll move in and pick them off. First thing is to pinpoint their location and get into a good firing position. He had an idea.

"This is Bravo Two. Vince, can you see our position?"

"That's affirmative, Chief. You're two hundred meters south of the schoolhouse. Hostiles are a hundred and fifty meters southwest of you. If you keep walking, take the next right, and then circle around the block, you'll come in right behind them. I can't see any kind of a rearguard. You should be able to reach them without them being any the wiser."

"Copy that. We're moving in now."

They walked quietly through the dark, empty streets.

The sounds of battle must have been terrifying for the locals, Nolan reflected.

There was no sign of any life. They were all indoors; keeping their shabby houses buttoned up tight and praying the soldiers of both sides left them alone. At least it meant the only Afghans they encountered would likely be hostiles. It made life more straightforward. They almost ran headlong into two armed men who were racing through the streets. The four Seals reacted automatically. Four suppressed shots snapped out, and both Afghans were hurled backward to slump to the ground.

"Zeke, make sure they're dead, then come after us. We're not too far away now."

"Copy that."

They reached a narrow alleyway. Nolan heard Vince's voice over the commo.

"Take it easy, Bravo Two. You're almost there. Go through the alleyway and look to your left. You'll be right behind them. They'll be about ten meters away."

"Copy that. Keep on them, Vince."

"No worries, buddy."

They reached the end of the alley, and Nolan peered around, snapping his head back as a hail of gunfire whistled past, but he only heard the muted sound of suppressed firing from Boswell's group.

"Bravo One, this is Two. Cease fire, I say again, cease fire. We're behind the hostiles. We can take them from here."

There was a slight pause, and then the shooting stopped. Boswell's voice sounded in his earpiece, "Copy that, Bravo Two. We'll go to ground, so you'll have a clear field of fire."

"Understood."

It meant they could angle their fire slightly upward and know they wouldn't accidentally target their own men. He explained to the three Seals what was required.

"We go around the corner and open fire immediately. Brad, when you open up with the Minimi, all hell's going to break loose. So wait until we've knocked down the flankers. Then you can hit them before they get a chance to run."

"Copy that."

"Okay, lock and load, let's go, and remember, angle the shots upward. The other guys are out there somewhere."

They went around the corner in a rush and flung themselves flat on the ground. Within two seconds, Nolan was singling out targets and had already knocked down two of the enemy. They were bunched together behind a low stonewall about a meter high in front of a house. He counted ten men in all. They'd started to pour fire in the direction of the new threat, Boswell's squad, who had almost reached the two beleaguered Seals. Bryce and Whitman were returning fire from where they were trapped inside some kind of a grain store, and he could see the muzzle flashes as they shot at the hostiles. But the stonewall was effective, and they'd not taken any casualties, until now. Dan and Zeke opened up with their HKs, and the Afghans began to bunch into the center as the withering gunfire blew away the fighters at either end of their firing line. Brad then opened up with the M249; a long burst that cut through more of the hostiles and blew them to hell, or to Paradise if that's what they believed, in little more than a few seconds. The four Seals stopped firing. It had taken ten seconds in all, and the insurgents were dead or dying several meters in front of them. Nolan called Boswell.

"This is Bravo Two, hostiles are all down. Area is clear."

"Copy that. Will, are you okay?"

Bryce's voice came over the commo. "Yeah, good one, guys. We had a nasty surprise back there."

He stepped out of a nearby doorway, his men right behind him, and joined Nolan's squad. It was time to go.

"Vince, how do things look from up there?"

There was no reply.

"Vince, do you copy?"

Nothing. Almost certainly his radio was u/s.

"Jack, I want you to go to Vince's location. He's on the roof of the mosque. We'll be pulling out soon, so find out what happened to his radio, and call us when you're with him."

"Sure thing, Chief."

He ran off, and Nolan called Boswell again. The radio was silent.

"Bravo Two to One, I repeat, come in."

There was no reply, just the muted sound of the carrier wave.

"We'll go over and join him. Will, I was just talking to you, try to reach me on the commo."

Bryce nodded and spoke into his mic. He came through loud and clear.

"It looks like the net's gone down. We've only got local communications. Let's join the Lieutenant and see if we can find the problem. And watch out for blue on blue. We can't alert them that we're on the way in."

They walked carefully to the end of the street and rounded a corner. Boswell's squad was still deployed in a defensive position, lying on the ground, their assault rifles pointing forward. But the NVG gear allowed them to identify his men, and they got up warily.

"I tried to reach you," Nolan explained. "The commo has gone dead, and we only have short range from headset to headset."

"I noticed," he replied. "What the hell happened? This gear is incredibly reliable. I've never known it go on the fritz."

"Me neither, but it's happened. We have to go past it. The problem is, we can't call in the helo."

Boswell nodded. "That's a bitch. The Chinook is waiting a few klicks away. It's going to be a hike to get to them, and we've no idea what lies between us and them." He shrugged. "We'll have to deal with it. I have their position marked on the map, so we can locate them, no problem. I guess we'd better get moving."

"And what if the helo has had to move position for some reason?" Nolan pointed out. "We'll be walking out into the Afghan badlands with no place to go."

He stared at Nolan. Finally, he nodded. "I guess you're right. We have to make contact somehow or get a message to Bagram. We could...hold it!" he delved into his pack and pulled out a portable phone. His satphone.

"Christ, I'd clean forgotten about this little toy. I only just had it fixed back at Kabul. I'll lock on the signal and put a call through. Damn, I thought this might come in useful. That was a useful repairman you found, Lucas. Would've taken weeks to fix it in the States."

Nolan said nothing; it sure turns a bad situation around. Boswell is one hell of a surprise.

It took ten minutes of wrangling and namedropping before the Lieutenant finally got patched through to the Chinook. He finished talking to them and ended the call.

"They're leaving now. They'll land the helo on the flat piece of ground to the south of the village, and they've asked us to get over there and make sure it's clean. Those guys are jumpy as hell about RPGs."

Nolan nodded. "Vince still isn't back yet. Whitman went out to find him. I hope there isn't a problem."

"You want to send someone else to take a look?" Boswell asked.

"No, Lt. You take the Platoon and head out to secure the landing ground. That's the priority. I'll go take a look, one man is enough."

"You'll be okay?"

"Yep. They know the score, and they're probably on their way in. I just need to make sure."

He left them and hurried toward the mosque. He jogged through the deserted streets, wondering again at the state of the inhabitants; a bunch of poor, terrified folks too frightened to walk out onto their own streets to investigate the sounds of battle. Like the population of some medieval French village in the dark days of the Hundred Years War, they bore the burden of the men with the guns and paid with their blood and their lives. They suffered from lack of food, from no medical care, poor housing, and zero sanitation. Their lot was to live out their lives in terror. Just who would show them any compassion? Not their own people, not the warlords, the Taliban. Or the corrupt officials of the Karzai government, who were too busy lining their own pockets, banking the billions of foreign aid money that came into the country into their offshore accounts. These folks had nothing, only an existence of suffering and fear, and likely a premature death through war, famine, or disease. There would be no comfortable old age, no honorable retirement. Probably the few who made it into their senior years waited only for the blessed release of death.

He heard a sound coming toward him and moved into

the shelter of a doorway. Vince Merano came into view, and he stepped out. His fellow sniper instantly raised his weapon when he saw the movement but lowered it.

"Christ, Chief, I nearly shot you."

Nolan grinned. "Not a chance. You're too slow by half, Vince. I gather you had radio problems too."

"Yeah, it's packed in completely. We pulling out?"

Nolan nodded. "The job's done, so yeah, we're rounding everybody up and getting out of Dodge. Where's Whitman?"

"Whitman? I didn't see him."

"Damn. He went to let you know we were leaving, but that was a while ago. Where the hell is he?"

"Beats me. He didn't come to my stand on the roof of the mosque."

"He can't have got lost. This place is not big enough. We'll head back to Boswell. He's waiting with the others at the assembly point. Whitman should be back there by now."

The retraced the route Nolan had taken when he came looking for Vince. They were only partway back before Vince stumbled.

"Shit!"

"What is it?"

"A body, it's okay, it's not Whitman. It's one of theirs."

"You sure he's dead?"

Vince bent down to check. "It's not a he, it's a she, one of their women. They use a lot of them to carry guns around for the fighters. She could even have been training to be a suicide bomber."

"Or she could be just an innocent," Nolan pointed out. "A girl out on some errand in the night. In the wrong place at the wrong time."

Vince knelt down at the body. She looked young, not much more than a kid.

"How did she die, a stray bullet, maybe?" Nolan asked him.

"No, that's really interesting."

"What's that?"

"Her throat. It's been cut."

Nolan went cold, and a chill sliced through his guts. His throat was dry, and his brain was numb. With an effort, he forced himself to speak normally.

"Did you see any activity around here while you were on that roof?"

Vince considered. "I didn't see any hostiles. Lucas Grant, he came by. Boswell, too."

And they could assume that Whitman had been past at some point, when he should have been carrying the recall to Vince. Could it have been one of them who killed her, or someone else entirely? Even one of the locals, the Afghans were no slouches when it came to using the knife.

"Okay, let's get rejoin the Platoon and hope Whitman got back okay."

The reached the rendezvous point and found Whitman was already there, waiting for them. They walked out of Bandez just as the Chinook was dropping down for a landing. Two hours later, Nolan was locked up in a cell.

CHAPTER FIVE

They were like a pair of tenacious bulldogs, Preston and Ashe. Because of the time difference, they'd been able to liaise with the Chief of Police in San Diego, who'd gone to speak to the Governor. Who'd got through to the Department of the Navy, who'd notified the JAG's department, who'd contacted the Base Commander at Bagram, who'd passed the order to the Commander of the Military Police Unit. The MPs had been waiting for him as he stepped off the helo.

"Chief Petty Officer Kyle Nolan?"

He'd nodded, tired and weary, and knowing in his gut what was coming.

"You're to come with us. Please remove all your weapons and equipment."

"What the fuck's going on here?" Boswell stormed, angry that they were once again trying again to undermine his platoon.

"Keep out of it, Lieutenant," the cop warned. He was a redcap captain, and Boswell would know that a Seal lieutenant couldn't trump even the lowest enlisted man, when that man carried the authority of the MPs in his pocket. Reluctantly, he stood back.

"I'll get to the bottom of this, Chief, don't worry. You'll be freed in no time."

"Thanks, Lt."

The MPs looked bored an uninterested. They'd seen it all too many times before, and they were always innocent. This one was no different, except he was a Seal. That was unusual, but too bad. The guy was under arrest. It didn't matter if he was the Base Commander himself. Orders were orders. Nolan shucked off his gear and waited for them to take him into detention. The MP Captain started to advise him of his rights.

"Under the Uniform Code of Military Justice, you are to be held pending certain inquiries." He looked closely at Nolan. "You gonna do this the easy way, or the hard way?"

"You can forget the handcuffs, Captain. I know you've got your job to do, and I also know that running won't help my case. Lead the way."

They'd taken him to the guardroom and locked him in a cell. After a half-hour, the two detectives came to see him. They stayed outside his cell, and Ashe was beaming as he set up a portable recorder and pressed the record button.

"Well, well, the runaway is finally back. You care to give us a statement now, Nolan? You don't mind me recording this interview?"

He stared at the gloating cop. "It's Chief Nolan. The only thing I object to is staring at your face, Detective Ashe."

"Not for much longer, my friend. You're on a flight back to the States. They're leaving you in our custody, and when we reach San Diego, you'll have a heap of questions to answer. It'd go much easier for you if you made a statement now and admitted it, got it all over with. We could even cut a deal with the DA when we get back."

Nolan nodded. "Sure, I can do that. You ready? Here it is. I didn't do it. This is a crock of shit, so fuck off, and find out who did do it."

"You'll regret that when we get back, Nolan. You're in no position to make enemies."

He laughed. "It's a little late for that, or did you think I counted you as one of my friends?"

The man snorted and stormed away, muttering, "I don't have to put up with this shit."

Nolan realized he'd achieve nothing by making enemies and cautioned himself to hold his anger in check. Preston looked in at him through the bars.

"Tell me about your problems, Nolan. You sound as if you're upset. Why don't we all settle down and sort this out?"

Nolan almost laughed at the poor pretense at good cop.

"Problems? I don't have any problems, only you and your partner."

The cop smiled. "I know it's not easy, any arrest is a difficult time, especially when you're in the service. But that's not what I meant. Your mental problems, what made you do it? You've had trouble, haven't you?"

There it is again. Where are they getting this from?

"I didn't do it. If you think I did, you're the one with mental problems."

"But at least I can remember what I was doing at any particular time, buddy. That's it, you see. Maybe that's the real problem, you know? Something's wrong, maybe a blow to the head you've taken in action, and it's caused you to go off the rails. It could be mitigating circumstances. It could rate a plea of diminished responsibility."

Nolan shook his head tiredly. "You're wrong."

"Am I? Are you telling me you don't get times when you lose your memory and can't recall what you were up to at any particular time?"

"Who've you been talking to?"

Preston looked surprised. "You mean how did we know you have problems? Detective Carol Summers, of course. Or did you think because you two were lovers, she'd cover for you for rape and murder? You must be crazy. She told us all about it. That's why we're here."

Something crumbled inside him then.

So it's Carol who betrayed me. Why? She knows I'm not capable of anything like rape or murder. Where is she coming from, and what have I done to her to deserve such a betrayal?

Preston made one last try. "A statement now will go a long way to easing your sentence, Nolan, and you'll feel better for clearing it up."

He knew then he had only one defense. He was like a boat, cast adrift on a stormy sea, and he needed to play for time until he could get his bearings and find the way to shore. He needed help.

"I don't want to talk to you, Preston. I want a lawyer before I say another word."

Preston nodded. He'd heard it too many times before to let it worry him. "I'll ask around for someone to talk to you, a legal representative. If you change your mind, and do want to talk, let me know."

He got up and left without another word. He had the

look of a satisfied man who was just tying up the loose ends, prior to moving on to the next case.

Nolan dozed for an hour; trying to push his troubles to the back of his mind and think of better, happier times. It didn't altogether work. Uppermost in his thoughts was the evidence that was stacked up against him. The rape in San Diego, the murders out here in Afghanistan, and he'd been on the scene when each one was committed. It wasn't perfect evidence, but the rape victim's description was definitely a mark on the cop's scoreboard. He wasn't finished yet, but he was still on the edge of a precipice. He looked up as a guard appeared in front of the bars.

"Visitor to see you, Nolan."

He nodded, swung his feet off the bunk and stood up. He was just Nolan now, no Mr., no Chief, just Nolan. Captain Mariko Noguchi came through the door and stood in front of the bars. She gave him a wan smile.

"How're you feeling?"

He grinned at her. "About as good as you'd expect."

"That bad, eh?"

"Yep."

"It's not looking too good, Kyle. Somehow, you have to clear this up before it gets any worse."

"I don't know how I can do that. This girl in San Diego. She gave a description that fits me, although it could also be several other guys in the Seals. They've decided I'm the perp, that's the problem, and they're not looking anywhere else. These murders in Afghanistan and Pakistan don't help."

"What happened in Bandez?"

He gave her a searching gaze. "Bandez, what do you mean? That was a successful operation. We went there, we killed the target, and we came back."

"There was another victim, not one of the hostiles. During the debriefs, it came out that a girl was killed, and her throat was cut in the same way as the others."

He recalled the body in the street. "Yeah, we did see a body, me and Vince, but there wasn't time to do anything about it. It looked like a local hassle."

"I doubt it was that. Piecing together all of the post-mission reports, it has all the hallmarks of another murder by the same person who did all the others."

He stared at her with a growing, horrified realization.

"You're not serious? They think it was me who killed her?"

She shook her head. "They haven't come to any conclusions about who killed her, and it's still possible it was a local murder and nothing to do with Bravo Platoon. But it doesn't help you, not at all."

He could see that the growing weight of evidence was becoming stronger almost by the day.

There has to be an answer. I know beyond any doubt I'm innocent of any of the murders committed during Bravo Platoon's missions. And I'm ninety-nine per cent sure that blackouts or no blackouts, I had nothing to do with the crime committed back in San Diego. He explained it all to Mariko.

"It looks to me as if they've made a decision that I'm the chief suspect, and they're not bothering to look elsewhere. I'm fucked."

"I agree they've made up their minds," she replied. "And I have to say they have some circumstantial evidence, but that's all it is. The connection is obviously Bravo Platoon, and yet there are twenty men in Bravo. It could have been any of them. I don't understand why they're pointing the finger at you."

He explained to her his problems with blackouts, after swearing her to secrecy. The cops may know, or were just guessing, but as far as he was aware, the Navy hadn't caught on yet.

"It hasn't happened recently, but I had to keep it under wraps before, otherwise they'd have taken me off operations. But when the girl in San Diego was raped, I'd had a blackout that was so severe I went to see my physician in the morning. So you see, I have no real recollection of what I was doing that night, and it's all on record."

"How the hell could they suspect you'd had the blackout?"

"My partner apparently told them. She's a detective on the San Diego force. I guess you'd say ex-partner, quite obviously we're not an item anymore. But I still can't believe she would have told them."

He saw Mariko's eyes look thoughtful. "It is strange that someone who loves you would do that to you."

Nolan shrugged. "That's all past tense. She's a cop before anything else, I guess. But the fact is, she did tell them something, and that made me the number one suspect. I have to accept that and move on from there. The problem now is disproving their suspicions."

"There's only one way you can do that, you realize that?"

He did. "Somehow, I have to uncover the killer. It has to be one of the Platoon."

She nodded. "Yep, it's the only explanation."

"I won't be able to do anything, not from behind bars."

"No, you won't. Kyle, I'll do my best to look into it.

You're not on your own. You have to roll with this. They'll take you back to San Diego, and almost certainly you'll be charged. You have to make bail somehow, and try to find out what you can from over there. Between us, I hope we can make some sense of it."

"Thanks, Mariko. Why are you doing this for me?"

He looked into her black Japanese eyes, and she stared back at him with a warmth that surprised him.

After all, I'm a murder suspect.

"I'm doing it because I don't like to see an innocent man going down for a crime he didn't commit. I believe we have a killer on the loose, and incarcerating you won't stop him killing. And I like you, Kyle Nolan. You're a good guy, and I hope when this is all over, we'll be able to meet for a drink and laugh about it. Maybe more than a drink, who knows?"

"Understood. It's appreciated, Mariko. And by the way, I feel the same way about you."

"But you have a girl back home, Kyle."

"Not anymore. There's a big difference between you and her, Mariko. You believe in me, and she thinks I'm a rapist murderer. That's a bit of a relationship killer."

She laughed. "I can't think of anything worse, that's true. I have to go now. I'm due back on duty. I'll try and visit before they fly you back stateside."

"Do you know when that is?"

"I'm sorry, no. I'll try and find out."

She left, and he felt the despair of isolation, trapped in a cell for something he hadn't done. He waited for two hours, and then the outer door to the cellblock clanged open. Boswell walked in. He gave Nolan a small nod of greeting. An MP followed him in and unlocked the cell.

Boswell entered, and the door was relocked. He looked at his Lieutenant.

"What gives, Lt? Why did they let you in here?"

"I'm your legal representative, Chief. At least, while you're still at Bagram. I heard you were looking for someone to protect your interests, and I volunteered."

Nolan felt both relief and unease.

At least he believes in me, but Boswell was present when all the crimes were committed, had to have been. That puts him in the frame. Would the description of the rapist fit Boswell? No, not very likely. And right now, I need someone on my side. Maybe the guy could be helpful, despite my misgivings about his lackluster performance on operations.

"Thanks, Lt, where do we go from here?"

"I'm not sure. You know they're taking you back to San Diego?"

He nodded. "Yeah, that's right."

"The brass have given them the go ahead," Boswell continued. "They say you have a case to answer, and they're sending a guy across from JAG to look at your case too, and see where it leads."

"Someone to defend me, you mean?"

He looked slightly embarrassed. "Er, no. They'll be looking at a separate prosecution. Once there's been further investigation, of course."

"So who'll represent me in the States?"

"You'll be able to appoint your own lawyer, or a public defender if you prefer. Do you have a lawyer experienced in criminal law?"

Nolan laughed. "My own lawyer deals with property transactions, corporate law, minor civil stuff, nothing much more than that. I've never needed a criminal attorney."

"Yeah, well, you need one now. My first piece of advice is to get yourself someone good. You need the best, and..." He stopped, and then went on, "in fact, I do know a guy in San Diego. I was at Harvard with him. Edward Oakley III. Do you want me to contact him?"

"Is he any good?"

Boswell considered. "He is good, if a little unconventional. But I'd say yes, in his own way, he's the best. If anyone can help you, it's Edward."

"In that case, I'd like to give him a shot."

"Okay, I'll fix it up. I'll get him to contact SDPD and fix up to talk to you when you arrive. Anything else I can do?"

"Get me out of here," Nolan grinned.

"I've no doubt most of the guys in Bravo Platoon would be more than happy to break you out. They're pretty pissed at all of this, and they know damn well it's all bullshit. But I'm afraid it would only be a temporary solution, and we'd all wind up behind bars."

"I'll be okay. This Oakley guy sounds good."

"He is."

* * *

They flew him back to the States on an American Airlines Boeing 767, flying coach, naturally. The cabin attendants, all pretty young women, viewed him with suspicion, and it occurred to him that Ashe had probably put the boot in and told them he was a suspected rapist and murderer. He was handcuffed to Detective Ashe the whole flight, except when Ashe needed the bathroom. They cuffed him to Preston, and Ashe unlocked his own cuff to leave his seat. Ashe spent the first part of the journey trying to put him off balance with grating observations.

"You'd better get used to the restraint, Nolan. They get a lot worse when you finish up in Pelican Bay. That's where they put scum like you."

Nolan forced a smile. "Do you get off on talking crap like that, Ashe? You playing with yourself right now? Have you got your hand inside your pants?"

Ashe scowled. "Very funny. You'll have plenty of time for that when they put you away. That's if you're not chosen to be someone's girlfriend."

"Is that it, Ashe? Are you gay, you get off on men?"

But the detective wasn't to be put off. "Why did you do it, Nolan? What makes a man like you with a good career, go rape a woman? And then kill those people while you were on operations? Yeah, the military guys told us all about you. They're going after you when we're done. You're gonna go down for so long, you'll never see the daylight ever again. Don't you have any regrets?"

"I do have one, Ashe."

"Yeah? What's that?" The man leaned closer, waiting for an admission.

"Sitting next to you on a long flight. You ever consider taking a shower?"

Ashe looked away, and Nolan felt he'd succeed in getting to him. That was good. The last thing he needed was the guy needling him throughout the entire flight. Ashe didn't bother him after that, and Nolan was left to his own thoughts. He made a mental list of priorities. He'd need it ready for when he talked to his lawyer.

I have to know what's bugging Carol Summers. It seems incredible that she changed so quickly from loving partner to betrayer. Damned Judas Iscariot has nothing on her. I'll try to talk to her as soon as I can after landing.

But the lawyer would come first, and number one on the list would be to get him out on bail. Number two was to start searching for the real killer. He had no illusions; the cops would do their utmost to get a conviction. They'd set their sights on him and wouldn't rest until he was in jail. And then he'd have the MPs to deal with. If JAG was sending in a lawyer, it wouldn't be long before they started making a case for a Military Court Martial. The more he thought about it, the more he came to realize there was only one surefire route to freedom. He had to find the real culprit, the rapist murderer who was still out there somewhere, still on the loose. And he didn't have far to look. It had to be a Bravo Platoon operative, there was little doubt about that. And some of them he could eliminate for a number of reasons. Will Bryce was black, which left him out. Zeke Murray, Hispanic. There were a half-dozen others who were out of the running, for reasons of color, height, and so on. At a stretch, there were maybe ten real candidates, including himself.

I have to get free and start checking them all out.

They landed in San Diego International in a squeal of brakes and kerosene fumes. There were no formal immigration facilities. The TSA uniforms had been briefed, and after a quick look at their passports, they were passed through and walked outside the bustling, modern, almost futuristic terminal. The cops had a marked patrol car waiting there, and a gang of reporters lounged nearby. They looked up quickly and pressed forward when Nolan came through with the detectives. It was then the normal bustle of the airport terminal became chaos. Reporters thrust recorders towards him, and he was conscious of a cluster of news cameras pointing his way.

"Mr. Nolan, why did you rape that woman?"

"Is it true you killed innocent civilians while you were out on legitimate missions?"

"Do you plan to plead guilty, Sir?"

"Chief Nolan, are you ashamed of what you have done to the image of the United States Navy?"

Ashe and Preston pushed him toward a waiting SDPD cruiser, a black and white with the full array of lights and sirens. Camera flashes lit up the interior as he sat in the back. The car squealed away in a blaze of strobe lights and sirens. Preston was in the front, and Ashe was beside him, still joined to him with the handcuffs. The detective looked aside at Nolan.

"You're a celebrity already, my friend. You'll make the late news. How does it feel to be a celebrity?"

Nolan ignored the sneering remark. It was the first salvo in what he knew would be the cop's intention to paint him blacker than black. They'd got their man, and they wanted everyone to know he was guilty before the inconvenience of a trial. They called it the perp walk. Ashe kept prodding him, but he kept his silence for the short journey to the headquarters of the Police Department at 1401 Broadway. Just before they hustled him inside, he looked up at the grim, gray building, built in modern American multi-story car park chic. Then they led him into the building and past the desk where several cops looked up and stared. His notoriety had preceded him, obviously, courtesy of Detective Ashe. The cop led him straight down to a cell and pushed him inside.

"Welcome home, Nolan. This is where you stay, my

friend, until the bus comes to take you to San Diego Central Jail."

"What about booking me, Ashe? I thought there were a lot of forms to be filled in."

"Already done. We shortcut the process and did the paperwork when we interviewed you in Afghanistan. Don't worry about it," he sneered. "We'll take good care of you."

"What about my lawyer? I want to talk to a lawyer. I want to make a phone call. I'm entitled to that."

"Yeah, you sure do need a lawyer. I'll arrange for you to get access to a phone. It'll be done in the next hour. Maybe a bit more," he grinned. "My memory is terrible, especially after a long flight."

He removed the handcuffs, left the cell, and Nolan heard the echoing clang of the steel door, as it slammed shut with a loud ratcheting noise as the lock engaged. He was now under the total control of the police and the prison system, and even worse, as good as convicted in the court of public opinion.

He paced around the cell. After the long flight, he needed to get his muscles working. He resolved to keep moving, and keep working on his fitness and strength. When he got out of here, he'd be straight back on operations, which was all he needed to keep in his head. He'd need every ounce of strength he could retain while he was cooped up inside this cramped cell. He was innocent, and he'd keep working at proving it until he was cleared. He estimated he'd been walking, stretching, and doing press ups for almost an hour when the door crashed open. A man stood there, accompanied by a guard. The guy looked distinguished, wearing a three thousand dollar suit, a shock of long, curly, barbered hair, polished handmade brogues, and the kind of watch worn by people with more money than sense. In fact, everything about him exuded wealth and power. He looked like an alien that had landed inside the prison.

"Who the hell are you?"

The man strode forward, his arm outstretched. "Edward Oakley III, Mr. Nolan, pleased to meet you. I'm your legal representative."

His voice was loud, and his grip firm. Before Nolan could answer, he turned to the guard. "I need some privacy here. Would you please leave us alone?"

The man looked unhappy. "This guy is a dangerous felon. They told me he's to be watched at all times."

"A felon, is that right?" Oakley raised an eyebrow. "Do you know the law? A felon is a man convicted of a felony, is he not?" The guard nodded uneasily. "And this man has not been convicted of anything, quite the opposite. The charge he is here for is manifestly ridiculous. So go and find yourself a felon, there's a good chap. And leave us alone, unless you want to explain to a Federal judge why you're trying to block this man's constitutional rights."

Oakley's voice was calm and measured, but each word was spoken in a precise East Coast Ivy League accent. The guard nodded, "Call out when you're done."

He pulled the door closed, and Nolan looked at the newcomer. He was of average height, but it was the only thing about him that was average. Oakley looked to be about thirty-five years old, and he told Nolan he'd started his law career late after pursuing a number of adventures to 'get some experience of life', as he put it. Tanned, lean, and fit, he had a pair of piercing blue eyes that Nolan felt were looking right through him. He was the epitome of the upper bracket lawyer, maybe with one exception to the average for that profession. There was nothing condescending about him. He was brisk, all business. Nolan got the impression it didn't make a difference to this man whether his client was a Navy Chief or a Washington Senator.

"May we sit on your bunk, Chief Nolan? They wouldn't allow me to speak to you in an interview room. They said there was a strong risk you'd try to escape. I'm sure they're breaking the law in that respect, but we'll deal with that one later. The first priority is to get you out of here. Any questions?"

Nolan was trying to adjust his thinking. For the first time, here was someone who was on his side for a change.

"Yes, how did you get to me? Who asked you to represent me?"

Oakley smiled. "My old college buddy, Will Boswell, of course. We were pretty close at Harvard, and he helped me out of more than a few scrapes, so I'm glad to help out one of his people. Anything else?"

Nolan shook his head.

"Good. To business, the first question. Am I defending a man who's guilty or not guilty?"

"I didn't do it, no way."

"Okay, but they have some evidence to the contrary. How do you explain that?"

"It's all circumstantial."

"But this business of the memory loss. That could be a problem. Why are they pushing this?"

He explained that Detective Carol Summers, his partner, or former partner, had passed information to them. Oakley made notes as he spoke, and then he looked up.

"I see. If she's your partner, why did she divulge personal information? She must have been pretty angry about something."

Nolan nodded. "I don't understand what it could be, but yeah, she's obviously pretty pissed."

Oakley made another note. "I'll look into that. Next, getting you out on bail is the first priority. Can you raise bail?"

"A few thousand dollars, maybe. I've got a house, that's about all. Not much by way of savings."

Oakley made another note. "Very well, I'll try and take care of that. Will Boswell said to make sure your bond was covered, and he'd talk to you about it later when this is cleared up."

"Boswell? Jesus Christ, I never thought he'd be that concerned, I mean…"

Oakley smiled. "You thought he was a rich kid working his ticket to a career in politics, I guess. It's partly true, but he told me he's become more and more convinced that the Seals are right for him. He just wants to make a success of running the Platoon, and he says that he has a lot to thank you for, including his life on more than one occasion. So don't worry about the bond. We'll be in court tomorrow for arraignment, and I'll take care of everything then. When you're out, we'll talk again. Any more questions?"

"None. And thanks, to you and Lieutenant Boswell."

"No problem. I'll see you in court."

He slept little that night. The cellblock was alive; the 'clang' of steel doors being locked and unlocked. The tramp of feet, and the sounds of curses and insults, sometimes silenced by what sounded suspiciously like a physical blow.

Then a short silence, as the faceless prisoners absorbed the reality of their position at the bottom of American society, and where they were vulnerable to whatever abuse the guards or other prisoners cared to dish out. After the brief pause, the noises would all start again. By the morning he was tired and haggard.

I'm astonished anyone lasts more than twenty-four hours in this hellhole. I'd almost prefer to spend time in an Arab village than here. Almost.

The door clanged open.

"You're due in court, Nolan. Face the wall. I have to fit cuffs on you."

It was a new guy, a guard he hadn't seen before. The guy looked young and mean, as if he'd enjoy the prisoner putting up resistance, so he could flex his muscles and put him down. Nolan did as he was told, and the wannabe redneck clamped on wrist and leg irons so that normal walking was impossible. He could only shuffle. It was done deliberately to hurt and humiliate. He kept calm.

If the time ever comes when I need to physically deal with these people, it's best not to let them know how a Navy Seal handles himself in a combat situation. But if the guy thinks the manacles would stop me, he'd have a surprise coming.

The courthouse appearance was another chance for the media circus to enjoy the disgrace of a Navy Seal. There was no secret now about his background. The detectives had seen to that. Probably Ashe, there was an enemy he was wary of. He grimaced to himself.

My training has sure given me the tools to take down the enemy, whoever they are. One day, maybe, I'll meet Ashe outside, and there'll be a settling of accounts.

As he was led into the courtroom, he took a deep breath. He realized he'd been daydreaming about taking revenge on the system. The system was the wrong target. He needed to focus on how this had all come about. He was convinced that there was someone who'd orchestrated the whole show, and right now, he needed a name. That was the enemy he had to take on, not blowhards like Ashe. His lawyer, Oakley, was in court to greet him with smile.

"How are you this morning, Chief Nolan?"

"I'm good. No problems."

"Uh huh," the lawyer replied uncertainly. "For a man with no problems, you look like hell."

"My cell didn't have an en suite shower."

He smiled again. "We'll see about getting you out of there. The bond is okay, as I said, so it's up to the judge."

They both looked up as the judge walked into court. "All rise!"

It took all of ten minutes, and he was almost free, temporarily, anyway. The prosecutor had objected, but Oakley had prevailed, and he was released on one million dollars bail. The lawyer turned to him.

"Don't worry, Mr. Nolan, the bond is taken care of. It's already on the way. We'd anticipated this. Give it an hour, no more, and you'll be out of here."

"Yeah, thanks, Mr. Oakley. You're telling me the Lieutenant put up one hundred thousand dollars, is that right?"

"That's about the size of it, yes."

"Okay. I mean that's pretty generous of him. I'll pay him back every cent."

"You already have, I told you. It's done, and that's an end to it. Will's not short of money. His trust fund is more money than most people see in a lifetime."

"Even so, it's a lot of cash."

"Not to him. If you want to repay him, keep him alive the next time you're on an operation."

"There may not be a next time."

Oakley fixed him with a stare. "That's crap. This whole case stinks to high heaven. When everything is unraveled, you'll be back with your unit. Just stay calm, and be patient."

"Thanks."

"Not a problem. What will you do now?"

"Now? I'll go and see my kids, and then I need to talk to Carol."

"That may not be a good idea. She'll be a prosecution witness, I would think."

"I have to talk to her. I need to find out who put her up to this."

Oakley nodded. "Just be careful when you speak to her. I'll catch you later."

They shook hands and parted. Nolan went to find a cab to take him to his home in San Diego. He was waiting on the street outside the courthouse when Carol approached him.

He tensed but forced himself to relax.

"What's going on, Carol? How could you think I'm a rapist and murderer?"

"Go to hell!"

He stared at her as she stormed off. He finally found a cab and reached his house, out in the 'burbs of San Diego. His first task was to check his car, a red Mustang convertible he kept running like a Swiss watch. After the kids, it was his pride and joy. Both children were at their grandparents. He hadn't expected to find anyone home, especially now that things were tricky between him and Carol. Normally, she'd taken time off to be home and make the house more welcoming, but the house was empty. He felt a brief pang of loneliness and pushed it to one side. That was weak-minded thinking, and he had to stay strong. For the time being, he needed to find out who the guilty party really was, that was the real crunch. He picked up his mail, nothing interesting there, so he tossed it to one side. He couldn't delay. It had to be done. He called Carol Summers, using the house phone he knew wouldn't show up on her caller id.

"Detective Summers, how may I help you?"

The familiar voice, his whole being ached for her, for what they'd once had.

"It's Kyle."

"What do you want?"

"Look, I didn't do what they're accusing me of. I have to see you and talk to you. It's all a crock of shit, a setup."

"A setup? You cannot be serious. You know exactly what you did. I found out the whole story, you bastard! You thought I'd never find out how my husband was killed? Don't you remember? He was in that bar in downtown Baghdad?"

He was puzzled, what was this? "You told me, sure, you said it was a suicide bomber that got him."

"Oh yeah, it got him alright. The bomb you planted to make it look as if it was a suicide attack. Maybe you thought it'd take out a high-ranking al Qaeda leader, but you got my husband instead, you fucker. You murdered him; so don't give me that shit about a conspiracy. You think I don't hear those stories every day in the precinct.

It's always a setup, and they're always innocent. Jesus Christ, to think I trusted you, and all the time you killed my husband! And you thought I wouldn't believe the rest of it, once I knew what you were capable of? You're just a worthless piece of shit, and I hope you get everything you deserve." She was almost shouting, her voice hot with rage and spite.

"It just isn't true, Carol, really. I don't understand any of it, and I don't know what you're talking about. I honestly know nothing about a bomb in a bar."

"No? Take a look at the website, 'Notable American War Criminals'. Take a good, long look at June 20th, 2009. You can see the pictures of you and your buddy planting the device. Then take another look, and you'll see a picture of Colin Summers, an officer, going into the bar later that day, just before it blew up. They told me it was a suicide bomber, but it wasn't anything of the kind. It was plain murder. I maybe can't prove it, but you'll sure as hell go to jail for raping that girl, Nolan. And then you have to answer for those murders you committed, I reckon you'll spend the rest of your life in a cell, if they don't tie you down and fill your veins with poison. I talked to Ashe and Preston. I was very careful to only give enough info that couldn't be suppressed in court, no reference to doctors. Memory loss! You're in more trouble than anyone would believe. You've done it this time. I hope you rot in hell, you bastard! Don't call me again."

She slammed the phone down, and he listened to the silent earpiece, stunned.

After a couple of minutes, he recovered enough to switch on and boot up his PC. He loaded Google on his browser page and keyed in Notable American War

Criminals. A bunch of results came in, so he added, 'Iraq', and after a moment's hesitation, 'Nolan'. Seconds later, he was staring an image of himself, several images, in fact. In one, he was with another Seal who had his back to the lens, but he could identify him as Zeke Murray. The two Seals were clearly planting an explosive device, but where? He was no stranger to planting explosives, but in a civilian bar? Never, not in a million years. In another image, the remains of the bar after the explosion were in evidence. He studied it carefully. It sure looked damning, except he knew they hadn't done it, the before and after pictures had obviously been fixed, but how? He needed a computer expert to look at them, to examine the entire site and see if there were any clues about how it had been done. The frame-up was so evil, so warped and complicated, that it required a warped and evil mind to put together. First things first, he took a few deep breaths and put through a call to the Robsons, his kids' grandparents who lived upstate. He asked to speak to his children, but they told him the kids were still in school. Their voices were cold, and they didn't invite him to call back. He briefly thought about explaining it all, but Carol was right. The story of a setup sounded like the lies of a desperate and very guilty man. And Carol would have talked to them, which would leave him double damned. He mumbled he'd call back later, and set to thinking again about those images. He didn't know anybody that may help, not outside of the service, and his pass had been automatically revoked so he couldn't get inside the base to talk to anyone. The only point of contact was Popeye's, the bar run by the former Navy Chief Art Winkelmann. He left the house, climbed into his Mustang, and drove across town to park outside the bar. He went inside. It was before the midday rush, and there were only three people sitting at the bar. Art smiled automatically, but when he recognized Nolan his smile faded.

"Kyle," he nodded.

"Art. I need your help."

Winkelmann nodded. "Sure you do, buddy. I'm sorry, Kyle, but I can't do anything for you. Maybe you'd better find somewhere else to do your drinking."

"What?"

"You heard me. A lot of the guys are not happy about the stain you've put on the Service. It's in your own interests to leave. I'm sorry."

He didn't look sorry, but Nolan knew he'd hit a brick wall. He nodded.

"So long, Art."

He climbed into the Mustang, started the engine, and kicked down savagely on the gas, slewing the wheel over to exit the car park in a hail of stones kicked up by the tires. He headed for home. It looked like the only place he could hide from the torrent of abuse the case had showered on his head. And he needed to think. His next court appearance was in two weeks, and by then he intended to make some progress in untangling the web that had ensnared him. But he had to have help, and every door was slammed shut in his face. He stopped at a liquor store on the way home and bought supplies of booze, four bottles of Jack Black. He got home and parked outside his house, went inside and broke the seal on the first bottle. The amber liquid slid down his throat, and for the first time since he'd arrived back in the US, he felt himself starting to relax. He poured more whiskey into his glass, and turned on the TV to watch an old movie, anything to take his mind off of his problems. When he awoke the next morning, the TV was still on, showing a repeat of some game show. He got up and stretched, and thought about a shower and change of clothes.

But what the hell for? I'm not about to show my face around the city, so I can be abused and told what a total bastard I am. If that's what they want to believe, I can't do anything about it.

But he wasn't about to be on the receiving end for another day. He had everything he needed there. His computer, so he could try and piece some of it together. The booze when he needed a break from the crushing misery and despair holding him in a viselike grip. He decided to start with the Internet, and see what he came up with. Nolan spent an hour looking around the War Criminals site, but all it did was make him feel worse, and he was no further forward in working out how it had been done. The photo of the bar looked familiar, and the shot of him and Zeke rung a bell in his memory.

Were we planting explosive charges, or was it something else? Like defusing a charge, maybe.

He just couldn't be sure. He looked at the time. It was long past midday, so he called a local pizza delivery and had them bring round a box of junk food to fill him with calories to keep him going. He ate it in front of the TV, washing it down with bourbon. At least he felt better afterward. It was a routine he easily slipped into, and the days sped by. During which time, he went nowhere fast.

* * *

It was two weeks later; two whole weeks that he'd squandered and got nowhere, and now he was astonished to realize it was the day of his court appearance.

Jesus Christ!

He checked his wristwatch. He had to be there in less than an hour. He showered and shaved, put on a clean shirt and tie, and climbed into the Mustang. He broke the speed limit all the way into the center of the city and left his car parked tight behind a delivery truck, hoping the hood wouldn't be dented when the driver came to drive away. He smiled.

It's the least of my problems. If I'm found guilty, I won't need a car, not for a long time, maybe never again.

He took a good, long look at his beautiful Mustang, possibly for the last time, and ran up the steps into court.

Edward Oakley III was waiting for him. He looked the same as when Nolan had seen him the first time, elegant, patrician, a picture of the successful Ivy League attorney.

"Where the hell have you been? You should have been here a half-hour ago."

"I got held up," he mumbled.

"Well okay, but I would've liked time to talk before we go into court. The case is about to be heard, so we'd…"

An usher who came out interrupted them. "State of California vs. Kyle Nolan."

Oakley turned to him. "I guess we'll have to play it by ear. We're on right now. Let's go."

Before he moved, Nolan popped the question that had haunted him the past fortnight.

"What do you think of my chances?"

Oakley shook his head. "I don't know. I just don't know. Let's see how this plays out."

So the guy's not optimistic.

He looked at the front door. Someone had just walked in off the street, and it was slowly swinging closed. He considered his options for a few moments, but Oakley saw the direction of his gaze.

"Don't even think about it, Mr. Nolan. I'll give it my best shot. We'll do everything we can to get you off."

"I'm innocent," he replied quietly.

Oakley nodded. "And I believe you, but we need to make the jury believe it."

Nolan followed him into the packed courtroom, and they sat down behind the defense table.

"All rise, the honorable Judge Edgar Reece presiding."

He got to his feet, and the judge marched in.

"What's he like?" Nolan whispered to Oakley.

"He's tough, and he's ex-Navy. He wouldn't have been my first choice," the lawyer replied gloomily. His buoyant optimism had already ratcheted down a notch, Nolan realized.

Great!

Judge Reece stared at the prosecutor's table adjacent to the defense.

"Is the District Attorney ready to proceed?"

"We are your honor."

"Very well, we'll…"

He stopped as the doors crashed open, and a man strode into the courtroom, another lawyer, no doubt. And then Nolan blinked as he saw the man behind him. Every head turned to watch the dramatic entrance of Rear Admiral Drew Jacks, USN, wearing spotless dress whites, emblazoned with the ribbons of numerous campaigns. On his shoulder he wore a single Admiral's star, with a single gold stripe on his shoulder. Jacks was the man who ran the entire Seal operation at Coronado. He was in his forties, short and bow-legged, but broad shouldered and rock-solid, with close cropped blonde hair. He walked fast, as if he was in a rush to get somewhere, which he usually was. He had just a hint of a swagger, but it was the swagger of pride in his men, not a personal boast. The crisp lines of his uniform were a perfect fit to a physique that was the result of constant training and long workouts, and more successful missions recorded in his jacket than most men would ever dream of. A Naval Aide who hesitated at the courtroom door followed the Admiral. Judge Reece stared down from his bench, obviously angry that someone had taken the spotlight off him in his own court, as the lawyer went up to him.

"What the hell is going on? We have a trial in progress. What is the meaning of this?"

The lawyer went up to the bench and put a document in front of him. "Not any more you haven't, your honor. This is a Federal warrant, sworn under the Patriot Act. This is a national security matter. The trial is over."

"You can't…"

"We can, Sir, and we are. The Patriot Act allows us to take over custody of this man. If you have any problems, you can take it up with Washington, but we are within the law as laid down by the Patriot Act. You will release him to our custody, or face a Federal court and explain why you have disobeyed the law."

The judge nodded his acceptance and sat back while the lawyer approached Nolan.

"You're to come with us, Chief Petty Officer Nolan."

Admiral Jacks caught his eye and nodded. Nolan got up

and joined them, and they walked out of the courtroom together. He looked aside at Jacks.

"What gives, Admiral? What's going on?" Nolan was conscious of a group of cops waiting in the hallway, giving him angry stares. The word had gone out in seconds, and they weren't exactly celebrating that their prisoner had escaped the net.

"Not now, Chief. We have to find a private room where we can talk."

"Here, Sir." The attorney opened a wood paneled door and ushered them in. He and the aide made to follow, but Jacks shook his head. "Wait outside you two. This is just for the ears of me and the Chief."

He shut the door and grinned at Nolan. "Better take a seat, Son. I expect you're a bit shaky after all this nonsense."

He sat down. "Okay, what's happening, Sir?"

"They want you, back at Bagram. There's a mission on the board, and you have to be in on it."

"Why me, Sir?"

"It's all to do with Neptune Spear, and the recon mission you did to check out the possibility of another bin Laden stepping into Osama's shoes?"

"I still don't understand."

"We want you to go back. The sighting has now been confirmed through other assets. This Riyad character is there, holed up in Abbottabad, there's no doubt. The problem is, we've done overflights, both high and low level, and we've scanned the place with everything we have. Yet we came up a blank, every time. We can't locate him."

"Maybe he's not there?"

"He's there. After your platoon went in, they increased

the defenses. The place is almost impregnable, and they wouldn't do that if they were just cultivating opium in the grounds. It's the perfect place for him, hell it's almost like a tourist site there now, and a brilliant smokescreen. Getting in by air like the last time is almost impossible, not without taking heavy losses. The target must be in that bunker system that was rumored to be underneath the grounds of the bin Laden compound, and we need someone to guide us in. The wounded Pakistani you brought back, Danial Masih, he worked as an engineer for the water and sanitation department in Abbottabad. They never understood then that he wasn't a Muslim, and he kept it very quiet, so he learned a lot. They'd have been real pissed if they knew he was Christian."

Nolan almost laughed. "I can imagine."

"Yes, they're not the most tolerant folk in the world, but back to his position in the water company. He says he's prepared to lead us through the underground tunnels to come out underneath the compound, and that hopefully, would lead us to this bunker. It can't be anywhere else."

Nolan nodded. "I see. But why do you need me, if you've got a guy to lead a team in?"

"It's this Masih guy. He'll do it, but the only man he trusts is you. Without you, he won't even think about going. We tried bribes, persuasion, you name it, but it's a no go. It has to be you."

"What about these charges against me? I'm still on bail. I can't just skip and leave the country."

"You're not on bail, not any more. It's been taken care of."

"So I'm in the clear?"

"Not exactly, no. There are still questions to be

answered, but when this operation is over, we'll put all of our resources into clearing it up. I know you're innocent, Chief. The problem is proving it. We need to go get this Riyad guy first. It's the priority, and then we'll deal with the other problem. Colonel Weathers told me he asked you to look for whoever did these crimes."

"That's right. Sir, you said, 'we'."

"Yeah, I'm coming back to Afghanistan, as far as Bagram, and I'll direct the operation from there. It's too important. We can't make a hash of it. And I guess they'll want someone to blame if it goes wrong," Jacks smiled. "I'm always good for that."

Nolan grinned back, the first time in a long time he'd felt able to lighten up. "When do we leave, Sir?"

"Right away, before that bastard gets on the move again and skips town. We're driving straight to San Diego International. There's a C-17 loaded on the tarmac, just waiting for us to join them."

"Sir, my Mustang is outside. I can't just leave it there."

Jacks opened the door and called the officer in. "Captain Barnes? Take this man's keys. You'll drive his car back to the base, and make sure it's secure until he comes home. Chief, give him the keys. We're leaving."

They left the room and started to walk out of the courthouse. He looked up, feeling a hostile gaze on him. Detective Carol Summers stood there.

"If you think you can pull a stunt like this and get away with it, Nolan, you're wrong. I'll pull every string I know how to get you back inside this court and indicted for the crimes you've committed. I intend to add my husband's murder to the list, so you can get yourself prepared for a long stay upstate."

"Carol, I…"

"Go fuck yourself, Nolan. I don't deal with rapists and murderers!"

She swung on her heel and left. Jacks raised his eyebrows.

"You're sure in her black books."

"Tell me about it, Admiral."

CHAPTER SIX

They flew back to Afghanistan on a C-17 cargo plane. Nolan was convinced that since they'd ended the interrogations at Abu Ghraib, a few hours spent in the hold of the Globemaster would make the most reluctant prisoner eager to talk, to spare them more pain and cramped misery. He had to lie on the floor for the entire journey, the aircraft had been stripped out to carry heavy equipment, and there were no seats, not even canvas jump seats. He made a bed on the metal floor of the cargo hold, but the noise was shatteringly loud, and the vibrations tore through his body, so he spent the most uncomfortable few hours he could recall in a long time. Even the police cell in San Diego was more comfortable than this, or less uncomfortable. In deference to the Admiral's rank, Jacks was fortunate enough to have a cot lashed up behind the cockpit, and he seemed to sleep most of the way. They landed at Ramstein in Germany for refueling and to take on more cargo. When the wheels touched down at Bagram, he had to spend long minutes massaging his legs to get the blood flowing around his body. They walked down the ramp, and the first person he saw was Lieutenant Boswell waiting to greet him. He was disappointed not to see Mariko Noguchi, but he swallowed any questions he wanted to ask after her. Boswell held out his hand.

"Good to see you again, Chief. I gather they gave you a hard time Stateside."

"Not half as hard as the ride on that torture machine," he nodded. Boswell smiled; he was no stranger to traveling in the giant aircraft. An aide drove up in a Humvee, and Jacks climbed inside. Nolan declined, telling the Admiral he needed a good long walk to get his blood pumping again. They started out toward the JSOC compound, and Boswell chatted to him as they strolled along.

"You know why we wanted you back?"

"Yeah, Jacks told me. So I guess the target is still there, in Abbottabad?"

"He is, we're pretty certain. At least, he's there somewhere. Our best guess he's well underground. That Pak we brought back, Danial Masih, he reckons he can lead us in through the tunnel system, but he'll only go along if you're in the party. He says he can rely on you to bring him back, after the last time. He's adamant he won't trust anyone else. At least it got the brass moving to get you out of San Diego."

"Yeah, that was no picnic. How is Danial? He was pretty bad when we brought him back."

"The medics worked a miracle, especially when we found out he was the key to unlocking Riyad's hideout. He's up and walking, and pretty mobile. He'll make out."

"I want to go see him."

"Sure, but make it quick, I want you to meet the Platoon.

They're waiting to buy you a beer, now that you've escaped the cops."

"About that. That was terrific, you fixing me up with the lawyer and putting up the bail."

Boswell waved it away. "Think nothing of it. Edward owes me a favor or two. I helped him out more than once at Harvard. You'd do it for any of the guys in Bravo. It's no big deal. So you want to go over to the hospital, right now?"

"Yep, right away."

They were almost at the medical facility, and Nolan reflected on what Boswell had said.

Maybe it's not a big deal if you're wealthy and connected, but for most people, putting up that kind of bail money, and organizing a high-end lawyer, is beyond their dreams. Yet there is something I can put my money on. Boswell is not quite the snotty kid as I first thought, and neither is he the killer. It would've been easy to let me rot in a San Diego cell, and he'd have been free and clear. No, the Lieutenant can be crossed off the list.

He felt he'd achieve something as they entered the pristine lobby of the base hospital. A nurse looked up, actually a pretty Air Force Corporal. Nolan forced himself not to give her the once over as Boswell stepped up to the desk.

"We're here to visit a Mr. Danial Masih. He's a civilian, being treated for wounds sustained during an operation. Would you direct us to his room?"

She looked up, surprised. "Mr. Masih? He left about an hour ago, Lieutenant."

"I'm sorry, I don't understand. What do you mean, left? How did he leave? Why did you let him go?"

"Well, Sir, it wasn't anything we could control. There were two men who came for him. One of them was the cab driver. The other was his imam. Apparently, Mr. Masih had expressed a wish to go to prayers at the central mosque in Kabul, so they took him away. I saw them wheel him out in a wheelchair. Even though he can walk, he was sleeping, as I recall. But there was no problem, they said he'd be back with him later for further treatment."

She saw their expressions and realized something was wrong. "You know we can't stop anyone asserting their religious rights, especially the Muslims. They tend to get pretty ornery."

Nolan stared at her. "We need descriptions of those men, right now, and the registration number of that cab he went in, if possible. Are you sure they headed into Kabul?"

"Well, yes, but why? Is something wrong?"

"You could say that. Danial Masih has vital intelligence for our military. He's an intelligence asset. He should never have left the hospital."

"But he'll be back later, and you can talk to him then."

"He won't be back."

She looked indignant. "How can you know that?"

"Because Danial Masih is not a Muslim. He's a Christian, and the enemy has just kidnapped him from under your nose. Write down everything you can remember. We may need that information later. We can get the vehicle registration from the main gate. They always record them." He turned to Boswell. "Let's go, they have an hour on us, but there might still be time."

They raced out of the hospital and ran across the base to the complex that housed the stores, restaurants, and bars. They headed to the bar, and Nolan was greeted by rousing cheers of welcome as he appeared. The noise died away when they saw his grim expression.

"What is it, Chief?" Will asked. "What's wrong?"

"You know how vital Danial Masih is to this mission?"

"Well, sure." Will looked around. "I wouldn't like to say too much in here, but yeah, we've been briefed."

"He's been taken, kidnapped from the base hospital."

He quickly explained how they'd done it, the ploy with the fake Imam.

"They're an hour ahead of us. If we move fast, we should be able to head them off. Lt, would you go across to JSOC intel? We need the names and addresses of known al Qaeda sympathizers in and around Kabul. We'll need to check them all."

"You're sure they won't have taken him out of the city?"

"Pretty sure, it's the obvious place to hide him, in a large city. Out in the countryside, they'd stick out like sore thumbs."

Boswell nodded. "I'll get right over there."

"Meet us at our quarters. We'll prepare everything for when you reach us." He turned to Bryce. "Will, we need transportation, weapons, and equipment for a fast operation; something that'll impress the locals. You know the drill, shock and awe. As soon as we've located these gomers, we'll go straight in. Any delay, and they're likely to kill him."

"Unless they already have."

"Not likely. They'll want to know how much he's told us. Somehow, they found out he was from Abbottabad. I'd think he might have given his original address to the nurse when he was admitted. He was pretty woozy, and it rang alarm bells in the local insurgent community. They have people in the base. It wouldn't be hard for a cleaner or a janitor to overhear a conversation and report back. I reckon he's alive, but not for long. We need to get to him fast. Vince, get over to the gate, and ask the MPs on duty for the registration of a taxi that left in the past hour or so. Let's move, people."

The mood had changed, from celebration, rounds of drinks and backslapping, to business. It was Seal business. Nolan chased the last of them out of the bar and sped over to his quarters. He'd been wearing his working uniform. He took a lightning fast, thirty-second ice-cold shower to freshen up, before he changed into his camo kit and went to work. Fifteen minutes later, they were assembling in the ready room. Boswell, Will, and Vince were still out; working on the resources they'd need to make the operation work. He'd just finished strapping on his armored vest and fending off questions about his incarceration when the big black PO1 appeared.

"It's all organized, Chief. I got 'em to lend us a Stryker and a couple of Humvees. They're enough to transport the Platoon with a bit of a squeeze."

Nolan raised his eyebrows. Using a Stryker to drive into the center of the city sure was going in mob-handed. The twenty-ton Stryker was a modern APC, designed to carry infantry into battle, with the protection of lightweight but strong hull armor. It also benefited from its most fearsome feature, the Protector M151 Remote Weapon Station with a mounted .50-cal M2 machine gun, together with a secondary 7.62mm M240 machine gun.

"What armament do we have on the Humvees?"

"They both have mounted .50 cals. We'll be packing a

lot of firepower."

Nolan nodded. "We may need all of it. You know what these people are like. They seem able to organize a rent-a-mob within minutes of an operation going in. If they see those .50 cals, they'll think twice before trying anything. What we need now is that intel, otherwise we'll be all dressed up with nowhere to go."

He picked up his Mk 11 Sniper Rifle and sighted down the scope. It all looked okay. He'd have liked more time to check it out after the armorer had worked on it, but more time was a luxury they didn't have. And the Mk 11 looked awful long for the kind of fight they were going into.

"Will, this could be cumbersome for CQB, I could use…"

"Already there, Chief. I drew an MP7 for you as a backup weapon, nice and compact. I thought you might want something small if we're fighting inside a building. Most of the guys have drawn MP7s for this one too. They're leaving their 416s in the armory."

Nolan smiled. "Copy that, thanks Will."

They both looked around as Boswell came bustling through the door.

"I've got it, the likely names and addresses of insurgent supporters. There are three in all, and one of them is the central mosque."

"You're not serious?" Nolan stared at him. "You mean to tell me the insurgents have a base inside the mosque?"

Boswell shrugged. "That's what they say at intel."

Nolan thought fast. "He's not likely to be there. The nurse said they mentioned the central mosque when they took him. That would've been a false lead. What else do we have?"

"A restaurant, they're not sure if it's still in use, and a repair workshop for motorcycles. Some of the guys here use it to service their bikes, especially the pilots. They like to think of themselves as hotshots," he grinned.

"I like the sound of the workshop. It sounds right. If our men go there, it'd be a good intelligence-gathering hub. You know how men like to talk. Even if he's not there, I'd put my money on them knowing where he is. Let's take the workshop first."

Boswell nodded. "The workshop it is. I'll take command of the Stryker and lead us in. Lucas, you'll man the remote weapons position. Nixon, handle the commo."

Richard Nixon nodded. A recent recruit to Bravo, he'd worked all his life to play down the unfortunate name he'd been given at birth. There'd been a lot of speculation about why his parents had chosen it. The best Nolan could come up with was they were Republicans with a warped sense of humor. But worse, he even looked like a young 'Tricky Dicky', complete with oiled, swept-back black hair and heavy growth of black beard on his chin, no matter what the time of day. Boswell turned from him to Dave Eisner. "Can you handle the Stryker?"

Dave nodded. "No sweat."

"Okay. Chief, I want you to bring up the rear in the second Humvee. Will, you'll take the other Humvee and follow right behind me."

"We're waiting for Vince," Nolan pointed out. He…"

"I got the registration," Vince called out as he entered the room. "It's a real Kabul registered cab, a black ten-year-old Mercedes."

Boswell nodded "Okay, people, you know what to do. Let's move out. And remember, time is not on our side.

We're running against the clock. There's no time to go in quietly. Shock and awe, guys, shock and awe."

They piled into the vehicles, and Nolan grinned as Boswell's head popped out of the top hatch of the Stryker.

"He reckons he's in command of an armored column," Zeke joked as he fired up the motor of their Humvee.

"Yeah, he does that, but he's doing well, the Lieutenant. Helped me out a lot when I hit trouble in San Diego. I reckon he's turned over a new leaf, so maybe he'll work out after all."

"Maybe," Zeke grunted in disbelief. Two more Seals clambered into the vehicle, Brad Rose and Dan Moseley. Brad manned the .50 caliber Browning, and Nolan heard him going through the motions of checking the action of the gun, loading an ammunition belt and preparing to fire. Already Boswell's Stryker was starting to roll out, almost before they were ready. The platoon leader's voice came over their earpieces.

"Commo check, call in. Anyone having any problems?"

A chorus of replies, 'loud and clear' came over the comms net.

"Move out!"

The journey from Bagram Base to Kabul was a little over thirty kilometers, and Boswell's Stryker kept up a fast pace along the busy highway. In less than a half hour, they were entering the outskirts of downtown Kabul. There was no immediate threat, and they kept their windows down to stare out at the bustling streets. Women in blue burqas, hideous and anonymous in their hot confinement, scurried to different destinations, carrying heavy loads in their arms or on their backs. Men sat on the pavements. Some of them in cafes, and many of them armed, but most of them were doing little or nothing. The scabrous buildings, many of them little more than ruins, were dilapidated, unpainted, and unrepaired after the Soviets had left their trail of destruction on the benighted country. The country that before the Islamic fanatics had begun to preach their bloody warpath to a paradise on earth, was in fact a paradise on earth, at least for some. For others, there was always hope. A hope that had disappeared, for the country had never recovered from the wars that began with the foreign invasions, wars that had seen tens of thousands of alien troops with their unfamiliar weapons of war and strange customs pouring into the country. From Alexander the Great, Genghis Khan, Timur, the Mughal Empire, the Russian Tsars, the British Empire, and the brutal repression of the Soviet Union. Now there was a well-meaning coalition force of NATO troops, and the majority from the United States, following the Taliban's ill-advised harboring of Osama bin Laden. Yet despite the all the effort, all they had to show was a country divided and ruined.

"Why the hell do they put up with this shit?" Zeke muttered. "It makes Mexico look like a good place to live. Christ, all the money they pour into this place, it sure doesn't get any better."

"Who knows? One thing's for sure, these Islamic folks know how to take a country and turn it into a poverty stricken shithole. It's not just Afghanistan."

Zeke grinned and twisted the wheel to avoid yet another pothole in the rutted street.

"Unless they hit oil, in which case it becomes a wealthy shithole."

Nolan thought of the oil-rich states he'd visited, the

abject and miserable poverty of the average Joe, compared to the opulent lifestyles of the rich.

Why do they put up with it? That's the million-dollar question and a question likely to go unanswered. But one thing's for sure, if the Islamic radicals stopped their unending, cruel, and pointless struggles, the money could be better spent. If their leaders ever allow it, and that just won't happen.

He stared out of the window, feeling an unaccountable sadness for these poor bastards who put up with so much, and had so little to live for. Then he brought his mind back to reality.

These people, or some of them at least, will be more than happy to kill me.

There seemed to be more of them in the streets than he'd seen a few minutes before. The locals had sent word ahead. The Americans were coming.

They rounded a corner, and the crowds were thicker than ever, more menacing, and many of the men were armed. The way ahead was almost completely blocked. Boswell called up on the commo.

"We're about a hundred meters from our objective, and it looks as if they're filling the streets to prevent us moving forward. This is a Taliban area, so they tell me. It's something of a no-go for ISAF troops. We're about to change their way of thinking."

"Go for it, Lt!" someone exclaimed on the commo.

Nolan and Zeke both exchanged a smile. Boswell continued.

"So button up, we're going in ready for battle. If you do need to open fire, the ROEs are simple. Aim high, and try to avoid collateral casualties, but these people are the enemy. So don't be fooled. They may look like civilians, but they're well armed, and I wouldn't be surprised if there isn't a machine gun or RPG not too far away. If it looks like trouble, it probably is, so don't spare the lead. Shoot the fuckers! Is that understood?"

There was a chorus of acknowledgments. Nolan nodded thoughtfully.

Boswell sure is changing fast.

"Move out!"

The Stryker's engine roared, and it waded into the crowd of civilians blocking the way, but they weren't civilians. Almost as if my magic, a score of men produced AKs from under their robes, and Nolan ducked instinctively as a hail of heavy 7.62mm rounds smashed into the side of the Humvee. Simultaneously, the street seemed to clear of people, and they saw in front of them a bus had been turned across it. The way was blocked. More rounds hit the vehicles, and Nolan saw a movement on a rooftop ahead of them. A missile shooter had appeared. They were aiming down at the Stryker, which had once again been forced to come to a stop.

"RPG! He's on a rooftop fifty meters ahead, ten o'clock."

Lucas replied, "I see him, I'm on it."

Nolan watched the turret on top of the APC turn under remote control to point the barrel up at the rooftop. Before the missile could be launched, Lucas opened fire. The massive .50 caliber bullets were devastating. The first rounds struck the building just below the missileer, and Lucas walked the fire upward. The man and his weapon were torn apart, shredded by the massive firepower. In the window of a room below, a machine gun barrel appeared. Nolan was about to call it in, but Lucas had seen the threat. He shifted his aim, and the machine gunner withdrew his weapon and ducked down inside behind cover. He shouldn't have wasted his time. The .50 caliber rounds slammed into and through the masonry, peppering the inside of the building, and he distinctly heard a chorus of screams as the fighters sheltering there were shredded. The turret turned again as Lucas looked for more targets of opportunity, but it seemed the building had been the main center of resistance. A few stray rounds were still hitting them, and .50 cal in Will's Humvee, returned fire. The enemy gunfire died away as the surviving insurgents realized how useless it was to hide behind a thin wall from the .50 caliber gunfire that could smash through and rip apart anything in its path. Abruptly, the street echoed again to the deafening noise of continuous firing from Lucas' heavy machine gun mounted in the Stryker turret. His target was the bus blocking the street, and the heavy rounds slammed into it, turning it into a twisted heap of wrecked junk. If anyone was sheltering behind it, they were dead.

"Move out!"

The Stryker pushed through the tangle of wreckage, and the remains of the bus were forced to the side of the street with a loud squealing of tortured metal. There in front of them, was the motorcycle repair shop, and with a taxi parked right outside. Fake taxis were one of the favored modes of transport for insurgents. They were anonymous and normally didn't rate a second glance. To one side of the building was a mosque, to the other, and empty, half ruined store.

"Vince, is that the vehicle we're looking for?"

"That's the one Lt. It's a genuine licensed cab, and the registration matches what they recorded at the gate."

"Good. Drive straight into that building, right through the front wall."

"Lt, there're some people sitting there, right out front."

"In that case, they'd better move their asses out the way mighty fast. My guess is they're there to watch the street, which makes them insurgents. If they don't move, roll right over them. Lucas, stand by with that gun, but be careful who you aim at. That goes for all of you. If we lose Mr. Masih, this will all be for nothing. Both Humvees, stop outside the front and cover both ends of the street with the .50 cals. Chief, I want you in here to look for Danial when we dismount. Vince, if you can find a good firing position, take it and listen out for orders. Okay, let's go, people! Let's nail these bastards!"

He didn't wait for acknowledgments, and the Stryker's engine roared as it hurtled forward; twenty tons of armor plate and heavy weaponry, powered by a massive Caterpillar 350 horsepower engine. Dave Eisner obeyed Boswell's orders, and his speed didn't slacken as he threw the wheel over, and the APC headed straight for the front wall of the building. Ten men sat drinking at tables placed in the front. Their sneers at the American column, confident they were untouchable in their civilian guise, turned to alarm, and then they ran like rabbits. Chairs and tables scattered as the armored monster bore down on them, a leviathan monster from the furthest reaches of hell. It struck the front wall with a shattering crash, and the masonry caved in as if it was made of cardboard. The nose of the Stryker disappeared inside, and the entire vehicle was swallowed up, leaving behind piles of shattered masonry and smashed furniture. Nolan leapt out of the Humvee, clutching his MP7, and ran forward into the workshop. He almost laughed at the scene that greeted him. A couple of mechanics, both Afghans, had been working on two motorcycles that were partially stripped down. They were frozen; their mouths open in disbelief. He saw a head look in on the chaos from a door in the rear of the building and quickly duck back out of sight. Nolan pointed.

"There's someone in there! I'm going after him!"

He sped through the workshop, ignoring the chaos, the shouts, and screams from inside and outside. Boswell had split Bravo into two units, one to deploy and cover any inbound threat from outside the building, the other to check out the two mechanics and search through the building. But Nolan didn't wait for backup. The face he'd seen didn't look too friendly, and he knew if they gave the enemy time to recover, they'd murder Danial out of hand. He ran to the doorway, paused and had the presence of mind to roll through it, landing a couple of meters inside, rising to sweep the room from a kneeling position. Bullets whizzed past his head, and he aimed almost reflexively at the shooter. It was a youth, probably no more than sixteen years of age, his face filled with hate. Nolan squeezed the trigger, fired a quick burst, and the boy went down. His AK47 fell to the ground on one side of him with a clatter. Nolan dashed over and kicked the gun away, but the boy was dead. He could see a narrow corridor leading further into the back of the building. Shouts and screams were coming from inside. He recognized the shouts. It was a voice he'd heard before. Danial Masih. He ran toward the direction of the noise and through a narrow door that was partially open. Inside, he found Danial. The Pakistani

Christian was hogtied into a kneeling position. A gag had covered his mouth, but he'd managed to work it to one side so he could shout out. Over him, an Afghan stood with a huge sword raised high. He was about to behead him. Nolan didn't hesitate. He fired a three-shot burst into the swordsman. He collapsed in a bloody heap, and his sword clanged to the floor, its blade unblooded. He ran over to Danial, put down his MP7 and lifted him up, taking out his combat knife to cut him free. He looked down at the elderly Pakistani.

"Danial, are you okay? Did they hurt you?"

The man's eyes were filled with tears, overcome by the emotion of his near-execution and last-minute release. His eyes changed as he recognized his rescuer.

"Nolan!"

The Chief whirled. A guy had come into the room and stood with a huge revolver pointed at his head. The man gave him an evil leer.

"He will not cheat our justice, infidel. And now you will die with him."

Nolan saw the hammer of the weapon draw back, and he threw the knife. He'd been aiming at the guys' eyes. It was the best way to distract them. Nothing distracts a man so much as a steel object hurtling toward your eyes. The guy tried to dodge at the last second, but he was too late. The knife took him in the throat and penetrated through the back of his mouth, severing a vital artery in his neck and skewer clean out the back of his head. He looked astonished.

"Chew on that, buddy," he muttered, as he retrieved the knife. He made sure the guy was dead and went back to help Danial.

"I thank you for this, Nolan," he said hoarsely. "I thought they would kill me."

He nodded. "Yeah, they had a pretty damn good try at it. What did they want? Do they know about Abbottabad?"

"No, that is the strange thing. An Afghan who cleans at the hospital was talking to me, and he was surprised when I told him I was a Christian. He asked why a Muslim Afghan was being treated inside a military facility. When I told him I was a Christian, he must have assumed I was a convert, and that I had deserted Islam. In their faith, the penalty for that is death."

Nolan nodded. "Yeah, they seem to prescribe the death penalty pretty freely for anyone who disagrees with them. It must play hell with their democracy."

Then he grimaced to himself as he realized how absurd that thought was.

What democracy?

He looked around fast as someone came into the room, but it was Boswell. He smiled with relief when he saw Danial.

"Mr. Masih, they didn't hurt you too badly?"

"Thanks to the timely intervention of you Americans, no, they didn't."

"Good. Chief, we've got a situation developing here. Bring Danial out and put him in the Stryker. We need to get out of here fast. There's a crowd gathering, and they look as angry as a swarm of hornets."

"We'll be right there. Are they armed?"

He started helping Danial toward the door.

"They're Muslims, and they're men."

He nodded. "Okay, they're armed. What's the plan?"

"Same tactic as when we came in. Shock and awe. Hit

them hard when we come out, and they'll get out of the way."

They reached the Stryker, and Nolan pushed Danial inside, making certain he was secure. Then he went to take a peep out of the door. Their two Humvees were still parked in the street outside the workshop. He could see both .50 cal gunners were alert, their guns manned, and the barrels constantly revolved as they hunted for threats. They were staring down a crowd that must have swelled to more than a couple of hundred people. Boswell came up behind him.

"How's it looking?"

"Lt, if we go out of here fast, those people won't be able to get out of the way. Even though most of 'em are insurgents, we don't need to risk running down the innocents. You know what they'll do afterwards, the old shoe trick."

Boswell nodded. They'd all seen it in the different Islamic conflicts they'd been involved with. After a successful attack, the beaten defenders protested it had been an 'innocent' target. And there was always one children's shoe left as a poignant signpost to the apparent 'slaughter of the innocents'. Always one shoe, always a child's shoe, and never two. Boswell looked at him.

"What do you suggest?"

"We need a diversion. Some of them may not have realized we have the Stryker in here if they didn't see it come in. And some of them that did may think it was wrecked when it drove through the wall. I know it's a tall order, but these people don't always think straight. If the two Humvees hightail it out of here with every gun firing, and making enough noise to wake the dead, they'll concentrate on them. As soon as they're away from here, the Stryker moves out in the opposite direction."

"I don't know," Boswell mused. "They get their thoughts in order mighty fast when they need to," he warned. "They've even been known to take out one of these Strykers."

"It's the best I can come up with, Lt."

Finally, Boswell sighed and nodded. "We'll try it your way, but with a slight variation. I want you and Vince up on the roof of this building to cover us. Find a good firing stand, and use the sound suppressors. If they don't know where the shots are coming from, they'll be as confused as hell. Do your best with the MP7. It's not a sniper rifle, but you're a sniper, so make it work. When the Humvees run into trouble, which they will forcing through that crowd, you can help them out from here. Hit them from behind. That'll make 'em think again. I'll redistribute the men. When I leave in the Stryker, you two can come with us. Get the men to their positions, Chief. We need to get this moving before they bring up any more hostiles."

"Copy that."

Nolan called Will inside and explained Boswell's plan and gave the orders. "You'll lead with your Humvee. Make plenty of noise, and try and clear the street. We don't want those civilians out there under the wheels."

"And if they're not civilians, Chief? You know as well as I do, these men all carry guns, hostile or not. What are the ROEs?"

Nolan thought hard how best to advise him.

Many of that mean crowd out there are armed with AK47s. How can we distinguish friend from foe? And yet, if they're out there, carrying a weapon, and a threat to an

American military patrol, they're hostile. Why else are they there? What would we do if it was happening in the US? We'd shoot.

He explained his thinking to Will.

"So if they're carrying a weapon and look like they may be a threat, we're cleared to fire."

"You got it. We can't play it any other way. I'll be up on the roof with Vince, and if we see anything we're unhappy with, we'll take care of as much as we can from there."

They both heard the shouting from outside become screams of pain. They couldn't hear the shooting; the gun was suppressed, which could only mean one thing.

"It looks like Vince has made an early start," Will grinned.

"Yeah. Get moving. We'll cover you as best we can. Just do your best to get out of here any way you can. And remember, the objective of this mission is to get Danial Masih out so that we can take care of the other business. That's the big one, nothing else matters. You have to draw off that crowd, Will, so we can get him out safely. Clear? I'll call you when I want you to move out."

The big, black PO1 nodded. "We'll pull their sting, don't worry about it. I'll see you back at Bagram."

He went back outside to prepare his vehicles, and Nolan started up to the roof. He first called the other sniper on the commo.

"This is Bravo Two, coming up."

"Copy that."

Like many rooftops in Afghanistan, this one was a flat terrace with a low and narrow wall running all the way around. Vince was at the corner, overlooking the street. He had made a stand by lying prone, pushing the barrel of his rifle through an ornamental slot in the parapet. He'd also covered himself with his lightweight camo net and sprinkled it with dust and debris. From a distance, he would have looked like a mound of rubble on the rooftop. Nolan crawled over to the edge and started preparing his own stand. Boswell's plan to make the crowd flee in chaos and panic would only work as long as they were unaware of who was shooting at them, and where the shots were coming from.

"How's it looking down there, Vince?"

"Much the same. I popped a couple of guys. They had AKs and looked like they were trying to get the crowd all riled up. But earlier, I saw at least one guy down there with an RPG."

Nolan groaned. "They should ban those fucking things."

"Tell me about it."

He looked down into the street. There were as many as five hundred demonstrators, many waving their AKs. Many others would be armed, but they'd keep their weapons out of sight until they needed them. The Humvees were in for a rough ride. He called down to Boswell.

"Lt, it's looking hot out there. We could do with something heavier up here, something that packs more punch. A SAW would be useful. Otherwise, I'm not sure we can hold them off for our guys to make it out."

The Platoon carried two of the SAWs, squad automatic weapons, M249 5.56 caliber Minimis. Vince turned his head aside to look at him as he spoke. "A gunship with a chain gun would be even better."

Nolan grinned. "Yeah, but that may be hard to explain away in a downtown Kabul street."

"Bravo One to Two." It was Boswell.

"Go ahead, Bravo One."

"I'm sending Jack Whitman up with an M249. The other one is going out with the Humvees."

"Copy that."

"I'll give the order for the Humvees to move out as soon as Jack's in position."

"Copy that, I'll call when we're set."

They heard, "Coming up," over the commo.

"Understood."

Jack Whitman appeared, clutching the M249 Minimi in one hand, and a pack containing ammunition belts in the other, his HK416 slung across his chest. Nolan signaled for him to drop down low out of sight. The Seal inched awkwardly toward the edge, laden with weapons and ammunition belts.

"What gives, Chief?"

"It's pretty simple. Vince and I are ready to take out targets of opportunity, as soon as the Humvees start to roll. We'd like for them to get out of here without any bloodshed, that's optimum. But I'm not too hopeful. It'll be chaos down there once they start rolling. Those guys are sure to press around them and start shooting the place up to try and force them to a stop. If that happens, they'll be dead meat. The .50 cals will open up if they get into trouble. If they have to resort to that, I want you to pour it on, so they're caught in a crossfire between us and the heavy weapons on the Humvees. One way or the other, we need to clear that street so the Stryker can drive out of here with Danial Masih. He's too important to lose. Stay back from the edge of the roof, and only come forward when you hear the .50 cals open up. Then you're free to open fire. Remember, the objective is to clear a path for those vehicles. Anyone looks like they're trying to get in their way, take 'em down."

Whitman nodded and moved back away from the edge. When Nolan looked around, the man was searching in his pack, apparently looking for some of his gear. Nolan ignored him, looked at the street, and called in to Boswell that they were ready. He looked back down at the crowd, as the shouting got louder, reaching a crescendo. The Humvees had started to roll.

"Any sign of the RPG?"

"Nothing," Vince grunted, as he loosed off the first half-dozen shots. Nolan saw three men slump to the ground, red blood beginning to stain their dirty white robes. Then he sighted the MP7. It was fitted with a modern Zeiss RSA reflex red dot sight, and as the first shooter loomed up, he aligned the dot on the guy's chest and fired. Two shots smacked into the guy, and he went straight down; it was no time for fancy shooting. The crowd was moving now, surging like a squirming, organic body; a mass of screaming, shouting, and threatening humanity. He killed another guy with an AK and then several more. He snatched out a clip to reload as he emptied the first twenty rounds. The Humvees were having a hard time of it, men pressing around the vehicles, and only his armored vest saved Brad Rose from serious hurt as he was struck on his ballistic plates twice by the incoming fire. Nolan continued to watch as things unfolded the way they'd planned. When men opened fire on a bunch of Seals, there was only one response, a whole new world of pain. Brad opened fire, and the awesome roar of the Browning .50 caliber drowned out the noise of the crowd. It was time for Whitman's machine gun to join in.

"Jack, get to it, and hit them hard. We have to clear a path for those vehicles."

"Copy that."

He squinted to the side and saw Jack putting the M249 into position. The bipod legs were unfolded ready, and the two hundred round box magazine containing the belt was in position. He nodded at Nolan.

"Do it!"

The Minimi began firing on full auto, adding the buzz of its higher speed, lighter 5.56 mm rounds to the heavy punch of the .50 caliber Browning that was roaring its awesome message of destruction and death. The crowd scattered, running for cover, and already the street was littered with bodies and dropped weapons.

"Those changed ROEs make a difference," Vince shouted as he fired, and another insurgent went down. "I guess we all thought it'd be more of the same. We'd be afraid to open fire on so called 'innocent' Afghans carrying AK47s and taking potshots at us." He snapped in a new clip and was already seeking the next target.

"I guess not, but this time Danial is too important to let these people stop us from getting him back to safety. Jesus Christ, all this because they thought he was converting from Islam to Christianity! Bunch of insane bastards. But I guess we'll have to take the heat for it later."

He began looking for the next target, but the north end of the street was almost clear of hostiles. Whitman snapped in another belt and started firing again, but Nolan stopped him, and the noise died away.

"There's nothing threatening left down there now. Let's get the Stryker on its way while the way is still clear."

He keyed his mic. "Lt, the street is open. Do you want us to come down? We ought to get going now."

"Sure thing, well done, Chief. I'll…"

Vince's shout chopped him off mid-sentence. "RPG, shooter coming in from the south end of the street. I say again, the south end of the street."

Nolan swiveled his gaze around in time to see a robed Afghan duck out of sight into a narrow alleyway. He looked to the north. The Humvees were making slow progress, picking their way through the debris of the running battle. There was no way out for the Stryker, no way other than past the missileer. And the APC would be an easy target.

"Lt, you heard? We have a guy with an RPG on the loose."

"Copy that. Can you deal with him? A short-range hit from one of those babies would hurt us bad."

"We'll do what we can, but it depends on him showing himself again. It would be best to go out and take him, man to man."

"Your call, Chief. Keep me posted."

"Copy that."

He turned to Whitman. "Jack, there's a chance we can scare him out of that alleyway. I want you to empty a belt into the entrance, and see if the ricochets buzzing around can scare him into running. Vince, you need to be ready if he shows."

"I'm on it, Chief."

Whitman nodded and swiveled the barrel of the M249 around to face the alleyway. He nodded at Nolan.

"Set."

"Fire!"

The M27 link belt used by the Minimi carried two

hundred 5.56mm rounds. Whitman fired in long, stuttering bursts, emptying the belt in less than two minutes. Nolan and Merano looked on, shocked. The gunfire had gone high. Instead of sending a raking hail of ricocheting bullets to gouge out the unseen part of the alleyway, his burst had only destroyed roofing tiles for several hundred meters around. Yet as far as they could see, he'd missed the target altogether.

"What the fuck are you doing?" Nolan shouted angrily. "What the hell made you shoot so high?"

Whitman shook his head. "I'm real sorry. A shower of grit flew into my eyes just as I pulled the trigger. I thought I was on target, but…"

He shrugged helplessly.

"Reload, and make sure you rake that alleyway good this time."

Nolan cursed. They'd just handed the missile shooter a free ticket to get out unscathed. Except that the guy may not be angling to get out. He wanted to get a shot at the hated American Humvees from behind. And when the Stryker appeared, it would be like a gift from the gods. Yes, he'd still be there. Jack snapped in a new box mag and took aim. They waited, nothing.

"What is it now?"

"I'm real sorry, Chief. She's jammed. It must have been a bad belt. It'll take me a half-hour to clear it."

"Fuck that. I'll call it in to Boswell."

The Lieutenant listened to what had gone wrong. Boswell was learning fast. It was a time for solutions, not recriminations. Nolan noted his voice was still confident. He was acquiring the skills needed to lead a Navy Seal unit in the field, and get them back home again.

"Can you take him, Chief?"

"Sure, I'll go out there and locate him. Vince is still up here. He'll keep me covered. It's the best place for him. I'm sending Whitman down to get ready to leave. I'll make my away across the roofs to try and come in behind him, so I'll keep you up to date.

"Copy that. Good luck."

Nolan coughed as a wind came up and gusted over the rooftop, swirling dust and sand into his throat. He shrugged and turned to Vince.

"You heard Boswell?"

"Sure. Whitman, get downstairs to the Stryker, and take that useless piece of shit gun with you." He turned back to Nolan. "I'll stay here, Chief, and if that bastard shows his ass, I'll blast it."

"Yeah."

Nolan loped off, running crouched down toward the back of the rooftop, and when he was out of sight of the street, he moved to the edge and stepped across the small gap onto the next roof. It was the mosque, and he could hear raised voices coming from inside.

I'd dearly like to know what they're up to. A Mosque in a Taliban controlled area sure won't be offering me a cold beer.

He weaved his way around roofing vents and curved minarets that had been added to the original building to make it look like an Islamic place of worship. There was a public address system fastened to the edge, overlooking the street. Four battered tin loudspeakers, which would convey the voice of the Muezzin to call the faithful to prayer.

And maybe a few of the unfaithful, he mused to himself.

These guys seem to make up their own rules about their beliefs. I can't believe the Prophet envisaged some of the outrages that have been perpetrated in his name.

He hid behind the largest of the minarets, and the angle was enough for him to look down the alleyway. He cursed. The shooter was there about ten meters back from the street, but this guy was a careful one. He was hidden inside the low-walled front yard of a stone house; thick walls with ornamental gaps in the stonework, angled so that he couldn't guarantee a hit, not with a carbine length weapon like the MP7.

Shall I try to clip the gomer through one of the gaps? But if I miss, he'll take off like a frightened rabbit. No, I'll have to do this the hard way. Mano a mano.

He crossed to the next rooftop, a small apartment block, and let himself into the stairwell through the roof access door. He was almost down to the first floor when a woman in a blue burqa came into view. She flinched, startled as he passed her, and he grinned to calm her fears. The sight of an armored, camouflaged trooper carrying a submachine gun was not what she'd expect to see outside her front door. Not every day, anyway. He put his finger to his lips. She nodded and stared at him through the mesh of her garment.

"You are American?"

She spoke English, which was unexpected.

"Yes, Ma'am. Go inside and keep your head down."

She stared at him through the mesh. "There is a man with a rocket waiting in the alleyway across the street."

"I know there is. Go inside your home, Ma'am."

"I can show you a way to get behind him, if you wish."

Nolan could hardly believe his ears. "You what? Why

would you do that?"

"I was a schoolteacher once, before the Taliban bombed my school. If I try to teach the girl children, they will kill me. If I do not wear this burqa, they will kill me. I hate them. I want to see them all dead, and this land rid of their evil kind."

He heard Boswell in his earpiece.

"Chief."

"Go ahead, Lt."

"We need to hurry it up. Danial doesn't look too good. It seems they hurt him bad, kicked him in the stomach, and maybe broke something. He needs treatment, and fast. Right now he's bleeding from the mouth."

"Copy that. I'm moving as quick as I can."

He looked at the woman. It could be a trap, but he had no time to waste. "Show me the way, Ma'am."

She led the way down the stairs and out the back door of the apartment block. Nolan had taken his pistol from the holster and was carrying it in his hand. The MP7 might be awkward for fighting inside the confined spaces. In addition, the Sig had a suppressor fitted that would give little away to the enemy. As they walked out the back door, a man walked in, and they almost ran into each other. He wore a black turban and carried an AK. Taliban for sure, the ID was near enough. Nolan raised his pistol. It coughed twice, and the guy was thrown back into the dirt. The woman turned briefly and looked down at him, and then she continued on. They walked along a narrow lane, so tight Nolan could feel his shoulders touching the walls either side. It was clogged with rubbish and debris, and stank to high heaven, but soon they came out on the main street, and the stench eased. In front of him was the alleyway he needed, around a slight bend that would shield him, so he could cross unseen.

"I'll take it from here, Ma'am. Thanks."

She shook her head. "I will show you the rest of the way. It is not so easy."

She ran lightly across the street and into the front door of another crumbling apartment block. He followed through the hallway and out another back door. They circled around and she stopped him.

"The man you seek is around the next corner. He is sheltering behind a low stonewall. If you are careful, he will not see you approach, and you will be able to kill him."

He nodded. "Ma'am, you have my sincere thanks. Anything I can do for you…"

"You already have, Mister American. That man you shot."

"Yeah, what about him?"

"He was my husband. He has been beating and abusing me badly ever since I was forced to marry him. He was a cruel, heartless bastard, and now he is dead, I can try to escape from this place."

"Well, yeah, right, anytime."

Her husband! Christ, these people!

He watched her walk back the way they'd come, still shaking his head in disbelief. He carried on working his way toward the shooter, holding his MP7 in the crook of his left hand and the Sig in the right. He'd only moved another ten meters when he ducked behind the cover of a stone pillar. He'd seen another insurgent clutching his AK-47 race across the alleyway to join the missile shooter behind the wall. Nolan called it in.

"Vince, do you copy?" He kept his voice to a low

murmur.

"Loud and clear."

"Can you see anything down here?"

"Negative, Chief."

"Understood. Listen up; I have two, repeat two, hostiles. I'm behind cover. Could you scatter a few rounds this way, and see if you can get them to make a move."

"Coming up, keep your head down."

Merano fired off ten rounds in rapid succession. The rifle hardly made a sound, but Vince's sniper rounds skidded all over the alleyway, sending chips of stone and pieces of lead flying and zinging around his position. One of the hostiles screamed. He'd just taken a ricochet; maybe just small piece of stone had clipped him, but enough was enough. It was sufficient incentive for them to move to a safer position. They came dashing into the alley once the firing had stopped and raced along toward the end, one man clutching the RPG, the other his assault rifle. Nolan stepped into their path and smiled. Their jaws dropped wide open.

"Salaam alaikum."

They stopped dead and stared at him. He put two rounds into each man. The guy with the AK must have had his finger on the trigger, as it fired off a short burst before it fell from his lifeless hands. Nolan picked up the fallen RPG and hightailed it back the way he'd come. Almost immediately, Boswell's voice came into his earpiece.

"Chief, what was that shooting?"

"Nothing to worry about, Lt. The missile shooter is dead, and I have his weapon. I didn't want anyone else tempted to give it another try."

"Nice job. I'll call Vince down from the roof. Come

229

right in, and we'll make tracks out of here."

He acknowledged and gave Vince the news they were leaving. He found Danial in a bad way when he finally climbed into the armored hull of the Stryker. Vince climbed aboard, and the hatch clanged shut while Nolan tried to talk to the wounded Pakistani. Whitman was doing his best to make him comfortable, but the old man's face was contorted in pain.

"Danial, hang in there, buddy."

He lowered his ear to the man's lips, to hear his whispered words.

"Nolan, if I don't make it, my son. You must…"

He lapsed into semi-consciousness. Boswell was watching, his face set with concern they might lose the old man, and he gave the order to move out fast. The Stryker lurched into motion, and Nolan bent back down close to Danial's head as his eyes flicked open again. He could see fresh blood coming from his mouth.

"How are you doing, Danial?"

The Pakistani grimaced at him. "I have been better, my friend," he whispered. "My stomach, it hurts bad. I wish I could help you before I die."

"You won't die. Stay with us, my friend. We've been through too much for you to give up now."

Nolan grimaced.

It's been a copybook hostage rescue so far, even taking down a score or more of enemy insurgents. The action was both furious and bloody, but then again, this is a Taliban controlled area, what else can you expect?

He recalled watching the film 'Black Hawk Down', about the debacle of Gothic Serpent. It was an operation carried out by Delta and US Rangers, with the primary objective of capturing warlord Mohamed Farrah Aidid. It was devised by JSOC, the Joint Special Operations Command who commanded the Navy Seals, as well as a number of other SpecOps units. In the film, hostile civilians gave minute-by-minute progress reports on the American incursion to their warlord leader. Whatever happened in the actual operation, the end result was the same. Both Rangers and Delta had to fight a running battle just to subdue the enemy enough to extract themselves and their wounded from a nightmare scenario, a seemingly endless procession of heavily armed civilians who took a ghoulish delight in desecrating the bodies of those Americans they managed to kill. The weapon that had caused them more trouble than any other was the RPG shoulder-launched missile system. Every soldier in a low flying helo or thinly armored vehicle had a healthy respect for these devastating weapons, which the Russians had sold in tens of thousands to emerging Third World countries. They could even cripple APCs with a single rocket, providing it was aimed at the correct place. And then a thought struck him.

That missile shooter I took out, he wouldn't have been alone, no way. It's not how they operate. The Taliban will have no shortage of the rockets in any area they control.

He leaned forward and tapped Boswell on the shoulder. "Lt."

The Lieutenant turned. "What is it?"

"That missile shooter I took care of. He can't be alone. There has to be more of them. We need to keep our eyes skinned moving out in the Stryker. We're a plum target for these people. I wouldn't mind betting they'll try and hit us again before we're away from here."

Boswell nodded thoughtfully. "I see your point. Did you see any more of them while you were out there?"

"No, it's just a hunch."

"Okay, that's good enough for me. We'll need better visibility. We won't see them coming from inside, so we'll have to open up the hull and hope they don't lob grenades down onto us from the rooftops."

"It's a possibility, but the RPG is almost a racing certainty."

"Yeah." He called up the rest of them. "Listen up, people. We're opening up the hatch. I want men outside on the hull to spy out any missiles pointed our way, or any way. I don't give a shit which way they're pointed. Whitman, is that M249 ready to fire?"

"It sure is, Lt. Locked, loaded, and set to go."

"Okay. Open the top hatch and get up top. You can cover our six, and make sure you don't get in the way of any dust flying toward your eyes this time. Lucas, you're to watch ahead with the remote system. We may need that .50 cal yet. Chief, I'd like you and Vince out there too. Those eyes of yours are our best defense against a shooter at long range."

They acknowledged, and Whitman flung open the hatch, clambering out with his Minimi and the bag of ammunition. Vince and Nolan followed him, and Boswell stuck his head out too.

To be fair to the Lieutenant, he's prepared to share the risks, Nolan acknowledged.

He wedged himself in the top of the turret with his MP7 held grimly in both hands, ready to loose off at the first sighting of the enemy. Nolan found a position on the hull where he could quarter the surrounding streets, and brace himself against the steel of the hull stanchions to get in a good shot. Vince followed suit on the other side, and Whitman set up at the rear of the hull.

"Lt!"

The voice came from down inside the hull, and it sounded like Dave Eisner.

"What is it?"

"The Paki, Masih. He's looking bad, and the bleeding looks even worse. I don't think he's going to make it."

"Shit! Can't you do anything about it?"

"It's internal, Lt. I just don't know."

He looked across at Whitman. "Jack, you were taking care of him. Get back inside the hull and try and fix him up. You can tell Eisner to come up and take over the Minimi."

"Copy that."

Nolan held the weapon while he scrambled inside. Seconds later, Dave appeared and took over the machine gun.

"Do you think he'll make it, Dave?"

Eisner shook his head. "It's touch and go. I don't know, maybe. He may get back to Bagram so they can patch him up, but his long-term prognosis is not real good. The Taliban roughed him up pretty bad, and at a guess, I'd say they've ruptured something inside. Whitman may be able to tell us more."

"So Danial isn't going to lead us through those tunnels into Abbottabad?"

"Not in this lifetime, no. But we can talk to him when we get back. Maybe he'll tell us what we need to know."

"Yeah."

Nolan settled his MP7 so that he could lay prone and

use the red dot sight. He looked toward the end of the street about a hundred meters ahead. The Stryker was hurtling toward it as fast as Zeke could push the screaming diesel engine. He settled his aim and saw movement, and then a distinctive shape appeared. Missile!

"RPG, dead ahead, one hundred meters."

Lucas was already on it. Nolan saw the remote turret turn to aim at the shooter, and a stream of .50 caliber rounds hammered out of the barrel to chew chunks of rock and woodwork out of the nearby houses as he tracked on the missile. Grant had been ready, and he was damn good. Lucas walked the fire right onto the target, and the huge rounds blew the shooter and his weapon to smithereens. Lucas ranged the turret around, seeking more targets, just as the first missile arced toward them. Nolan jerked his gaze up to the rooftop. He'd seen the missile trail as it descended before he had a chance to react. The missile exploded in the street, ten meters behind them. There was a shout of pain. Dave was back there, and a fragment had obviously hit him, but it was no time to stop to ask if he was hurt bad. He and Vince sighted up to the rooftop, located a single shooter in the process of reloading his launcher, and both men fired. The hostile was thrown back just as his loader stepped into view. Nolan double tapped him, and immediately began searching for more targets.

"Two o'clock, third floor window," Vince shouted as he squeezed off a couple more shots.

"Copy that, we have activity in the street. Looks like they're coming at us in force."

"Jesus Christ," Boswell breathed. "What the fuck is this?"

'This' was a crowd, marching slowly and resolutely toward them, a crowd of children, veiled women, and old cripples. A crowd that was at least two hundred strong, and growing.

"They must have rounded up every non-combatant in Kabul," he snarled angrily.

"They'll have shooters and RPGs at the back of that crowd," Nolan warned. "It's a repeat of the tactic they used at Parachinar." He looked keenly into the distance at the outskirts of the crowd. And saw another problem.

"Heads up! There's a CNN News team right at the back of the crowd. They're hugging the edge, next to the buildings. I see two of them, a guy with a camera and a woman, and they're both wearing armor and blue Kevlar helmets."

Boswell raised his eyes skyward. "As if we haven't got enough problems." He raised his binoculars and scanned the crowd. "Yep, they're there, reporters at the back of the crowd, and a bunch of armed Taliban close by. Shit!"

"Lt, you should see this. There's another bunch of people coming up behind us," Dave exclaimed.

Nolan turned his head to look at Eisner. The Seal had a deep gouge in his armored vest on the shoulder, just above the front ballistic plate. Some of the fragment that hit him must have penetrated. His left side was covered in blood. Past him, he could see a further group of insurgents blocking the street behind them. They waited, uncertain as to how they could respond. If they opened fire, the newsies would capture it all on camera, and they'd be screwed for opening fire on civilians. If they didn't open fire, the Taliban shooters would destroy them in a shower of missiles augmented by incoming fire from their

Russian assault rifles. Boswell scanned up and down the street, desperately searching for a solution. He keyed his mic.

"Zeke, turn right now."

"Turn right? But it's…"

"I don't give a shit! I said turn right. That's an order, Mister. Pedal to the fucking metal, and get us out of here. You men on the hull, keep your heads down low."

Nolan threw himself flat on the steel platform, just as Dave and Vince heard the order and followed suit. Boswell's head popped down inside the hatch, and the vehicle shuddered as it hit the front wall of an adjacent house. Bricks, rubble, masonry, and timber framing all showered down on the Stryker. Nolan peered out from where he was hugging the steel deck, in time to see a family of Afghans sitting at a table, open mouthed and about to eat their meal. They screamed and ran as the abrupt realization hit them. A twenty-ton military behemoth had just crashed through the front wall and invaded their home. The Stryker shuddered again as it hit the wooden staircase a glancing blow, and the whole structure began to collapse. Zeke kept his foot pressed down, and the APC crashed through out the rear wall, staggering as chunks of masonry threatened to block its progress. Zeke gave it the gun, and the massive wheels rode over the broken masonry and broke free. There was another street at the back of the house. He smashed through a rear garden wall and turned into it. The street was empty.

"Keep it going, Zeke," Boswell shouted. "Take us all the way back to Bagram."

Nolan remembered Zeke's words, about Boswell imaging himself in command of an armored column.

Maybe that was true, but he's done well, the Lieutenant, as well as anyone could have done. He kept his head and got us out of a real tight spot.

Someone shouted, "Hostiles, three hundred meters ahead. They've just seen us."

Boswell was back up in the turret, surveying the way ahead for targets. They were driving toward an open square, and once again men with guns blocked their way. Men they could shoot at. He spoke quietly.

"Open fire, men. Kill those bastards. Clear them out of our way."

Nolan sighted on a guy who was out front. He was waving an AK in the air and seemed to be shouting encouragement at his people. Before he shot him, he searched the crowd and saw why he was shouting. They were retreating, edging back, clearly unhappy about taking on an armored Stryker APC with only assault rifles and maybe a couple of RPGs. He squeezed the trigger, and the guy went down. The man behind him followed. He was unlucky to be in the wrong place at the wrong time. As Nolan's target dropped, Vince had been sighting on the guy next to him, and the two sniper rounds felled his target and a man stood next to him.

Nolan searched for the next target but relaxed his trigger finger. They'd turned and were running, leaving the street littered with abandoned weapons and equipment. He focused on some of the fleeing group and saw the reason why. They were young, very young; some looked no more than twelve years old. Just like Hitler's last-ditch defense of Berlin, when the SS had forced children armed with no more than a Panzerfaust to do battle with hardened Soviet Tank Divisions. He smiled as he thought of the primitive weapon. After firing, the launcher was discarded, making the Panzerfaust the first disposable anti-tank gun. They were not effective, and German generals commented sarcastically that the tubes could be used more usefully as clubs after firing, when they may kill more of the enemy. The Russian built RPGs were a huge advance on the Panzerfaust, but the motivation and training of the boy soldiers that fired them was little different from that of their predecessors. The hate-filled rhetoric of the religious leaders soon evaporated in the face of a trained and well-equipped enemy. Nolan couldn't open fire on the fleeing boys, couldn't add to the death and misery that had arrived in this Kabul suburb. The other Seals kept shooting as Boswell urged them on.

"Pour it on, don't let them get away. Chief, what's going on? Keep firing. I haven't given the order to cease fire."

Nolan glanced in his direction. "They're only kids, Lt."

"Kids with AKs and RPGs. You leave them to run away, and they'll be back killing our guys. Is that what you want?"

Boswell was right, and in his head, Nolan knew it. But in his heart, it wasn't so easy.

"Copy that." Loathing himself, he nodded and opened fire on semi auto. He wasn't particular about aiming. Even so, he was aware that some of his single shots would have hit their mark. He emptied the clip and rammed in a new one, then sighed with relief as the Lieutenant ordered the ceasefire.

"It looks as if they're either dead or ran away. Zeke, move forward again, but take it easy. The rest of you, keep alert, some of those casualties could be faking. Let's go."

Zeke gunned the engine. The APC rolled forward, and

soon they were adjacent with the scene of the carnage. Bodies were strewn in the street, dropped weapons, AKs, and several RPGs. Nolan recalled the Duke of Wellington's famous dispatch after the battle of Waterloo. 'Nothing except a battle lost can be half so melancholy as a battle won.'

Yeah, this is sure melancholy, Nolan reflected.

They were all looking at the bodies carefully, watching in case one of them was waiting to hit them with a sucker punch, to leap up and lob a grenade at the American APC. Nobody moved, and they started to relax. The Stryker was almost past the last of the fallen Taliban. Boswell nodded to himself and looked at Nolan with a grin. He'd done well, as well as could be expected, and he knew it.

"I reckon that does it, Chief. We're almost home." He clicked his mic. "Zeke, you can step on it now. Take us back to Bagram as fast as you can, and with any luck we'll be there in time to save our Pakistani friend."

"Copy that."

Nolan felt the tremble of power as the massive engine picked up, and he clutched at a rail for support as the Stryker lurched forward, picking up speed.

"Missile launch, on our six!"

He raised his MP7 automatically and whirled around, searching for the threat. Then the missile struck before he even saw the shooter. Dave had opened fire a fraction of a second before it hit, and to Nolan, it was like watching a movie in slow motion. The trail of smoke from the missile, the robed Afghan clutching the launcher and standing on a balcony overlooking the street. Eisner scored a hit, stitching a line of bullets that split his body apart, and the missileer fell dead before he had the satisfaction of seeing his rocket hit the target. Then the RPG exploded, and Nolan was thrown off the hull. He remembered landing in the street next to Dave Eisner. It crossed his mind that he was injured, lying in the street, almost unprotected, in a Taliban controlled area of Kabul. He recalled looking up at the sky, and seeing a roiling cloud of smoke blowing in the gentle breeze from the mortally damaged APC. He tested his limbs and found he couldn't move them. It was strange, he couldn't hear anything either. It was like he was floating in some middle world, between Earth and Heaven. Or maybe it was Hell. And then he blacked out.

CHAPTER SEVEN

He opened his eyes, looked around, and saw he was lying on a gurney. He took in the furnishings and equipment, and understood he was inside a military ambulance. An attractive black female nurse, a corporal, sat opposite, managing to look pretty even inside her helmet and body armor.

"What happened?" But his voice came out in a strained whisper. He tried again. "What happened back there?"

She smiled. "You're awake, Chief Nolan. That's good. You know your vehicle was destroyed?"

He could barely hear her, as if she was whispering quietly to him. His ears rang, and he realized his eardrums were still recovering from the explosion.

"I remember it, yeah."

"You were lucky. The men you sent away in the Humvees stayed in the area in case you needed help. They heard the explosion and came and found your unit in and around the burning Stryker. They helped them get out before it blew and called in medical assistance. Then they stayed to form a defensive perimeter to make sure we got to you before the Taliban."

He nodded his thanks. "We going back to Bagram?"

"We sure are. They'll fix you up. There's nothing broken, but you suffered a concussion. We'll keep you in the hospital overnight, just in case you're thinking along those lines. You'll be good to go in a few days."

Good to go, providing the explosion doesn't trigger a repeat of the blackouts that plagued me before. Thank Christ the Navy isn't aware of them.

"Did all the men make it out?"

"It was a miracle, but yes, the Stryker soaked up the worst of the explosion, and they were almost able to walk away. One of the men was thrown into the street along with you, but he seems to be okay too. A few cuts and bruises, but nothing more serious."

"Thank Christ for that."

"Thank the General Dynamics Land Systems Company. Since they brought those Strykers to Afghanistan, our casualty rate has fallen dramatically. With most other APCs, those guys inside would have been in body bags by now, and on their way back to the States."

"I guess you're right." And then he remembered the purpose of their mission. "What about the Pakistani civilian? He was inside the hull."

Her eyes looked troubled. "The old man? Yeah, I forgot. He's not so good, and he's in the ambulance ahead of us. He's unconscious, and I'm afraid he's not expected to make it."

So it looks as if those bastards may win out after all, if Danial dies.

"How bad is he?"

She looked solemn. "He has internal bleeding. The explosion seemed to tear him apart internally, which is strange. The others next to him inside the vehicle weren't hurt so bad."

Nolan explained the torture the Taliban had subjected him to. She nodded.

"That explains a lot. If something were already broken, the explosion that occurred when the rocket hit would have done a lot more damage. Poor old man, he wouldn't have stood a chance."

"Does he have a chance?"

"I don't know. He may not even regain consciousness."

So there goes the entire objective of the mission, and an essential part of the operation to eliminate Riyad bin Laden may just go down the toilet. Not to mention the life of a sick old man who just wants to live out his life in peace, away from the Muslims who so want to persecute him.

They reached the hospital, and the nurse found a medic to help her move Nolan's gurney inside. He had a bad moment when they insisted on carrying out an MRI scan on his brain to check for any damage or bleeding, but when the doc came back, a guy about ten years older than Nolan, he was all smiles.

"You're in the clear, Chief. Nothing too serious showing up on the scan. There is something curious though, a couple of old scars. Have you had any trouble before, headaches, anything like that?"

"Nothing, no."

The doc pursed his lips and assumed a dubious expression. He had the look of the old fashioned family physician, calm and confident. Reliable. The kind of guy who would make a fortune when he set up his practice in some middle class suburb, treating stressed executives and obese women. Graying hair, steel rimmed glasses, trim looking and fit, but too pale; probably didn't get out of the hospital enough.

"Nothing? You sure about that?"

"Yep, I try to keep myself pretty fit."

"I see, that's real strange, the MRI scan showed…" And then understanding dawned in his eyes. "I guess if you did have any problems, they'd rule you out of operations, that right?"

Nolan stared straight at him. "That's exactly right."

The doc shrugged. "Okay, in that case I have no objections to your being released tomorrow. We'll just keep you under observation overnight. Call me if you want to talk about anything off the record, Chief."

"I'm okay, really."

The doc looked thoughtful. "If that's good enough for you, I'm fine with it. But if you do experience any problems, as a result of that explosion, of course, make sure you speak to a physician."

"I will."

He nodded and left the room. Minutes later, Rear Admiral Jacks walked in, followed by Boswell. Both men looked grim. Nolan nodded a greeting, but it came out as more of a grimace.

"How are you feeling, Chief?"

"I'm fine, Admiral. No problems, they said I'll be out of here tomorrow."

"Yeah, we talked to the doc." Jacks got right down to business. "You know we have a problem?"

"Danial Masih? I guess he's still unconscious."

"He's dead, Chief."

Nolan closed his eyes, thinking of the poor old guy, his quest for freedom, and the son he'd left behind. As well as the intel locked inside his head; the layout of the service tunnels that lay underneath Abbottabad.

"So we're fucked."

Jacks sighed. "It's not looking so good, that's for sure." He turned to Boswell. "Lieutenant, close that door. This is confidential material."

Boswell obeyed, and Jacks continued. "Chief, we're outta ideas. We looked at other alternatives, ways to attack that compound, and so far none of them look too hopeful. There are several problems we have to take into account. It's Pakistani sovereign territory, of course. Whatever we do, it has to be a lightning fast raid, in and out in a blink of an eye before they know we're there. And after the last time, it'll be that much more difficult."

"You see the main problem as Al Qaeda or the Pakistanis?"

"Is there a difference? This is Waziristan we're talking about. They're all in it together."

Nolan nodded his understanding. "These defenses they've installed, do we know anything more?"

"Since Seal Team Six took out Osama, they've put in an advanced and very sophisticated Russian anti-aircraft missile system, with sensitive, wide area defensive radar that would pick anything up from fifteen kilometers out or more. It can't be done again, not like before."

"We could infiltrate. It's what we're trained to do, dress and wander around like locals."

"Not this time. On the ground, they have a ring of checkpoints, and Christ knows how many police guarding the area surrounding the place. They may be checking id documents, who knows? Maybe you could get through, but the political fallout would be worse than leaving the guy alone to direct his terrorist fantasies. And that's not all. We don't know where he is! Or to put it more accurately, we don't know how to locate his bunker. Okay, we presume it's underground, but it's anyone's guess as to where. Without Danial Masih, we're back to square one."

He stopped and they turned as there was a knock at the door. Boswell looked out, murmured a few words, and then turned back to Jacks.

"Admiral, it's Captain Mariko Noguchi. She wanted to see Chief Nolan. She's…"

Jacks nodded. "It's okay, I know who she is. Marine Intelligence. Tell her to come in. She knows pretty well everything anyway."

Mariko walked in, crisp and pretty in her working uniform. She saluted Jacks. "Sir, I came to see the patient. I can always call back later if you prefer."

"I want you to stay, Captain, and listen to what we're talking about. Maybe you'll think of something we've missed. I understand you were on that first recon to Abbottabad, correct?"

"Yes, Sir."

"So none of this is news to you."

She shook her head. "No, Sir."

"Good. We have a problem, Captain. How to quietly locate this Riyad character, get into the compound, and eliminate him. If we don't bump him off, he'll pop up again like a jack in the box, and it'll be like a second coming to these Islamic fanatics sat around waiting for rapture. Except that this character won't be preaching love thy neighbor. We can't go in by air since they expanded their air defenses. And we can't go in by road. They've saturated the town with checkpoints. The local cops are all over the place."

"Sir, we went in by means of a HAHO jump last time. Why not do it that way again?"

"It's tempting, Captain. I know it worked then, and it may even work again. But if their radar is half decent, and we know it is, they may spot those MC-6 parachutes. Even if it doesn't pick them up, they have to locate the bunker, and we haven't got a clue where it is. Then they have to blast their way inside, identify Riyad bin Laden, take him out, and get out in a mighty hurry. If the Pakistanis are as prepared as our intelligence suggests, whoever goes in there may strike lucky and eliminate the target, but they wouldn't get out so easily, no way. Those air defenses would blast the helos we send in right out of the sky. Some damn fool sold them a bunch of M42 Self-Propelled tracked anti-aircraft guns. Our UAV imagery shows a dozen of them hidden around the outskirts of the town. They're obsolete, but they'd have no problem shooting down any of the helos sent in for exfil. They're don't intend to be caught with their pants down a second time."

She nodded thoughtfully. "In that case, Sir, there's only one option. If we can't go in by air, or by road, underground is the only option."

"You mean the sanitation tunnels, but the problem is, we know nothing about them, and now we have no chance of finding out. We have no idea where they are, how large or how safe they are, the layout, you name it, and we have no intelligence. It died with Mr. Masih."

Nolan lifted his head. He flinched as pain knifed

through him, but he shook it off before they noticed. "But we could get that intelligence."

Three heads swiveled to look in his direction. "What the hell do you know that Military, Naval and Air Force Intelligence, the NSA and the CIA don't?" Jacks asked sharply.

Nolan explained what Danial had told him about his son.

"Apparently, he spent a lot of time with his father, and he knows the network inside out and back to front. His ambition when he grew up was to follow in his father's footsteps. It's the way it works out here, jobs pass from father to son. They're kind of inherited."

"I don't know," the Admiral pondered. "We know nothing about him. Where is he, this guy, and why would he help us?"

"He'd sure help us. Danial told me how much his family despised the Muslims for the way they persecuted him almost on a daily basis. So he's seen what the Muslims have done to his family, and all his life they've abused them. But as to where he is, well, I don't know, Sir."

Jacks raised his eyes. "You don't know? So it's all for nothing, and we're still no further forward."

Boswell edged forward. "Sir, that's not entirely true. I understand this guy was a civil engineer for the water company, so he'll be on local records somewhere in the town. How hard could it be to run down the son? Don't we have intel people to do that kind of thing? How about CIA, or NSA? It's time they earned their keep."

"Lieutenant," Jacks snapped, "you're not in California now. This is the asshole of Asia. These people don't keep centralized records on computer like we do. They may have records, sure, but they're chaotic. The only way would be a local records check in the town itself, and we don't have a way of doing that."

Mariko interrupted. "I could get in there."

The Admiral stared at Captain Noguchi. "What, are you going to take the bus?"

She grinned. "Why not, Sir? I wore a burqa before to disguise myself as a local. I speak perfect Dari and Urdu. And if Bravo Platoon was on the ground in support not too far away, they could come right in and finish the job as soon as I have the data we need."

He shook his head. "No! No way, that is the most cockamamie plan I've ever heard. Anything could go wrong, and you'd be going in totally unprepared. There has to be another way." He smiled at Mariko. "But thanks for the offer, Captain. I'm going to talk to Randall Weathers, and see if he has any better ideas than using women in burqas. Lieutenant Boswell, come with me. We'll leave these two and go find the Colonel. Chief, I'll see you in the morning. I assume you'll be back on duty then?"

Nolan nodded. "I will, yes, Sir."

"Good. Captain Noguchi, nice meeting you."

They saluted, and the two men left. Mariko looked at Nolan.

"Was it bad, that dust up in the town?"

He nodded. "Bad enough. We got the Platoon out in one piece, but we lost Danial, so overall it was a bust."

She grimaced. "I'm so sorry. He came a long way to get away from those people, and they got him in the end. It looks like the operation may be over, at least for the time being."

"You're right, they did get him, but I still like your idea.

I reckon it could be done. You and I could go in together, dressed and disguised as Pakis. Well, you wouldn't have any problems, not in a burqa, so I guess those stupid garments do have a use." He smiled. "But I could do a better job of the disguise, make it look more convincing, not such a rush job this time. With your knowledge of the language, and me to back you up, we could get in, locate the son and bring in Bravo Platoon. We'd be in and out before anyone knew what was going on."

"Except for one small problem. Jacks laughed it off."

He swung his legs out of bed. "The hell with Jacks. I'm getting out of here now. I'll go and see the Admiral and make him see sense."

"Kyle! You're supposed to be staying in overnight. You could die if you check yourself out and suffer a blood clot, or something bad."

He searched in the locker for his uniform, started to remove the hospital nightshirt, and began pulling on his pants. Partially dressed, he felt better already. He turned to face her.

"Mariko, I can tell you someone's going to die, but it isn't going to be me. There's one big, bad, bearded bastard out there in Abbottabad and I'm going to nail his ass. Help me locate my gear. I need my shoes and jacket. They must be around here somewhere."

She grinned and gave him a mocking salute. "Yes, Sir!" She found what he needed in a closet on the other side of the room.

"I'll come with you to find the Admiral. I imagine Colonel Weathers will be with him, and I do have some influence with him."

He nodded, finished dressing, and moved to the door

to vacate the hospital room when the nurse returned, with an expression of anger.

"You can't leave the hospital, Chief Nolan. Not until tomorrow at the earliest. You've had a nasty concussion. You'll kill yourself it you're not careful! Get back into bed and finish your treatment."

"Sorry, Nurse, I do have to go. Tell you what, I'll come back here when I'm done."

"And how long will that be?"

He grinned at her. "Ask the enemy, Ma'am. They don't keep me informed."

They were told to wait outside Admiral Jacks' office. Inside, they could hear the sounds of a heated argument raging. It was obvious Jacks and Weathers weren't in agreement about something. After a half-hour, the door opened, and Jacks' aide beckoned for them to enter. The Admiral was sitting behind a desk, Weathers stood across from him, his hands on the battered military issue desk, leaning toward the Admiral almost as if to menace him.

"Captain Walker and Chief Nolan, Sir."

They came to attention, and Jacks nodded. "At ease. What is it? I'm busy right now."

Mariko led off. "Sir, about getting in to Abbottabad. We think it's entirely feasible to do it the way I suggested." She used a ploy that was guaranteed to get his sympathy and support. "It's a classic Navy Seal operation, Sir. A couple of operatives go in undercover to gather intel, and then the assault team comes in to finish the job. It has a great chance of success."

"And a great chance of failure," he grumbled. "Colonel Weathers has been trying to convince me it would work as well, or should I say General Weathers? You both know his real rank and department. The problem is I have to deal with the fallout, political fallout from Pakistan if they find out what we're up to, and a lot of service flak from the Pentagon if they think I'm responsible for mounting a rogue operation."

Nolan edged nearer. "What would be the fallout if a born-again bin Laden were to appear? And we'd done nothing about it, even when we had a chance to try."

"Exactly what I've been saying," Weathers agreed. "We have to give it our best shot."

"And you'll take the hit when the shit flies, Randall? Is that what you're saying?"

Weathers grinned. "We're all in trouble if it doesn't work, Drew. But a lot less trouble than if we don't even make the attempt."

Jacks nodded thoughtfully. Then he smiled. "You're right, I guess. I just needed to be persuaded a little more." He looked at Nolan. "Okay, so what exactly do you propose? What's the plan?"

"We go in tomorrow, into Abbottabad by public transport, all innocent and above board. Captain Noguchi and me will be disguised as Pakis, and as soon as we get there, we find Danial's son. Bravo Platoon makes a night drop to an LZ outside of Abbottabad, and they lie up ready for us to make contact. We'll pick them up, and the son will be able to show us the start of the main tunnel system, which I understand is just outside the town. We go inside. Danial told me it goes right underneath the bin Laden compound. We come up inside the compound, locate this Riyad and take him out. Exfil along the same route. We obviously can't have helos flying low over the town to pick us up. They can land well outside the town, and we'll meet them somewhere quiet."

Jacks nodded thoughtfully. "A couple of points you may not have thought of. First, Bravo's LZ will have to be well outside of the town. You'll need transport to collect them and get them to wherever this tunnel system starts."

"That'd be no problem, Sir. Captain Noguchi and I could drive over from J-Bad. In fact, we could take a jingle truck and just blend in with the locals."

"A what?" Weathers interjected.

"Jingle truck, Sir. It's those colorfully decorated trucks. They use them all over Pakistan and Afghanistan. The customized trucks and buses you see everywhere, with chains and stuff hanging down from them, it jingles. They're kind of like psychedelic painted hippy trucks."

Weathers nodded. "Yeah, I know what you mean. One of those would sure blend in."

"I hate to put problems in your way," Jacks interrupted. "But have you considered that the Pakis won't take too kindly to one of our helos overflying Waziristan again? Not after Neptune Spear. We'd need something big, like a CH-47 Chinook to bring out the personnel, and it'd be at risk from any Paki fighter jock that decides to take an interest. They're not very forgiving over there these days. It's likely to be a hot extraction. In fact, I'd bet my paycheck on it. They're not going to let you just stroll out of there."

They were silent for a few moments. Then Mariko spoke. "The helo would need a fighter escort, Sir. A couple of F/A18s to provide an overhead air defense. It's the only way."

He raised his eyes to the roof. "Jesus Christ, you're not serious! The Pakis would go ballistic if we sent our fighters. Christ, a combat air patrol to provide cover for a returning SpecOps mission! They'll have kittens."

"Fuck 'em, Drew," Weathers snapped. "If they're that serious about fighting terror, they should go in and terminate this bastard once and for all, and dynamite his compound. Not leave it up to us every fucking time. No, they always leave the dirty work for us to take care of. Well all right, if that's the case, let's not disappoint them. We'll do what needs to be done, and fuck the consequences."

They all stared at him. His emotive outburst and strong language hinted at the huge frustration he must have felt at being constantly blocked from doing what was needed to win this war.

Jacks broke the shocked silence. "Randall, I agree with you." He grinned, "I wouldn't put it quite like that to our masters in the Pentagon, but whatever. I'll lend my support to the fighters if you'll clear it with the Department of the Navy, just so our asses are covered."

Weathers nodded. "It's a deal. Nothing on paper, of course, you know the way the game's played. I'll arrange for my people in Jalalabad to buy a jingle truck from someone who needs a quick sale." He looked at Nolan. "Anything else you need?"

"A good makeup artist. I need to look like a local, the whole works. Clothing, skin color, beard, you name it."

"What about your eye color? Not many Pakistanis with blue eyes."

"I'll wear sunglasses, that should do it."

Weathers nodded. "That'll work in the daytime. You'd better pray no one sees you after dark."

"I'll keep 'em on. The right kind of lenses will allow me to see out, but they won't be able to see my eyes."

Jacks looked worried. "You don't want colored contact

lenses? I'm sure our people could organize it."

"I'll be fine, Sir. If it comes to a fight, I can take off sunglasses fast. Contacts could be a problem."

"In that case, there's nothing more to be said. I'll fix it all up for you. The mission is a go. I'll talk to Lieutenant Boswell in and sort out the arrangements for infil, and we'll need to pinpoint the LZ." He picked up the phone and shouted for someone to tell Lieutenant Boswell to get his ass in right away.

"I'd imagine a HAHO drop from a long ways out would fit the bill," he continued. "We'll need to make sure the LZ is somewhere real quiet, but not too far out. You don't need to be driving fifty klicks to locate the Platoon. You'll have to sync with Boswell, so you'll know where to pick them up. I'd suggest a satellite phone to keep in contact while you're driving over there. I'll have them bring in your commo gear with the rest of your equipment when you meet up with them. Or maybe we can stow it in the truck if there's a suitable secret compartment. The sixty-four dollar question, Chief, is do you think you can find this kid? And if you do, will he definitely help us? Right now, there are too many maybes."

Nolan though for a few moments, of Danial Masih, of everything he'd told him, but he didn't know the son's name, only the family name, Masih. Didn't know where he lived, only that his father had worked for the water company in the town.

What if the son also works for the water company? It is possible. How can we find out? Go to the admin office and hold them at gunpoint while Mariko demands to know his address? Yeah, that's exactly what we'll do.

He stared at Admiral Jacks.

"Yes, Sir. We can find him, and I know he'll help us."

Jacks nodded. "Good enough. I'll get onto my people in J-Bad. They can run down one of these crazy jingle trucks for you. I'll get them to bring it in and give it the once over to make sure it's one hundred percent mechanically fit before you leave. I want…"

"No, Sir," Nolan interrupted. "Just get the truck and park it up somewhere. I don't want it anywhere near an American base."

"If that's what you want, I'll tell them. It makes sense, I know, but if you break down halfway there," he shrugged. "The whole mission goes down the toilet."

"In that case, make sure they pay for a damn good truck that won't break down. And I'll need to carry a cargo of goods to make it look good. Machinery parts would be fine. Some old military surplus stuff that our people don't want, and the Pakis would likely want to buy. I'll need paperwork too, and money for bribes."

"Consider it done. What about weapons?"

"I'll carry my Sig-Sauer under my coat, and I could do with something heavier concealed in the truck. Yeah, an MP7 would be ideal, with a half-dozen spare clips. And my sniper rifle, the Mk 11, it could come in useful if we get into a scrap. But the weapons will need to be well hidden."

"Okay, I'll ask them to locate a friendly workshop that can weld up a couple of hidden lockers underneath the chassis. That should do it, together with a few big bribes. What about you, Captain? What will you need?"

"I have a small pistol I can carry underneath my burqa, Sir. It's a Glock 26, the Baby Glock, ideal for a concealed carry. The armorers fitted it with a suppressor which makes it a little more bulky, but it'll do the job without making too much of a fuss."

He nodded. Someone knocked on the door and opened it. Lieutenant Boswell walked in and saluted.

"At ease, Lieutenant. Here's the deal. The Abbottabad mission is a go. We're just going over the details right now."

Boswell smiled. "That's great news, Sir." He looked at Nolan. "Are you okay, Chief? I thought you were supposed to stay in that hospital overnight?"

"And let you guys have all the fun? No way, Lieutenant. Captain Noguchi and I are going into the town to locate Danial's son. He'll be able to lead us through those tunnels to the target. When we have him, we'll meet up with you at the LZ and guide you in." He looked at Jacks. "Admiral, we should be making a start for J-Bad. We have a lot to organize there, and we need that truck, pronto."

"Sure. Randall, would you go with them and fix everything up? They'll need transportation and so on, and someone the other end to take care of things."

"Sure, I'll do that. In fact, how about we move our operational control to J-Bad, so we'll be on the spot?"

"Sounds good to me. You go ahead and fix it up. I'll make arrangements for the infil. They can leave direct from here in a C-17. They can't fly out of J-Bad, so I'll see them off and join you after I've fixed up the helo and escort for the return. Yeah, it'll have to be Chinook with that number of people. I'll detail one from here and travel over to Jalalabad when Bravo has left. I'll meet you on the ground tomorrow about midday, and we can go over the final plans. Anything I've forgotten?"

Weathers shook his head. "I think that covers it." He nodded at Nolan and Mariko. "I'll get that truck arranged before we leave for J-Bad. We need to make certain we sync your infil and the HAHO drop so you link up okay. This is important. When you locate the target, we can assume the mission is close to completion. I want you to call it in, and we'll get our people on standby." He thought for a few moments. "No, call it in as soon as you begin the assault on the compound. We'll be ready for you, whatever you need."

Nolan grinned at Boswell. "We'll meet you at the LZ, Lieutenant. Take it easy, and don't be late."

"You too, Chief. Try not to get lost."

They shook hands and left. Weathers barked orders at his Marine aide, who arranged for an available Black Hawk to carry them across to Jalalabad. The operation took on the characteristics of a whirlwind. Everything happened so fast once the brass had made up their minds to go. They stood by as Weathers picked up the phone and made the arrangements for them to be received at J-bad. He left the office to hustle his people into finalizing the arrangements, and the Black Hawk was soon spooling up to transport them to their destination. They boarded the helo, and an hour later, they were eating lunch in JSOC's compound at J-bad. The Joint Special Operations Command had its own chow hall, gym, operations center, and a number of wooden huts, one of which had been allocated to them. Mariko glanced across the table at Nolan. Her eyes were troubled.

"Do you think we can pull this off, Chief?"

He took his time answering. "Exactly what are you worried about, Mariko?"

Her face was pale. "It's just that getting in there is one thing, but we have to locate the utilities company, find the person in charge of records, and persuade him to give us

Danial Masih's address. He may not be there; he could be on vacation, off work with the flu, not even work there, who knows? And all the while, we'll be in a hostile town with a strong police presence. They'll be checking out everything. I could even wind up incarcerated in a Pakistani prison, and for a woman that's not good."

He tried to reassure her. "It's normal to get last minute worries, especially on an operation like this. Don't worry about it. We'll find the place, go in there, and I'll persuade them to tell us what we need to know. That's all there is to it. And there's one other thing."

She looked up. "What's that?"

"You'll have me to take care of you. I won't let any harm come to you, trust me."

"You mean that?" Her eyes met his. "You really mean it?"

She was holding in her fear, and right then, he appreciated the courage of this woman for even thinking about going disguised into the cauldron of Abbottabad.

"I do, Mariko. Any girl that's with me, well," he shrugged. "No one gets in the way. You hear, no one. Period." He relaxed, and smiled. "Besides, when we went in for that recon you did real well. You've nothing to worry about, you're a pro."

She regarded him for a few moments. "Since that time, I've had a dream, a nightmare really, that they'll catch me disguised in a burqa and torture me as a spy. They're not kind to women, the Muslims."

"No, they're not, but as long as you're with me, you'll be fine."

She nodded. "Yes, I think I will be. Thank you, Kyle."

They finished their food. He wanted to check out the

progress of acquiring the jingle truck, but she suggested they go look out their disguises first. He nodded.

"Sure, if you want. I'll need some extra stuff, a false beard, and something to darken my skin. I can pick up some sunglasses from the store later, but the skin coloring is essential, even if I'm to pass at a distance. Remember, it'll be daylight."

"First off, we need to check to see that the ethnic clothes look right. I don't want you going over there wearing something several sizes too small. Or even an outfit that's entirely wrong for the region."

They walked over to the wooden hut they'd been allocated at J-Bad. Inside it was pretty basic, just a couple of beds, two chairs, and a rickety closet. The place smelled of damp and mildew, the smell of Asia. She stared at him.

"Take off your clothes, Kyle. I need to see how that costume can be made to fit better." Her voice was throaty.

He stared back at her. The previous time he'd changed in his own quarters.

"Are you sure about this?"

She stared back, and when she spoke, her voice almost cracked. "I'm sure."

There was a world of meaning in those two words. He abruptly realized how slow he'd been. So preoccupied with the mission and with calming her fears, that he hadn't understood the signals she'd been sending him. It was by no means unusual for troops going into danger to want to feel the warmth and intimacy of sexual contact. He'd felt that way himself in the early days. It was clear she felt it too. He finished undressing, removing his pants to strip down to his underwear. She'd pulled out the blue burqa and was stripping off her clothes too, but not to put on her disguise, not yet. He watched her strip off until she only wore her bra and panties. She stared at him.

"Kyle, please. Come to me, I need you."

He went to her and pushed her down on the bed. She wriggled out of her underwear so that she was naked, and she helped him out of his shorts and took hold of his engorged penis. He looked at her face and saw she was smiling.

"My word, Chief Petty Officer Nolan, show that to the enemy, and they'll be terrified. It's a large caliber weapon."

He chuckled. "I appreciate the thought, Captain Walker, but I'll be showing them something a bit more useful than this, like my Sig."

"It's useful enough for me, don't worry. Fuck me, Kyle. Oh, God, I need this. I need you."

"Anything to oblige a lady."

She guided him. She was already soaking wet with arousal, and he slid inside. She quivered in ecstasy, catching her breath in a gulp as she felt the full hardness of him slide right up inside her. Then they fucked, a long, slow sensual joining that for a brief while took her mind off the terrors that had assaulted her. And for him, it was a chance to be a man, a man with a beautiful girl, maybe for the last time. Despite his words, neither of them had too many illusions. If they were caught by the Pakistanis, and wearing disguise, the end would be long and painful. As Mariko had said, Muslims were cruel to women, and to spies.

Afterward, she dressed quietly.

"Do you want me to put on my ethnic gear, see how it looks?" he asked her.

She smiled. "Sure, if you want. I'm sorry…"

"Hey, don't apologize. That was fantastic, and Mariko…"

"Yes?"

"You're fantastic. I'm a lucky guy."

He kissed her and felt her tongue sliding inside his mouth. He responded, and felt the familiar feeling returning to his loins. He broke away.

"I think we'd better get the show on the road before we get too carried away again."

She looked at him, but before she could reply, there was a knock on the door.

"You'd better find somewhere to stand out of sight, and I'll see who it is."

He grinned and stood behind the door. Mariko opened it, to see a Marine corporal stood there.

"Ma'am, message from Colonel Weathers. I'm to take you across to the operations room for a briefing."

"Right now?"

"Yes, Ma'am."

"Give us a few minutes, Corporal. We'll be right out."

There was a short silence as he digested the meaning of 'we'. Then he cleared his throat. "Er, yes, Ma'am."

The door closed, and she grinned at him. "Better get your gear on. We're needed. Now the whole base will know what we're up to."

He shook his head. "Only JSOC, I'd imagine. What comes in here, stays in here."

"I hope you're right."

Weathers had taken someone's office to use as a temporary operations room at J-Bad. First off, he went over the infil and exfil once more, using huge maps he'd pinned to the wall. Then he got down to specifics.

"A couple of CIA operatives here in Jalalabad have bought the jingle truck. It's stored in a downtown warehouse. The word is it's as new and reliable as they could get without arousing suspicion. I want you to get over to the warehouse after dark. You can get some rest inside and leave town before first light, so no one sees you leave. They've arranged for the extras you wanted, the secret compartments and the weapons, and we transferred your Mk 11 rifle over there so they could make everything fit. They'll be waiting for you when you get there, and they'll have everything you need, the money, and the satphone. They'll give you a verbal briefing on the route, as well as anything you'll need to be looking for when you go over. Whatever you do, stay out of trouble. Just get to the town, find the son, bring in Bravo Platoon, and go take out Riyad."

"What can we offer this guy, Sir? I mean if he's not that enthusiastic about helping us?"

"Anything! This is too important to fail. Anything at all."

"Like a new life in America?"

Weathers sighed. "Why the hell do these people fight us, when all most of them want is to come to America and share our lifestyle, the benefits of a free, Christian society?" Neither of them answered. There was no answer. "Okay, yeah, whatever. If he wants it, he can have a Green Card and a few dollars to settle him when he gets there. Anything else?"

"Rules of engagement, Colonel."

He nodded and smiled. "Yeah, that's the real question. I take it you're referring to the Paki cops, military, and so on."

"That's right."

"We don't have a choice. If anyone gets in the way of this mission, you take them out. I don't care if it's the fucking Pakistani national cricket team, no one, but no one gets in the way. If they do, it's too bad. They go down. Is that clear enough for you?"

They both nodded.

"Good. It's not long to dark, so go back to your room and get some rest. I'll have an Afghan civilian vehicle pick you up in a couple of hours and take you to the truck. One of the CIA people in the warehouse is an escape and evasion specialist. He'll have all the stuff you need to be convincing when you go across." He came toward Mariko and Nolan. "Good luck to both of you. I'll be here, controlling the operation at first hand, and Admiral Jacks will be joining me. I'm expecting him at first light tomorrow."

He shook their hands, and they left to walk through the JSOC compound to their quarters. Neither made any comment on the fact that Weathers obviously knew about their temporary bunking arrangements. But it was as Mariko had said; there were few secrets in a place such as this. They lay on the bunk, fully dressed, and he held her until their transport arrived, occasionally whispering words of encouragement into her ear. When the knock came on the door, she held on to him briefly, and then let him go. He stared at her inky-black eyes, shining in the gloom like two black gemstones.

"Are you gonna be okay?"

She nodded. "Just don't wander too far away. Stay with me, Nolan."

"I'll be there."

They climbed into the enclosed truck and suffered a bumpy journey into downtown Jalalabad.

Do they never repair any roads in this asshole country?

When the vehicle stopped, the back doors opened, and they found themselves inside a dimly lit space. Two men helped them down; both wore the unmistakable stamp of CIA mercenaries. The paramilitary clothing, complete with shoulder holsters and ice cold stares, as hard as the steel of the weapons inside the holsters, was more than a giveaway. They may as well have worn id badges. The light was so poor they could hardly see the sides of the almost empty warehouse. Almost empty, apart from the jingle truck. The vehicle itself was by far the brightest object in the room. It was based on a medium size commercial truck, but the similarity to a Western counterpart ended there. The bodywork was painted in a gaudy blaze of color, reds, yellows, oranges, greens, and blues of every shade. Chains hung down from the front fender, and Nolan knew they would jingle like crazy as they made their way along the poorly maintained roads. Maybe it would help keep them awake. It was going to be a long drive. Over the cab, a semi-circular arch had been constructed with more decorative artwork and wind chimes hanging down. It was like some monstrous sun canopy. A sun canopy when the truck was moving with the sun behind it. Otherwise it would be useless, except for the sound effects. Nolan nodded to the nearest CIA man.

"Does it run?"

"Sweet as a nut. It'll get you there, and back if you want."

Nolan nodded but said nothing.

"This is Wes," the operative continued. "He's the

makeup and disguise king. If you'd like to step into the cab of the jingle truck, he'll show you how everything works. His stuff is all in there, and there's a good interior light, so he can get to work on you and make you look like a raghead. Only problem is, one of our guys might start taking pot shots at you, but there you go." He shrugged. "It's a chance you have to take."

Nolan wasn't sure if he was making a joke. He decided he wasn't. He climbed into the truck, and the other guy, Wes, climbed in, spent a minute showing him the controls and pulled a make up box from behind the seat. When he switched the light on, it was enough for the man to see his work by, and he spent a half-hour working on Nolan's face, neck and hand color, his hair, and gluing a false beard to his chin.

"How long will this stay on?" he asked the guy.

"Long enough. Mind you, the last one who wore one of these got himself killed, so he didn't need it for too long," the man grunted.

Very funny! Thank Christ Mariko can't hear this.

He finished up by winding a turban around Nolan's head, and he was done. When Nolan climbed down from the truck, Mariko was waiting for him.

"You look good, real good, Kyle. I'd take you for a native any day. What do you think?" she asked the first CIA operative.

He grunted, "Yeah, I guess I'd shoot him if I caught him in my sights, so he must look pretty good."

They both gave up.

"You want to see the false compartments, buddy?"

"I would. Was it difficult to get them welded into the chassis?"

"Didn't have to do a goddamn thing. Most of these trucks smuggle goods both ways across the border, and they all have false compartments fitted. Mainly, they're for show. They know they're there, but it's the bribe money that'll get you across. This way, the border guards can pretend they weren't aware you were carrying anything."

Nolan checked underneath, and the guy showed him how the hatches could be opened. Inside, his Mk 11 rifle and an MP7 had been stowed, with supplies and ammunition. There was also a metal box of grenades, and no one made any comment when Nolan took out two of them and stuffed them inside his robes. There was a small leather case for documents. He took out his and Mariko's Afghan ID cards and the satphone to check them over. Satisfied, he got back in the cab and started the engine. The motor fired straight away.

It'll do.

It sounded as healthy as they could expect. He nodded at the two operatives.

"It all looks pretty good, thanks. We want to stay here until an hour before dawn. Is there somewhere we can get some rest?"

"You don't stay here, buddy, not if you want to get to somewhere in Pakiland by anytime tomorrow. The trucks like this one that carry NATO supplies clog up the passes, and you'll be queuing for hours just to get across. You need to go now and drive through the night. You'll cross while it's dark if it's not too busy. That way, you'll be able to get where you're going. Otherwise, you can easy add an extra day. You seen the roads over there?"

Nolan shook his head. "Not lately."

Christ, this isn't a great start.

"It's a lie."

He stiffened. "I'm sorry?"

"It's a lie, to call them roads. They ain't. I wouldn't use 'em to send pigs into a pigsty back home. I'd get going if I were you. You'll need all the time you can get."

Nolan nodded and climbed into the cab. Mariko got in the other side. The two CIA operatives opened the street doors and watched dispassionately as they drove out.

"Chatty pair," she said to him. She sounded as if she was smiling, but he couldn't see.

"Yeah, they obviously enjoy their work."

They drove off in a deafening crescendo of diesel engine noise and rattling chains. Every nut and bolt on the bodywork seemed loose, adding to the cacophony. The exhaust leaking diesel fumes added to their discomfort. They tried to ignore the irritations, and Nolan drove grimly through the night. Four hours later, they were at the front of the queue to cross into Pakistan, high in the mountains, so high that the air was thin. It took an effort just to breathe in the chill night air. It was a small border town called Torkham, three miles west of the highest peak of the Hindu Kush, and lined with refreshment stalls selling everything from food and drink to girls, boys, and as much raw opium as you could carry. An Army officer stepped up to the truck and signaled them to get down. Outside the truck, a soldier stood with his rifle trained on Nolan. He spoke to them in a mangled dialect of Pashto and Urdu, and Mariko whispered, "He says we are smugglers, and we are under arrest."

CHAPTER EIGHT

Nolan did his best to feign ignorance as the officer began shouting in his face. Then Mariko intervened. He could hear the pleading note in her voice and knew she was doing her best to persuade him to release them. He replied with more shouted abuse, and when she interrupted him again, he backhanded her to send her sprawling to the ground. In time, Nolan remembered where he was. This was Muslim Central, where women were chattels and of less value than a horse or a goat. He forced himself not to draw his Sig and shoot the guy on he spot. Instead, he helped her up.

"I think he wants a big bribe," she whispered. "Do you have money in your coat? If we have to go to the hidden cache on the truck, he'll take the lot, and probably seize the truck as well."

"I have five hundred dollars ready, loose in my pocket."

"Okay, get it out, and offer it all to him. Try to look deaf, dumb, and stupid."

"I'll do my best," he murmured. He dragged out the

money, a creased bundle of notes, and offered it to the officer. The man's eyes lit up. Then his expression sobered, and he shouted at Mariko again.

"He says it is an insult, and it will cost us double if we want to get back over the border."

"Yeah, tell him it's just the one-way rate we're looking for. We don't need a return ticket. Next time we'll cross in a gunship and unload a few thousands rounds of ammo on his stinking border post."

"Schh. Get in the cab and drive. And smile at the bastard, as if you're grateful."

He grinned and nodded at the guy. But his eyes were not smiling.

The next time we meet, you'll be staring at the wrong end of my gun barrel. You fuck with Kyle Nolan's girl, and you better start saying your prayers, motherfucker.

He drove on, down the N-5 National Highway that linked the Hindu Kush and Afghanistan to the thriving Pakistani city of Peshawar. The road was as poorly maintained as most of the highways in Pakistan. That is to say, there was no maintenance, only potholes that were filled when the locals could be bribed or cajoled into coming out to do some hard work. Despite the rutted road, the traffic was heavy, even in the early hours of the morning.

"Why the hell don't they maintain their highways?" Nolan grumbled, as he constantly wrestled with the wheel, trying to avoid yet another hole that could potentially fracture the rear axle.

"This route, the N-5, is Pakistan's longest highway. It runs from the port city of Karachi to the border crossing back there at Torkham," Mariko explained. "Its total length is over fifteen hundred kilometers, from Karachi through Hyderabad, Gujarat, and Rawalpindi. It runs through Peshawar before entering the Khyber Pass and reaching the border town of Torkham. It's one of their most important roads, so if you think this is bad," she said, he thought she was grinning but he couldn't read her expression through the mesh of the burqa, "you should see the others."

He grunted. "Any idea of how long we have to drive?"

"About four hours if nothing goes wrong. We should be there just after midday."

"That'll give us a few hours to run this guy to earth. When we get there, I guess we'll just park up and go knocking on the door of the local water company."

"If they're not on their four hour lunch break. They don't like to work long hours over here. After the morning shift, these folks are pretty much finished for the day, but a bribe should bring them out of the woodwork. And if that doesn't work, you can do the other thing."

He nodded. Damn right I'll do the other thing. Jesus Christ, what a shithole!

He was exhausted by the time they reached Abbottabad, but the exhilaration of being close enough to the target to almost spit in Riyad's face gave him new life. There was a truck park outside the town, and Mariko arranged the payment of five dollars to persuade the watchman to look after their vehicle.

Probably about five times the going rate, but what the hell, at least we'll still have four wheels when we get back.

When Mariko asked him the directions to the water company, he looked disgusted that a mere woman had spoken to a man such as him, a high-ranking car park security guard. He spoke to her like he was talking to a dog, and she dragged Nolan away before he hit the guy.

"Take it easy. That's the way these men treat women around here," she whispered urgently. "You need to act like it's normal. Otherwise, they'll wonder who the hell you are."

He nodded. "Yeah, you're right. I'll kick his ass to hell and back on the way out."

"Fair enough, but I've got directions to the water company, and it's not too far away from here. Let's see who we can bribe there to give us the address of Danial's family home."

It took them less than five minutes to reach the Abbottabad Water Company Central Office, with Mariko walking behind Nolan and whispering directions to make it look right. Like most places, other than the homes of the wealthy, the building was crumbling and badly maintained. They went through the front door and found themselves in a reception hall. A man stood behind the single counter. He looked to be in his twenties, and he gave Mariko's burqa clad form a friendly nod as she approached.

Nolan smiled to himself. That's different! Maybe they aren't all misogynist scum around here.

She talked with him for several minutes, and then Mariko gestured for Nolan to step back with her, out of his hearing.

"It's astonishing. We're in luck."

"About time something changed for the better," Nolan acknowledged.

"Yes, well it has. When I mentioned the name Danial Masih, everything changed, and he was very suspicious at first. But I made it clear there was no problem. I just had a message from Danial to give to his son. It turns out this guy actually is Danial's son, which I guess is not surprising. Families tend to work for the same company. He runs the central office. There are other staff, but they're not here. I guess they're on the four hour lunch break, but he's more conscientious."

"Does he know yet his father is dead?"

"No, I thought it best to tell him when we're better acquainted. The question is, do we trust this man?"

He looked across at the Paki who was staring at them curiously. "Yeah, we'll have to for now. If we can't trust him, the mission will be a complete bust. Give it a try, and see how he responds. If he kicks up, I'll have to take care of him."

"Okay, I'll try it."

She went back to the counter, where the younger Masih was still watching them intently, and spoke to him in his language. At first, he didn't reply, but then he looked across at Nolan and spoke in good English.

"You are not an Afghan, my friend."

Nolan shook his head.

"American?"

He nodded.

"I see. You are here because of my father. Where is he?"

He took a deep breath. "I'm very sorry, Mr. Masih. He's dead, murdered."

The man nodded. It obviously didn't surprise him. "Who killed him?"

"Islamic terrorists, probably al Qaeda. They kidnapped and murdered him in Kabul."

"You didn't come here to tell me this." His expression

was strange, and finally Nolan understood what it was. It wasn't sadness; it was a deep, raging hate.

"No, Sir, we didn't."

"What do you want from me?"

"We need you to help us, to guide us through the underground tunnel system."

He looked puzzled. "Us? Who do you mean? You two people? Why would you wish to go through the tunnels?"

"That's classified, I'm afraid," Nolan replied gently. "I'm sorry, but I can't tell you at this stage."

"Then I cannot help you."

Mariko stood directly in front of him and touched his arm. "Mr. Masih, we're real sorry about your father. We intend to destroy the bin Laden compound, to finish it off for all time, and kill any al Qaeda operatives we find inside it."

He stared at her and then at Nolan. "You're after Riyad." It wasn't a question.

Nolan sighed and nodded. "We are, yes."

"His people killed my father?"

Nolan inclined his head. "Yes."

"In that case, there's no problem. I will help you. When do you wish to go in?"

"After dark, tonight. There are some of our people we need to meet up with. We have a truck to collect them and transport them to the entrance to the tunnels. Where is it?"

Masih opened the gate that led behind the counter. "Come, you can look at the map. It is inside the office."

They followed him through the door into an inner room. On the wall, there was a large square map with colored lines indicating the routes of the main underground passages, pipes, and tunnels. He pointed to a thick green line.

"This is the main service tunnel. It is accessible. If you follow it here," he pointed with his finger, "it travels along this route, branches off here, and here, until it reaches this point."

He looked around triumphantly. Nolan was bewildered. "What's that?"

"It is what you seek. The bin Laden compound."

"And we can get there without any problems?"

"My name is Nazir. Yes, I can get you there, but there may be patrols in the tunnel system. People in the compound are very concerned for their security, especially after the American raid that killed Osama."

"We'll deal with the patrols. I understand that Riyad bin Laden may be using an underground command bunker, do you know anything about that?"

"If there is such a bunker, it would have to be accessed through the tunnel system, I suppose. Yes, it is logical, as a means of escape if they have to flee. I do not know of it, but if it exists, it should not be too hard to find. There is a service shaft that leads up into the grounds of the compound, so I assume it will be connected to that."

"We'll check it all out." Nolan replied. "Where do we meet you?"

Nazir pointed with his finger. "Here, it is one of the old tunnel entrances, part of our storm drain system, and just over a kilometer from the compound. I can be there at nightfall. That will be about eight-thirty tonight. But listen; there is something you should be aware of. The Minister of Foreign Affairs is in Abbottabad, some kind of official visit. It means there will be added security, and even more patrols, so you should be very careful. This man has a residence in Abbottabad. It is quite close to the tunnel entrance, and there is no other way to reach it. Make sure you do nothing suspicious to alert the police."

Nolan nodded. "We'll keep a look out for any cops, don't worry. Nazir, make it 2200, that's ten o clock tonight. We have to have time to meet up with the Platoon."

He stared again at the map and exchanged glances with Mariko.

There's a wooded area close to the tunnel entrance. That will enable us to hide the jingle truck. We can collect the team and drive straight back. From there, say a half-hour to reach the compound through the underground tunnel system. Then we'll begin the real work we came here to do. Start the killing.

She inclined her head and looked back at him out of the mesh of her burqa.

"It'll work."

They returned to the vehicle park, retrieved the truck, and drove out of town to the area of the LZ. It was an abandoned factory, built with American money to manufacture water pumps for remote areas. An ideal business venture for a third world country. One that could be exported to other third world countries to help them help themselves, but the Islamic terrorists had destroyed it and threatened death to anyone who tried to rebuild it or benefit in any way from the American investment. It seemed they were frightened that drinking water brought up by American financed water pumps may carry the taint of the infidel. Better for the civilian population to go thirsty and die, if necessary. Next to the bombed out factory was a weed strewn sports field, now designated as the LZ for Team Bravo. He parked up and they waited, sweating in the hot cab of the jingle truck. To get some shelter from the sun, he'd driven inside the burned out shell of the buildings, but it didn't appear to lower the temperature much. Occasionally, Nolan patrolled the area to check for any signs of life, anyone who may be watching them, but the place was empty. Apparently, the locals had been sufficiently intimidated to prevent them from going near the place. It suited him. Back in the truck, they talked about home, and about their plans for the future. He found himself telling Mariko everything, even the mocked up images of him planting that bomb when Carol's husband was killed. Nolan had never worked it out, only that it was a straightforward Photoshop job, not uncommon in the time of the Internet, and they'd used it to add to the damning evidence against him. But still, she was supposed to be his partner. Shouldn't she judge him innocent until proven guilty? Mariko had removed her stifling burqa to be more comfortable, and he talked more about Carol Summers, and about the way she'd helped build the case against him that led to his arrest. She tried to defend her, pointing out that as a cop she'd see the evidence leading to Nolan as the guilty party and come to the inevitable conclusion. But he wasn't buying any of it.

"I don't accept that line of argument, Mariko. Either she knows me or she doesn't. Period. If she doesn't realize that I'm not capable of rape and murder, then as far as I'm concerned, the relationship was always a non-starter. There's nothing else to discuss."

She nodded. "Knowing you as I do, I don't understand how she could think something like that. It does seem weird," she murmured.

He made no reply. This was getting too close to the

business of the blackouts. It was not for public airing. As far as he was concerned, it was irrelevant. Either he was a rapist murderer, or he wasn't, blackouts or no blackouts. There was such a thing as trust, a fundamental principle he'd lived his life believing in. No exceptions. To his relief, she indicated her agreement and understanding. Partnership was about trust, without it, there was nothing. They sat in silence when they'd finished talking. He spent some time checking his weapons and pulling out equipment from the hidden compartments to make everything ready for instant use. He also dragged out the load of machine parts they'd carried as cover so that the truck was empty, and the Platoon would find enough space inside. He put his uniform, helmet and vest, into the cab; ready to change into when they reached the tunnels. Mariko declined to change into her Marine camo and armor.

"I'll wear the burqa the whole time. If we get into a tight spot, it may give me an edge. They don't expect women wearing these things to start shooting back," she'd grinned.

Darkness crept over them, lit only by a quarter moon, and the outlines of the ruined buildings were dark shadows that chased away the last of the light and finally surrounded them. The satphone buzzed.

"Bravo Two."

"This is One." It was Boswell's voice, no question. In the background, he could hear the roar of the turboshaft engines. "We're dropping in five, and we'll be with you in fifteen. Everything okay?"

"We're prepped to go down here, Lt."

"Copy that. Bravo One, out."

It was twenty minutes before the first Seal touched

down, and Nolan used his NV goggles to recognize in the neat landing the hard competence of Will Bryce, the huge, black rock that was the tough, indestructible core of Bravo Platoon. Boswell landed next, and the rest came down soon after, all touching the ground and taking a couple of steps to get their balance, looking around to check their landing space. He went out to meet them. Boswell nodded a greeting.

"How're things fixed, Chief? Any problems on the ground?"

"None, Lt. We located Danial's son, Nazir, and he's happy to help us."

"What did he want? What did you offer him?"

"He only wanted revenge for his father."

Boswell nodded. "That makes sense. I'd have wanted the same."

"Yeah. The jingle truck is inside the building. We have to get aboard. He's meeting us soon at the entrance to the tunnel system." He looked around as Will came up to them. He nodded at Nolan and then turned to the Lieutenant.

"They're all down, Lt. No problems."

"Copy that. The truck is inside the building. Get them aboard, and we'll move out."

He nodded, assembled the men, and they went inside the dark ruin where they had their first sight of their ride, the jingle truck. Amidst groans and catcalls, 'Jesus Christ', and 'What a fucking heap', they tumbled into the back. Without an order, they started knocking small loopholes through the sides of the bodywork. If the shit hit the fan, they'd need to see the target. Zeke gave Nolan his commo system, and he pushed in the earpiece, glad to be in touch with the Platoon again. Mariko put on a commo rig inside her burqa and climbed into the cab. Nolan joined her, started the engine, and they drove off. He followed the road into town and took the turn for the tunnel entrance. They were at the end of a street of wealthy houses. There was no other road, and in the distance, Nolan could see the place they were headed. It stood alone in an area of empty ground a few hundred meters away. He drove along carefully, but then they ran into trouble. A cop stepped out and flagged them down. He braked to a stop; thanking the stars he was still wearing the ethnic clothes. A limousine traveling in the same direction had collided with an ancient auto. It looked antique, like something from half a century ago, an elderly, somber black saloon. The driver had stepped out and was cowering at the side of the street, while another man stood shouting at him in rage. With astonishment, Nolan recognized the man. Chutani Muhammad, the Pakistani Minister he'd met after the raid on Kabul International Airport.

What the hell is he doing out here?

Short, plump and obese bodyguards idly looked on as he harangued the shabbily dressed driver of the saloon that had collided with his limo. And then Nolan got it. It all clicked. The fat Paki Minister was going the same direction as they were. The compound! It didn't take a genius to add two and two together; almost certainly he was heading for the secret tunnel entrance that would lead them to Riyad bin Laden's compound.

So this is how these al Qaeda terrorists and their Pakistani allies can come and go at will, without being seen by an arsenal of American surveillance technology. Interesting!

A cop stormed up to his vehicle, gesticulating wildly, and diverted his attention. He shouted, and Mariko quietly translated. Fortunately, the cop couldn't see what they were doing in the dark cab.

"He says we have to turn around and go back."

"Shit! We can't. There's no other way around. Tell him we'll edge carefully around the damaged vehicles."

She spoke to him, but the cop shouted some more and put his hand on his holster.

"He says turn back, or he'll arrest us."

Nolan began to calculate the odds. Chutani Muhammad had a driver and two bodyguards, and there were four cops. Eight men in all, and they were twenty Seals, plus Mariko. First, they needed to get them off guard.

"Tell him we're turning around."

He heard Mariko talking to the cop, pleading with him. Then the Pakistani lost interest and turned away, satisfied. Nolan heard the click as the commo was activated.

"What's going on, Chief?" Boswell asked from the back.

"Cops, there's been an accident. They want us to turn back."

"Is there another way through?"

"No."

"We'll have to clear them out the way. How many are there?"

He told them and explained about the high-ranking politician and the civilian.

"Copy that. Mariko, that cop you're talking to, can you take him?"

"Sure."

"Okay, on my order. Chief, try and keep the Paki

Minister alive. We may be able to use him. Vince, get out the back so no one sees you, and find a good place to target those gomers. The rest of you, shoot through the holes in the side of the vehicle. As soon as you're ready, Vince, call it in, and we'll take 'em."

"Copy that."

A couple of minutes later, Nolan heard Vince Merano.

"This is Merano, I'm ready. I'm lined up on the two bodyguards."

"Copy that. Open fire!"

His command was not overly loud, but the effect was awesome. Merano's sniper rifle spat out four bullets, and both bodyguards went down like broken dolls. Mariko's pistol coughed twice, and the cop confronting her lurched back and slumped to the ground. The rest of the Platoon opened fire, and more than a dozen sound-suppressed assault rifles fired short, targeted bursts that tossed the remaining cops into bloody ruin. Chutani Muhammad stood stock still, his mouth opening and closing in shock. Nolan could see his legs were visibly shaking. The driver of the old sedan was trembling too, actually rocking and moaning with fear. Boswell came back on the commo.

"Nice shooting men. We need to get those bodies off the street. Chief, get the Minister, and make sure he doesn't try to run. Move, people, I want the area cleared fast so we can push on. You can drive the limo. I'll get someone in the cop car to follow us, and we'll find somewhere to lose them when we reach that wood near the tunnel entrance."

They tossed the bodies into the rear of the cars, and the Seals piled into the front seats and started the engines. Mariko went to the civilian and told him to get out, fast. If he cleared the area, they wouldn't kill him. He gratefully jumped into his vehicle and drove off. Nolan ran up to the Minister of Foreign Affairs.

"You're our prisoner, Sir. Come with us."

He stared at the Pakistani who wasn't a Pakistani. "You're an American!"

"Yeah, an ally. Isn't life strange? Let's go, Minister. Climb up, you can sit in the center of the cab."

"You, you can't do this to me. I am a government minister."

"Sure I can. Like I said, we're allies."

Nolan pushed him up, and with a length of thin cord, tied his wrists. Mariko climbed in beside him, and they continued along the street to their destination. The tarmac petered out, and there was the building they sought that housed the tunnel entrance just a few meters ahead, exactly as Nazir had described it. He drove up and doused the lights. Nazir was waiting for them, and he glanced at the procession of vehicles with apprehension.

"What is this? Police, a government vehicle, what is happening?"

"We're good, Nazir. Don't worry about it," Nolan told him.

"But they will link this all to me. They know I have access to these tunnels."

"Yeah, it's tough. You got family here?"

"No, no one."

"Then you'd better come back with us. We can offer you US citizenship."

Nazir was astonished. "You would do this for me?"

"It's yours if you want it."

"I accept. Thank you."

"No problem. I have to get out of these clothes and

into my gear. Give me a few minutes, then you can show us the way, and we can move off. You do know where we're going?"

"Yes."

"Good. While I'm changing, you'd better talk to the Lieutenant, and give him some idea of where we're going."

He sent Nazir across to Boswell, ripped off his robes and turban, and thankfully donned his camo kit and armor. Mariko, still anonymous in her blue burqa, helped him remove some of his skin makeup, and he strapped on his weapons. He carried his Mk 11 barrel down on his back, and the MP7 across his chest, ready for instant use. He felt better in his normal gear. Wearing the ethnic gear made him feel alien, naked. He joined the rest of the men who were preparing their weapons to go in. Chutani Muhammad caught sight of Nolan in his Multicam and gaped as he recognized him, the soldier from Bagram Air Base.

"You!"

"Yeah, me."

"I know your name. I will contact the authorities and have you arrested and imprisoned when I return to Islamabad. This action is criminal. It's nothing short of kidnap! I am a government minister. You can't do this to me."

"I'd suggest you get yourself an attorney, my friend. But you're not going to Islamabad, I can tell you that much."

His eyes narrowed. "Where are you taking me? Why are you doing this?"

"As for the why, I guess you know that well enough. We both know this street only leads in one direction, unless you were planning on taking a walk in the countryside through the night. As for the where, option one, if you cooperate, is we find you a tropical retreat in the Caribbean, and you can take a nice long holiday. It's called Guantanamo Bay. Option two, if you're unlucky, is you'll be going straight to hell." He saw the man shiver. "Yeah, it kind of limits your freedom of action. If I were you, I'd think about cooperating. Tell us about Riyad bin Laden."

"I will tell you nothing," he muttered. "I know nothing of this man. You cannot do this to me."

"If that's the way you want it, then it'll be option two. It's your choice, Muhammad. I'd think seriously if I were you."

"We're ready to move off," Boswell's voice came over the commo. "Zeke, contact J-bad. Tell them we're moving into the tunnel system, and we'll be in position shortly to start the assault on the compound. I'll take the lead, along with Nazir to guide us. Chief Nolan, bring up the rear."

"Copy that. I'll bring this prisoner along. He's one of Riyad's buddies."

"You'd better keep him quiet," Boswell warned.

"Either he sees sense and keeps his mouth shut, or he gets a bullet between the eyes."

"Fine by me."

Muhammad shuddered again, and then they entered the tunnel system. Nolan felt the tightening of his own muscles as adrenaline poured through his body, the classic 'fight or flight' effect. They were closing the target. The tunnel, green in his night vision goggles, was about two meters high, enough for most of them to walk upright or with only a slight stoop. There were numerous branches, and without Nazir, they would have been hopelessly lost. They'd been walking for about five hundred meters when he heard Boswell's whispered warning in his earpiece.

"Hostiles approaching. I'd guess about four men, so keep it quiet! All of you, get out of sight in one of the side tunnels."

Nolan pushed Muhammad into a side tunnel, and Mariko held her small pistol to his head.

"What's going on, Muhammad?" Nolan murmured. "Four men, is this a normal patrol, or do they suspect something's up?"

"I will not…"

He smashed the butt of his MP7 across the man's face; a cruel blow, meant to stun and terrify rather than to seriously injure.

"Last chance. The next one breaks your skull. Tell me about them."

"I think it will is a special group sent out to investigate something. Normal patrols are in ones and twos."

"Good."

He passed it on to Boswell and turned his attention back to Muhammad. "That's good. You have one chance to get out of here alive, Minister. That's to cooperate, and next time make it snappier. Got it?"

The man nodded sullenly. Boswell's whisper sounded in his earpiece.

"We're letting them go past us. Stay out of the main tunnel, and we'll hit them from behind. Chief, as soon as the shooting stops, I want you to block any leakers."

"Copy that."

He turned to Mariko. "Keep this guy quiet. If he makes a sound, shoot him dead. And stay in here, they'll be firing along the main tunnel in a few seconds."

She nodded and put the barrel of her Baby Glock

against his forehead, between his eyes; the first time a woman in a burqa had threatened the Pakistani, but the Minister was a fast learner. He kept his mouth shut.

They waited, silent and out of sight in the branch tunnel. Then Nolan heard the 'phut, phut' sounds, as Boswell's group took down the patrol with precise, well-aimed double taps. His earpiece replayed the action as they called it in.

"First guy is down, the other three don't know where it came from. They've started to run." Vince Merano's soft voice.

The sound of more suppressed gunfire, "Two down, we have a squirter running on toward the entrance. He's carrying an assault rifle. If he gets off a shot, it'll make one hell of a noise."

Nolan could hear footsteps racing toward him.

"I'm on him. Leave him to me. Keep the main tunnel clear."

He waited. The footsteps came nearer and nearer. At last, he stepped out into the tunnel, and in the wash of green light saw the man racing toward him, his expression one of both fear and triumph. He'd evaded the silent and terrifying ambush from whoever had invaded the tunnel system, and was making his escape. At the last moment, he spotted Nolan in the gloom, and his thick lips drew back in a snarl. He raised his assault rifle and prepared to gun down the man standing in front of him. Nolan saw his fingers curl around the trigger. He couldn't allow the sound of a shot that would alert the compound. They would be waiting for the patrol to call in, and so far they had nothing to alert them to the Seals' presence. With a fluid motion, he put the selector to 'auto' and aimed the suppressed submachine gun. He emptied the clip into the man's hand, the one with the trigger finger about to squeeze. And then there was no trigger finger; it was blown off, shredded along with most off his hand. All that was left was a bleeding, ruined mess. Part of the burst hit his body, protected only by a chest rack of spare clips. He opened his mouth to scream in shock and terrorized agony. In a single, flowing movement Nolan drew his combat knife and lunged, taking him in the mouth with a powerful, arcing slash. The victim's eyes, a ghostly green in the goggles, dilated even wider, showing his agony as the heavy blade slashed through his mouth, all the way to his throat, then drew back across and ripped back out the way it had gone in. But no sound emerged through the ruined vocal chords. Nolan gripped him as a gush of green blood poured out of his neck, and the body went limp. As he gasped his last breaths, his heart pumped the lifeblood onto the dusty floor of the tunnel. He eased him to the ground, pulling the body back into the side tunnel and out of sight.

"Bravo One, this is Two. Target is down."

"Copy that. Move out."

Nolan pulled Muhammad out of the side tunnel by the collar, and Mariko kept hold of his arm to stop him running. He was more docile now. He'd seen enough through the gloom, enough to realize that the Seals meant business, and he hurried along in silent obedience.

They moved almost without a sound, keeping up a fast pace to get to their target before whoever had sent out the patrol began wondering where they were. They reached their destination, and Boswell called over the commo net.

"This is One. Nazir says we're right under the

compound. If the command bunker exists, it has to be here. Hold your positions. We're taking a look around."

Nolan gripped the prisoner by the throat. "If you want to live, you have one chance. Where is bin Laden's underground bunker?"

"I can't…"

He drew out his combat knife, still wet with blood from the encounter with the patrol. Even in the darkness, the man could see it, or more accurately, smell it, the rank, metallic odor of fresh blood.

"Yes, you can. This is your last chance. Where is it? You're no use to us if you can't help."

He put the sharp edge of the blade against his neck and applied pressure.

"I will show you," the man muttered hoarsely.

"Okay, let's go forward."

Mariko followed as Nolan dragged him along the dark, narrow space. They reached Boswell, who heard them coming.

"What's this?"

"He's going to show us the bunker."

The Lieutenant smiled. "Go ahead." He looked at Moseley, standing next to him. "Dan, take care of Nazir, and don't let anything happen to him. He's coming out with us when this is over."

The son of Danial Masih looked anxious. "It feels strange, to contemplate leaving here, even though the Muslims make life hard for Christians. My home is here, my job…"

"They'll kill you if you stay."

He shut up, and Dan Moseley pulled him into the entrance of yet another branch tunnel, away from any possible gunfire. Chutani Muhammad walked slowly forward, his hands feeling the contours of the side of the tunnel. Nolan kept a tight hold of his collar with one hand, the huge knife held in the other hand, ready to slash down if he looked as if he was about to shout a warning. But the man was cowed, a professional politician to his fingertips. He'd clearly worked out what was to his best advantage. He was already calculating how to make the new arrangement work for him, and even turn it into a profit. He stopped and looked at Nolan.

"What will you give me if I show you this place?"

"We let you live."

Muhammad shook his head. "I want more than that. Give me something worth helping you for, a reason to join you. You will not find the bunker without me."

Nolan smiled inwardly; obviously loyalty to his own people was not this guy's main priority.

"We'll get you to the States, American citizenship."

"I want one million dollars, enough for me to start a new life. And a US passport."

Yeah, along with ninety percent of the Muslim world.

"How about a Manhattan apartment and a late model Chevrolet?"

The Pakistani sensed the irony in his words. "I have told you what I want, a million dollars and a passport. Do we have a deal?"

Nolan nodded without any hesitation. Killing Riyad bin Laden was beyond price, and he knew the Pentagon would okay any arrangement, if the Minister lived. "Deal. Where is it?"

"It's along here, about another ten meters up ahead." He started to go forward, but Nolan gripped him harder.

"Be careful! If you want to live long enough to spend that money, don't do anything stupid."

"Don't worry, I won't."

They crept forward until Muhammad whispered they should stop. There was a right-hand branch leading off from the tunnel, but he ignored it and looked to the left. A section of the tunnel wall had been repaired recently with new metal beams and signs of fresh concrete. He pointed to a piece of rusting steel, part of the reinforcing structure.

"You press down hard on that metal, and a section of wall opens out to a doorway. On the other side is the bunker system. It is soundproofed, so they cannot hear us, and we cannot hear them."

"Does it lead up to the surface?"

"Yes, of course it does. The entrance is in front of the stairwell of the main house, a trapdoor concealed in the floor."

Boswell was watching and listening nearby. Nolan turned to him. "That should take care of getting inside, if he's telling the truth. Can you get someone to take care of this guy, Lt? It's about time we started the assault."

"Yeah, Whitman, where are you?"

Jack Whitman appeared a couple of seconds later.

"Take care of this prisoner, Jack. We may need him again, so don't let anything happen to him."

"I've got it."

He took hold of the man's arm and led the Minister into the right-hand tunnel branch. Boswell called the Platoon to cluster around him.

"Brad, I need a rearguard. Stay here and watch our six. You're designated," he paused, and smiled. "Bravo Six. I don't want to get trapped inside the compound if anyone comes in behind us."

Brad Rose cursed under his breath, "Who the hell wants to be left behind at this moment?" But he nodded his agreement.

"We'll go in hard and fast," Boswell continued. "I want you right behind me. I'll pull the door open. Will, you can go in first and clear any obstacles in our way. Lucas, you stay with him. Remember, this is it. There are hostiles the other side, so keep sharp. And if you see this Riyad character, you know what is required of us."

Bryce nodded. "Copy that."

"Chief, you'll come in behind me with Captain Noguchi. We may need her language skills if we have to question anyone. The rest of you, we'll split into two squads when we're inside. I want half the men to follow me, the rest go with Will. If we don't find Riyad the other side of this door, and the action spreads through the main house, I'll take the first floor and hold it. Will, you take the second and third floors. Chief, you hold the rear with Mariko and wait for orders. Make sure you guard against anyone coming into the house from outside. Any questions?"

There were no questions. It was a simple plan, and simple plans were always the best. Boswell nodded, satisfied.

"Will, Lucas, do it. Let's go."

The Lieutenant put his hand on the rusty metal bar. At first nothing happened. He pushed harder and hammered hard until it finally gave and slid back. The wall swung out into the tunnel, revealing a short passage, no more than a meter long. They pointed their weapons inside. All that was revealed was an empty space with no signs of life. Will ran forward with his squad on his heels, and entered. A few seconds later, his voice came over the commo.

"There's no one in here, but we're in the right place. The bunker system looks like it has several rooms. We'll check them out one by one, but I don't see anyone down here."

"Copy that," Boswell replied. "Second squad, stand by. We're moving in."

They crept forward, and then Nolan's whole world erupted in smoke and flame. As his brain registered 'stun grenade', he was automatically diving for cover as a huge shockwave sucked the breath out of his body. Everything went dark as his NV goggles overloaded, and he wrenched them off. Mariko was lying on the ground groaning, and he crawled over to her.

"Are you okay?"

"Yes, it wasn't the grenade. Someone hit me."

She got to her feet, and he looked around.

Chutani Muhammad, the bastard's gone. So much for making deals with politicians. Where the hell is Whitman?

"Lt, watch yourself, the Minister has legged it. He may come up behind you."

"Copy that," Boswell replied. "If he tries to get out of the tunnels, Brad and Vince will nail his ass. Is anyone down?"

A chorus of negatives came over the commo. Two men were missing.

"Jack? Come in, Whitman, where are you? Nixon, what's the deal? Were you injured in that blast? Over."

There was only silence.

"All of you, keep your eyes skinned for any sign of Jack or Richard. They may be hurt. We'll have to check out what happened to them on the way back. There's no time now. The enemy will have heard that stun grenade explode, so let's nail the big bad bastard before he hightails it. And if anyone sees that fucking Pakistani Minister, Muhammad, give him a heavy caliber present from me. Let's move, people."

There was no need to look further for one of the missing men. They came across the body of Nixon. Nolan bent down to examine him, and his heart missed a beat. The Seal's throat had been cut!

How the hell did anyone manage to catch him off guard? The Minister, we searched him, and he didn't possess a knife. Surely it wasn't him! Besides, he didn't seem the physical type to take down a Navy Seal. It's highly unlikely it was him, but if not, who killed him?

He made a note to take Nixon's body out when they left, and he wondered about Whitman.

Will we be carrying his body away? Has he been taken the same way, from behind, maybe by the same guy who threw the grenade? And if so, where is he, has he run out of the tunnel system? In which case Boswell was right, Brad and Vince will stop him. God only knows what other traps this bunker system has in store for us.

But there was no time to check around further. There were no signs of any further opposition in the bunker system, and they had to react fast before the principal target ran. Time was 'a wasting', as the saying went. Will led the way and threw open the trapdoor that led upward. They surged up into the house, and Nolan was struck by the importance of such a historic occasion. The second battle of the Abbottabad compound was about to begin, the battle for the leadership of America and the World's number one enemy. He climbed out of the trapdoor, pulling Mariko up behind him. She was still shaky after the blast of the stun grenade. He ducked as a burst of gunfire whistled overhead, dragging her away from the trapdoor to take shelter in the stairwell. It was protected by the concrete staircase. In front of it, there were heavy iron gates guarding the route to the upper floors to prevent unwelcome visitors. They'd been thrown open, and the unwelcome visitors had arrived.

"That gunfire, it came from upstairs," Mariko murmured to him. "It can only mean he's still here. He's trapped."

"Let's hope so."

Will's squad hurtled up the stairs, firing on the run. They heard a scream, and a body tumbled down from the next floor. The man, a native, lay at an unnatural angle on the floor. He was still wearing a chest rack for his spare clips and a canvas pistol holster. The fall had broken his neck, but his body was also riddled with wounds, so he was probably dead before he fell. The commo was alive with reports. Boswell's squad ran from room to room, searching for their targets, shouting 'clear!' above the increasing din of gunfire from the defenders as the firefight intensified. And then the outside door of the residence was flung open, and four armed men dashed inside. Nolan called Boswell, keeping his voice to a low murmur.

"Lt, we got trouble. Four hostiles just came in the main door, and they're right behind you."

A burst of firing came from one of the first floor rooms, and Boswell's voice came back to him, almost drowned by the sounds of the shots. The enemy was fighting back hard.

"Copy that, Chief. We have our own problems. The

place is full of guards. We've found a dozen or more of them, and they're everywhere. Can you hold those shooters who came in the front door? We need time to settle this bunch in here."

"Understood, I'll take care of it."

They hadn't seen him or Mariko as yet. They'd slowed down and were creeping further inside the house, their assault rifles held ready to fire.

"You got that pistol of yours ready?" he whispered to Mariko. "I'll try and knock them all down, but if any get past me, you'll have to deal with them."

She nodded nervously. "I'm ready."

He knelt unseen in the shadows of the stairwell and leveled the MP7 as they crept nearer. He sighted on the first man, squeezed the trigger, and was already shifting his aim as they started to react. The second man went down, but the last two managed to get off a burst of fire, forcing him back into cover. He felt a hammer blow as one of the 7.62mm rounds impacted on his vest, but he ducked back out and fired off the last bullets in his clip. He saw another of the men go down. The HK MP7 clicked on empty, and he ripped out a spare mag. As he was ramming it into the weapon, he looked up. The fourth man was only two meters away and coming toward him. He smiled as he saw Nolan reloading, ignoring the blue-burqa clad woman as he aimed straight at the Seal's head. Nolan tensed, ready to throw himself to one side, as the man stepped nearer to be certain of the shot. Mariko was a woman, anonymous inside the burqa and of no consequence. Until her hand emerged from the voluminous folds of material, clutching the Baby Glock. She fired twice. The first bullet hit the guy in the chest, and he staggered but still kept hold of his rifle. The second bullet impacted in the center of his face, shattering his nose as it drilled forward and up into the brain. He crashed to the floor. Nolan ran out, kicked his rifle away from the body, just in case, and sped out toward the main door. It was slightly ajar, and when he peered out, he saw a band of fighters rushing to the house.

"Bravo One, this is Two. More hostiles inbound. I count at least ten, probably more on the way."

"Copy that. Try and hold them off. We're still heavily engaged here."

"I'm on it, Lt."

Where the hell are they all coming from? They're like lice pouring out of the woodwork. We'll just have to kill them like lice, but these lice are armed with assault rifles. The odds are not looking good.

He keyed his mic. "Will, how are things going up there?"

The big black PO1 sounded hassled, maybe for the first time since Nolan had been working with him.

"We got a real fight on our hands, Chief. The target is barricaded into some kind of a safe room. They're defending it like crazy. As soon as we get through to it, I'll get Zeke to blow the door, but it'll take time."

"We'll come up and lend a hand, Will," Boswell informed him. "We're pretty much clear down here."

"Make it as fast as you can. They're coming in from everywhere."

"We're on the way. They're like a bunch of mad dogs, these guys."

Nolan listened to the exchange. It was true. They were fighting fanatically. It made him think of what he knew about the end of World War Two, when Hitler's fanatic SS legions had fought almost to the last man.

Why do these men fight to defend bloodthirsty, crazed and tyrannical despots? Despots who can turn a nation into a heap of rubble and misery, in no time at all. No one knows, but there's only one way to deal with mad dogs. Put them down.

"Copy that."

He peered out of the door again. The hostiles were nearer, only a few meters away. He stepped out, emptied the MP7 into the group, and stepped back inside the heavy oak doors, just as the return fire chewed chunks of wood from the timber. He rammed a fresh clip in the HK and handed it to Mariko.

"Time to get out of that fancy dress. We're going to need every gun we've got. And then some."

She nodded quickly and began to remove the burqa. Underneath, she was wearing Multicam gear like the rest of them. But she had no vest, no ballistic plates, and no half helmet.

Shit!

Nolan resolved to do everything in his power to keep her safe. He took his Mk 11 off his back and found a tiny window, more of an open vent that overlooked the front of the house. It was a perfect firing position, and he leveled the weapon though the makeshift firing loop and opened fire on the fighters milling outside. The suppressed gunfire took them by surprise, and he knocked down four of the hostiles before they realized what was happening and rushed for cover. He could see yet more of them coming into the compound, and it hit him that they'd vastly underestimated the numbers they'd face. Once more, intelligence had proved wrong, and men's lives would likely be lost as a result. Assault rifles blazed away in front of him, and bullets hammered at the house. Some shots came through the window he'd been firing from, and he was forced to pull back inside. He looked around for Mariko and saw she was right behind him. He opened his mouth to speak to her, but several AKs fired from somewhere inside the house, and the building echoed to the sounds of gunfire and screams. He could hear the thuds of the Seals' suppressed weapons as they fired repeatedly, and the screams of the defenders as the murderous barrage of fire cut them down in droves.

But it's close, too close. We haven't killed Riyad bin Laden, and the enemy is still arriving, and in even greater numbers.

"Mariko, we're going to need more time to get this bastard, and those shooters outside are pouring in. We need help. I'll ask Zeke to bring the satcom. I want you to call for air support."

She nodded as he called their comms man, Zeke Murray.

"This is Bravo Two. Zeke, can you make it to the first floor hallway. We're in the stairwell, and I need the radio."

A loud explosion shook the building, and chunks of plaster rained down on them. Zeke's voice replied, "I'm pretty close to you, in the room next to the kitchen. One of our guys just tossed a grenade into the next room and cleared out the opposition. There's a door opens onto the hallway. I'm coming through now."

"Copy that."

The door close to them opened cautiously. "This is Zeke, I'm coming out!"

"I've got you, go ahead."

Zeke came slowly through the door, and Nolan relaxed.

It wasn't always possible to guess when the enemy might try something inventive and pretend to be a friend. Zeke handed over the encrypted satcom that would connect them with Jacks and Weathers at Jalalabad JSOC headquarters.

"Anything I can do?"

"Just kill as many of the bastards as you can. We're calling in air support. We can't do the job with so many of the bastards queuing up to take potshots at us."

He grinned. "Good plan. I'll get back to it."

He turned and went back through the door he'd just emerged from, diving to one side as he entered. There was a renewed burst of suppressed firing, and an agonized scream. Another hostile had gone down.

"Mariko, get on that radio. We need support, and we need it now! They'll have to send in something to target those hostiles and clear the ground outside to stop any more of them coming at us. We'll also need a watch on the tunnel exit. They may try to stage a blocking action there."

She nodded. "Understood, I'll get onto it right away. Kyle, I could instruct them to target the missile launchers inside the compound, and they could send the helo right in here and take us off the roof. No need to go back through the tunnel."

He thought for a few seconds. "Yeah, get through to them, and see what they can do. An exfil from here would be sweet. Try 'em."

She made the connection with Jalalabad. Nolan looked away and peered through the tiny window overlooking the courtyard as an explosion sounded from above, from somewhere up on the roof. He was in time to see a body crash down to the ground from the roof, a robed body.

What the hell?

"This is Bravo Two, what's going on up on the roof?"

Vince's voice came back to him. "We just got out here, Chief, Dave Eisner and me. There were a couple of hostiles on the rooftop, but Dave lobbed a grenade, and it took them out, blew one of them clean over the top. We're setting up a position to cover the ground around the house, just give us a moment."

"Copy that. Outstanding, Vince. Those hostiles have to be stopped before they can counterattack the main house. There are too many of the bastards."

"We're on it."

As he watched, the fighters in the courtyard started to fall to the hail of fire from above. There was little cover from the two men; one a sniper perched so high he could overlook the entire compound. The enemy fighters fell. One man was thrown backward to sprawl in a heap of bloody rags and broken flesh, then another, and another. Dave fired a series of short burst with his HK416, reloaded, and then emptied a clip on full auto that decimated another group of fighters who were running for cover from the devastating sniper fire. Boswell's urgent shout came over the commo.

"Heads up, people. Zeke has the safe room door wired ready to blow. Stand by, with any luck we can finish this and go home. We're almost there, so hang in there. Okay, Zeke, let her go."

Zeke's voice instantly came into his earpiece. "Fire in the hole!"

Nolan ducked automatically even though he was nowhere near the site of the explosion. A massive blast shook the building. There was renewed firing, as Riyad bin Laden's guards desperately tried to block the final assault on their Sheikh's last refuge. Grenades went off, and Nolan heard the gunfire, the shouts and screams as the endgame fought through its last moments.

And then it was done. Will's exultant voice came over the commo, "Target is down, I repeat, the target is down. That's a confirmed kill. We're taking photos right now and getting the DNA swabs. I can't see the Lieutenant, does anyone know where he is?"

"This is Grant, he's been hurt. He's with me. We're out on the landing."

"How bad is he, Lucas?"

"A round went right through his vest. I dunno, maybe it was faulty, or the range was just too short. He's bleeding badly. We need to get him out of here."

Nolan interrupted. "Do your best with him. We're calling in the helo to exfil from the roof."

He started toward the stairs, but Mariko stopped him. "It's Admiral Jacks on the radio from J-bad. He says they have a pair of RAF Reapers standing by to lend a hand. They were the nearest aircraft they had available. They're both overhead right now."

"Understood, patch me through to the controller."

A few seconds later, he heard an unfamiliar British voice in his earpiece. "This is Groves, 39 Squadron, RAF Creech Air Force Base. How can we help you, Chief Petty Officer Nolan?"

"What are you carrying, Groves?"

"Hellfires, Chief. Both Reapers are over your position. They're carrying a full load of missiles."

"Can you see the action around the compound?"

"Yes. I have the main house in sight, and I can see

what looks like two of your men on the rooftop. In the courtyard, there are several groups of fighters forming up. It looks like two units at the front of the house, about forty men, and another fifteen or so hostiles at the rear."

"What about anti-aircraft missiles? I heard they had missile sites around the compound."

There was a hesitation, then, "Searching now. Yes, I have them, two sites; both are manned and look as if they're ready to shoot. Chief, there could be another problem. There's a convoy of vehicles headed your way. It's safe to assume they're reinforcements on their way to pitch in."

"Copy that, RAF. Take them both out."

"Two missile sites to be targeted, understood. Confirm your order to destroy both of them, Bravo."

"Bravo confirmed."

Nolan looked around the hallway where he was still holding tight with Mariko.

We're safe for the present, but things are rapidly going to hell. There's still a good chance we can get out with the unit intact if the Predators are effective. And if the attack is successful, and if no more fighters come to reinforce the compound. It's too many 'ifs'.

He thought of Vince and Dave up on the roof, exposed to any secondary effects of the Hellfire bombardment, and called them.

"This is Bravo Two. Vince, Dave, get off that roof. There's a bunch of Hellfires coming down around us. There'll be metal and debris flying every which way all over the compound."

"Copy that," Vince's voice replied. "We'll come down inside and hunker down until it's over."

"Understood. When the Reapers are finished, you'll

need to secure the roof again. I'm fixing up an exfil direct from right here. We'll get the Chinook to come straight in when the missile sites have been taken out."

"Copy that."

It's close, very close, but there are still too many 'ifs'.

He keyed his mic. "Lucas, how's the Lieutenant doing?"

"Not good. He needs help. We could do with a corpsman."

Nolan thought of Jack Whitman. He'll know how to keep him going, but where the hell is he?

"This is Bravo Two, Whitman, what's your situation?"

The radio hissed with static but no reply.

"Has anyone seen Whitman? He's supposed to be with Nazir. He should be looking for that Paki Minister." The silence mocked him.

What is he up to? If he's alive. Unless he's somewhere, like in the tunnel system where his radio won't work properly. That must be it. Another 'if'.

"Will, what's your twenty?"

"We're holding on the third floor. Vince and Dave just came down to join us. All quiet here."

As if to contradict him, a burst of firing came from the second floor.

"Hostiles, hostiles in the media center," someone shouted.

He could hear the sound of renewed firing, echoing down the stairwell. Dan called him.

"Chief, a bunch of guys were hiding in the media center. We're dealing with them now."

"Are you..."

"Grenade!"

Another burst of firing, and then there was silence.

Before he could ask, Dan came back on the commo.

"We got them all, second floor is clear, repeat clear."

"Copy that."

He turned to Mariko. "We need that Chinook here mighty fast, as soon as the Reapers have taken out the defenses. We have to get out before they attack again."

She nodded and turned to the satcom to call Jalalabad. Nolan remembered the men downstairs.

"This is Two, Brad, can you hear me? Come in, Bravo Six."

A silence, and nothing.

"Bravo Six, do you read, over?"

And then there was a faint signal. "This is Six. The tunnel is breaking up the signal, but I can just about hear you."

"Good. Come through the tunnel and join us inside the main residence. We're fixing up an exfil from the roof. We've called in a Chinook."

"Understood, I'll to come through to the residence."

"Yeah. Brad, watch out for Whitman. He was with Nazir, guarding the Paki Minister before he escaped. He may have recaptured him by now. Bring them up to join us."

Mariko caught his attention. "Hold it, Brad. What is it, Captain?"

"I got through to Jacks. The Chinook is on the way, and it's almost here."

"Understood, I'll…"

He stopped as the compound erupted with a series of explosions. The Hellfires had struck their targets.

"Bravo Six, hurry it up. That sounds like the air defenses just went down, so we'll be getting out of here real soon."

His voice came over even more faintly. "Copy...., I'm ...…."

It would have to do. Nolan assumed he was on the way. It was time to get the evacuation organized.

"Lucas, get Boswell up to the roof. The helo is on the way in. I'll secure everything down here and come up. Brad is on his way. He's rounding up Whitman and Nazir Masih. Hopefully, he'll have recaptured the prisoner."

"I'll need some help to lift the Lieutenant."

A new voice interrupted.

"This is Will. My boys and me will lend a hand. We're close by."

"Copy that. Brad, how're you making out?"

Silence.

"Brad, come in. Any sign of Whitman?"

The silence mocked him. He decided Brad must still be in the tunnel, where'd he be out of contact. He was worried about Whitman.

The guy is probably out of radio contact for the same reason, but all the same, he's been quiet for a long time. He'll have to take care of himself, he shrugged.

He walked over to check the double doors that guarded the entrance. They were the only way in or out, with the exception of the hatch into the tunnel. The doors were solid oak, furnished with heavy iron fastenings. There was a wide, heavy bolt top and bottom, still slid across. It should hold anyone trying to get in, at least for long enough for them to make their getaway. He keyed his mic.

"Vince, how's it looking down on the ground?"

"Chief, those Hellfires did a good job. The anti aircraft sites are heaps of junk, and the scores of fighters were wiped out when they hit. There're a few squirters running around, darting from place to place and taking potshots at us. I expect they're trying to figure out how to come at us again. Chief, they'll have more fighters on the way, that's for sure. They can't be too pleased we've pissed all over their backyard. Lucas has just joined us with Will's unit. They've brought up Boswell."

"Understood. I'll stay down here and wait for Brad and Jack to get in."

"They in trouble?"

"I'm not certain. They may be okay. Let me know when that helo turns up."

"You can be sure of that. We'll make it out, Chief."

"Even Boswell? Will he make it?"

"Lucas reckons if he gets back to civilization pretty soon, his chances are good."

"Copy that. I'll hold here and call as soon as Whitman and Rose arrive, and then we'll come on up."

"Sure."

He went around the ground floor, checking the shutters were securely closed, and then went to recheck the heavy oak entrance door. It was just as secure as the last time he'd checked it, but something bugged him. An eerie silence had descended on the house.

It feels like, what? He had to work it through his brain. Yeah, it feels like the house is holding its breath. It's too quiet. Waiting for the shitstorm that's about to hit. Where the hell is that Chinook?

He noticed Mariko staring at him.

"What?"

She smiled, a tired smile, and her face was covered in dirt. "Nothing. You're doing okay, Nolan. You've got a situation out front, upstairs, underground, and Christ knows where else, and you're holding it all together. Impressive."

"It will be if we get out of here."

"We will. Give me a moment. I want to check something out in the next room. I thought I heard something a moment ago. I'll take a last look around before we leave. I don't think it's anything to worry about."

He nodded, "Be careful."

His attention was diverted when a new voice came into his earpiece. "Bravo, this is 160th Special Operations Aviation Regiment, inbound from Jalalabad. Do you copy?"

Thank Christ for that.

"This is Bravo, I copy. What is your ETA?"

"Eight minutes, Bravo. Make sure you're ready to exfil. The Paks have fighters in the area. I don't want to tangle with them. This flying bus would be hard put to fight off an angry buzzard."

"Understood, I'll make sure our people are all on the roof ready to climb aboard. Our location is the largest building in the compound."

A short pause, and then the voice replied in a flat tone. "We've been there before, Bravo."

Of course they have, the 160th, Neptune Spear, the mission that successfully eliminated Osama bin Laden.

"Copy that."

He looked back as a loud noise echoed through the hallway. The hatch had been thrown open, and Brad Rose's familiar head appeared.

"Brad, thank Christ, did you see…"

He realized that Brad carried no weapon, and he'd lost his helmet and armored vest. Behind him, Jack Whitman followed, carrying his Sig Sauer pointed at Brad's back. They climbed out of the hatch, and Nazir Masih followed. Then Chutani Muhammad climbed out, also clutching a pistol. This one pressed into Nazir's back.

"Jack, what the hell?"

But he didn't need to ask. In that fraction of a second, it all clicked into place. His mind flashed back to the artist's sketches of the rapist he'd seen when he was taken into custody. The pictures had been released to his defense attorney, Edward Oakley III. It could have been Nolan, sure, but it was also a perfect fit for Whitman. He thought back to the missions when Whitman had been on the same operation. When there'd been a killing.

I thought Lucas Grant was the most likely candidate, but I was blind. It was Whitman!

"Drop the weapon, Chief."

"And if I don't?"

"Then your friend Bradford Rose gets a bullet in his head. I've no doubt Mr. Muhammad will be happy to do the honors for Nazir. He can go to meet his late father, so maybe it's not such a bad idea."

Nolan needed time, time to get on top of this.

"Don't kill anyone, Whitman. Just tell me what you want. We can discuss it, and maybe we can all get out of here."

Brad's eyes were almost closed, his face partially covered in blood where Whitman had probably taken him by surprise. He tried to catch Brad's attention, but Rose looked as if he was still stunned. Nazir appeared uninjured so far, and Chutani Muhammad wore an expression of triumph, now that the tables were turned.

"I want you to drop the weapon, Nolan," Whitman

repeated.

"No. I do that, and you'll just kill me. Tell me what you want. We can strike a deal and part company."

"No, you cannot do that," Muhammad shouted. "Kill him, you must kill him. He has insulted me. You agreed!"

"Shut up," Whitman snarled. "Are you on your own down here?"

Nolan thought of Mariko. He nodded. "They're on the roof."

"Waiting for exfil?"

So he didn't know. It meant he'd somehow lost his radio or switched it off.

"Just tell me what you want, Jack."

"Okay, you got it. I want five million dollars to set up a new life."

"And what makes you think we'd give it to you, once we've left here?"

Whitman grinned. "Because I'll keep ol' Brad here as a guarantee. Soon as the money is paid, he goes home."

"It was you who raped those women, Whitman, wasn't it?"

He laughed. "You only just worked that out, did you? Damn, I covered that up pretty well. Who did you think it was, Lucas Grant?" He saw the flicker in Nolan's eyes. "Yeah, I thought so. I planted a few hints, just in case I needed a scapegoat. Didn't do too badly setting you up on that website either, did I? Got your cop girlfriend pretty pissed at you too!"

"And those people, those poor bastards you killed while we were on operations. Why did you do it?" Nolan was white with rage.

He laughed out loud. "Why do it? For the best reason

in the world, that's why. Because I could, and because I loved it, every second. Do you know what it feels like, to hold that kind of power over people? It's better than sex, although," he laughed again, "sometimes I get the sex as well. I don't always kill those women, not if they please me. I might want 'em again. I don't want to have to screw a corpse. That'd be gross, even for me."

His laugh was grating now, and crazed.

"You must kill him," the Minister insisted.

"Must I?" Whitman gazed at the Pakistani. Then he pointed his Sig and fired, a single bullet that took the Minister in the gut. He fell to the ground, screaming shrilly, blood pouring from his belly. He lay there, and his screams echoed around the house. Whitman laughed again.

"I never could stand people telling me what to do, especially a fucking raghead."

He looked at the man and fired a single shot into his forehead. Muhammad slumped, and they heard the last breath sigh out of his body.

"Those screams annoyed me. Now, me and Brad here are going back into the tunnel. We'll just, kind of, disappear into the night. I'll call you, Nolan, say in a day or two. I've got my own satphone, so when I make the call, you'll never know where it's coming from. We'll…"

"Chinook in sight, Chief. You have to come up here!"

Will's voice, calling down the staircase from the roof.

Whitman screwed the gun barrel hard into Brad's neck.

"You stay where you are, Chief. Don't move."

"I need to leave, and I have to take Brad and Nazir with me."

"Oh, sure, the fuck you do. Tell you what. You can take the kid. He's no use to me."

He pushed Nazir at Nolan, who thrust him out of the line of fire. Then Whitman started back toward the hatch that descended to the tunnel, pulling Brad in front of him. And he cannoned into Mariko, who'd moved unseen into position right behind him.

"What the…"

She fired, emptying the whole of the Baby Glock clip into him. The first rounds took Whitman under his arm, and he dropped his gun. She shifted her aim, and the rest of the shots embedded themselves into his head so that when he hit the floor, he was dead. Behind him, Mariko stood shaking. She was breathing hard and clicking the firing pin of the empty pistol, again and again. Nolan went and took from her shaking fingers.

"It's okay, it's all over."

She nodded, but she was still shaking badly. Nolan held her and looked at Brad.

"Can you get up to the roof?"

"Yeah, I'll make it. Bastard jumped me. I didn't realize what he was up to until it was too late. He'd made a deal with that Paki Minister. I wonder why the hell he changed his mind."

"He thought he could get more money from the US government. How much did Muhammad offer him?"

"A hundred thousand dollars to help him escape."

Nolan nodded. "That explains it. If Muhammad could have offered him six million dollars, he would have shot one of us instead. Is the tunnel clear, no one else inside?"

"There was just us, except for the body of Richard Nixon down there, at the foot of the staircase."

"I'll go get him. I'm not leaving him here. Go up to the roof. Mariko, you go with Brad. Nazir, you go too."

Mariko shook her head. "I'm staying with you, Kyle. You may need a hand with that body."

"That's a negative, get up top."

"Sorry, Chief, I outrank you. I'm coming. Brad, Nazir, go up to the roof and get ready to leave."

Nolan watched helplessly as she rushed down the staircase into the bunker. He followed her and found her trying to pick up Nixon's body. He pushed her to one side and hoisted the corpse onto his shoulders in the classic fireman's lift. Then he nodded at Mariko.

"Time to move. If that's okay with you, Captain."

She gave him a small smile. "I'll be right behind you."

His earpiece clicked. "Chinook is overhead, Chief. We're winching Boswell inside right now. They've lowered a ladder, so we'll start climbing aboard as soon as the Lieutenant is clear."

"Copy that. I'm on the way up. I'll need the winch for Nixon's body. He comes with us."

"Understood. Any other bodies?"

He thought of Whitman.

Traitor and murderous rapist.

"None."

As he rushed past the second floor, he could see out of the windows. Flames were licking around the compound, most of them started by the detonations of the Hellfires. He ducked back as several bullets whistled past him. A few of them had regrouped outside and were already firing at them. He couldn't make out the location of the shooters, but it was enough to know they'd brought in more fighters. They were clearly determined to keep up the pressure in an attempt to make the Americans pay for daring to mount a second attack on their precious 'Sheikh'. He ran up the last staircase, his muscles screaming with the weight of the heavy body. Willing hands helped him put Nixon down on the concrete, ready to winch up. But they weren't out of trouble yet. Will loomed over him.

"We've got more trouble, Chief. They've brought up a machine gun. They're going to try to bring down the helo."

Nolan looked up. Boswell was just being winched aboard, and the first of the Seals were scaling the ladder.

"Can we do anything about it?"

"That's a negative. They're keeping well behind cover, but they can hardly miss the Chinook. It's a mighty big target. I'd guess they'll be ready to open fire any second."

"How many machine guns and how many fighters?"

"Maybe ten or so, and just the one machine gun so far."

He heard the rattle of automatic fire, and the Chinook rocked as a line of bullets stitched across the fuselage. It wouldn't take too many hits like that to bring it down.

"Okay, here's the deal. We'll have to let the helo get away from here now before it's hit badly. We'll go out through the tunnel, so the helo can pick us up from the other end. That was the original plan. Get Nixon's body on the winch line fast, and the rest of us will go out underground. It's the only way, otherwise we'll lose that Chinook, and it's our ticket home. Mariko, call up the crew and tell 'em what we want them to do."

She nodded and began talking to the Chinook.

Nolan could see that Will looked doubtful.

"What is it?"

"The gomers in the compound. There are more of them arriving all the time. They'll follow us down into the tunnel system and come after us. They could even try to take down the Chinook the other end if they get that far."

"In that case, we'd better make sure they don't get the chance."

Nixon's body had gone aboard. The crew chief's face appeared in the open ramp, looking down, and Nolan waved him away. The engine sound changed as the pilot adjusted the collective and hauled the big craft away into the night, pursued by sporadic gunfire. He looked around his dwindling command. There were a dozen of them left on the rooftop, including Nazir Masih, who he'd kept back in case they needed help finding their way out. It was time to head out. He'd had enough of the bin Laden compound anyway, more than enough to last any man a lifetime.

"Let's move out!"

They hurtled down the staircase, and Nolan called Zeke alongside him as they ran.

"We need to stop those hostiles from following us down the tunnel system. Can you rig anything?"

Zeke grinned. "I'd guess a booby trap would fit the bill, bury a few of the bastards. If I lay everything I have, it'll take down the residence as well and bury the bunker for good and all."

"Sounds good to me." He shouted at Merano. "Vince, stay with Zeke while he fixes the charges. They'll be right on our tail, so stay sharp."

"Copy that."

When they reached the ground floor, the oak doors were already starting to buckle as the enemy made frantic attempts to get inside.

"It'll hold them for a short time," Will noted, as he ripped out the half empty clip from his HK and slammed in a new one. He gave Zeke a worried look. "Five minutes, maybe ten, that's about all we've got. It's going to be tight. I wouldn't take too much time, if I were you."

"I hear you. Don't worry, fear will lend me wings, as they say."

"It better," the big PO1 mumbled as the thick door shuddered to a furious attempt to break it down. They reached the hatch that led down into the tunnels. Nolan sent Mariko ahead with Nazir to make certain they used the correct route back. Then he checked his men as they dropped down the narrow stairway. Zeke finally dropped down with Vince still watching his back. Then there was just him and Will.

"After you," he invited Bryce.

"You want the honor of being the last person to see this place intact?"

"Not really. I'm not planning on writing it up when we get back. I just like to see my people go out first. It's a commander's prerogative."

"That it is." Will went ahead. He jumped down and ran through the bunker, following the huge, armored back of Will Bryce. Zeke was already at work just outside the start of the tunnels, planting what looked like enough explosives to take down a shopping mall. He looked up as Nolan came abreast of him.

"I found this stuff in a couple of wooden crates in the corner of the bunker. It's what the Afghans use to make IEDs, so I thought it'd be a way to put it to better use. It's ex-Soviet stuff, probably they left it behind when they bailed out of the region."

"As long as it makes a big bang."

"Oh yeah, I guarantee it."

"Just make it quick, Zeke. We're running out of time here. Three minutes, no more."

"Copy that."

"And remember, we're out of radio contact in this place, so just plant it and get out."

"Understood."

Will was jogging along the tunnel, his head bent to stop banging his helmet on the stone roof. Nolan followed him, and it seemed endless, but finally he saw the starlit sky ahead, and the dark shapes of the Platoon gathered just outside the entrance. Two men had positioned a Minimi M247 pointing back along the tunnel, in case any hostiles leaked through. The rest had formed a defensive perimeter around the outside to watch for any wayward Pakistani patrols. As he emerged into the night, he heard the welcome clatter of the CH-47 dropping down gently for a landing.

"As soon as the wheels touch the ground, let's go," he shouted. "The timing on this is operation is shot to hell. If we don't get out of here fast, we'll have the Pakistan military taking an interest. And they've got an Air Force with fast jets, guys, don't forget that."

"They're already taking an interest," Mariko called over to him. She'd been talking to the Chinook crew while she waited to board. She put the commset down and walked across. "The Pakistani Air Force has launched a couple of air superiority fighters. One of our AWACS aircraft over the border picked them up taking off from Peshawar. The electronic warfare guys say they've been targeted to investigate the airspace around Abbottabad for a suspected incursion."

"Damn. How long before they get here?"

"Five minutes, no more."

"Got it."

He looked around as the Chinook landed, and the men started piling aboard. He looked along the tunnel, but there was no sign of Zeke and Vince. He ran to the tunnel entrance, shouting for them to hurry. Nothing. The machine gun was still staring into the darkness. He told the crew to get aboard the helo, and when he looked again, there was only Mariko on the ground waiting. He shouted across to her.

"Get on board. We'll be leaving any second."

She nodded, but she still waited. She was holding an assault rifle, an HK416, obviously mounting guard against anything unexpected. Nolan seethed, but there was nothing more he could do, except wait. Wait for his two men to arrive. Wait for the hostiles to come out of the tunnel shooting if anything went wrong with the explosives. Wait for the Pakistani Air Force to arrive and force the Chinook to land and take them into captivity. Or wait to get back to J-Bad, where the military cops may be waiting to take him in for murder. He thought back to Whitman's confession.

Mariko heard it, but will they believe her, if the cops know we've been intimate? We can't hide it. There are few secrets on a base. Nazir overheard Whitman, but did he understand? And will they believe him? It's ironic. We killed a rapist murderer, and yet that may have prevented me from dragging Whitman to justice and proving my innocence.

He felt his anger and frustration mounting. Mariko was on the encrypted commo again, maybe talking to J-Bad. They'd got what they wanted, the big bad wolf, Riyad bin Laden, was dead. All that was left was to get Bravo

Platoon home safe, as well as the valuable Chinook helo and its crew, and all in the face of a pair of supersonic fighter interceptors. The irony was they were likely to be missile-armed F-16 Fighting Falcons, supplied to them originally by the US. The General Dynamics Company and subsequently Lockheed built fighters were obsolete inside the US Air Force, but it was still a lightning fast, highly maneuverable, and heavily armed combat aircraft. The Chinook would be a dead duck if they met up in the skies of Waziristan.

Suddenly Zeke and Vince ran out of the tunnel.

"We're set, Chief. We have to get out of there before they trip the charge. It's going to be one mighty big bang."

"Understood, get aboard the helo. We're leaving."

They ran up the ramp, and he took Mariko's arm, hustling her up into the fuselage. Boswell lay on a heap of improvised bedding behind the cockpit bulkhead, being tended to by two of the Seals, Lucas and Dave. He didn't see the body of Richard Nixon, but he knew it would be close by. The twin turboshafts whined as the rotors picked up speed, and within seconds, the heavy aircraft was climbing slowly into the night sky of Waziristan. The nose tilted as the pilot banked and turned north, right at the moment their pursuers ran into Zeke's booby trap. The sky lit up with jets of flame, followed by roiling clouds of dense black smoke. The Chinook was thrown over on its side by the force of the pressure wave that hit them, and they clung on to the internal struts for support. The pilot was no rookie, the 160th Special Aviation Regiment was chosen from the very best to be the finest in their profession. He hauled the aircraft around, tilting the fuselage along the outward direction of the explosion, running with it, riding it like an expert surfer on one of the mighty waves that periodically broke on the beaches at Maui. He twisted the heavy craft this way and that, following the invisible air currents that tore at the fragile airframe. Finally, he managed to regain full control, and the Chinook steadied on a northerly course, toward the distant mountains of the Hindu Kush, and Afghanistan. They were going home. The crew chief touched his arm, and he looked around.

"Skipper wants you up front, Chief. Go on up to the cockpit."

"Is there a problem?"

"Could be, yeah."

The nose was tilted up as the helo continued to claw for height. Nolan grabbed for handholds and swung his way forward. The co-pilot saw him coming and handed him a headset. He removed his helmet and clipped it on his head, immediately the pilot began speaking to him.

"You're the guy in charge of this outfit?"

"I am, our platoon leader is back there injured."

"Yep, I heard about that. I hope he'll be okay."

"He will if we get him back to a hospital fast."

"Yeah, see, that's the problem. You know they launched a couple of fighters to come chasing our tail."

"Yes."

"I've just had a heads-up from the AWACS aircraft watching this area. They're heading this way like bears toward a honey pot. They will have picked us up on their radar already."

"Can we hide from them?"

The pilot laughed. "In a Chinook? You jest, my friend. No, we can't hide, not in the air. We can't outrun them, outshoot them, or even outshit them if it comes to that."

Nolan smiled.

"What can we do?"

"Two options, Chief. We land somewhere we can go to ground and wait them out. It's not guaranteed because they have their own AWACS systems and onboard lookdown radars. Chances are they'll know where we are. Option two, we surrender."

"How about option three?"

They both looked around at the new voice in their headsets. Captain Mariko Noguchi stood behind them, holding onto the co-pilots seat for support. She'd donned a spare headset to join in, apparently. The pilot glanced at her.

"What's option three, Ma'am? You want us to take them on in air-to-air combat, shoot them down?"

She ignored his sarcasm. "Not quite, but we may be able to arrange someone else to do it for us. I talked to Admiral Jacks in Jalalabad. He's trying to get an escort up to lead us back."

"They'd need some heavy firepower to frighten off those Pakis."

"He knows. He said he'll do his best, so we have to wait and see. But we haven't lost, not yet."

The co-pilot leaned over and spoke in the pilot's ear. He nodded and turned back to them.

"You tell that Admiral they'll need to get here mighty fast. The Paki birds are only a minute or so out. They're already within range if they're carrying air-to-air missiles, and last time I checked, they never left home without them."

"Do you have any defensive capability?" Nolan asked.

"Some," he admitted. "Chaff, not a whole heap more. It may help us, at first anyway, until they get too close. Then their missiles will home on our engines, and they won't be diverted for anything at all. It may still be better to land and sit this out until the escort turns up."

"No!"

He looked at Nolan, surprised at his vehemence.

"What's up?"

"If we land and wait, Lieutenant Boswell will die. He's on the edge as it is. We keep going."

The pilot shrugged. "I hope you know what you're doing, buddy."

They all heard the Pakistani accented English in their headsets.

"Unidentified aircraft, you are in restricted airspace. You are ordered to identify yourself and turn around and land at Peshawar."

The pilot looked at him. "What's it to be?"

"Keep going."

Every second in the air took them a little nearer home, and Boswell to a hospital.

"Unidentified aircraft, acknowledge and turn around, or we will launch our missiles and destroy you."

"He means business, Chief," the pilot warned.

"So do we. Keep it going, Skipper. The escort should be along soon, any second."

"Soon may be too late. We've barely got seconds. Seconds, not minutes or hours. They're about to launch. I may outfly the first pair of missiles, but this flying bus is not designed to go head-to-head with these fighters."

"Missile, missile, incoming!"

The crewmember had picked up the first launch, and

the Chinook crew went into evasive maneuvers. The pilot rammed the collective over, and the helo swooped low and banked hard to starboard, just as the co-pilot activated the automatic chaff dispensers. Nolan and Mariko held on grimly with both hands as the lumbering craft seemed to stand on its end, then fall out of the sky. Above and to the side of them they watched the two missile trails burn past, and there was a blinding explosion as the warheads exploded harmlessly inside the cloud of chaff.

"That's it, we're fucked," the pilot shouted. "Now they've seen how it's done, they'll come in close next time before they launch, and we'll take a hit."

"How far to Afghanistan?"

He looked at the panel. "Maybe thirty kilometers."

"Keep going, do your best to avoid the next missile launch. Just one more, Skipper, and I reckon Jacks will get those fighters here."

"He'd better," he scowled. He looked across at the co-pilot. "Jerry, when they launch again, dump all of the chaff, everything we have. It's a small chance, but it's all we've got."

"Acknowledged, dump all the chaff."

Nolan heard the man mutter, "May as well throw fucking MREs at them, all the good it'll do."

He smiled. MREs, Meals Ready to Eat, were the famous, or infamous, sealed ration packs given out to troops in the field. Most were not enamored of them.

Have I got it wrong? Should we land? But if we do, Boswell will die. If we stay aloft, we might all die. Will Jacks get them here? What the hell should I do?

"Missiles launched, two missiles inbound, estimated six seconds to impact."

Nolan tensed.

Is this the end of a long road? Have I called it wrongly and consigned these people to their deaths? Where are our fighters?

He grabbed Mariko as the sudden lurch of the helo flew her toward him, and he held her tight. The vapor trail stormed past, less than twenty meters off the port side, another miss.

The fourth missile exploded on the aft rotor shaft. The Pakistani pilot had come in from above them, and his missile was attracted to the aft engine. It was interrupted in its plunge at the rear turboshaft engine, or rather the heat given off by that engine, to hit the rotor shaft. The craft staggered in the air, but they all knew the hit was a mortal wound. They were finished. Every man aboard knew that. The only question was whether the pilot could bring down the unwieldy helo intact and keep them alive. Nolan held Mariko to him and watched as the two men fought the controls, trying every trick in the book, and a few that had never been written, to make a soft landing. The fuselage began to turn, picking up speed as the counter-rotating effect of the surviving engine and rotors made it more and more impossible to fly straight and level. They were losing height fast, and when he looked down, there was maybe thirty meters of sky beneath them, and then the possible safety of a flat plain. He pulled Mariko closer to him.

We're going in hard, but it might be survivable if we can get away fast from the wreck. The risk of fire's heavy. We might just walk away from the crash. Well, crawl away.

But the damage was too severe. The rear turboshaft was still trying to turn. The pilot had cut the engine and stopped the fuel supply in an effort to minimize the danger. Their speed worked against them, the rotors were still turning fast. Abruptly, the aft transmission assembly screeched in a parody of an animal in pain, then the bearings seized solid. Fragments of steel and aluminum ripped through the cabin as the engine and gearbox disintegrated, and he pushed Mariko into the co-pilots lap, where the guy's body would shelter her. Nolan was still wearing the headset, but his helmet lay on the tilting floor of the aircraft. He'd removed it to don the headset. When a heavy chunk of the Chinook's shaft finally broke adrift and slammed into his head, he pitched forward. Into blackness, into failure.

CHAPTER NINE

The pain was terrible. The lights shone in his eyes, like the questing gaze of a nightmarish demon. He was being tortured. He realized that.

They can forget it! I won't say anything, not a single word. Fuck 'em!

"You have to talk to us," the voice commanded. The voice hidden behind the lights.

"No, not a word. Fuck you!"

The pain, oh God, it's almost too much to bear. Almost. What have they done to me? It feels like they're using chemicals. Yeah, that's what it is. Let them try; I'll die before I tell them a single thing.

He vaguely remembered the crash, inside Waziristan. Pakistani territory.

So this is a Pakistani torture cell. So much for fucking allies. They shelter a worthless piece of shit like bin Laden, with his misogynistic bunch of religious crazies, but when an American soldier comes in to do something about it, they shoot at him and then torture him. Dear God, it hurts. Bastards!

"You feel bad, do you?"

The voice isn't unkind, oh no. They try to be sympathetic, pump me full of chemicals, and pile on the charm. Fuck 'em! Forget it, you bastards.

"No! I won't tell you!"

"Kyle."

He recognized the voice.

Is it some kind of trick?

He tried opening his eyes, but they'd been glued together. He tried again, and the small effort of lifting his eyelids sent a shaft of pain ripping through his head. He tried yet again, and this time he got them open a fraction. He squinted up at Mariko.

"What…"

"Kyle, it's okay. We made it back. We're at Bagram Air Base. This is the hospital."

"But, how? We're in Pakistan, I know."

"No. They sent another helo to pick us up."

Another helo? How could they do that? There were missile-armed Pakistani fighters, supersonic F-16s? He winced as he felt a sharp pain in his arm, and then it was all black again.

When he awoke, he could see. They'd done something to his eyes. He could open the lids, and it didn't hurt quite so much. Mariko Noguchi stood in front of him, wearing a khaki US Marine officer's working uniform. She looked good, and as she leaned over him, he smelt her, and she smelled good too. He gripped her arm, and she winced at first, but he couldn't let her go, couldn't. He stared into her eyes.

"It's not a trick, we got back?"

"We sure did, yes. Those fighters didn't get to us, but when the Chinook went down, an AWACS aircraft was watching the action, and they vectored a flight of F/A18s in to help us out. The Pakistanis didn't like it, and they threatened all sorts of retaliation, but in the end they backed down. The F-16s returned to their base after our pilots threatened to blast them out of the sky. When it was clear, they sent in a replacement Chinook and got everyone home. "

I'm home. We made it!

"Boswell? What about him?"

"He's okay. He was badly hurt, but they've patched up his wounds, and he'll make a full recovery. As will you."

"How did I get hurt? Where?"

He felt a momentary panic and reached down to check his limbs were all intact.

"You were hit on the head, a piece of flying metal. You've been in a coma, but they say that now you've woken up, you'll begin to recover pretty fast."

"A coma? How long?"

She hesitated. "It's been a while."

"How long?" He didn't mean to shout, and he noticed the nurse who was making notes on his chart throw him a sharp look.

"Six weeks."

Six weeks of my life! Gone, gone for good. No! He closed his eyes. In six weeks, anything could happen, and probably had. Like I could have been discharged from the Seals, from the Navy, even. After all, those cops wanted my ass. Am I about to be court martialed? He realized she was still talking.

"Because you were under so long, your wounds have

healed without you experiencing the worst of the pain."

He looked up at her. "Believe me, I'm experiencing it now."

"It would have been worse if you were conscious. They've had to repair a lot of damage, and with you out of it, your wounds healed naturally."

He nodded, or tried to. But his head hurt too much.

"How long before I can get out of here?"

"They say another week. If there're no problems, you can go then. But you'll need a lot of R&R, at least three months."

"I can't take three months off work. That's impossible."

She smiled. "Doctor's orders. You don't have a choice. Admiral Jacks has been in to visit several times, and he concurred. He said it's either that, or you'll be discharged from the Seals. If you're not fully recovered, you're no use to him. Besides, there is another reason you'll need three months R&R."

"Yeah? What's that, to defend myself when it comes to my arraignment, for rape and murder?"

Her face creased up in concern. "Of course, you don't know. It's been cleared up. They know now it was Whitman who did it all. He tried to blame you and laid a false trail to Lucas Grant as well. But you recall when he boasted about it, in that stairwell inside the residence? I got it on my cellphone. I heard him talking, and when I realized what he was saying, it was a golden opportunity to record what he said so it would clear you afterward. Nazir Masih also swore an affidavit that it was the truth, and you've been completely exonerated. It's finished, Kyle. All over, except for one thing."

He looked up, suspicious. "What's that?"

She glanced around the hospital room, but the nurse had gone. "Your R&R. If it's okay with you, I've booked us into a hotel in Hawaii, four weeks of sunshine, sea and surf. And fucking."

"What!"

She grinned. "You heard."

"Excuse me!"

She jumped as someone cleared his throat behind her. Rear Admiral Drew Jacks stood in the doorway, watching them.

"Admiral! How long have you been there?"

Her face had gone beetroot red, and she hunched her shoulders and looked away in shame.

"Only just got here," he said cheerfully. "Didn't hear a thing. How's the patient?"

She smiled faintly. "You're a liar, Admiral Jacks, but a kind one, so I'll forgive you. He's doing well."

"He'd better be." He looked quizzically at Nolan. "How's the head, Son? How do you feel?"

"I've been better, thank you, Sir."

"You did a fine job back there, all of you. If that bastard Riyad had made an appearance, it would have fired up the religious lunatics, and we'd have had our work cut out beating them. As it is now, as far as the world is concerned, he never existed."

"Why do you think he didn't show himself sooner?" Nolan asked. His head was clearing fast, and there were parts of the operation he still couldn't fathom.

"Same reason we sent you in there to deal with him, and the same reason we launched Neptune Spear and sent Seal Team Six in to take out his brother. They're fighting a coward's war, Chief. They only emerge from their dark holes to attack and kill anyone who disagrees with them. And then they disappear back into the shadows. These people don't want to stay around and answer awkward questions, like when are their people going to get water, electric power, maybe an education and a job. They attack our Western values, with IEDs and suicide bombers, but give 'em half a chance, and all they want in life is to come to the States and enjoy some of the benefits of being American. If they came out and stood for election in their own countries, like they do back in the States, they'd lose every time. So they hide in their holes, and they know that when we get wind of them, we'll go in and deal with them. It's all a power play, and they're a bunch of sickos for using their own people's suffering to achieve their own ends. Like Yasser Arafat, in Palestine. You remember, after he died, they found he had more money than Bill Gates in his Swiss bank account. You go figure."

"It makes sense, Admiral," Mariko nodded.

He smiled at her. "Captain Noguchi, it makes a lot of sense. Listen, my Chief Petty Officer won't be able to take a full three months R&R. We have a war to fight here. But I do agree with your prescription for his recovery, so you get to it."

She reacted as if he'd thrown a bucket of hot water at her.

"Aw, Jesus, Admiral, you were listening."

He nodded. "Only the end bit."

She ran out of the room, and he smiled. "Don't worry, Chief. I'll make it right with her. She's good people."

"She is all of that, Sir, but I have a partner back in California."

"That still on? Last I heard, it sounded like the big

heave-ho."

Nolan thought about Carol.

He's right. There's nothing left there, but old habits die hard. Like loyalty and trust between two partners. And when I needed her trust, it was notably absent.

"You could be right, yeah. In fact, you are right. It is all over."

"It looks that way to me, sure. Enjoy your pretty Marine Captain while you can, Chief. She's a real find, and there're not many like her around. Life's too short to pass up a good thing, and she sure is a good thing."

"I'll remember that, Sir."

"You can have a month."

"A month! But Mariko, Captain Noguchi, she said the doctor had ordered me to take three months before I can return to duty. I have to see my kids as well, and sort a few things out."

Jacks fixed him with a stare that seemed to drill right through him. "Last I heard; an Admiral trumps a physician. Your guy is a Major, anyway."

"I guess that's right. Why the hurry, what's going down?"

"Your ears only, Chief. It's Yemen. Our Islamic friends have found a convenient bolthole down there, and it's become something of a mainstream terrorist hub. I want a small unit to go in and locate their main base of operations, then destroy it. This one's been on the table for several months. We've been looking at putting a crimp in their operations, and our masters are concerned to make sure this one works. You'll have all the help you need. The Navy will have a Carrier Group offshore, so once you've located the target, there'll be unlimited air and artillery support, and anything else you need."

"It sounds like a tough call for a single platoon."

"Yeah, but we can't send in a larger unit. The second they get wind of impending attack, they'll run for the hills, like bin Laden at Tora Bora, and you know how long it took to nail his ass. So it'll be a tight group, well trained, well disciplined, and that means you, my friend. Your success is maybe working against you. The word is that when you need results, you call in Bravo. The Pentagon and the White House, they want these people destroyed, wiped off the face off the earth. So your job is to find them, call it in, and sit back and watch the fun."

Nolan stared back at Jacks. He made it sound too easy, much too easy. Something didn't gel.

"What aren't you telling me, Admiral?"

Jacks looked annoyed and a little embarrassed.

"What do you mean? We'll spell it all out when you come back."

"Sir, it stinks. The timescale, I mean. Why not go in now? Why wait for me? There's something you're not telling me."

Jacks thought for a few moments and then sighed. "Okay, you're right, here it is. They'll know you're coming. We sent in Alpha Platoon. They were caught, and their men are due to go on trial in Yemen, in the town of Lawdar in eight weeks time. At the moment, they're held in a maximum-security prison, and we can't get to them. When they're brought for trial, we'll have a chance to get them out."

"But, why can't we do this diplomatically? What's the big deal?"

"The big deal, Chief, is that Lawdar is currently part of

an Islamic Emirate under the control of al Qaeda. This emirate, they call it the Abyan Governorate, is like the Wild West, and they're literally a law unto themselves in that stinking hellhole. Our guys won't expect or get any justice when they come up for trial."

"What are they facing, life?"

Jacks regarded him coldly. "Death. It's the only penalty for what they're accused of. Essentially, it's spying and attempting to topple this phony emirate. The Arabs won't deal, not at any price. If you can't get them out when they come up for trial, they'll be taken out and executed. There are eighteen men who survived the fight with the Islamists, and we can't let them die. You will locate that headquarters first and call it in. Our air assets will take care of it while you haul your asses over to Lawdar and secure the release of those men, by any means. So you see, we're on a timetable. One month, Chief. Get yourself fit, I mean, real fit. Go easy on, well, you know what I mean. You'll be out of here in a week, and I want you back in uniform five weeks from today. You'll have two weeks maximum to prepare, and then you go into Yemen. Any questions?"

"Lieutenant Boswell, Sir? How is he? Will he be fit enough to lead the Team in?"

Jacks shook his head. "It's doubtful, but not impossible. I don't suppose you'd consider a commission? I could get them to jump a rank, under the circumstances?"

Nolan laughed. "I took a blow to the head, Sir, but it wasn't that bad. Why would I give up the best job in the Navy?"

Jacks laughed with him. "I guess not. I'll leave you now with Captain Noguchi. I guess you two have a lot to talk about, or something."

"Yeah."

A few minutes later, Mariko returned to the hospital room.

"You're going back to the Seals?"

"I am, yes."

She forced a smile. "I'd hoped maybe something less stressful, but maybe not. At least we have three months."

"One."

"One? What...I don't understand."

"It's called being a Navy Seal, Mariko. It's what we're trained for, to go anywhere, anytime."

She looked crestfallen. "I guess so."

"But I also have other skills. You know, I've been real lucky. I love doing what I do in the Navy Seals. So they must have lied to me."

"What do you mean?"

"When they said, 'make love not war'. I'm pretty good at doing both."

She brightened and chuckled. "You'd better prove that statement, Mister."

"I'm looking forward to it.

CPSIA information can be obtained
at www.ICGtesting.com
Printed in the USA
LVOW08s0305060717
540414LV00001B/124/P